ALL-TIME FAVORITE
DETECTIVE
STORIES

EDITED AND WITH AN INTRODUCTION BY
ROCHELLE KRONZEK

DOVER PUBLICATIONS, INC.
Mineola, New York

Acknowledgments

"The Gioconda Smile" by Aldous Huxley is reprinted with permission by the George Burchardt Agency.
"Suspicion" by Dorothy L. Sayers is reprinted with permission by David Higham Associates.

Bibliographical Note

All-Time Favorite Detective Stories, first published by Dover Publications, Inc., in 2010, is a new anthology of twelve stories reprinted from standard sources. The original sources and first publication dates are provided in the introduction.

Library of Congress Cataloging-in-Publication Data

All-time favorite detective stories / edited by Rochelle Kronzek.
   p. cm.
  ISBN-13: 978-0-486-47274-4
  ISBN-10: 0-486-47274-4
   1. Detective and mystery stories, English.   2. Detective and mystery stories, American.   I. Kronzek, Rochelle.
PR1309.D4A55 2010
823'.0872'08—dc22

                          2009038324

Manufactured in the United States by Courier Corporation
47274402
www.doverpublications.com

Contents

Introduction

*"The mind is master of all things. When science fully recognizes
that fact a great advance will have been made."*
—The Thinking Machine from "The Problem of Cell 13"

To BRING THE essence of mystery, sufficient plot, surprise, and clever
twists into a detective short story takes literary skill, wit, ingenuity,
and imagination. In 1950, *Ellery Queen's Mystery Magazine* selected a
panel of eleven mystery story experts, among them Vincent Starrett,
Anthony Boucher, Charles Honce, John Dickson Carr, and Lewis D.
Feldman, to choose the top detective stories ever written. From the
eighty-three detective stories initially nominated, twelve stories were
chosen, and the results were published in the July 1950 issue of *Ellery
Queen Magazine*. A full sixty years have elapsed since the expert crime
genre panel convened, and the twelve celebrated tales contained in
this volume have endured the test of time. The stories that follow are
not macabre or nightmarish, but clever, intellectual detective tales
that deftly unravel in skillfully interwoven scenarios.

Orphaned as an infant, Thomas Burke (1886–1945) lived with his
uncle in a working-class neighborhood of London until he was nine.
He was then placed in an orphanage until he left at fourteen to work
in a boardinghouse. Burke developed an intimate knowledge of Lime-
house and London's East End, where Jack the Ripper committed his
crimes. Though Burke wrote many stories in different genres, mystery
and crime were his gift. First published in February 1929 in *Story-Teller
Magazine*, this story, which portrays the horrific Ripper murders, was
voted the greatest mystery story of all time by the Ellery Queen panel.

"The Purloined Letter" by Edgar Allan Poe (1809-1849) was published in 1844 and is one of the earliest known detective genre tales.
Poe is credited with giving the world a more psychological type of

detective story—less about gore and gritty details and more intellectual in nature, whereby clues are gathered through careful analysis and witty conversation. This story centers on a stolen letter taken from a woman who is being blackmailed. Poe considered "The Purloined Letter" to be his best detective story.

"The Red-Headed League" by Sir Arthur Conan Doyle (1859–1930) was first published in *The Strand* in August 1891. It was republished in 1892, along with eleven other Sherlock Holmes stories, in the collection, *The Adventures of Sherlock Holmes*. As the creator of the inimitable Sherlock Holmes and his associate, Dr. Watson, Conan Doyle is inextricably linked with the most popular fictional sleuth of all time.

Anthony Berkeley (1893–1971) was an English crime writer. After serving in the army in World War I, he worked as a journalist for many years, contributing stories to magazines. "The Avenging Chance" was published in the September 1929 issue of *Pearson's Magazine*. Berkeley's novels and short stories feature the debonair detective Roger Sheringham and Inspector Moresby.

Robert Barr (1849–1912) was a Scottish author, editor, journalist, and creator of the infamous sleuth, Eugene Valmont. "The Absent-Minded Coterie" is chapter 5 from *The Triumphs of Eugene Valmont* (1906). Against the backdrop of thick London fog, this story leads the reader from a fake case into a real crime. Barr also wrote under the name of Luke Sharp. His stories are well-seasoned with colorful narration, irony, and humor.

Jacques Futrelle (1875–1912) was an American journalist and mystery writer. He is best known for writing short stories featuring the "Thinking Machine," Professor Augustus S. F. X. Van Dusen. Van Dusen was a master logician with many credentials to show for it: a Ph.D., an LL.D., an F.R.S., an M.D., and an M.D.S.! In "The Problem of Cell 13" (1907), Professor Van Dusen is willingly locked into Chisholm prison, which his friends have wagered he cannot escape. Tragically, Futrelle perished in the Atlantic on April 12, 1912, while returning from Europe aboard the RMS *Titanic*.

Prolific English critic and author of verse, essays, novels, and short stories, G[ilbert] K[eith] Chesterton (1874–1936) gained fame for his series about the priest-detective Father Brown, who appeared in fifty stories. "The Invisible Man" was published in 1910 as a chapter in *The Innocence of Father Brown*. All twelve stories were first published individually in Philadelphia's *Saturday Evening Post*.

"Naboth's Vineyard" by Melville D. Post (1871–1930) was first published in *Metropolitan Magazine* in December 1912. His many stories featuring the character of Uncle Abner appeared between 1913 and 1918. The American-born Post also created the recurring characters of Sir Henry Marquis of Scotland Yard and Randolph Mason.

"The Gioconda Smile" by Aldous Huxley (1894–1963) was published in 1922 and is widely considered to be Huxley's best short story. As a writer, Huxley's output was impressive. In addition to novels, he also published travel books, histories, poems, plays, and essays. One of Huxley's best-known novels, *Brave New World* (1932), stands as a classic work of science fiction.

H[enry] C[hristopher] Bailey (1878–1961) was an English author of detective and historical fiction. He wrote mainly short stories and a few novels that starred Reggie Fortune, a detective with extensive medical knowledge and training. Bailey was at one time the most popular British detective writer during a period that spanned between 1918 and 1945. "The Yellow Slugs" first appeared in the volume, *Mr. Fortune Objects*, published by Doubleday in 1935.

E[dmund] C[lerihew] Bentley (1875–1956) was a British journalist and humorist and a main contributor to the British magazine, *Punch*. He became famous for his first detective novel, *Trent's Last Case*, published in 1913. Philip Trent was the detective appearing in many of the Bentley tales, as is the case with "The Genuine Tabard," which was first published in *The Strand* in January 1938.

"Suspicion" by Dorothy L. Sayers (1893–1957) is a short story in which a man suspects that the household cook plans to poison both his wife and himself. Sayers, a noted British essayist, novelist, critic, scholar, and playwright, made her reputation with her Lord Peter Wimsey detective stories. She wrote a dozen detective novels and two dozen detective short stories during the 1920s and 1930s that remain extremely popular to this day.

In light of such prolific and successful contemporary authors such as James Patterson and Robert B. Parker, do the stories included here still represent the best detective short stories ever written sixty years after the prestigious contest that was sponsored by the writing team of two cousins known by the pen name of Ellery Queen? I'll let you each judge for yourselves.

August 2009   ROCHELLE KRONZEK

The Hands of Mr. Ottermole

Thomas Burke

"Murder (said old Quong)—oblige me by passing my pipe—murder is one of the simplest things in the world to do. Killing a man is a much simpler matter than killing a duck. Not always so safe, perhaps, but simpler. But to certain gifted people it is both simple and entirely safe. Many minds of finer complexion than my own have discolored themselves in seeking to name the identity of the author of those wholesale murders which took place last year. Who that man or woman really was, I know no more than you do, but I have a theory of the person it could have been; and if you are not pressed for time I will elaborate that theory into a little tale."

As I had the rest of that evening and the whole of the next day for dalliance in my ivory tower, I desired that he would tell me the story; and, having reckoned up his cash register and closed the ivory gate, he told me—between then and the dawn—his story of the Mallon End murders. Paraphrased and condensed, it came out something like this.

At six o'clock of a January evening Mr. Whybrow was walking home through the cobweb alleys of London's East End. He had left the golden clamor of the great High Street to which the tram had brought him from the river and his daily work, and was now in the chessboard of byways that is called Mallon End. None of the rush and gleam of the High Street trickled into these byways. A few paces south—a flood tide of life, foaming, and beating. Here—only slow shuffling figures and muffled pulses. He was in the sink of London, the last refuge of European vagrants.

As though in tune with the street's spirit, he too walked slowly with head down. It seemed that he was pondering some pressing trouble, but he was not. He had no trouble. He was walking slowly because he had been on his feet all day; and he was bent in abstraction because he was wondering whether the Missis would have herrings

1

for his tea, or haddock; and he was trying to decide which would be the more tasty on a night like this. A wretched night it was, of damp and mist, and the mist wandered into his throat and his eyes, and the damp had settled on pavement and roadway, and where the sparse lamplight fell it sent up a greasy sparkle that chilled one to look at. By contrast it made his speculations more agreeable, and made him ready for that tea—whether herring or haddock. His eye turned from the glum bricks that made his horizon, and went forward half a mile. He saw a gas-lit kitchen, a flamy fire, and a spread tea table. There was toast in the hearth and a singing kettle on the side and a piquant effusion of herrings, or maybe of haddock, or perhaps sausages. The vision gave his aching feet a throb of energy. He shook imperceptible damp from his shoulders, and hastened toward its reality.

But Mr. Whybrow wasn't going to get any tea that evening—or any other evening. Mr. Whybrow was going to die. Somewhere within a hundred yards of him, another man was walking: a man much like Mr. Whybrow and much like any other man, but without the only quality that enables mankind to live peaceably together and not as madmen in a jungle. A man with a dead heart eating into itself and bringing forth the foul organisms that arise from death and corruption. And that thing in man's shape, on a whim or a settled idea—one cannot know—had said within himself that Mr. Whybrow should never taste another herring. Not that Mr. Whybrow had injured him. Not that he had any dislike of Mr. Whybrow. Indeed, he knew nothing of him save as a familiar figure about the streets. But, moved by a force that had taken possession of his empty cells, he had picked on Mr. Whybrow with that blind choice that makes us pick one restaurant table that has nothing to mark it from four or five other tables, or one apple from a dish of half-a-dozen equal apples; or that drives nature to send a cyclone upon one corner of this planet and destroy five hundred lives in that corner, and leave another five hundred in the same corner unharmed. So this man had picked on Mr. Whybrow as he might have picked on you or me, had we been within his daily observation; and even now he was creeping through the blue-toned streets, nursing his large white hands, moving ever closer to Mr. Whybrow's tea table, and so closer to Mr. Whybrow himself.

He wasn't, this man, a bad man. Indeed, he had many of the social and amiable qualities, and passed as a respectable man, as most successful criminals do. But the thought had come into his moldering mind that he would like to murder somebody, and as he held no fear of God or man, he was going to do it, and would then go home to *his* tea. I don't say that flippantly, but as a statement of fact. Strange as it may seem to the humane, murderers must and do sit down to meals after a murder. There is no reason why they shouldn't, and many reasons why they should. For one thing, they need to keep their physical and mental vitality at full beat for the business of covering their crime. For another, the strain of their effort makes them hungry, and satisfaction at the accomplishment of a desired thing brings a feeling of relaxation toward human pleasures. It is accepted among nonmurderers that the murderer is always overcome by fear for his safety and horror at his act; but this type is rare. His own safety is, of course, his immediate concern, but vanity is a marked quality of most murderers, and that, together with the thrill of conquest, makes him confident that he can secure it; and when he has restored his strength with food, he goes about securing it as a young hostess goes about the arranging of her first big dinner—a little anxious, but no more. Criminologists and detectives tell us that *every* murderer, however intelligent or cunning, always makes one slip in his tactics—one little slip that brings the affair home to him. But that is only half-true. It is true only of the murderers who are caught. Scores of murderers are not caught: therefore, scores of murderers do not make any mistake at all. This man didn't.

As for horror or remorse, prison chaplains, doctors, and lawyers have told us that of murderers they have interviewed under condemnation and the shadow of death, only one here and there has expressed any contrition for his act or shown any sign of mental misery. Most of them display only exasperation at having been caught when so many have gone undiscovered, or indignation at being condemned for a perfectly reasonable act. However normal and humane they may have been before the murder, they are utterly without conscience after it. For what is conscience? Simply a polite nickname for superstition, which is a polite nickname for fear. Those who associate remorse with murder are, no doubt, basing their ideas on the world-legend of the remorse of Cain, or are projecting their own frail minds into the mind of the murderer, and getting false reactions. Peaceable folk cannot hope to make contact with this mind, for they are not merely different in mental type from the murderer; they are different in their personal chemistry and construction. Some men can and do kill— not one man, but two or three—and go calmly about their daily affairs. Other men could not, under the most agonizing provocation,

bring themselves even to wound. It is men of this sort who imagine
the murderer in torments of remorse and fear of the law, whereas he
is actually sitting down to his tea.

The man with the large white hands was as ready for his tea as
Mr. Whybrow was, but he had something to do before he went to it.
When he had done that something, and made no mistake about it, he
would be even more ready for it, and would go to it as comfortably
as he went to it the day before, when his hands were stainless.

Walk on, then, Mr. Whybrow, walk on; and as you walk, look your
last upon the familiar features of your nightly journey. Follow your
jack-o'-lantern tea table. Look well upon its warmth and color and
kindness; feed your eyes with it and tease your nose with its gentle
domestic odors, for you will never sit down to it. Within ten minutes'
pacing of you, a pursuing phantom has spoken in his heart, and you
are doomed. There you go—you and phantom—two nebulous dabs
of mortality moving through green air along pavements of powder-
blue, the one to kill, the other to be killed. Walk on. Don't annoy
your burning feet by hurrying, for the more slowly you walk, the
longer you will breathe the green air of this January dusk, and see the
dreamy lamplight and the little shops, and hear the agreeable commerce of the London crowd and the haunting pathos of the street
organ. These things are dear to you, Mr. Whybrow. You don't know
it now, but in fifteen minutes you will have two seconds in which to
realize how inexpressibly dear they are.

Walk on, then, across this crazy chessboard. You are in Lagos Street
now, among the tents of the wanderers of Eastern Europe. A minute
or so, and you are in Loyal Lane, among the lodging houses that
shelter the useless and the beaten of London's camp followers. The
lane holds the smell of them, and its soft darkness seems heavy with
the wail of the futile. But you are not sensitive to impalpable things,
and you plod through it, unseeing, as you do every evening, and come
to Blean Street, and plod through that. From basement to sky rise
the tenements of an alien colony. Their windows slot the ebony of
their walls with lemon. Behind those windows, strange life is moving,
dressed with forms that are not of London or of England, yet, in
essence, the same agreeable life that you have been living, and tonight
will live no more. From high above you comes a voice crooning *The
Song of Katta*. Through a window you see a family keeping a religious
rite. Through another you see a woman pouring out tea for her hus-

band. You see a man mending a pair of boots; a mother bathing her baby. You have seen all these things before, and never noticed them. You do not notice them now, but if you knew that you were never going to see them again, you would notice them. You never *will* see them again, not because your life has run its natural course, but because a man whom you have often passed in the street has at his own solitary pleasure decided to usurp the awful authority of nature, and destroy you. So perhaps it's as well that you don't notice them, for your part in them is ended. No more for you these pretty moments of our earthly travail: only one moment of terror, and then a plunging darkness.

Closer to you this shadow of massacre moves, and now he is twenty yards behind you. You can hear his footfall, but you do not turn your head. You are familiar with footfalls. You are in London, in the easy security of your daily territory, and footfalls behind you, your instinct tells you, are no more than a message of human company.

But can't you hear something in those footfalls—something that goes with a widdershins beat? Something that says: *Look out, look out. Beware, beware.* Can't you hear the very syllables of *murd-er-er, murd-er-er*? No; there is nothing in footfalls. They are neutral. The foot of villainy falls with the same quiet note as the foot of honesty. But those footfalls, Mr. Whybrow, are bearing on to you a pair of hands, and there *is* something in hands. Behind you that pair of hands is even now stretching its muscles in preparation for your end. Every minute of your days, you have been seeing human hands. Have you ever realized the sheer horror of hands—those appendages that are a symbol of our moments of trust and affection and salutation? Have you thought of the sickening potentialities that lie within the scope of that five-tentacled member? No, you never have; for all the human hands that you have seen have been stretched to you in kindness or fellowship. Yet, though the eyes can hate and the lips can sting, it is only that dangling member that can gather the accumulated essence of evil and electrify it into currents of destruction. Satan may enter into man by many doors, but in the hands alone can he find the servants of his will.

Another minute, Mr. Whybrow, and you will know all about the horror of human hands.

You are nearly home now. You have turned into your street—Caspar Street—and you are in the center of the chessboard. You can see the front window of your little four-roomed house. The street is dark, and its three lamps give only a smut of light that is more confusing than darkness. It is dark—empty, too. Nobody about; no lights in the front parlors of the houses, for the families are at tea in their kitchens; and only a random glow in a few upper rooms occupied by lodgers. Nobody about but you and your following companion, and you don't notice him. You see him so often that he is never seen. Even if you turned your head and saw him, you would only say "Good evening" to him, and walk on. A suggestion that he was a possible murderer would not even make you laugh. It would be too silly.

And now you are at your gate. And now you have found your door key. And now you are in, and hanging up your hat and coat. The Missis has just called a greeting from the kitchen, whose smell is an echo of that greeting (herrings!), and you have answered it, when the door shakes under a sharp knock.

Go away, Mr. Whybrow. Go away from that door. Don't touch it. Get right away from it. Get out of the house. Run with the Missis to the back garden, and over the fence. Or call the neighbors. But don't touch that door. Don't, Mr. Whybrow, don't open. . . .

Mr. Whybrow opened the door.

That was the beginning of what became known as London's Strangling Horrors. Horrors they were called because they were something more than murders: they were motiveless, and there was an air of black magic about them. Each murder was committed at a time when the street where the bodies were found was empty of any perceptible or possible murderer. There would be an empty alley. There would be a policeman at its end. He would turn his back on the empty alley for less than a minute. Then he would look round and run into the night with news of another strangling. And in any direction he looked, nobody to be seen and no report to be had of anybody being seen. Or he would be on duty in a long-quiet street, and suddenly be called to a house of dead people whom a few seconds earlier he had seen alive. And, again, whichever way he looked nobody to be seen; and although police whistles put an immediate cordon around the area and searched all houses, no possible murderer to be found.

The first news of the murder of Mr. and Mrs. Whybrow was brought by the station sergeant. He had been walking through Caspar Street on his way to the station for duty, when he noticed the open door of No. 98. Glancing in, he saw by the gaslight of the passage a motionless body on the floor. After a second look he blew his whistle; and when the constables answered him, he took one to join him in search of the house, and sent others to watch all neighboring streets and make inquiries at adjoining houses. But neither in the house nor in the streets was anything found to indicate the murderer. Neighbors on either side, and opposite, were questioned, but they had seen nobody about, and had heard nothing. One had heard Mr. Whybrow come home—the scrape of his latchkey in the door was so regular an evening sound, he said, that you could set your watch by it for half-past six—but he had heard nothing more than the sound of the opening door until the sergeant's whistle. Nobody had been seen to enter the house or leave it, by front or back, and the necks of the dead people carried no fingerprints or other traces. A nephew was called in to go over the house, but he could find nothing missing; and anyway his uncle possessed nothing worth stealing. The little money in the house was untouched, and there were no signs of any disturbance of the property, or even of struggle. No signs of anything but brutal and wanton murder.

Mr. Whybrow was known to neighbors and workmates as a quiet, likable, home-loving man; such a man as could not have any enemies. But, then, murdered men seldom have. A relentless enemy who hates a man to the point of wanting to hurt him seldom wants to murder him, since to do that puts him beyond suffering. So the police were left with an impossible situation: no clue to the murderer and no motive for the murders, only that they had been done.

The first news of the affair sent a tremor through London generally, and an electric thrill through all Mallon End. Here was a murder of two inoffensive people, not for gain and not for revenge; and the murderer, to whom, apparently, killing was a casual impulse, was at large. He had left no traces, and provided he had no companions, there seemed no reason why he should not remain at large. Any clearheaded man who stands alone and has no fear of God or man, can, if he chooses, hold a city, even a nation, in subjection; but your everyday criminal is seldom clearheaded and dislikes being lonely. He needs, if not the support of confederates, at least somebody to talk to; his vanity needs the satisfaction of perceiving at first hand the effect of his work. For this he will frequent bars and coffee shops and other public places. Then, sooner or later, in a glow of comradeship, he will utter the one word too much; and the nark, who is everywhere, has an easy job.

But though the doss-houses and saloons and other places were "combed" and set with watches, and it was made known by whispers that good money and protection were assured to those with information, nothing attaching to the Whybrow case could be found. The murderer clearly had no friends and kept no company. Known men of this type were called up and questioned, but each was able to give a good account of himself; and in a few days the police were at a dead end. Against the constant public gibe that the thing had been done almost under their noses, they became restive, and for four days each man of the force was working his daily beat under a strain. On the fifth day they became still more restive.

It was the season of annual teas and entertainments for the children of the Sunday Schools; and on an evening of fog, when London was a world of groping phantoms, a small girl, in the bravery of best Sunday frock and shoes, shining face and new-washed hair, set out from Logan Passage for St. Michael's Parish Hall. She never got there. She was not actually dead until half-past six, but she was as good as dead from the moment she left her mother's door. Somebody like a man, pacing the street from which the passage led, saw her come out; and from that moment she was dead. Through the fog somebody's large white hands reached after her, and in fifteen minutes they were about her.

At half-past six a whistle screamed trouble, and those answering it found the body of little Nellie Vrinoff in a warehouse entry in Minnow Street. The sergeant was first among them, and he posted his men to useful points, ordering them here and there in the tart tones of repressed rage, and berating the officer whose beat the street was. "I saw you, Magson, at the end of the lane. What were you up to there? You were there ten minutes before you turned." Magson began an explanation about keeping an eye on a suspicious-looking character at that end, but the sergeant cut him short: "Suspicious characters be damned. You don't want to look for suspicious characters. You want to look for *murderers*. Messing about . . . and then this happens right where you ought to be. Now think what they'll say."

With the speed of ill news came the crowd, pale and perturbed; and on the story that the unknown monster had appeared again, and this time to a child, their faces streaked the fog with spots of hate and horror. But then came the ambulance and more police, and swiftly they broke up the crowd; and as it broke, the sergeant's thought was thickened into words, and from all sides came low murmurs of

"Right under their noses." Later inquiries showed that four people of the district, above suspicion, had passed that entry at intervals of seconds before the murder, and seen nothing and heard nothing. None of them had passed the child alive or seen her dead. None of them had seen anybody in the street except themselves. Again the police were left with no motive and with no clue.

And now the district, as you will remember, was given over, not to panic, for the London public never yields to that, but to apprehension and dismay. If these things were happening in their familiar streets, then anything might happen. Wherever people met—in the streets, the markets, and the shops—they debated the one topic. Women took to bolting their windows and doors at the first fall of dusk. They kept their children closely under their eye. They did their shopping before dark, and watched anxiously—while pretending they weren't watching—for the return of their husbands from work. Under the cockney's semi-humorous resignation to disaster, they hid an hourly foreboding. By the whim of one man with a pair of hands, the structure and tenor of their daily life were shaken, as they always can be shaken by any man contemptuous of humanity and fearless of its laws. They began to realize that the pillars that supported the peaceable society in which they lived were mere straws that anybody could snap; that laws were powerful only so long as they were obeyed; that the police were potent only so long as they were feared. By the power of his hands this one man had made a whole community do something new: he had made it think, and left it gasping at the obvious.

And then, while it was yet gasping under his first two strokes, he made his third. Conscious of the horror that his hands had created, and hungry as an actor who has once tasted the thrill of the multitude, he made fresh advertisement of his presence; and on Wednesday morning, three days after the murder of the child, the papers carried to the breakfast tables of England the story of a still more shocking outrage.

At 9:32 on Tuesday night a constable was on duty in Jarnigan Road, and at that time spoke to a fellow officer named Petersen at the top of Clemming Street. He had seen this officer walk down that street. He could swear that the street was empty at that time, except for a lame bootblack whom he knew by sight, and who passed him and entered a tenement on the side opposite that on which his fellow officer was walking. He had the habit, as all constables had just then, of looking constantly behind him and around him, whichever way he was walking, and he was certain that the street was empty. He passed his sergeant at 9:33, saluted him, and answered his inquiry for anything seen. He reported that he had seen nothing, and passed on. His beat ended at a short distance from Clemming Street, and having paced it, he turned and came again at 9:34 to the top of the street. He had scarcely reached it before he heard the hoarse voice of the sergeant: "Gregory! You there? Quick. Here's another. My God, it's Petersen! Garroted. Quick, call 'em up!"

That was the third of the Strangling Horrors, of which there were to be a fourth and a fifth; and the five horrors were to pass into the unknown and unknowable. That is, unknown as far as authority and the public were concerned. The identity of the murderer *was* known, but to two men only. One was the murderer himself; the other was a young journalist.

This young man, who was covering the affairs for his paper, the *Daily Torch*, was no smarter than the other zealous newspapermen who were hanging about these byways in the hope of a sudden story. But he was patient, and he hung a little closer to the case than the other fellows, and by continually staring at it he at last raised the figure of the murderer like a genie from the stones on which he had stood to do his murders.

After the first few days the men had given up any attempt at exclusive stories, for there were none to be had. They met regularly at the police station, and what little information there was they shared. The officials were agreeable to them, but no more. The sergeant discussed with them the details of each murder; suggested possible explanations of the man's methods; recalled from the past those cases that had some similarity; and on the matter of motive reminded them of the motiveless Neil Cream and the wanton John Williams, and hinted that work was being done which would soon bring the business to an end; but about that work he would not say a word. The Inspector, too, was gracefully garrulous on the thesis of Murder, but whenever one of the party edged the talk toward what was being done in this immediate matter, he glided past it. Whatever the officials knew, they were not giving it to newspapermen. The business had fallen heavily upon them, and only by a capture made by their own efforts could they rehabilitate themselves in official and public esteem. Scotland Yard, of course, was at work, and had all the station's material; but the station's hope was that they themselves would have the honor of settling the affair; and however useful the cooperation of the press might be in other cases, they did not want to risk a defeat by a premature disclosure of their theories and plans.

So the sergeant talked at large, and propounded one interesting theory after another, all of which the newspapermen had thought of themselves.

The young man soon gave up their morning lectures on the philosophy of crime, and took to wandering about the streets and making bright stories out of the effect of the murders on the normal life of the people. A melancholy job made more melancholy by the district. The littered roadways, the crestfallen houses, the bleared windows— all held the acid misery that evokes no sympathy: the misery of the frustrated poet. The misery was the creation of the aliens, who were living in this makeshift fashion because they had no settled homes, and would neither take the trouble to make a home where they *could* settle, nor get on with their wandering.

There was little to be picked up. All he saw and heard were indignant faces, and wild conjectures of the murderer's identity and of the secret of his trick of appearing and disappearing unseen. Since a policeman himself had fallen a victim, denunciations of the force had ceased, and the unknown was now invested with a cloak of legend. Men eyed other men as though thinking: It might be *him*. It might be *him*. They were no longer looking for a man who had the air of a Madame Tussaud murderer; they were looking for a man, or perhaps some harridan woman, who had done these particular murders. Their thoughts ran mainly on the foreign set. Such ruffianism could scarcely belong to England, nor could the bewildering cleverness of the thing. So they turned to Rumanian gypsies and Turkish carpet-sellers. There, clearly, would be found the "warm" spot. These Eastern fellows—they knew all sorts of tricks, and they had no real religion— nothing to hold them within bounds. Sailors returning from those parts had told tales of conjurors who made themselves invisible; and there were tales of Egyptian and Arab potions that were used for abysmally queer purposes. Perhaps it *was* possible to them; you never knew. They were so slick and cunning, and they had such gliding movements; no Englishman could melt away as they could. Almost certainly the murderer would be found to be one of that sort—with some dark trick of his own—and just because they were sure that he *was* a magician, they felt that it was useless to look for him. He was a power, able to hold them in subjection and to hold himself untouchable. Superstition, which so easily cracks the frail shell of reason, had got into them. He could do anything he chose; he would never be discovered. These two points they settled, and they went about the streets in a mood of resentful fatalism.

They talked of their ideas to the journalist in half-tones, looking right and left, as though HE might overhear them and visit them. And though all the district was thinking of him and ready to pounce upon him, yet, so strongly had he worked upon them, that if any man in the street—say, a small man of commonplace features and form—had cried "*I* am the Monster!" would their stifled fury have broken into flood and have borne him down and engulfed him? Or would they not suddenly have seen something unearthly in that everyday face and figure, something unearthly in his everyday boots, something unearthly about his hat, something that marked him as one whom none of their weapons could alarm or pierce? And would they not momentarily have fallen back from this devil, as the devil fell back from the cross made by the sword of Faust, and so have given him time to escape? I do not know; but so fixed was their belief in his invincibility that it is at least likely that they would have made this hesitation, had such an occasion arisen. But it never did. Today this commonplace fellow, his murder lust glutted, it still seen and observed among them as he was seen and observed all the time; but because nobody then dreamt, or now dreams, that he was what he was, they observed him then, and observe him now, as people observe a lamppost.

Almost was their belief in his invincibility justified; for, five days after the murder of the policeman Petersen, when the experience and inspiration of the whole detective force of London were turned toward his identification and capture, he made his fourth and fifth strokes.

At nine o'clock that evening, the young newspaperman, who hung about every night until his paper was away, was strolling along Richards Lane. Richards Lane is a narrow street, partly a stall-market, and partly residential. The young man was in the residential section, which carries on one side small working-class cottages, and on the other the wall of a railway goods-yard. The great wall hung a blanket of shadow over the lane, and the shadow and the cadaverous outline of the now deserted market stalls gave it the appearance of a living lane that had been turned to frost in the moment between breath and death. The very lamps, that elsewhere were nimbuses of gold, had here the rigidity of gems. The journalist, feeling this message of frozen eternity, was telling himself that he was tired of the whole thing, when in one stroke the frost was broken. In the moment between one pace and another, silence and darkness were racked by a high scream and through the scream a voice: "Help! help! *He's here!*"

Before he could think what movement to make, the lane came to life. As though its invisible populace had been waiting on that cry, the door of every cottage was flung open, and from them and from the alleys poured shadowy figures bent in question-mark form. For a second or so they stood as rigid as the lamps; then a police whistle gave them direction, and the flock of shadows sloped up the street. The journalist followed them, and others followed him. From the main street and from surrounding streets they came, some risen from unfinished suppers, some disturbed in their ease of slippers and shirtsleeves, some stumbling on infirm limbs, and some upright and armed with pokers or the tools of their trade. Here and there above the wavering cloud of heads moved the bold helmets of policemen. In one dim mass they surged upon a cottage whose doorway was marked by the sergeant and two constables; and voices of those behind urged them on with "Get in! Find him! Run round the back! Over the wall!" And those in front cried, "Keep back! Keep back!"

And now the fury of a mob held in thrall by unknown peril broke loose. He was here—on the spot. Surely this time he *could not* escape. All minds were bent upon the cottage; all energies thrust toward its doors and windows and roof; all thought was turned upon one unknown man and his extermination. So that no one man saw any other man. No man saw the narrow, packed lane and the mass of struggling shadows, and all forgot to look among themselves for the monster who never lingered upon his victims. All forgot, indeed, that they, by their mass crusade of vengeance, were affording him the perfect hiding place. They saw only the house, and they heard only the rending of woodwork and the smash of glass at back and front, and the police giving orders or crying with the chase; and they pressed on.

But they found no murderer. All they found was news of murder and a glimpse of the ambulance, and for their fury there was no other object than the police themselves, who fought against this hampering of their work.

The journalist managed to struggle through to the cottage door, and to get the story from the constable stationed there. The cottage was the home of a pensioned sailor and his wife and daughter. They had been at supper, and at first it appeared that some noxious gas had smitten all three in mid-action. The daughter lay dead on the hearth rug, with a piece of bread and butter in her hand. The father had fallen sideways from his chair, leaving on his plate a filled spoon of rice pudding. The mother lay half under the table, her lap filled with the pieces of a broken cup and splashes of cocoa. But in three seconds the idea of gas was dismissed. One glance at their necks showed that this was the Strangler again; and the police stood and looked at the room and momentarily shared the fatalism of the public. They were helpless.

This was his fourth visit, making seven murders in all. He was to do, as you know, one more—and to do it that night; and then he was to pass into history as the unknown London horror, and return to the decent life that he had always led, remembering little of what he had done and worried not at all by the memory. Why did he stop? Impossible to say. Why did he begin? Impossible again. It just happened like that; and if he thinks at all of those days and nights, I surmise that he thinks of them as we think of foolish or dirty little sins that we committed in childhood. We say that they were not really sins because we were not then consciously ourselves: we had not come to realization; and we look back at that foolish little creature that we once were and forgive him because he didn't know. So, I think, with this man.

There are plenty like him. Eugene Aram, after the murder of Daniel Clarke, lived a quiet, contented life for fourteen years, unhaunted by his crime and unshaken in his self-esteem. Dr. Crippen murdered his wife, and then lived pleasantly with his mistress in the house under whose floor he had buried the wife. Constance Kent, found Not Guilty of the murder of her young brother, led a peaceful life for five years before she confessed. George Joseph Smith and William Palmer lived amiably among their fellows untroubled by fear or by remorse for their poisonings, and drownings. Charles Peace, at the time he made his one unfortunate essay, had settled down into a respectable citizen with an interest in antiques. It happened that, after a lapse of time, these men were discovered; but more murderers than we guess are living decent lives today, and will die in decency, undiscovered and unsuspected. As this man will.

But he had a narrow escape, and it was perhaps this narrow escape that brought him to a stop. The escape was due to an error of judgment on the part of the journalist.

As soon as he had the full story of the affair, which took some time, he spent fifteen minutes on the telephone, sending the story through, and at the end of the fifteen minutes, when the stimulus

of the business had left him, he felt physically tired and mentally
disheveled. He was not yet free to go home; the paper would not go
away for another hour; so he turned into a bar for a drink and some
sandwiches.

It was then, when he had dismissed the whole business from his
mind and was looking about the bar and admiring the landlord's taste
in watch chains and his air of domination, and was thinking that the
landlord of a well-conducted tavern had a more comfortable life than
a newspaperman, that his mind received from nowhere a spark of
light. He was not thinking about the Strangling Horrors; his mind
was on his sandwich. As a public-house sandwich, it was a curiosity.
The bread had been thinly cut, it was buttered, and the ham was not
two months stale; it was ham as it should be. His mind turned to
the inventor of this refreshment, the Earl of Sandwich, and then to
George the Fourth, and then to the Georges, and to the legend of
that George who was worried to know how the apple got into the
apple dumpling. He wondered whether George would have been
equally puzzled to know how the ham got into the ham sandwich,
and how long it would have been before it occurred to him that
the ham could not have got there unless somebody had put it there.
He got up to order another sandwich, and in that moment a little
active corner of his mind settled the affair. If there was ham in his
sandwich, somebody must have put it there. If seven people had been
murdered, somebody must have been there to murder them. There
was no aeroplane or automobile that would go into a man's pocket;
therefore, that somebody must have escaped either by running away
or standing still; and again therefore—

He was visualizing the front-page story that his paper would carry
if his theory was correct, and if—a matter of conjecture—his editor
had the necessary nerve to make a bold stroke, when a cry of "Time,
gentlemen, please! All out!" reminded him of the hour. He got up
and went out into a world of mist, broken by the ragged discs of
roadside puddles and the streaming lightning of motor buses. He was
certain that he had *the* story, but even if it was proved, he was doubtful
whether the policy of his paper would permit him to print it. It had
one great fault. It was truth, but it was impossible truth. It rocked
the foundations of everything that newspaper readers believed and
that newspaper editors helped them to believe. They might believe
that Turkish carpetsellers had the gift of making themselves invisible.
They would not believe this.

As it happened, they were not asked to, for the story was never written. As his paper had by now gone away, and as he was nourished by his refreshment and stimulated by his theory, he thought he might put in an extra half hour by testing that theory. So he began to look about for the man he had in mind—a man with white hair and large white hands; otherwise an everyday figure whom nobody would look twice at. He wanted to spring his idea on this man without warning, and he was going to place himself within reach of a man armored in legends of dreadfulness and grue. This might appear to be an act of supreme courage—that one man, with no hope of immediate outside support, should place himself at the mercy of one who was holding a whole parish in terror. But it wasn't. He didn't think about the risk. He didn't think about his duty to his employers or loyalty to his paper. He was moved simply by an instinct to follow a story to its end.

He walked slowly from the tavern and crossed into Fingal Street, making for Deever Market, where he had hope of finding his man. But his journey was shortened. At the corner of Lotus Street he saw him—or a man who looked like him. This street was poorly lit, and he could see little of the man: but he *could* see white hands. For some twenty paces he stalked him; then drew level with him; and at a point where the arch of railway crossed the street, he saw that this was his man. He approached him with the current conversational phrase of the district: "Well, seen anything of the murderer?" The man stopped to look sharply at him; then, satisfied that the journalist was not the murderer, said:

"Eh? No, nor's anybody else, curse it. Doubt if they ever will."

"I don't know. I've been thinking about them, and I've got an idea."

"So?"

"Yes. Came to me all of a sudden. Quarter of an hour ago. And I'd felt that we'd all been blind. It's been staring us in the face."

The man turned again to look at him, and the look and the movement held suspicion of this man who seemed to know so much. "Oh? Has it? Well, if you're so sure, why not give us the benefit of it?"

"I'm going to." They walked level, and were nearly at the end of the little street where it meets Deever Market when the journalist turned casually to the man. He put a finger on his arm. "Yes, it seems to me quite simple now. But there's still one point I don't understand. One little thing I'd like to clear up. I mean the motive. Now, as man to man, tell me, Sergeant Ottermole, just *why* did you kill all those inoffensive people?"

The sergeant stopped, and the journalist stopped. There was just enough light from the sky, which held the reflected light of the continent of London, to give him a sight of the sergeant's face, and the sergeant's face was turned to him with a wide smile of such urbanity and charm that the journalist's eyes were frozen as they met it. The smile stayed for some seconds. Then said the sergeant, "Well, to tell you the truth, Mister Newspaperman, I don't know. I really don't know. In fact, I've been worried about it myself. But I've got an idea—just like you. Everybody knows that we can't control the workings of our minds. Don't they? Ideas come into our minds without asking. But everybody's supposed to be able to control his body. Why? Eh? We get our minds from lord-knows-where—from people who were dead hundreds of years before we were born. Mayn't we get our bodies in the same way? Our faces—our legs—our heads—they aren't completely ours. We don't make 'em. They come to us. And couldn't ideas come into our bodies like ideas come into our minds? Eh? Can't ideas live in nerve and muscle as well as in brain? Couldn't it be that parts of our bodies aren't really us, and couldn't ideas come into those parts all of a sudden, like ideas come into . . . into"—he shot his arms out, showing the great white-gloved hands and hairy wrists; shot them out so swiftly to the journalist's throat that his eyes never saw them—"into *my hands!*"

The Purloined Letter

Edgar Allan Poe

Nil sapientiæ odiosius acumine nimio.—SENECA.

AT PARIS, just after dark one gusty evening in the autumn of 18———,
I was enjoying the twofold luxury of meditation and meerschaum, in
company with my friend, C. Auguste Dupin, in his little back library,
or book-closet, *au troisième*, No. 33 Rue Dunôt, Faubourg St. Ger-
main. For one hour at least we had maintained a profound silence;
while each, to any casual observer, might have seemed intently and
exclusively occupied with the curling eddies of smoke that oppressed
the atmosphere of the chamber. For myself, however, I was mentally
discussing certain topics which had formed matter for conversation
between us at an earlier period of the evening; I mean the affair of the
Rue Morgue and the mystery attending the murder of Marie Roget.
I looked upon it, therefore, as something of a coincidence when
the door of our apartment was thrown open and admitted our old
acquaintance, Monsieur G———, the Prefect of the Parisian police.

We gave him a hearty welcome; for there was nearly half as much
of the entertaining as of the contemptible about the man, and we had
not seen him for several years. We had been sitting in the dark, and
Dupin now arose for the purpose of lighting a lamp, but sat down
again, without doing so, upon G———'s saying that he had called to
consult us, or rather to ask the opinion of my friend, about some
official business which had occasioned a great deal of trouble.

"If it is any point requiring reflection," observed Dupin, as he for-
bore to enkindle the wick, "we shall examine it to better purpose in
the dark."

"That is another of your odd notions," said the Prefect, who had
the fashion of calling everything "odd" that was beyond his comprehension, and thus lived amid an absolute legion of "oddities."

"Very true," said Dupin, as he supplied his visitor with a pipe and
rolled toward him a comfortable chair.

"And what is the difficulty now?" I asked. "Nothing more in the assassination way, I hope?"

"Oh, no; nothing of that nature. The fact is, the business is very simple indeed, and I make no doubt that we can manage it sufficiently well ourselves; but then I thought Dupin would like to hear the details of it, because it is so excessively odd."

"Simple and odd?" said Dupin.

"Why, yes; and not exactly that either. The fact is, we have all been a good deal puzzled because the affair is so simple, and yet baffles us altogether."

"Perhaps it is the very simplicity of the thing which puts you at fault," said my friend.

"What nonsense you do talk!" replied the Prefect, laughing heartily.

"Perhaps the mystery is a little too plain," said Dupin.

"Oh, good heavens! who ever heard of such an idea?"

"A little too self-evident."

"Ha! ha! ha!—ha! ha! ha—ho! ho! ho!" roared our visitor, profoundly amused. "Oh, Dupin, you will be the death of me yet."

"And what, after all, is the matter on hand?" I asked.

"Why, I will tell you," replied the Prefect, as he gave a long, steady, and contemplative puff and settled himself in his chair,—"I will tell you in a few words; but, before I begin, let me caution you that this is an affair demanding the greatest secrecy, and that I should most probably lose the position I now hold were it known that I confided it to any one."

"Proceed," said I.

"Or not," said Dupin.

"Well, then; I have received personal information, from a very high quarter, that a certain document of the last importance had been purloined from the royal apartments. The individual who purloined it is known—this beyond a doubt; he was seen to take it. It is known, also, that it still remains in his possession."

"How is this known?" asked Dupin.

"It is clearly inferred," replied the Prefect, "from the nature of the document and from the non-appearance of certain results which would at once arise from its passing out of the robber's possession, that is to say, from his employing it as he must design in the end to employ it."

"Be a little more explicit," I said.

"Well, I may venture so far as to say that the paper gives its holder a certain power in a certain quarter where such power is immensely valuable." The Prefect was fond of the cant of diplomacy.

"Still I do not quite understand," said Dupin.

"No? Well; the disclosure of the document to a third person, who shall be nameless, would bring in question the honor of a personage of most exalted station; and this fact gives the holder of the document an ascendency over the illustrious personage whose honor and peace are so jeopardized."

"But this ascendency," I interposed, "would depend upon the robber's knowledge of the loser's knowledge of the robber. Who would dare—"

"The thief," said G——, "is the Minister D——, who dares all things, those unbecoming as well as those becoming a man. The method of the theft was not less ingenious than bold. The document in question,—a letter, to be frank,—had been received by the personage robbed while alone in the royal boudoir. During its perusal she was suddenly interrupted by the entrance of the other exalted personage from whom especially it was her wish to conceal it. After a hurried and vain endeavor to thrust it in a drawer, she was forced to place it, open as it was, upon a table. The address, however, was uppermost, and, the contents thus unexposed, the letter escaped notice. At this juncture enters the Minister D——. His lynx eye immediately perceives the paper, recognizes the handwriting of the address, observes the confusion of the personage addressed, and fathoms her secret. After some business transactions, hurried through in his ordinary manner, he produces a letter somewhat similar to the one in question, opens it, pretends to read it, and then places it in close juxtaposition to the other. Again he converses for some fifteen minutes upon the public affairs. At length, in taking leave, he takes also from the table the letter to which he had no claim. Its rightful owner saw, but, of course, dared not call attention to the act, in the presence of the third personage, who stood at her elbow. The Minister decamped, leaving his own letter, one of no importance, upon the table."

"Here, then," said Dupin to me, "you have precisely what you demand to make the ascendency complete, the robber's knowledge of the loser's knowledge of the robber."

"Yes," replied the Prefect; "and the power thus attained has, for some months past, been wielded, for political purposes, to a very dangerous extent. The personage robbed is more thoroughly convinced every day of the necessity of reclaiming her letter. But this, of course, cannot be done openly. In fine, driven to despair, she has committed the matter to me."

"Than whom," said Dupin, amid a perfect whirlwind of smoke, "no more sagacious agent could, I suppose, be desired or even imagined."

"You flatter me," replied the Prefect; "but it is possible that some such opinion may have been entertained."

"It is clear," said I, "as you observe, that the letter is still in the possession of the Minister; since it is this possession, and not any employment of the letter, which bestows the power. With the employment the power departs."

"True," said G——; "and upon this conviction I proceeded. My first care was to make thorough search of the Minister's hotel; and here my chief embarrassment lay in the necessity of searching without his knowledge. Beyond all things, I have been warned of the danger which would result from giving him reason to suspect our design."

"But," said I, "you are quite *au fait* in these investigations. The Parisian police have done this thing often before."

"Oh, yes: and for this reason I did not despair. The habits of the Minister gave me, too, a great advantage. He is frequently absent from home all night. His servants are by no means numerous. They sleep at a distance from their master's apartment, and, being chiefly Neapolitans, are readily made drunk. I have keys, as you know, with which I can open any chamber or cabinet in Paris. For three months a night has not passed, during the greater part of which I have not been engaged, personally, in ransacking the D—— Hotel. My honor is interested, and, to mention a great secret, the reward is enormous. So I did not abandon the search until I had become fully satisfied that the thief is a more astute man than myself. I fancy that I have investigated every nook and corner of the premises in which it is possible that the paper can be concealed."

"But is it not possible," I suggested, "that although the letter may be in possession of the Minister, as it unquestionably is, he may have concealed it elsewhere than upon his own premises?"

"This is barely possible," said Dupin. "The present peculiar condition of affairs at court, and especially of those intrigues in which D—— is known to be involved, would render the instant availability of the document, its susceptibility of being produced at a moment's notice, a point of nearly equal importance with its possession."

"Its susceptibility of being produced?" said I.

"That is to say, of being destroyed," said Dupin.

"True," I observed; "the paper is clearly, then, upon the premises. As for its being upon the person of the minister, we may consider that as out of the question."

"Entirely," said the Prefect. "He has been twice waylaid, as if by footpads, and his person rigidly searched under my own inspection."

"You might have spared yourself this trouble," said Dupin. "D——, I presume, is not altogether a fool, and, if not, must have anticipated these waylayings, as a matter of course."

"Not altogether a fool," said G——, "but then he is a poet, which I take to be only one remove from a fool."

"True," said Dupin, after a long and thoughtful whiff from his meer-schaum, "although I have been guilty of certain doggerel myself."

"Suppose you detail," said I, "the particulars of your search."

"Why, the fact is, we took our time, and we searched everywhere. I have had long experience in these affairs. I took the entire build-ing, room by room; devoting the nights of a whole week to each. We examined, first, the furniture of each apartment. We opened every possible drawer; and I presume you know that, to a properly trained police-agent, such a thing as a 'secret' drawer is impossible. Any man is a dolt who permits a 'secret' drawer to escape him in a search of this kind. The thing is so plain. There is a certain amount of bulk, of space, to be accounted for in every cabinet. Then we have accurate rules. The fiftieth part of a line could not escape us. After the cabinets we took the chairs. The cushions we probed with the fine long needles you have seen me employ. From the tables we removed the tops."

"Why so?"

"Sometimes the top of a table or other similarly arranged piece of furniture is removed by the person wishing to conceal an article; then the leg is excavated, the article deposited within the cavity, and the top replaced. The bottoms and tops of bedposts are employed in the same way."

"But could not the cavity be detected by sounding?" I asked.

"By no means, if, when the article is deposited, a sufficient wad-ding of cotton be placed around it. Besides, in our case, we were obliged to proceed without noise."

"But you could not have removed, you could not have taken to pieces all articles of furniture in which it would have been possible to make a deposit in the manner you mention. A letter may be compressed into a thin spiral roll, not differing much in shape or bulk from a large knitting-needle, and in this form it might be inserted into the rung of a chair, for example. You did not take to pieces all the chairs?"

"Certainly not, but we did better: we examined the rungs of every chair in the hotel, and, indeed, the jointings of every description of furniture, by the aid of a most powerful microscope. Had there been any traces of recent disturbance we should not have failed to detect it instantly. A single gram of gimlet-dust, for example, would have been as obvious as an apple. Any disorder in the gluing, any unusual gaping in the joints, would have sufficed to insure detection."

"I presume you looked to the mirrors, between the boards and the plates, and you probed the beds and the bedclothes, as well as the curtains and carpets."

"That of course; and when we had absolutely completed every particle of the furniture in this way, then we examined the house itself. We divided its entire surface into compartments, which we numbered, so that none might be missed; then we scrutinized each individual square inch throughout the premises, including the two houses immediately adjoining, with the microscope, as before."

"The two houses adjoining!" I exclaimed; "you must have had a great deal of trouble."

"We had; but the reward offered is prodigious."

"You include the grounds about the houses?"

"All the grounds are paved with brick. They gave us comparatively little trouble. We examined the moss between the bricks and found it undisturbed."

"You looked among D——'s papers, of course, and into the books of the library?"

"Certainly; we opened every package and parcel; we not only opened every book, but we turned over every leaf in each volume, not contenting ourselves with a mere shake, according to the fashion of some of our police officers. We also measured the thickness of every book-cover with the most accurate measurement, and applied to each the most jealous scrutiny of the microscope. Had any of the bindings been recently meddled with, it would have been utterly impossible that the fact should have escaped observation. Some five or six volumes, just from the hands of the binder, we carefully probed, longitudinally, with the needles."

"You explored the floors beneath the carpets?"

"Beyond doubt. We removed every carpet and examined the boards with the microscope."

"And the paper on the walls?"

"Yes."

"You looked into the cellars?"

"We did."

"Then," I said, "you have been making a miscalculation, and the letter is not upon the premises, as you suppose."

"I fear you are right there," said the Prefect. "And now, Dupin, what would you advise me to do?"

"To make a thorough research of the premises."

"That is absolutely needless," replied G——. "I am not more sure that I breathe than I am that the letter is not at the hotel."

"I have no better advice to give you," said Dupin. "You have, of course, an accurate description of the letter?"

"Oh, yes!" and here the Prefect, producing a memorandum-book, proceeded to read aloud a minute account of the internal, and especially of the external, appearance of the missing document. Soon after finishing the perusal of this description he took his departure, more entirely depressed in spirits than I had ever known the good gentleman before.

In about a month afterward he paid us another visit, and found us occupied very nearly as before. He took a pipe and a chair and entered into some ordinary conversation. At length I said:

"Well, but, G——, what of the purloined letter? I presume you have at last made up your mind that there is no such thing as over-reaching the Minister?"

"Confound him! say I—yes; I made the reëxamination, however, as Dupin suggested, but it was all labor lost, as I knew it would be."

"How much was the reward offered, did you say?" asked Dupin.

"Why, a very great deal, a very liberal reward; I don't like to say how much, precisely: but one thing I will say,—that I wouldn't mind giving my individual check for fifty thousand francs to any one who could obtain me that letter. The fact is, it is becoming of more and more importance every day; and the reward has been lately doubled. If it were trebled, however, I could do no more than I have done."

"Why, yes," said Dupin, drawlingly, between the whiffs of his meerschaum, "I really—think, G——, you have not exerted yourself—to the utmost in this matter. You might—do a little more, I think, eh?"

"How? In what way?"

"Why—puff, puff—you might—puff, puff—employ counsel in the matter, eh?—puff, puff, puff. Do you remember the story they tell of Abernethy?"

"No; hang Abernethy!"

"To be sure, hang him and welcome. But, once upon a time, a certain rich miser conceived the design of sponging upon this Abernethy for a medical opinion. Getting up, for this purpose, an ordinary conversation in a private company, he insinuated his case to the physician as that of an imaginary individual.

"'We will suppose,' said the miser, 'that his symptoms are such and such; now, Doctor, what would you have directed him to take?

"'Take,' said Abernethy, 'why, take advice, to be sure.'"

"But," said the Prefect, a little discomposed, "I am perfectly willing to take advice and to pay for it. I would really give fifty thousand francs to any one who would aid me in the matter."

"In that case," replied Dupin, opening a drawer and producing a checkbook, "you may as well fill me up a check for the amount mentioned. When you have signed it I will hand you the letter."

I was astounded. The Prefect appeared absolutely thunderstricken. For some minutes he remained speechless and motionless, looking incredulously at my friend with open mouth, and eyes that seemed starting from their sockets; then, apparently recovering himself in some measure, he seized a pen, and after several pauses and vacant stares finally filled up and signed a check for fifty thousand francs and handed it across the table to Dupin. The latter examined it carefully and deposited it in his pocketbook; then, unlocking an escritoire, took thence a letter and gave it to the Prefect. This functionary grasped it in a perfect agony of joy, opened it with a trembling hand, cast a rapid glance at its contents, and then, scrambling and struggling to the door, rushed at length unceremoniously from the room and from the house without having uttered a syllable since Dupin had requested him to fill up the check.

When he had gone, my friend entered into some explanations.

"The Parisian police," he said, "are exceedingly able in their way. They are persevering, ingenious, cunning, and thoroughly versed in the knowledge which their duties seem chiefly to demand. Thus, when G—— detailed to us his mode of searching the premises at the Hotel D——, I felt entire confidence in his having made a satisfactory investigation, so far as his labors extended."

"'So far as his labors extended?'" said I.

"Yes," said Dupin. "The measures adopted were not only the best of their kind, but carried out to absolute perfection. Had the letter been deposited within the range of their search, these fellows would, beyond a question, have found it."

I merely laughed, but he seemed quite serious in all that he said.

"The measures, then," he continued, "were good in their kind and well executed; their defect lay in their being inapplicable to the case and to the man. A certain set of highly ingenious resources are, with the Prefect, a sort of Procrustean bed, to which he forcibly adapts his designs. But he perpetually errs by being too deep or too shallow for the matter in hand; and many a schoolboy is a better reasoner than he. I knew one about eight years of age, whose success at guessing in the game of 'even and odd' attracted universal admiration. This game is simple, and is played with marbles. One player holds in his hand a number of these toys and demands of another whether that number is even or odd. If the guess is right, the guesser wins one; if wrong, he loses one. The boy to whom I allude won all the marbles of the school. Of course he had some principle of guessing; and this lay in mere observation and admeasurement of the astuteness of his opponents. For example, an arrant simpleton is his opponent, and, holding up his closed hand, asks, 'Are they even or odd?' Our school-boy replies, 'Odd,' and loses; but upon the second trial he wins, for he then says to himself: 'The simpleton had them even upon the first trial, and his amount of cunning is just sufficient to make him have them odd upon the second; I will therefore guess odd'; he guesses odd and wins. Now, with a simpleton a degree above the first, he would have reasoned thus: 'This fellow finds that in the first instance I guessed odd, and in the second he will propose to himself, upon the first impulse, a simple variation from even to odd, as did the first simpleton; but then a second thought will suggest that this is too simple a variation, and finally he will decide upon putting it even as before. I will therefore guess even';—he guesses even and wins. Now this mode of reasoning in the schoolboy, whom his fellows termed 'lucky,'—what, in its last analysis, is it?"

"It is merely," I said, "an identification of the reasoner's intellect with that of his opponent."

"It is," said Dupin; "and upon inquiring of the boy by what means he effected the thorough identification in which his success consisted, I received answer as follows: 'When I wish to find out how wise, or how stupid, or how good, or how wicked is any one, or what are his thoughts at the moment, I fashion the expression of my face, as accurately as possible, in accordance with the expression of his and then wait to see what thoughts or sentiments arise in my mind or heart, as if to match or correspond with the expression.' This response of the schoolboy lies at the bottom of all the spurious profundity which has been attributed to Rochefoucauld, to La Bruyère, to Machiavelli, and to Campanella."

"And the identification," I said, "of the reasoner's intellect with that of his opponent depends, if I understand you aright, upon the accuracy with which the opponent's intellect is admeasured."

"For its practical value it depends upon this," replied Dupin; "and the Prefect and his cohort fail so frequently, first, by default of this identification, and, secondly, by ill-admeasurement, or rather through non-admeasurement, of the intellect with which they are engaged. They consider only their own ideas of ingenuity; and, in searching for anything hidden, advert only to the modes in which they would have hidden it. They are right in this much, that their own ingenuity is a faithful representative of that of the mass; but when the cunning of the individual felon is diverse in character from their own the felon foils them, of course. This always happens when it is above their own, and very usually when it is below. They have no variation of principle in their investigations; at best, when urged by some unusual emergency, by some extraordinary reward, they extend or exaggerate their old modes of practice without touching their principles. What, for example, in this case of D——, has been done to vary the principle of action? What is all this boring, and probing, and sounding, and scrutinizing with the microscope, and dividing the surface of the building into registered square inches; what is it all but an exaggeration of the application of the one principle or set of principles of search, which are based upon the one set of notions regarding human ingenuity, to which the Prefect, in the long routine of his duty, has been accustomed? Do you not see he has taken it for granted that all men proceed to conceal a letter, not exactly in a gimlet-hole bored in a chair-leg, but, at least, in some out-of-the-way hole or corner suggested by the same tenor of thought which would urge a man to secrete a letter in a gimlet-hole bored in a chair-leg? And do you not see, also, that such *recherchés* nooks for concealment are adapted only for ordinary occasions, and would be adopted only by ordinary intellects; for, in all cases of concealment, a disposal of the article concealed, a disposal of it in this *recherché* manner, is, in the very first instance, presumable and presumed; and thus its discovery depends, not at all upon the acumen, but altogether upon the mere care, patience, and determination of the seekers; and where the case is of importance, or, what amounts to the same thing in the policial eyes, when the reward is of magnitude, the qualities in question have never been known to fail. You will now understand what I meant in suggesting that, had the purloined letter been hidden anywhere within the limits of the Prefect's examination,—in other words, had the principle of its concealment been comprehended within the principles of the Prefect,—its discovery would have been a matter altogether beyond question. This functionary, however, has been thoroughly mystified; and the remote source of his defeat lies in the supposition that the Minister is a fool, because he has acquired renown as a poet. All fools are poets; this the Prefect feels; and he is merely guilty of a *non distributio medii* in thence inferring that all poets are fools."

"But is this really the poet?" I asked. "There are two brothers, I know; and both have attained reputation in letters. The Minister, I believe, has written learnedly on the Differential Calculus. He is a mathematician and no poet."

"You are mistaken; I know him well; he is both. As poet and mathematician, he would reason well; as mere mathematician, he could not have reasoned at all, and thus would have been at the mercy of the Prefect."

"You surprise me," I said, "by these opinions, which have been contradicted by the voice of the world. You do not mean to set at naught the well-digested idea of centuries? The mathematical reason has long been regarded as the reason *par excellence*."

"'*Il y a à parier,*'" replied Dupin, quoting from Chamfort, "'*que toute idée publique, toute convention reçue, est une sottise, car elle a convenue au plus grand nombre.*' The mathematicians, I grant you, have done their best to promulgate the popular error to which you allude, and which is none the less an error for its promulgation as truth. With an art worthy a better cause, for example, they have insinuated the term 'analysis' into application to algebra. The French are the originators of this particular deception; but if a term is of any importance, if words derive any value from applicability, then 'analysis' conveys 'algebra' about as much as, in Latin, '*ambitus*' implies 'ambition,' '*religio*' 'religion,' or '*homines honesti*' a set of honorable men."

"You have a quarrel on hand, I see," said I, "with some of the algebraists of Paris; but proceed."

"I dispute the availability, and thus the value of that reason which is cultivated in any especial form other than the abstractly logical. I dispute, in particular, the reason educed by mathematical study. The mathematics are the science of form and quantity; mathematical reasoning is merely logic applied to observation upon form and quantity. The great error lies in supposing that even the truths of what is called pure algebra are abstract or general truths. And this error is so egregious that I am confounded at the universality with which it has been received. Mathematical axioms are not axioms of general truth. What is true of relation, of form and quantity, is often grossly false in regard to morals, for example. In this latter science it is very usually untrue that the aggregated parts are equal to the whole. In chemistry, also, the axiom fails. In the consideration of motive it fails; for two motives, each of a given value, have not, necessarily, a value, when united, equal to the sum of their values apart. There are numerous other mathematical truths which are only truths within the limits of relation. But the mathematician argues from his finite truths, through habit, as if they were of an absolutely general applicability, as the world indeed imagines them to be. Bryant, in his very learned *Mythology*, mentions an analogous source of error when he says that 'although the pagan fables are not believed, yet we forget ourselves continually and make inferences from them as existing realities.' With the algebraists, however, who are pagans themselves, the 'pagan fables' are believed, and the inferences are made, not so much through lapse of memory as through an unaccountable addling of the brains. In short, I never yet encountered the mere mathematician who could be trusted out of equal roots, or one who did not clandestinely hold it as a point of his faith that $x^2 + px$ was absolutely and unconditionally equal to q. Say to one of these gentlemen, by way of experiment, if you please, that you believe occasions may occur where $x^2 + px$ is not altogether equal to q, and, having made him understand what you mean, get out of his reach as speedily as convenient, for, beyond doubt, he will endeavor to knock you down.

"I mean to say," continued Dupin, while I merely laughed at his last observations, "that if the Minister had been no more than a mathematician, the Prefect would have been under no necessity of giving me this check. I knew him, however, as both mathematician and poet, and my measures were adapted to his capacity with refer-

ence to the circumstances by which he was surrounded. I knew him
as a courtier, too, and as a bold intriguant. Such a man, I considered,
could not fail to be aware of the ordinary policial modes of action.
He could not have failed to anticipate—and events have proved that
he did not fail to anticipate—the waylayings to which he was sub-
jected. He must have foreseen, I reflected, the secret investigations
of his premises. His frequent absences from home at night, which
were hailed by the Prefect as certain aids to his success, I regarded
only as ruses to afford opportunity for thorough search to the police,
and thus the sooner to impress them with the conviction, to which
G——, in fact, did finally arrive,—the conviction that the letter was
not upon the premises. I felt, also, that the whole train of thought,
which I was at some pains in detailing to you just now, concerning the invariable principle of policial action in searches for articles
concealed,—I felt that this whole train of thought would necessarily
pass through the mind of the Minister. It would imperatively lead
him to despise all the ordinary nooks of concealment. He could
not, I reflected, be so weak as not to see that the most intricate and
remote recess of his hotel would be as open as his commonest closets
to the eyes, to the probes, to the gimlets, and to the microscopes
of the Prefect. I saw, in fine, that he would be driven, as a matter
of course, to simplicity, if not deliberately induced to it as a matter of
choice. You will remember, perhaps, how desperately the Prefect
laughed when I suggested, upon our first interview, that it was just
possible this mystery troubled him so much on account of its being
so very self-evident."

"Yes," said I, "I remember his merriment well. I really thought he
would have fallen into convulsions."

"The material world," continued Dupin, "abounds with very strict
analogies to the immaterial and thus some color of truth has been
given to the rhetorical dogma that metaphor, or simile, may be made
to strengthen an argument as well as to embellish a description. The
principle of the *vis inertiæ*, for example, seems to be identical in phys-
ics and metaphysics. It is not more true in the former, that a large
body is with more difficulty set in motion than a smaller one, and
that its subsequent momentum is commensurate with this difficulty,
than it is, in the latter, that intellects of the vaster capacity, while
more forcible, more constant, and more eventful in their movements
than those of inferior grade, are yet the less readily moved, and more
embarrassed, and full of hesitation in the first few steps of their prog-

ress. Again: have you ever noticed which of the street signs, over the shop doors, are the most attractive of attention?"

"I have never given the matter a thought," I said.

"There is a game of puzzles," he resumed, "which is played upon a map. One party playing requires another to find a given word, the name of town, river, state, or empire,—any word, in short, upon the motley and perplexed surface of the chart. A novice in the game generally seeks to embarrass his opponents by giving them the most minutely lettered names; but the adept selects such words as stretch, in large characters, from one end of the chart to the other. These, like the over-largely lettered signs and placards of the street, escape observation by dint of being excessively obvious; and here the physical oversight is precisely analogous with the moral inapprehension by which the intellect suffers to pass unnoticed those considerations which are too obtrusively and too palpably self-evident. But this is a point, it appears, somewhat above or beneath the understanding of the Prefect. He never once thought it probable, or possible, that the Minister had deposited the letter immediately beneath the nose of the whole world by way of best preventing any portion of that world from perceiving it.

"But the more I reflected upon the daring, dashing, and discriminating ingenuity of D——; upon the fact that the document must always have been at hand, if he intended to use it to good purpose; and upon the decisive evidence, obtained by the Prefect, that it was not hidden within the limits of that dignitary's ordinary search, the more satisfied I became that, to conceal this letter, the Minister had resorted to the comprehensive and sagacious expedient of not attempting to conceal it at all.

"Full of these ideas, I prepared myself with a pair of green spectacles, and called one fine morning, quite by accident, at the ministerial hotel. I found D—— at home, yawning, lounging, and dawdling, as usual, and pretending to be in the last extremity of *ennui*. He is, perhaps, the most really energetic human being now alive; but that is only when nobody sees him.

"To be even with him, I complained of my weak eyes, and lamented the necessity of the spectacles under cover of which I cautiously and thoroughly surveyed the whole apartment, while seemingly intent only upon the conversation of my host.

"I paid especial attention to a large writing-table near which he sat, and upon which lay confusedly some miscellaneous letters and

other papers, with one or two musical instruments and a few books.
Here, however, after a long and very deliberate scrutiny, I saw nothing
to excite particular suspicion.

"At length my eyes, in going the circuit of the room, fell upon a
trumpery filigree card-rack of pasteboard, that hung dangling by a
dirty blue ribbon from a little brass knob just beneath the middle of
the mantelpiece. In this rack, which had three or four compartments,
were five or six visiting-cards and a solitary letter. This last was much
soiled and crumpled. It was torn nearly in two, across the middle,
as if a design, in the first instance, to tear it entirely up as worthless,
had been altered, or stayed, in the second. It had a large black seal,
bearing the D—— cipher very conspicuously, and was addressed, in
a diminutive female hand, to D——, the Minister, himself. It was
thrust carelessly, and even, as it seemed, contemptuously, into one of
the uppermost divisions of the rack.

"No sooner had I glanced at this letter than I concluded it to be that
of which I was in search. To be sure, it was, to all appearance, radically
different from the one of which the Prefect had read us so minute a
description. Here the seal was large and black, with the D—— cipher,
there it was small and red, with the ducal arms of the S—— family. Here, the address, to the Minister, was diminutive and feminine;
there the superscription, to a certain royal personage, was markedly
bold and decided; the size alone formed a point of correspondence.
But, then, the radicalness of these differences, which was excessive:
the dirt; the soiled and torn condition of the paper, so inconsistent
with the true methodical habits of D——, and so suggestive of a
design to delude the beholder into an idea of the worthlessness of the
document,—these things, together with the hyperobtrusive situation
of this document, full in the view of every visitor, and thus exactly in
accordance with the conclusions to which I had previously arrived;
these things, I say, were strongly corroborative of suspicion, in one
who came with the intention to suspect.

"I protracted my visit as long as possible, and, while I maintained
a most animated discussion with the Minister upon a topic which
I knew well had never failed to interest and excite him, I kept my
attention really riveted upon the letter. In this examination, I committed to memory its external appearance and arrangement in the rack;
and also fell, at length, upon a discovery which set at rest whatever
trivial doubt I might have entertained. In scrutinizing the edges of
the paper, I observed them to be more chafed than seemed necessary.

They presented the broken appearance which is manifested when a stiff paper, having been once folded and pressed with a folder, is refolded in a reversed direction, in the same creases or edges which had formed the original fold. This discovery was sufficient. It was clear to me that the letter had been turned, as a glove, inside out, redirected and resealed. I bade the Minister good-morning, and took my departure at once, leaving a gold snuff-box upon the table.

"The next morning I called for the snuff-box, when we resumed, quite eagerly, the conversation of the preceding day. While thus engaged, however, a loud report, as if of a pistol, was heard immediately beneath the windows of the hotel, and was succeeded by a series of fearful screams, and the shoutings of a terrified mob. D—— rushed to a casement, threw it open, and looked out. In the meantime I stepped to the card-rack, took the letter, put it in my pocket, and replaced it by a facsimile (so far as regards externals) which I had carefully prepared at my lodgings, imitating the D—— cipher very readily by means of a seal formed of bread.

"The disturbance in the street had been occasioned by the frantic behavior of a man with a musket. He had fired it among a crowd of women and children. It proved, however, to have been without a ball, and the fellow was suffered to go his way as a lunatic or a drunkard. When he had gone, D—— came from the window, whither I had followed him immediately upon securing the object in view. Soon afterward I bade him farewell. The pretended lunatic was a man in my own pay."

"But what purpose had you," I asked, "in replacing the letter by a facsimile? Would it not have been better, at the first visit, to have seized it openly and departed?"

"D——," replied Dupin, "is a desperate man, and a man of nerve. His hotel, too, is not without attendants devoted to his interests. Had I made the wild attempt you suggest, I might never have left the ministerial presence alive. The good people of Paris might have heard of me no more. But I had an object apart from these considerations. You know my political prepossessions. In this matter, I act as a partisan of the lady concerned. For eighteen months the Minister has had her in his power. She has now him in hers, since, being unaware that the letter is not in his possession, he will proceed with his exactions as if it was. Thus will he inevitably commit himself, at once, to his political destruction. His downfall, too, will not be more precipitate than awkward. It is all very well to talk about the *facilis descensus Averni*;

but in all kinds of climbing, as Catalani said of singing, it is far more easy to get up than to come down. In the present instance I have no sympathy, at least no pity, for him who descends. He is that *monstrum horrendum*, an unprincipled man of genius. I confess, however, that I should like very well to know the precise character of his thoughts, when, being defied by her whom the Prefect terms 'a certain personage,' he is reduced to opening the letter which I left for him in the card-rack."

"How? Did you put anything particular in it?"

"Why, it did not seem altogether right to leave the interior blank; that would have been insulting. D——, at Vienna once, did me an evil turn, which I told him, quite good-humoredly, that I should remember. So, as I knew he would feel some curiosity in regard to the identity of the person who had outwitted him, I thought it a pity not to give him a clue. He is well acquainted with my MS., and I just copied into the middle of the blank sheet the words

"'—Un dessein si funeste,
S'il n'est digne d'Atrée, est digne de Thyeste.'

They are to be found in Crébillon's *Atrée*."

The Red-Headed League

Sir Arthur Conan Doyle

I HAD called upon my friend, Mr. Sherlock Holmes, one day in the autumn of last year, and found him in deep conversation with a very stout, florid-faced elderly gentleman, with fiery red hair. With an apology for my intrusion, I was about to withdraw, when Holmes pulled me abruptly into the room and closed the door behind me.

"You could not possibly have come at a better time, my dear Watson," he said, cordially.

"I was afraid that you were engaged."

"So I am. Very much so."

"Then I can wait in the next room."

"Not at all. This gentleman, Mr. Wilson, has been my partner and helper in many of my most successful cases, and I have no doubt that he will be of the utmost use to me in yours also."

The stout gentleman half rose from his chair and gave a bob of greeting, with a quick little questioning glance from his small, fat-encircled eyes.

"Try the settee," said Holmes, relapsing into his armchair, and putting his finger-tips together, as was his custom when in judicial moods. "I know, my dear Watson, that you share my love of all that is bizarre and outside the conventions and humdrum routine of every-day life. You have shown your relish for it by the enthusiasm which has prompted you to chronicle, and, if you will excuse my saying so, somewhat to embellish so many of my own little adventures."

"Your cases have indeed been of the greatest interest to me," I observed.

"You will remember that I remarked the other day, just before we went into the very simple problem presented by Miss Mary Sutherland, that for strange effects and extraordinary combinations we must go to life itself, which is always far more daring than any effort of the imagination."

"A proposition which I took the liberty of doubting."

"You did, doctor, but none the less you must come round to my view, for otherwise I shall keep on piling fact upon fact on you, until your reason breaks down under them and acknowledges me to be right. Now, Mr. Jabez Wilson here has been good enough to call upon me this morning, and to begin a narrative which promises to be one of the most singular which I have listened to for some time. You have heard me remark that the strangest and most unique things are very often connected not with the larger but with the smaller crimes, and occasionally, indeed, where there is room for doubt whether any positive crime has been committed. As far as I have heard, it is impossible for me to say whether the present case is an instance of crime or not, but the course of events is certainly among the most singular that I have ever listened to. Perhaps, Mr. Wilson, you would have the great kindness to recommence your narrative. I ask you, not merely because my friend, Dr. Watson, has not heard the opening part, but also because the peculiar nature of the story makes me anxious to have every possible detail from your lips. As a rule, when I have heard some slight indication of the course of events I am able to guide myself by the thousands of other similar cases which occur to my memory. In the present instance I am forced to admit that the facts are, to the best of my belief, unique."

The portly client puffed out his chest with an appearance of some little pride, and pulled a dirty and wrinkled newspaper from the inside pocket of his greatcoat. As he glanced down the advertisement column, with his head thrust forward, and the paper flattened out upon his knee, I took a good look at the man, and endeavored, after the fashion of my companion, to read the indications which might be presented by his dress or appearance.

I did not gain very much, however, by my inspection. Our visitor bore every mark of being an average commonplace British tradesman, obese, pompous, and slow. He wore rather baggy gray shepherd's check trousers, a not over-clean black frock-coat, unbuttoned in the front, and a drab waistcoat with a heavy brassy Albert chain, and a square pierced bit of metal dangling down as an ornament. A frayed top hat and a faded brown overcoat with a wrinkled velvet collar lay upon a chair beside him. Altogether, look as I would, there was nothing remarkable about the man save his blazing red head and the expression of extreme chagrin and discontent upon his features.

Sherlock Holmes's quick eye took in my occupation, and he shook his head with a smile as he noticed my questioning glances. "Beyond the obvious facts that he has at some time done manual labor, that he takes snuff, that he is a Freemason, that he has been in China, and that he has done a considerable amount of writing lately, I can deduce nothing else."

Mr. Jabez Wilson started up in his chair, with his forefinger upon the paper, but his eyes upon my companion.

"How, in the name of good fortune, did you know all that, Mr. Holmes?" he asked. "How did you know, for example, that I did manual labor? It's as true as gospel, for I began as a ship's carpenter."

"Your hands, my dear sir. Your right hand is quite a size larger than your left. You have worked with it and the muscles are more developed."

"Well, the snuff, then, and the Freemasonry?"

"I won't insult your intelligence by telling you how I read that, especially as, rather against the strict rules of your order, you use an arc and compass breastpin."

"Ah, of course, I forgot that. But the writing?"

"What else can be indicated by that right cuff so very shiny for five inches, and the left one with the smooth patch near the elbow where you rest it upon the desk."

"Well, but China?"

"The fish which you have tattooed immediately above your wrist could only have been done in China. I have made a small study of tattoo marks, and have even contributed to the literature of the subject. That trick of staining the fishes' scales of a delicate pink is quite peculiar to China. When, in addition, I see a Chinese coin hanging from your watch-chain, the matter becomes even more simple."

Mr. Jabez Wilson laughed heavily. "Well, I never!" said he. "I thought at first that you had done something clever, but I see that there was nothing in it after all."

"I begin to think, Watson," said Holmes, "that I make a mistake in explaining. 'Omne ignotum pro magnifico,' you know, and my poor little reputation, such as it is, will suffer shipwreck if I am so candid. Can you not find the advertisement, Mr. Wilson?"

"Yes, I have got it now," he answered, with his thick, red finger planted half-way down the column. "Here it is. This is what began it all. You just read it for yourself, sir."

I took the paper from him and read as follows:

"To THE RED-HEADED LEAGUE: On account of the bequest of the late
Ezekiah Hopkins, of Lebanon, Pa., U.S.A., there is now another vacancy
open which entitles a member of the League to a salary of four pounds a
week for purely nominal services. All red-headed men who are sound in
body and mind and above the age of twenty-one years are eligible. Apply in
person on Monday, at eleven o'clock, to Duncan Ross, at the offices of the
League, 7 Pope's Court, Fleet Street."

"What on earth does this mean?" I ejaculated, after I had twice
read over the extraordinary announcement.

Holmes chuckled and wriggled in his chair, as was his habit when
in high spirits. "It is a little off the beaten track, isn't it?" said he. "And
now, Mr. Wilson, off you go at scratch, and tell us all about yourself,
your household, and the effect which this advertisement had upon
your fortunes. You will first make a note, doctor, of the paper and the
date."

"It is *The Morning Chronicle* of April 27, 1890. Just two months
ago."

"Very good. Now, Mr. Wilson."

"Well, it is just as I have been telling you, Mr. Sherlock Holmes,"
said Jabez Wilson, mopping his forehead, "I have a small pawnbroker's
business at Coburg Square, near the City. It's not a very large affair,
and of late years it has not done more than just give me a living. I
used to be able to keep two assistants, but now I only keep one; and
I would have a job to pay him but that he is willing to come for half
wages, so as to learn the business."

"What is the name of this obliging youth?" asked Sherlock
Holmes.

"His name is Vincent Spaulding, and he's not such a youth either.
It's hard to say his age. I should not wish a smarter assistant, Mr.
Holmes; and I know very well that he could better himself, and earn
twice what I am able to give him. But, after all, if he is satisfied, why
should I put ideas in his head?"

"Why, indeed? You seem most fortunate in having an employee
who comes under the full market price. It is not a common experience among employers in this age. I don't know that your assistant is
not as remarkable as your advertisement."

"Oh, he has his faults, too," said Mr. Wilson. "Never was such a
fellow for photography. Snapping away with a camera when he ought

to be improving his mind, and then diving down into the cellar like a rabbit into its hole to develop his pictures. That is his main fault; but, on the whole, he's a good worker. There's no vice in him."

"He is still with you, I presume?"

"Yes, sir. He and a girl of fourteen, who does a bit of simple cooking, and keeps the place clean—that's all I have in the house, for I am a widower, and never had any family. We live very quietly, sir, the three of us; and we keep a roof over our heads, and pay our debts, if we do nothing more.

"The first thing that put us out was that advertisement. Spaulding, he came down into the office just this day eight weeks, with this very paper in his hand, and he says:

"'I wish to the Lord, Mr. Wilson, that I was a red-headed man.'

"'Why that?' I asks.

"'Why,' says he, 'here's another vacancy on the League of the Red-headed Men. It's worth quite a little fortune to any man who gets it, and I understand that there are more vacancies than there are men, so that the trustees are at their wits' end what to do with the money. If my hair would only change color here's a nice little crib all ready for me to step into.'

"'Why, what is it, then?' I asked. You see, Mr. Holmes, I am a very stay-at-home man, and, as my business came to me instead of my having to go to it, I was often weeks on end without putting my foot over the door-mat. In that way I didn't know much of what was going on outside, and I was always glad of a bit of news.

"'Have you never heard of the League of the Red-headed Men?' he asked, with his eyes open.

"'Never.'

"'Why, I wonder at that, for you are eligible yourself for one of the vacancies.'

"'And what are they worth?' I asked.

"'Oh, merely a couple of hundred a year, but the work is slight, and it need not interfere very much with one's other occupations.'

"Well, you can easily think that that made me prick up my ears, for the business has not been over good for some years, and an extra couple of hundred would have been very handy.

"'Tell me all about it,' said I.

"'Well,' said he, showing me the advertisement, 'you can see for yourself that the League has a vacancy, and there is the address where you should apply for particulars. As far as I can make out, the League was founded by an American millionaire, Ezekiah Hopkins, who was very peculiar in his ways. He was himself red-headed, and he had a great sympathy for all red-headed men; so, when he died, it was found that he had left his enormous fortune in the hands of trustees, with instructions to apply the interest to the providing of easy berths to men whose hair is of that color. From all I hear it is splendid pay, and very little to do.'

"'But,' said I, 'there would be millions of red-headed men who would apply.'

"'Not so many as you might think,' he answered. 'You see it is really confined to Londoners, and to grown men. This American had started from London when he was young, and he wanted to do the old town a good turn. Then, again, I have heard it is no use your applying if your hair is light red, or dark red, or anything but real, bright, blazing, fiery red. Now, if you cared to apply, Mr. Wilson, you would just walk in; but perhaps it would hardly be worth your while to put yourself out of the way for the sake of a few hundred pounds.'

"Now it is a fact, gentlemen, as you may see for yourselves, that my hair is of a very full and rich tint, so that it seemed to me that, if there was to be any competition in the matter, I stood as good a chance as any man that I had ever met. Vincent Spaulding seemed to know so much about it that I thought he might prove useful, so I just ordered him to put up the shutters for the day, and to come right away with me. He was very willing to have a holiday, so we shut the business up, and started off for the address that was given us in the advertisement.

"I never hope to see such a sight as that again, Mr. Holmes. From north, south, east, and west every man who had a shade of red in his hair had tramped into the City to answer the advertisement. Fleet Street was choked with red-headed folk, and Pope's Court looked like a coster's orange barrow. I should not have thought there were so many in the whole country as were brought together by that single advertisement. Every shade of color they were—straw, lemon, orange, brick, Irish-setter, liver, clay; but, as Spaulding said, there were not many who had the real vivid flame-colored tint. When I saw how many were waiting, I would have given it up in despair; but Spaulding would not hear of it. How he did it I could not imagine, but he pushed and pulled and butted until he got me through the crowd, and right up to the steps which led to the office. There was a double stream upon the stair, some going up in hope, and some coming back dejected; but we wedged in as well as we could, and soon found ourselves in the office."

"Your experience has been a most entertaining one," remarked Holmes, as his client paused and refreshed his memory with a huge pinch of snuff. "Pray continue your very interesting statement."

"There was nothing in the office but a couple of wooden chairs and a deal table, behind which sat a small man, with a head that was even redder than mine. He said a few words to each candidate as he came up, and then he always managed to find some fault in them which would disqualify them. Getting a vacancy did not seem to be such a very easy matter after all. However, when our turn came, the little man was much more favorable to me than to any of the others, and he closed the door as we entered, so that he might have a private word with us.

"'This is Mr. Jabez Wilson,' said my assistant, 'and he is willing to fill a vacancy in the League.'

"'And he is admirably suited for it,' the other answered. 'He has every requirement. I cannot recall when I have seen anything so fine.' He took a step backward, cocked his head on one side, and gazed at my hair until I felt quite bashful. Then suddenly he plunged forward, wrung my hand, and congratulated me warmly on my success.

"'It would be injustice to hesitate,' said he. 'You will, however, I am sure, excuse me for taking an obvious precaution.' With that he seized my hair in both his hands, and tugged until I yelled with the pain. 'There is water in your eyes,' said he, as he released me. 'I perceive that all is as it should be. But we have to be careful, for we have twice been deceived by wigs and once by paint. I could tell you tales of cobbler's wax which would disgust you with human nature.' He stepped over to the window and shouted through it at the top of his voice that the vacancy was filled. A groan of disappointment came up from below, and the folk all trooped away in different directions, until there was not a red head to be seen except my own and that of the manager.

"'My name,' said he, 'is Mr. Duncan Ross, and I am myself one of the pensioners upon the fund left by our noble benefactor. Are you a married man, Mr. Wilson? Have you a family?'

"I answered that I had not.

"His face fell immediately.

"'Dear me!' he said, gravely, 'that is very serious indeed. I am sorry to hear you say that. The fund was, of course, for the propagation and spread of the redheads as well as for their maintenance. It is exceedingly unfortunate that you should be a bachelor.'

"My face lengthened at this, Mr. Holmes, for I thought that I was not to have the vacancy after all; but, after thinking it over for a few minutes, he said that it would be all right.

"'In the case of another,' said he, 'the objection might be fatal, but we must stretch a point in favor of a man with such a head of hair as yours. When shall you be able to enter upon your new duties?'

"'Well, it is a little awkward, for I have a business already,' said I.

"'Oh, never mind about that, Mr. Wilson!' said Vincent Spaulding. 'I shall be able to look after that for you.'

"'What would be the hours?' I asked.

"'Ten to two.'

"Now a pawnbroker's business is mostly done of an evening, Mr. Holmes, especially Thursday and Friday evenings, which is just before pay-day; so it would suit me very well to earn a little in the mornings. Besides, I knew that my assistant was a good man, and that he would see to anything that turned up.

"'That would suit me very well,' said I. 'And the pay?'

"'Is four pounds a week.'

"'And the work?'

"'Is purely nominal.'

"'What do you call purely nominal?'

"'Well, you have to be in the office, or at least in the building, the whole time. If you leave, you forfeit your whole position forever. The will is very clear upon that point. You don't comply with the conditions if you budge from the office during that time.'

"'It's only four hours a day, and I should not think of leaving,' said I.

"'No excuse will avail,' said Mr. Duncan Ross, 'neither sickness, nor business, nor anything else. There you must stay, or you lose your billet.'

"'And the work?'

"'Is to copy out the "Encyclopædia Britannica." There is the first volume of it in that press. You must find your own ink, pens, and blotting-paper, but we provide this table and chair. Will you be ready to-morrow?'

"'Certainly,' I answered.

"'Then, good-by, Mr. Jabez Wilson, and let me congratulate you once more on the important position which you have been fortunate

enough to gain.' He bowed me out of the room, and I went home
with my assistant hardly knowing what to say or do, I was so pleased
at my own good fortune.

"Well, I thought over the matter all day, and by evening I was in
low spirits again; for I had quite persuaded myself that the whole
affair must be some great hoax or fraud, though what its object might
be I could not imagine. It seemed altogether past belief that any
one could make such a will, or that they would pay such a sum for
doing anything so simple as copying out the 'Encyclopædia Britannica.' Vincent Spaulding did what he could to cheer me up, but by
bedtime I had reasoned myself out of the whole thing. However, in
the morning I determined to have a look at it anyhow, so I bought a
penny bottle of ink, and with a quill pen and seven sheets of foolscap
paper I started off for Pope's Court.

"Well, to my surprise and delight everything was as right as possible. The table was set out ready for me, and Mr. Duncan Ross was
there to see that I got fairly to work. He started me off upon the letter
A, and then he left me; but he would drop in from time to time to
see that all was right with me. At two o'clock he bade me good-day,
complimented me upon the amount that I had written, and locked
the door of the office after me.

"This went on day after day, Mr. Holmes, and on Saturday the
manager came in and planked down four golden sovereigns for my
week's work. It was the same next week, and the same the week
after. Every morning I was there, at ten, and every afternoon I left at
two. By degrees Mr. Duncan Ross took to coming in only once of
a morning, and then, after a time, he did not come in at all. Still, of
course, I never dared to leave the room for an instant, for I was not
sure when he might come, and the billet was such a good one, and
suited me so well, that I would not risk the loss of it.

"Eight weeks passed away like this, and I had written about Abbots,
and Archery, and Armor, and Architecture and Attica, and hoped with
diligence that I might get on to the B's before very long. It cost me
something in foolscap, and I had pretty nearly filled a shelf with my
writings. And then suddenly the whole business came to an end."

"To an end?"

"Yes, sir. And no later than this morning. I went to my work as
usual at ten o'clock, but the door was shut and locked, with a little
square of cardboard hammered onto the middle of the panel with a
tack. Here it is, and you can read for yourself."

He held up a piece of white cardboard, about the size of a sheet of note-paper. It read in this fashion:

"The Red-headed League Dissolved.
Oct. 9, 1890."

Sherlock Holmes and I surveyed this curt announcement and the rueful face behind it, until the comical side of the affair so completely overtopped every consideration that we both burst out into a roar of laughter.

"I cannot see that there is anything very funny," cried our client, flushing up to the roots of his flaming hair. "If you can do nothing better than laugh at me, I can go elsewhere."

"No, no," cried Holmes, shoving him back into the chair from which he had half risen. "I really wouldn't miss your case for the world. It is most refreshingly unusual. But there is, if you will excuse my saying so, something just a little funny about it. Pray what steps did you take when you found the card upon the door?"

"I was staggered, sir. I did not know what to do. Then I called at the offices round, but none of them seemed to know anything about it. Finally, I went to the landlord, who is an accountant living on the ground floor, and I asked him if he could tell me what had become of the Red-headed League. He said that he had never heard of any such body. Then I asked him who Mr. Duncan Ross was. He answered that the name was new to him.

"'Well,' said I, 'the gentleman at No. 4.'

"'What, the red-headed man?'

"'Yes.'

"'Oh,' said he, 'his name was William Morris. He was a solicitor, and was using my room as a temporary convenience until his new premises were ready. He moved out yesterday.'

"'Where could I find him?'

"'Oh, at his new offices. He did tell me the address. Yes, 17 King Edward Street, near St. Paul's.'

"I started off, Mr. Holmes, but when I got to that address it was a manufactory of artificial knee-caps, and no one in it had ever heard of either Mr. William Morris, or Mr. Duncan Ross."

"And what did you do then?" asked Holmes.

"I went home to Saxe-Coburg Square, and I took the advice of my assistant. But he could not help me in any way. He could only say that if I waited I should hear by post. But that was not quite good enough, Mr. Holmes. I did not wish to lose such a place without a struggle, so, as I had heard that you were good enough to give advice to poor folk who were in need of it, I came right away to you."

"And you did very wisely," said Holmes. "Your case is an exceedingly remarkable one, and I shall be happy to look into it. From what you have told me I think that it is possible that graver issues hang from it than might at first sight appear."

"Grave enough!" said Mr. Jabez Wilson. "Why, I have lost four pound a week."

"As far as you are personally concerned," remarked Holmes, "I do not see that you have any grievance against this extraordinary league. On the contrary, you are, as I understand, richer by some thirty pounds, to say nothing of the minute knowledge which you have gained on every subject which comes under the letter A. You have lost nothing by them."

"No, sir. But I want to find out about them, and who they are, and what their object was in playing this prank—if it was a prank—upon me. It was a pretty expensive joke for them, for it cost them two-and-thirty pounds."

"We shall endeavor to clear up these points for you. And, first, one or two questions, Mr. Wilson. This assistant of yours who first called your attention to the advertisement—how long had he been with you?"

"About a month then."

"How did he come?"

"In answer to an advertisement."

"Was he the only applicant?"

"No, I had a dozen."

"Why did you pick him?"

"Because he was handy and would come cheap."

"At half wages, in fact."

"Yes."

"What is he like, this Vincent Spaulding?"

"Small, stout-built, very quick in his ways, no hair on his face, though he's not short of thirty. Has a white splash of acid upon his forehead."

Holmes sat up in his chair, in considerable excitement. "I thought as much," said he. "Have you ever observed that his ears are pierced for earrings?"

"Yes, sir. He told me that a gypsy had done it for him when he was a lad."

"Hum!" said Holmes, sinking back in deep thought. "He is still with you?"

"Oh, yes, sir; I have only just left him."

"And has your business been attended to in your absence?"

"Nothing to complain of, sir. There's never very much to do of a morning."

"That will do, Mr. Wilson. I shall be happy to give you an opinion upon the subject in the course of a day or two. To-day is Saturday, and I hope that by Monday we may come to a conclusion.

"Well, Watson," said Holmes, when our visitor had left us, "what do you make of it all?"

"I make nothing of it," I answered, frankly. "It is a most mysterious business."

"As a rule," said Holmes, "the more bizarre a thing is the less mysterious it proves to be. It is your commonplace, featureless crimes which are really puzzling, just as a commonplace face is the most difficult to identify. But I must be prompt over this matter."

"What are you going to do, then?" I asked.

"To smoke," he answered. "It is quite a three-pipe problem, and I beg that you won't speak to me for fifty minutes." He curled himself up in his chair, with his thin knees drawn up to his hawk-like nose, and there he sat with his eyes closed and his black clay pipe thrusting out like the bill of some strange bird. I had come to the conclusion that he had dropped asleep, and indeed was nodding myself, when he suddenly sprang out of his chair with the gesture of a man who has made up his mind, and put his pipe down upon the mantelpiece.

"Sarasate plays at St. James's Hall this afternoon," he remarked. "What do you think, Watson? Could your patients spare you for a few hours?"

"I have nothing to do to-day. My practice is never very absorbing."

"Then put on your hat and come. I am going through the City first, and we can have some lunch on the way. I observe that there is a good deal of German music on the program, which is rather more to my taste than Italian or French. It is introspective, and I want to introspect. Come along!"

We traveled by the Underground as far as Aldersgate; and a short walk took us to Saxe-Coburg Square, the scene of the singular story which we had listened to in the morning. It was a poky, little, shabby-genteel place, where four lines of dingy, two-storied brick houses looked out into a small railed-in inclosure, where a lawn of weedy grass, and a few clumps of faded laurel bushes made a hard fight against a smoke-laden and uncongenial atmosphere. Three gilt balls and a brown board with JABEZ WILSON in white letters, upon a corner house, announced the place where our red-headed client carried on his business. Sherlock Holmes stopped in front of it with his head on one side, and looked it all over, with his eyes shining brightly between puckered lids. Then he walked slowly up the street, and then down again to the corner, still looking keenly at the houses. Finally he returned to the pawnbroker's and, having thumped vigorously upon the pavement with his stick two or three times, he went up to the door and knocked. It was instantly opened by a bright-looking, clean-shaven young fellow, who asked him to step in.

"Thank you," said Holmes, "I only wished to ask you how you would go from here to the Strand."

"Third right, four left," answered the assistant, promptly, closing the door.

"Smart fellow, that," observed Holmes as we walked away. "He is, in my judgment, the fourth smartest man in London, and for daring I am not sure that he has not a claim to be third. I have known something of him before."

"Evidently," said I, "Mr. Wilson's assistant counts for a good deal in this mystery of the Red-headed League. I am sure that you inquired your way merely in order that you might see him."

"Not him."

"What then?"

"The knees of his trousers."

"And what did you see?"

"What I expected to see."

"Why did you beat the pavement?"

"My dear doctor, this is a time for observation, not for talk. We are spies in an enemy's country. We know something of Saxe-Coburg Square. Let us now explore the parts which lie behind it."

The road in which we found ourselves as we turned round the corner from the retired Saxe-Coburg Square presented as great a contrast to it as the front of a picture does to the back. It was one of the main arteries which convey the traffic of the City to the north and west. The roadway was blocked with the immense stream of

commerce flowing in a double tide inward and outward, while the
footpaths were black with the hurrying swarm of pedestrians. It was
difficult to realize, as we looked at the line of fine shops and stately
business premises, that they really abutted on the other side upon the
faded and stagnant square which we had just quitted.

"Let me see," said Holmes, standing at the corner, and glancing
along the line, "I should like just to remember the order of the houses
here. It is a hobby of mine to have an exact knowledge of London.
There is Mortimer's, the tobacconist; the little newspaper shop, the
Coburg branch of the City and Suburban Bank, the Vegetarian Restaurant, and McFarlane's carriage-building depot. That carries us right
on to the other block. And now, doctor, we've done our work, so it's
time we had some play. A sandwich and a cup of coffee, and then off
to violin-land, where all is sweetness, and delicacy, and harmony, and
there are no red-headed clients to vex us with their conundrums."

My friend was an enthusiastic musician, being himself not only a
very capable performer, but a composer of no ordinary merit. All the
afternoon he sat in the stalls wrapped in the most perfect happiness,
gently waving his long thin fingers in time to the music, while his
gently smiling face and his languid, dreamy eyes were as unlike those
of Holmes the sleuth-hound, Holmes the relentless, keen-witted,
ready-handed criminal agent, as it was possible to conceive. In his
singular character the dual nature alternately asserted itself, and his
extreme exactness and astuteness represented, as I have often thought,
the reaction against the poetic and contemplative mood which occasionally predominated in him. The swing of his nature took him from
extreme languor to devouring energy; and, as I knew well, he was
never so truly formidable as when, for days on end, he had been
lounging in his armchair amid his improvisations and his black-letter
editions. Then it was that the lust of the chase would suddenly come
upon him, and that his brilliant reasoning power would rise to the
level of intuition, until those who were unacquainted with his methods would look askance at him as on a man whose knowledge was not
that of other mortals. When I saw him that afternoon so enwrapped
in the music at St. James's Hall, I felt that an evil time might be coming upon those whom he had set himself to hunt down.

"You want to go home, no doubt, doctor," he remarked, as we
emerged.

"Yes, it would be as well."

"And I have some business to do which will take some hours. This business at Coburg Square is serious."

"Why serious?"

"A considerable crime is in contemplation. I have every reason to believe that we shall be in time to stop it. But to-day being Saturday rather complicates matters. I shall want your help to-night."

"At what time?"

"Ten will be early enough."

"I shall be at Baker Street at ten."

"Very well. And, I say, doctor! there may be some little danger, so kindly put your army revolver in your pocket." He waved his hand, turned on his heel, and disappeared in an instant among the crowd.

I trust that I am not more dense than my neighbors, but I was always oppressed with a sense of my own stupidity in my dealings with Sherlock Holmes. Here I had heard what he had heard, I had seen what he had seen, and yet from his words it was evident that he saw clearly not only what had happened, but what was about to happen, while to me the whole business was still confused and grotesque. As I drove home to my house in Kensington I thought over it all, from the extraordinary story of the red-headed copier of the "Encyclopædia" down to the visit to Saxe-Coburg Square, and the ominous words with which he had parted from me. What was this nocturnal expedition, and why should I go armed? Where were we going, and what were we to do? I had the hint from Holmes that this smooth-faced pawnbroker's assistant was a formidable man—a man who might play a deep game. I tried to puzzle it out, but gave it up in despair, and set the matter aside until night should bring an explanation.

It was a quarter-past nine when I started from home and made my way across the Park, and so through Oxford Street to Baker Street. Two hansoms were standing at the door, and, as I entered the passage, I heard the sound of voices from above. On entering his room, I found Holmes in animated conversation with two men, one of whom I recognized as Peter Jones, the official police agent; while the other was a long, thin, sad-faced man with a very shiny hat and oppressively respectable frock-coat.

"Ha! our party is complete," said Holmes, buttoning up his pea-jacket, and taking his heavy hunting crop from the rack. "Watson,

I think you know Mr. Jones, of Scotland Yard? Let me introduce you to Mr. Merryweather, who is to be our companion in to-night's adventure."

"We're hunting in couples again, doctor, you see," said Jones, in his consequential way. "Our friend here is a wonderful man for starting a chase. All he wants is an old dog to help him do the running down."

"I hope a wild goose may not prove to be the end of our chase," observed Mr. Merryweather, gloomily.

"You may place considerable confidence in Mr. Holmes, sir," said the police agent, loftily. "He has his own little methods, which are, if he won't mind my saying so, just a little too theoretical and fantastic, but he has the makings of a detective in him. It is not too much to say that once or twice, as in that business of the Sholto murder and the Agra treasure, he has been more nearly correct than the official force."

"Oh, if you say so, Mr. Jones, it is all right!" said the stranger, with deference. "Still, I confess that I miss my rubber. It is the first Saturday night for seven-and-twenty years that I have not had my rubber."

"I think you will find," said Sherlock Holmes, "that you will play for a higher stake to-night than you have ever done yet, and that the play will be more exciting. For you, Mr. Merryweather, the stake will be some thirty thousand pounds; and for you, Jones, it will be the man upon whom you wish to lay your hands."

"John Clay, the murderer, thief, smasher, and forger. He's a young man, Mr. Merryweather, but he is at the head of his profession, and I would rather have my bracelets on him than on any criminal in London. He's a remarkable man, is young John Clay. His grandfather was a Royal Duke, and he himself has been to Eton and Oxford. His brain is as cunning as his fingers, and though we meet signs of him at every turn, we never know where to find the man himself. He'll crack a crib in Scotland one week, and be raising money to build an orphanage in Cornwall the next. I've been on his track for years, and have never set eyes on him yet."

"I hope that I may have the pleasure of introducing you to-night. I've had one or two little turns also with Mr. John Clay, and I agree with you that he is at the head of his profession. It is past ten, however, and quite time that we started. If you two will take the first hansom, Watson and I will follow in the second."

Sherlock Holmes was not very communicative during the long drive, and lay back in the cab humming the tunes which he had heard in the afternoon. We rattled through an endless labyrinth of gas-lit streets until we emerged into Farringdon Street.

"We are close there now," my friend remarked. "This fellow Merryweather is a bank director and personally interested in the matter. I thought it as well to have Jones with us also. He is not a bad fellow, though an absolute imbecile in his profession. He has one positive virtue. He is as brave as a bulldog, and as tenacious as a lobster if he gets his claws upon any one. Here we are, and they are waiting for us."

We had reached the same crowded thoroughfare in which we had found ourselves in the morning. Our cabs were dismissed, and following the guidance of Mr. Merryweather, we passed down a narrow passage, and through a side door which he opened for us. Within there was a small corridor, which ended in a very massive iron gate. This also was opened, and led down a flight of winding stone steps, which terminated at another formidable gate. Mr. Merryweather stopped to light a lantern, and then conducted us down a dark, earth-smelling passage, and so, after opening a third door, into a huge vault or cellar, which was piled all round with crates and massive boxes.

"You are not very vulnerable from above," Holmes remarked, as he held up the lantern and gazed about him.

"Nor from below," said Mr. Merryweather, striking his stick upon the flags which lined the floor. "Why, dear me, it sounds quite hollow!" he remarked, looking up in surprise.

"I must really ask you to be a little more quiet," said Holmes, severely. "You have already imperiled the whole success of our expedition. Might I beg that you would have the goodness to sit down upon one of those boxes, and not to interfere?"

The solemn Mr. Merryweather perched himself upon a crate, with a very injured expression upon his face, while Holmes fell upon his knees upon the floor, and, with the lantern and a magnifying lens, began to examine minutely the cracks between the stones. A few seconds sufficed to satisfy him, for he sprang to his feet again, and put his glass in his pocket.

"We have at least an hour before us," he remarked, "for they can hardly take any steps until the good pawnbroker is safely in bed. Then they will not lose a minute, for the sooner they do their work the longer time they will have for their escape. We are at present, doctor—as no doubt you have divined—in the cellar of the City branch of one of the principal London banks. Mr. Merryweather is the chairman of directors, and he will explain to you that there are reasons why the more daring criminals of London should take a considerable interest in this cellar at present."

"It is our French gold," whispered the director. "We have had several warnings that an attempt might be made upon it."

"Your French gold?"

"Yes. We had occasion some months ago to strengthen our resources, and borrowed, for that purpose, thirty thousand napoleons from the Bank of France. It has become known that we have never had occasion to unpack the money, and that it is still lying in our cellar. The crate upon which I sit contains two thousand napoleons packed between layers of lead foil. Our reserve of bullion is much larger at present than is usually kept in a single branch office, and the directors have had misgivings upon the subject."

"Which were very well justified," observed Holmes. "And now it is time that we arranged our little plans. I expect that within an hour matters will come to a head. In the meantime, Mr. Merryweather, we must put the screen over that dark lantern."

"And sit in the dark?"

"I am afraid so. I had brought a pack of cards in my pocket, and I thought that, as we were a *partie carrée*, you might have your rubber after all. But I see that the enemy's preparations have gone so far that we cannot risk the presence of a light. And, first of all, we must choose our positions. These are daring men, and, though we shall take them at a disadvantage, they may do us some harm, unless we are careful. I shall stand behind this crate, and do you conceal yourself behind those. Then, when I flash a light upon them, close in swiftly. If they fire, Watson, have no compunction about shooting them down."

I placed my revolver, cocked, upon the top of the wooden case behind which I crouched. Holmes shot the slide across the front of his lantern, and left us in pitch darkness—such an absolute darkness as I have never before experienced. The smell of hot metal remained to assure us that the light was still there, ready to flash out at a moment's notice. To me, with my nerves worked up to a pitch of expectancy, there was something depressing and subduing in the sudden gloom, and in the cold, dank air of the vault.

"They have but one retreat," whispered Holmes. "That is back through the house into Saxe-Coburg Square. I hope that you have done what I asked you, Jones?"

"I have an inspector and two officers waiting at the front door."

"Then we have stopped all the holes. And now we must be silent and wait."

What a time it seemed! From comparing notes afterwards, it was but an hour and a quarter, yet it appeared to me that the night must have almost gone, and the dawn be breaking above us. My limbs were weary and stiff, for I feared to change my position, yet my nerves were worked up to the highest pitch of tension, and my hearing was so acute that I could not only hear the gentle breathing of my companions, but I could distinguish the deeper, heavier inbreath of the bulky Jones from the thin, sighing note of the bank director. From my position I could look over the case in the direction of the floor. Suddenly my eyes caught the glint of a light.

At first it was but a lurid spark upon the stone pavement. Then it lengthened out until it became a yellow line, and then, without any warning or sound, a gash seemed to open and a hand appeared, a white, almost womanly hand, which felt about in the center of the little area of light. For a minute or more the hand, with its writhing fingers, protruded out of the floor. Then it was withdrawn as suddenly as it appeared, and all was dark again save the single lurid spark, which marked a chink between the stones.

Its disappearance, however, was but momentary. With a rending, tearing sound, one of the broad white stones turned over upon its side, and left a square, gaping hole, through which streamed the light of a lantern. Over the edge there peeped a clean-cut, boyish face, which looked keenly about it, and then, with a hand on either side of the aperture, drew itself shoulder-high and waist-high, until one knee rested upon the edge. In another instant he stood at the side of the hole, and was hauling after him a companion, lithe and small like himself, with a pale face and a shock of very red hair.

"It's all clear," he whispered. "Have you the chisel and the bags? Great Scott! Jump, Archie, jump, and I'll swing for it!"

Sherlock Holmes had sprung out and seized the intruder by the collar. The other dived down the hole, and I heard the sound of rending cloth as Jones clutched at his skirts. The light flashed upon the barrel of a revolver, but Holmes's hunting crop came down on the man's wrist, and the pistol clinked upon the stone floor.

"It's no use, John Clay," said Holmes, blandly, "you have no chance at all."

"So, I see," the other answered, with the utmost coolness. "I fancy that my pal is all right, though I see you have got his coat-tails."

"There are three men waiting for him at the door," said Holmes.

"Oh, indeed. You seem to have done the thing very completely. I must compliment you."

"And I you," Holmes answered. "Your red-headed idea was very new and effective."

"You'll see your pal again presently," said Jones. "He's quicker at climbing down holes than I am. Just hold out while I fix the derbies."

"I beg that you will not touch me with your filthy hands," remarked our prisoner, as the handcuffs clattered upon his wrists. "You may not be aware that I have royal blood in my veins. Have the goodness also, when you address me, always to say 'sir' and 'please.'"

"All right," said Jones, with a stare and a snigger. "Well, would you please, sir, march upstairs where we can get a cab to carry your highness to the police station."

"That is better," said John Clay, serenely. He made a sweeping bow to the three of us, and walked quietly off in the custody of the detective.

"Really, Mr. Holmes," said Mr. Merryweather, as we followed them from the cellar, "I do not know how the bank can thank you or repay you. There is no doubt that you have detected and defeated in the most complete manner one of the most determined attempts at bank robbery that have ever come within my experience."

"I have had one or two little scores of my own to settle with Mr. John Clay," said Holmes. "I have been at some small expense over this matter, which I shall expect the bank to refund, but beyond that I am amply repaid by having had an experience which is in many ways unique, and by hearing the very remarkable narrative of the Red-headed League."

"You see, Watson," he explained, in the early hours of the morning, as we sat over a glass of whisky and soda in Baker Street, "it was perfectly obvious from the first that the only possible object of this rather fantastic business of the advertisement of the League, and the copying of the 'Encyclopædia,' must be to get this not over-bright pawnbroker out of the way for a number of hours every day. It was a curious way of managing it, but really it would be difficult to suggest a better. The method was no doubt suggested to Clay's ingenious mind by the color of his accomplice's hair. The four pounds a week was a lure which must draw him, and what was it to them, who were playing for thousands? They put in the advertisement, one rogue has the temporary office, the other rogue incites the man to apply for it, and together they manage to secure his absence every morning in the week. From the time that I heard of the assistant having come for half wages, it was obvious to me that he had some strong motive for securing the situation."

"But how could you guess what the motive was?"

"Had there been women in the house, I should have suspected a mere vulgar intrigue. That, however, was out of the question. The man's business was a small one, and there was nothing in his house which could account for such elaborate preparations, and such an expenditure as they were at. It must then be something out of the house. What could it be? I thought of the assistant's fondness for photography, and his trick of vanishing into the cellar. The cellar! There was the end of this tangled clue. Then I made inquiries as to this mysterious assistant, and found that I had to deal with one of the coolest and most daring criminals in London. He was doing something in the cellar—something which took many hours a day for months on end. What could it be, once more? I could think of nothing save that he was running a tunnel to some other building.

"So far I had got when we went to visit the scene of action. I surprised you by beating upon the pavement with my stick. I was ascertaining whether the cellar stretched out in front or behind. It was not in front. Then I rang the bell, and, as I hoped, the assistant answered it. We have had some skirmishes, but we had never set eyes upon each other before. I hardly looked at his face. His knees were what I wished to see. You must yourself have remarked how worn, wrinkled, and stained they were. They spoke of those hours of burrowing. The only remaining point was what they were burrowing for. I walked round the corner, saw that the City and Suburban Bank abutted on our friend's premises, and felt that I had solved my problem. When you drove home after the concert I called upon Scotland Yard, and upon the chairman of the bank directors, with the result that you have seen."

"And how could you tell that they would make their attempt tonight?" I asked.

"Well, when they closed their League offices that was a sign that they cared no longer about Mr. Jabez Wilson's presence; in other words, that they had completed their tunnel. But it was essential that they should use it soon, as it might be discovered, or the bullion might be removed. Saturday would suit them better than any other day, as it would give them two days for their escape. For all these reasons I expected them to come to-night."

"You reasoned it out beautifully," I exclaimed, in unfeigned admiration. "It is so long a chain, and yet every link rings true."

"It saved me from ennui," he answered, yawning. "Alas! I already feel it closing in upon me. My life is spent in one long effort to escape from the commonplaces of existence. These little problems help me to do so."

"And you are a benefactor of the race," said I. He shrugged his shoulders. "Well, perhaps, after all, it is of some little use," he remarked. "'L'homme c'est rien—l'œuvre c'est tout,' as Gustave Flaubert wrote to Georges Sand."

The Avenging Chance

Anthony Berkeley

WHEN HE was able to review it in perspective Roger Sheringham was inclined to think that the Poisoned Chocolate Case, as the papers called it, was perhaps the most perfectly planned murder he had ever encountered. Certainly he plumed himself more on its solution than on that of any other. The motive was so obvious, when you knew where to look for it—but you didn't know; the method was so significant, when you had grasped its real essentials—but you didn't grasp them; the traces were so thinly covered, when you had realized what was covering them—but you didn't realize. But for the merest piece of bad luck, which the murderer could not possibly have foreseen, the crime must have been added to the classical list of great mysteries.

This was the story of the case, as Chief Inspector Moresby told it one evening to Roger in the latter's rooms in the Albany a week or so later. Or rather, this is the raw material of Moresby's story as it passed through the crucible of Roger's vivid imagination:

On Friday morning, the fifteenth of November, at half-past ten in the morning, Graham Beresford walked into his club in Piccadilly, the very exclusive Rainbow Club, and asked for his letters. The porter handed him one and a couple of circulars. Beresford walked over to the fireplace in the big lounge to open them.

While he was doing so, a few minutes later, another member entered the club, a Sir William Anstruther, who lived in rooms just round the corner in Berkeley Street and spent most of his time at the Rainbow. The porter glanced at the clock, as he always did when Sir William entered, and, as always, it was exactly half-past ten to the minute. The time was thus definitely fixed by the porter beyond all doubt. There were three letters for Sir William and a small parcel, and he also strolled over to the fireplace, nodding to Beresford but not

57

speaking to him. The two men only knew each other very slightly, and had probably never exchanged more than a dozen words in all.

Having glanced through his letters Sir William opened the parcel and, after a moment, snorted with disgust. Beresford looked at him, and Sir William thrust out a letter which had been enclosed in the parcel, with an uncomplimentary remark upon modern trade methods. Concealing a smile (Sir William's ways were a matter of some amusement to his fellow members), Beresford read the letter. It was from a big firm of chocolate manufacturers, Mason and Sons, and set forth that they were putting on the market a new brand of liqueur chocolates designed especially to appeal to men; would Sir William do them the honor of accepting the enclosed two-pound box and letting the firm have his candid opinion on them?

"Do they think I'm a blank chorus-girl?" fumed Sir William. "Write 'em testimonials about their blank chocolates, indeed! Blank 'em! I'll complain to the blank committee. That sort of blank thing can't blank well be allowed here." Sir William, it will be gathered, was a choleric man.

"Well, it's an ill wind so far as I'm concerned," Beresford soothed him. "It's reminded me of something. My wife and I had a box at the Imperial last night and I bet her a box of chocolates to a hundred cigarettes that she wouldn't spot the villain by the end of the second act. She won. I must remember to get them this morning. Have you seen it, by the way—*The Creaking Skull*—? Not a bad show."

"Not blank likely," growled Sir William, unsoothed. "I've got something better to do than sit and watch a lot of blank fools with phosphorescent paint on their faces popping off silly pop-guns at each other. Got to get a box of chocolates, did you say? Well, take this blank one. I don't want it."

For a moment Beresford demurred politely and then, most unfortunately for himself, accepted. The money so saved meant nothing to him, for he was a wealthy man; but trouble was always worth saving.

By an extraordinarily lucky chance neither the outer wrapper of the box nor its covering letter were thrown into the fire, and this was the more fortunate in that both men had tossed the envelopes of their letters into the flames. Sir William did, indeed, make a bundle of wrapper, letter and string, but he handed it over to Beresford with the box, and the latter simply dropped it inside the fender. This bundle the porter subsequently extracted and, being a man of orderly habits, put it tidily away in the waste-paper basket, whence it was retrieved later by the police. The bundle, it may be said at once, comprised two out of the only three material clues to the murder, the third of course being the chocolates themselves.

Of the three unconscious protagonists in the impending tragedy, Sir William was without doubt the most remarkable. Still a year or two under fifty he looked, with his flaming red face and thick-set figure, a typical country squire of the old school, and both his manners and his language were in accordance with tradition. There were other resemblances too, but always with a difference. The voices of the country squires of the old school were often slightly husky towards late middle-age; but it was not with whiskey. They hunted, and so did Sir William. But the squires only hunted foxes; Sir William was more catholic. Sir William, in short, was no doubt a thoroughly bad baronet. But there was nothing mean about him. His vices, like such virtues as he had, were all on the large scale. And the result, as usual, was that most other men, good or bad, liked him well enough (except a husband here and there, or a father or two) and women openly hung on his husky words.

On comparison with him Beresford was rather an ordinary man, a tall, dark, not unhandsome fellow of two-and-thirty, quiet and reserved; popular in a way but neither inviting nor apparently reciprocating anything beyond a rather grave friendliness. His father had left him a rich man, but idleness did not appeal to him. He had inherited enough of the parental energy and drive not to allow his money to lie softly in gilt-edged securities and had a finger in a good many business pies, out of sheer love of the game.

Money attracts money. Graham Beresford had inherited it, he made it, and, inevitably, he had married it too. The daughter of a late ship-owner in Liverpool, with not far off half a million in her own right. That half-million might have made some poor man incredibly happy for life, but she had chosen to bring it to Beresford, who needed it not at all. But the money was incidental, for he needed her and would have married her just as inevitably (said his friends) if she had not a farthing.

She was so exactly his type. A tall, rather serious-minded, highly cultured girl, not so young that her character had not had time to form (she was twenty-five when Beresford married her, three years ago), she was the ideal wife for him. A bit of a Puritan, perhaps, in some ways, but Beresford, whose wild oats, though duly sown, had been a sparse crop, was ready enough to be a Puritan himself by that time, if she was. To make no bones about it, the Beresfords succeeded in achieving that eighth wonder of the modern world, a happy marriage.

And into the middle of it there dropped, with irretrievable tragedy, the box of chocolates. Beresford gave her the chocolates after the meal as they were sitting over their coffee in the drawing-room, explaining how they had come into his possession. His wife made some laughing comment on his meanness in not having bought a special box to pay his debt, but approved the brand and was interested to try the new variety. Joan Beresford was not so serious-minded as not to have a healthy feminine interest in good chocolates.

She delved with her fingers among the silver-wrapped sweets, each bearing the name of its filling in neat blue lettering, and remarked that the new variety appeared to consist of nothing but Kirsch and Maraschino taken from the firm's ordinary brand of liqueur choco-lates. She offered him one, but Beresford, who had no interest in chocolates and did not believe in spoiling good coffee, refused. His wife unwrapped one and put it in her mouth, uttering the next moment a slight exclamation.

"Oh! I was wrong. They are different. They're twenty times as strong. Really, it almost burns. You must try one, Graham. Catch!" She threw one across to him and Beresford, to humor her, consumed it. A burning taste, not intolerable but far too strong to be pleasant, followed the release of the liquid filling.

"By Jove," he exclaimed, "I should think they are strong. They must be filled with neat alcohol."

"Oh, they wouldn't do that, surely," said his wife, unwrapping another. "It must be the mixture. I rather like them. But that Kirsch one tasted far too strongly of almonds; this may be better. You try a Maraschino too." She threw another over to him.

He ate it and disliked it still more. "Funny," he remarked, feeling the roof of his mouth with the tip of his tongue. "My tongue feels quite numb."

"So did mine at first," she agreed. "Now it's tingling rather nicely. But there doesn't seem to be any difference between the Kirsch and the Maraschino. And they do burn! The almond flavoring's much too strong too. I can't make up my mind whether I like them or not."

"I don't," Beresford said with decision. "I shouldn't eat any more of them if I were you. I think there's something wrong with them."

"Well, they're only an experiment, I suppose," said his wife.

A few minutes later Beresford went out, to keep a business appointment in the City. He left her still trying to make up her mind whether she liked the new variety or not. Beresford remembered that conversation afterwards very clearly, because it was the last time he saw his wife alive.

That was roughly half-past two. At a quarter to four Beresford arrived at his club from the City in a taxi, in a state of collapse. He was helped into the building by the driver and the porter, and both described him subsequently as pale to the point of ghastliness, with staring eyes and livid lips, and his skin damp and clammy. His mind seemed unaffected, however, and when they had got him up the steps he was able to walk, with the porter's help, into the lounge.

The porter, thoroughly alarmed, wanted to send for a doctor at once, but Beresford, who was the last man in the world to make a fuss, refused to let him, saying that it must be indigestion and he would be all right in a few minutes. To Sir William Anstruther, however, who was in the lounge at the time, he added after the porter had gone: "Yes, and I believe it was those infernal chocolates you gave me, now I come to think of it. I thought there was something funny about them at the time. I'd better go and find out if my wife's all right."

Sir William, a kind-hearted man, was much perturbed at the notion that he might be responsible for Beresford's condition and offered to ring up Mrs. Beresford himself, as the other was plainly in no fit state to move. Beresford was about to reply when a strange change came over him. His body, which had been leaning back limply in his chair, suddenly heaved rigidly upright; his jaws locked together, the livid lips drawn back in a horrible grin, and his hands clenched on the arms of his chair. At the same time Sir William became aware of an unmistakable smell of bitter almonds.

Believing that the man was dying under his eyes, Sir William raised an alarmed shout for the porter and a doctor. The other occupants of the lounge hurried up, and between them they got the convulsed body of the unconscious man into a more comfortable position. They had no doubt that Beresford had taken poison, and the porter was sent off post-haste to find a doctor. Before the latter could arrive a telephone message was received at the club from an agitated butler asking if Mr. Beresford was there, and if so would he come home at once as Mrs. Beresford had been taken seriously ill. As a matter of fact she was already dead.

Beresford did not die. He had taken less of the poison than his wife, who after his departure must have eaten at least three more of the chocolates, so that its action in his case was less rapid and the doctor had time to save him. Not that the latter knew then what the poison was. He treated him chiefly for prussic acid poison, on the strength of the smell of bitter almonds, but he wasn't sure and threw in one or two others things as well. Anyhow it turned out in the end that he could not have had a fatal dose, and by about eight o'clock that night he was conscious; the next day he was practically convalescent. As for the unfortunate Mrs. Beresford, the doctor arrived too late to save her and she passed away very rapidly in a deep coma.

At first it was thought that the poisoning was due to a terrible accident on the part of the firm of Mason & Sons. The police had taken the matter in hand as soon as Mrs. Beresford's death was reported to them and the fact of poison established, and it was only a very short time before things had become narrowed down to the chocolates as the active agent. Sir William was interrogated, the letter and wrapper were recovered from the waste-paper basket, and, even before the sick man was out of danger, a detective inspector was asking for an interview just before closing-time with the managing director of Mason & Sons. Scotland Yard moves quickly.

It was the police theory at this stage, based on what Sir William and two doctors had been able to tell them, that by an act of criminal carelessness on the part of one of Mason's employees, an excessive amount of oil of bitter almonds had been included in the filling mixture of the chocolates, for that was what the doctors had decided must be the poisoning ingredient. Oil of bitter almonds is used a good deal, in the cheaper kinds of confectionery, as a flavoring. However, the managing director quashed this idea at once. Oil of bitter almonds, he asserted, was never used by Mason's. The inspector then produced the covering letter and asked if he could have an interview with the person or persons who had filled the sample chocolates, and with any others through whose hands the box might have passed before it was dispatched.

That brought matters to a head. The managing director read the letter with undisguised astonishment and at once declared that it was a forgery. No such letter, no such samples had been sent out by the firm at all; a new variety of liqueur chocolates had never even been mooted. Shown the fatal chocolates, he identified them without hesitation as their ordinary brand. Unwrapping and examining one more closely, he called the inspector's attention to a mark on the underside, which he suggested was the remains of a small hole drilled in the case through which the liquid could have been extracted and the fatal filling inserted, the hole afterwards being stopped up with softened chocolate, a perfectly simple operation.

The inspector agreed. It was now clear to him that somebody had been trying deliberately to murder Sir William Anstruther.

Scotland Yard doubled its activities. The chocolates were sent for analysis, Sir William was interviewed again, and so was the now conscious Beresford. From the latter the doctor insisted that the news of his wife's death must be kept till the next day, as in his weakened condition the shock might be fatal, so that nothing very helpful was obtained from him. Nor could Sir William, now thoroughly alarmed, throw any light on the mystery or produce a single person who might have any grounds for tying to kill him. The police were at a dead end.

Oil of bitter almonds had not been a bad guess at the noxious agent in the chocolates. The analysis showed that this was actually nitrobenzene, a kindred substance. Each chocolate in the upper layer contained exactly six minims, the remaining space inside the case being filled with a mixture of Kirsch and Maraschino. The chocolates in the lower layers, containing the other liqueurs to be found in one of Mason's two-pound boxes, were harmless.

"And now you know as much as we do, Mr. Sheringham," concluded Chief Inspector Moresby; "and if you can say who sent those chocolates to Sir William, you'll know a good deal more."

Roger nodded thoughtfully. "It's a brute of a case. The field of possible suspects is so wide. It might have been anyone in the whole world. I suppose you've looked into all the people who have an interest in Sir William's death?"

"Well, naturally," said Moresby. "There aren't many. He and his wife are on notoriously bad terms and have been living apart for the last two years, but she gets a good fat legacy in his will and she's the residuary legatee as well (they've got no children). But her alibi can't be got round. She was at her villa in the South of France when it happened. I've checked that, from the French police."

"Not another Marie Lafarge case, then," Roger murmured. 'Though of course there never was any doubt as to Marie Lefarge really being innocent, in any intelligent mind. Well, who else?"

"His estate in Worcestershire's entailed and goes to a nephew. But there's no possible motive there. Sir William hasn't been near the place for twenty years, and the nephew lives there, with his wife and family, on a long lease at a nominal rent, so long as he looks after the place properly. Sir William couldn't turn him out if he wanted to."

"Not a male edition of the Mary Ansell case, then," Roger commented. "Well, two other possible parallels occur to me. Don't they to you?"

"Well, sir," Moresby scratched his head. "There's the Molineux case, of course, in New York, where a poisoned phial of bromo-seltzer was sent to a Mr. Cornish at the Knickerbocker Club, with the result that a lady to whom he gave some at his boarding-house for a headache died and Cornish himself, who only sipped it because she complained of it being bitter, was violently ill. That's as close a parallel as I can call to mind."

"By Jove, yes." Roger was impressed. "And it had never occurred to me at all. It's a very close parallel indeed. Have you acted on it at all? Molineux, the man who was put on trial, was a fellow member of the same club, if I remember, and it was said to be a case of jealousy. Have you made enquiries about any possibilities like that among Sir William's fellow members at the Rainbow?"

"I have, sir, you may be sure; but there's nothing in it along those lines. Not a thing," said Moresby with conviction. "What were the other two possible parallels you had in mind?"

"Why, the Christina Edmunds case, for one. Feminine jealousy. Sir William's private life doesn't seem to be immaculate. I daresay there's a good deal of off with the old light-o'-love and on with the new. What about investigations round that idea?"

"Why, that's just what I have been doing, Mr. Sheringham, sir," retorted Chief Inspector Moresby reproachfully. "That was the first thing that came to me. Because if anything does stand out about this business it is that it's a woman's crime. Nobody but a woman would send poisoned chocolates to a man. Another man would never think of it. He'd send a poisoned sample of whiskey, or something like that."

"That's a very sound point, Moresby," Roger meditated. "Very sound indeed. And Sir William couldn't help you?"

"Couldn't," said Moresby, not without a trace of resentment, "or wouldn't. I was inclined to believe at first that he might have his suspicions and was shielding some woman. But I don't know. There may be nothing in it."

"On the other hand, there may be quite a lot. As I feel the case at present, that's where the truth lies."

Moresby looked as if a little solid evidence would be more to his liking than any amount of feelings about the case. "And your other parallel, Mr. Sheringham?" he asked, rather dispiritedly.

"Why, Sir William Horwood. You remember that some lunatic sent poisoned chocolates not so long ago to the Commissioner of Police himself. A good crime always gets imitated. One could bear in mind the possibility that this is a copy of the Horwood case."

Moresby brightened. "It's funny you should say that, Mr. Sheringham, sir, because that's about the conclusion I'm being forced to myself. In fact I've pretty well made up my mind. I've tested every other theory there is, you see. There's not a solitary person with an interest in Sir William's death, so far as I can see, whether it's from motives of gain, revenge, hatred, jealousy or anything else, whom I haven't had to rule out of the question. They've all either got complete alibis or I've satisfied myself in some other way that they're not to blame. If Sir William isn't shielding someone (and I'm pretty sure now that he isn't) there's nothing else for it but some irresponsible lunatic of a woman who's come to the conclusion that this world would be a better place without Sir William Anstruther in it—some social or religious fanatic, who's probably never even seen Sir William personally. And if that's the case," sighed Moresby, "a fat lot of chance we have of laying hands on her."

Roger reflected for a moment. "You may be right, Moresby. In fact I shouldn't be at all surprised if you were. But if I were superstitious, which I'm not, do you know what I should believe? That the murderer's aim misfired and Sir William escaped death for an express purpose of providence: so that he, the destined victim, should be the ironical instrument of bringing his own intended murderer to justice."

"Well, Mr. Sheringham, would you really?" said the sarcastic chief inspector, who was not superstitious either.

Roger seemed rather taken with the idea. "*Chance, the Avenger.* Make a good film title, wouldn't it? But there's a terrible lot of truth in it. How often don't you people at the Yard stumble on some vital piece of evidence out of pure chance? How often isn't it that you are led to the right solution by what seems a series of sheer coincidences? I'm not belittling your detective work; but just think how often a piece of brilliant detective work which has led you most of the way but not the last vital few inches, meets with some remarkable stroke of sheer luck (thoroughly well-deserved luck, no doubt, but *luck*), which just makes the case complete for you. I can think of scores of instances. The Milsom and Fowler murder, for example. Don't you see what I mean? Is it chance every time, or is it Providence avenging the victim?"

"Well, Mr. Sheringham," said Chief Inspector Moresby, "to tell you the truth, I don't mind what it is, so long as it lets me put my hands on the right man."

"Moresby," laughed Roger, "you're hopeless. I thought I was rais-ing such a fruitful topic. Very well, we'll change the subject. Tell me why in the name of goodness the murderess (assuming that you're right every time) used nitrobenzene, of all surprising things?"

"There, Mr. Sheringham," Moresby admitted, "you've got me. I never even knew it was so poisonous. It's used a good deal in various manufactures, I'm told, confectionery for instance, and as a solvent; and its chief use is in making aniline dyes. But it's never reckoned among the ordinary poisons. I suppose she used it because it's so easy to get hold of."

"Isn't there a line of attack there?" Roger suggested. "The infer-ence is that the criminal is a woman who is employed in some fac-tory or business, the odds favoring an aniline dye establishment, and who knew of the poisonous properties of nitrobenzene because the employees have been warned about it. Couldn't you use that as a point of departure?"

"To interrogate every employee of every establishment in this country that uses nitrobenzene in any of its processes, Mr. Shering-ham? Come, sir. Even if you're right the chances are we should all be dead before we reached the guilty person."

"I suppose we should," regretted Roger, who had thought he was being rather clever.

They discussed the case for some time longer, but nothing further of importance emerged. Naturally it had not been possible to trace the machine on which the forged letter had been typed, nor to ascertain how the piece of Mason's notepaper had come into the criminal's possession. With regard to this last point, Roger suggested, as an out-side possibility, that it might not have been Mason's notepaper at all but a piece with a heading especially printed for the occasion, which might give a pointer towards a printer as being concerned in the crime. He was chagrined to learn that this brilliant idea had occurred to Moresby as a mere matter of routine, and the notepaper had been definitely identified by Merton's, the printers concerned, as their own work. He produced the piece of paper for Roger's inspection, and the latter commented on the fact that the edges were distinctly yellowed, which seemed to suggest that the sheet was an old one.

Another idea occurred to Roger. "I shouldn't be surprised, Moresby," he said, with a certain impressiveness, "if the murderer never *tried* to get hold of this sheet at all. In other words, it was the chance possession of it which suggested the whole method of the crime."

It appeared that this notion had also occurred to Moresby. If it were true, it only helped to make the crime more insoluble than before. From the wrapper, a piece of ordinary brown paper with Sir William's name and address hand-printed on it in large capitals, there was nothing at all to be learnt beyond the fact that the parcel had been posted at the office in Southampton Street, Strand, between the hours of eight-thirty and nine-thirty p.m. Except for the chocolates themselves, which seemed to offer no further help, there was nothing else whatsoever in the way of material clues. Whoever coveted Sir William's life had certainly no intention of purchasing it with his or her own.

If Moresby had paid his visit to Roger Sheringham with any hope of tapping that gentleman's brains, he went away disappointed. Rack them as he might, Roger had been unable to throw any effective light on the affair.

To tell the truth Roger was inclined to agree with the chief inspector's conclusion, that the attempted murder of Sir William Anstruther and the actual death of the unfortunate Mrs. Beresford must be laid to the account of some irresponsible criminal lunatic, actuated by a religious or social fanaticism. For this reason, although he thought about it a good deal during the next few days, he made no attempt to take the case in hand. It was the sort of affair, necessitating endless enquiries, that a private person would have neither the time nor the authority to carry out, which can only be handled by the official police. Roger's interest in it was purely academic.

It was hazard, two chance encounters, which translated this interest from the academic to the personal.

The first was at the Rainbow Club itself. Roger was lunching there with a member, and inevitably the conversation turned on the recent tragedy. Roger's host was inclined to plume himself on the fact that he had been at school with Beresford and so had a more intimate connection with the affair than his fellow members. One gathered, indeed, that the connection was a trifle closer even than Sir William's. Roger's host was that kind of man.

"And just as it happened I saw the Beresfords in their box at the Imperial that night. Noticed them before the curtain went up for the first act. I had a stall. I may even have seen them making that fatal bet." Roger's host took on an even more portentous aspect. One gathered that it was by no means improbably due to his presence in the stalls that the disastrous bet was made at all.

As they were talking a man entered the dining room and walked past their table. Roger's host became abruptly silent. The newcomer threw him a slight nod and passed on. The other leant forward across the table.

"Talk of the devil! That was Beresford himself. First time I've seen him in here since it happened. Poor devil! It knocked him all to pieces, you know. I've never seen a man so devoted to his wife. Did you notice how ghastly he looked?" All this in a hushed, tactful whisper, that would have been far more obvious to the subject of it, had he happened to have been looking their way, than the loudest shouts.

Roger nodded shortly. He had caught a glimpse of Beresford's face and been shocked by it even before he learned his identity. It was haggard and pale and seamed with lines of bitterness, prematurely old. "Hang it all," he now thought, much moved, "Moresby really must make an effort. If the murderer isn't found soon it'll kill that chap too."

He said aloud, somewhat at random and certainly without tact: "He didn't exactly fall on your neck. I thought you two were such bosom friends?"

His host looked uncomfortable. "Oh, well, you must make allowances, just at present," he hedged. "Besides, we weren't *bosom* friends exactly. As a matter of fact he was a year or two senior to me. Or it might have been three. We were in different houses, too. And he was on the modern side of course, while I was a classical bird."

"I see," said Roger, quite gravely, realizing that his host's actual contact with Beresford at school had been limited, at the very most, to that of the latter's toe with the former's hinder parts.

He left it at that.

The next encounter took place the following morning. Roger was in Bond Street, about to go through the distressing ordeal of buying a new hat. Along the pavement he suddenly saw bearing down on him Mrs. Verreker-le-Flemming. Mrs. Verreker-le-Flemming was small, exquisite, rich and a widow, and she sat at Roger's feet whenever he gave her the opportunity. But she talked. She talked, in fact, and talked, and talked. And Roger, who rather liked talking himself, could not bear it. He tried to dart across the road, but there was no opening stream. He was cornered.

Mrs. Verreker-le-Flemming fastened on him gladly. "Oh, Mr. Sheringham! *Just* the person I wanted to see. Mr. Sheringham, *do* tell me. In confidence. *Are* you taking up this dreadful business of *poor* Joan Beresford's death? Oh, don't—*don't* tell me you're not!" Roger was trying to do so, but she gave him no chance. "It's too dreadful. You must—you simply *must* find out who sent those chocolates to that dreadful Sir William Anstruther. You *are* going to, aren't you?"

Roger, the frozen and imbecile grin of civilized intercourse on his face, again tried to get a word in; without result.

"I was horrified when I heard of it—simply horrified. You see, Joan and I were such *very* close friends. Quite intimate. We were at school together—Did you say anything, Mr. Sheringham?"

Roger, who had allowed a faint groan to escape him, hastily shook his head.

"And the awful thing, the truly *terrible* thing is that Joan brought the whole business on herself. Isn't that *appalling?*"

Roger no longer wanted to escape. "What did you say?" he managed to insert, incredulously.

"I suppose it's what they call tragic irony. Certainly it was tragic enough, and I've never heard anything so terribly ironical. You know about that bet she made with her husband of course, so that he had to get her a box of chocolates, and if he hadn't Sir William would never have given him the poisoned ones and he'd have eaten them and died himself and good riddance? Well, Mr. Sheringham—" Mrs. Verreker-le-Flemming lowered her voice to a conspirator's whisper and glanced about her in the approved manner. "I've never told anybody else this, but I'm telling you because I know you'll appreciate it. You're interested in irony, aren't you?"

"I adore it," Roger said mechanically. "Yes?"

"Well—*Joan wasn't playing fair!*"

"How do you mean?" Roger asked, bewildered.

Mrs. Verreker-le-Flemming was artlessly pleased with her sensation. "Why, she ought not to have made that bet at all. It was a judgment on her. A terrible judgment, of course, but the appalling thing is that she did bring it on herself, in a way. She'd seen the play before. We went together, the very first week it was on. She *knew* who the villain was all the time."

"By Jove!" Roger was as impressed as Mrs. Verreker-le-Flemming could have wished. "Chance the Avenger, with a vengeance. We're none of us immune from it."

"Poetic justice, you mean?" twittered Mrs. Verreker-le-Flemming, to whom these remarks had been somewhat obscure. "Yes, it was, wasn't it? Though really, the punishment was out of all proportion to the crime. Good gracious, if every woman who cheats over a bet is to be killed for it, where would any of us be?" demanded Mrs. Verreker-le-Flemming with unconscious frankness.

"Umph!" said Roger, tactfully.

"But Joan Beresford! That's the extraordinary thing. I should never have thought Joan *would* do a thing like that. She was such a *nice* girl. A little close with money, of course, considering how well off they were, but that isn't anything. Of course it was only fun, and pulling her husband's leg, but I always used to think Joan was such a *serious* girl, Mr. Sheringham. I mean, ordinary people don't talk about honor, and truth, and playing the game. Well, she paid herself for not playing the game, poor girl, didn't she? Still, it all goes to show the truth of the old saying, doesn't it?"

"What old saying?" said Roger, hypnotized by this flow.

"Why, that still waters run deep. Joan must have been deep, I'm afraid." Mrs. Verreker-le-Flemming sighed. It was evidently a social error to be deep. "I mean, she certainly took me in. She can't have been quite so honorable and truthful as she was always pretending, can she? And I can't help wondering whether a girl who'd deceive her husband in a little thing like that might not—oh, well, I don't want to say anything against poor Joan now she's dead, poor darling, but she can't have been quite such a plaster saint after all, can she? I mean," said Mrs. Verreker-le-Flemming, in hasty extenuation of these suggestions, "I do think psychology is so *very* interesting, don't you, Mr. Sheringham?"

"Sometimes, very," Roger agreed gravely. "But you mentioned Sir William Anstruther just now. Do you know him, too?"

"I used to," Mrs. Verreker-le-Flemming replied, with an expression of positive vindictiveness. "Horrible man! Always running after some woman or other. And when he's tired of her, just drops her——biff!—like that. At least," added Mrs. Verreker-le-Flemming hastily, "so I've heard."

"And what happens if she refused to be dropped?"

"Oh, dear, I'm sure I don't know. I suppose you've heard the latest?" Mrs. Verreker-le-Flemming hurried on, perhaps a trifle more pink than the delicate aids to nature on her cheeks would have warranted. "He's taken up with that Bryce woman now. You know, the wife of the oil man, or petrol, or whatever he made his money in. It began about three weeks ago. You'd have thought that dreadful business of being responsible, in a way, for poor Joan Beresford's death would have sobered him up a little, wouldn't you? But not a bit of it; he——"

"I suppose Sir William knew Mrs. Beresford pretty well?" Roger remarked casually.

Mrs. Verreker-le-Flemming stared at him. "Sir William? No, he didn't know Joan at all. I'm sure he didn't. I've never heard her mention him."

Roger shot off on another tack. "What a pity you weren't at the Imperial with the Beresfords that evening. She'd never have made that bet if you had been." Roger looked extremely innocent. "You weren't, I suppose?"

"I?" queried Mrs. Verreker-le-Flemming in surprise. "Good gracious, no. I was at the new revue at the Pavilion. Lady Gavelstoke had a box and asked me to join her party."

"Oh, yes. Good show, isn't it? I thought that sketch *The Sempiternal Triangle* very clever. Didn't you?"

"*The Sempiternal Triangle*?" wavered Mrs. Verreker-le-Flemming.

"Yes, in the first half."

"Oh! Then I didn't see it. I got there disgracefully late, I'm afraid. But then," said Mrs. Verreker-le-Flemming with pathos, "I always do seem to be late for simply everything."

Once more Roger changed the subject. "By the way, I wonder if you've got a photograph of Mrs. Beresford?" he asked carelessly.

"Of Joan? Yes, I have. Why Mr. Sheringham?"

"You haven't got one of Sir William too, by any chance?" asked Roger, still more carelessly.

The pink on Mrs. Verreker-le-Flemming's cheeks deepened half a shade. "I—I think I have. Yes, I'm almost sure I have. But——"

"Would you lend them to me some time?" Roger asked, with a mysterious air, and looked around him with a frown in the approved manner.

"Oh, Mr. Sheringham! Yes, of course I will. You mean—you mean you *are* going to find out who sent those chocolates to Sir William?"

Roger nodded, and put his finger to his lips. "Yes. You've guessed it. But not a word, Mrs. Verreker-le-Flemming. Oh, excuse me, there's a man on that bus who wants to speak to me. *Scotland Yard*," he hissed in an impressive whisper. "Good-bye." He dived for a passing bus and clung on with difficulty. With awful stealth he climbed up the steps and took his seat, after an exaggerated scrutiny of the other passengers, beside a perfectly inoffensive man in a bowler hat. The man in the bowler hat, who happened to be a clerk in the employment of a builder's merchant, looked at him resentfully: there were plenty of quite empty seats all round them.

Roger bought no new hat that morning.

For probably the first time in her life Mrs. Verreker-le-Flemming had given somebody a constructive idea.

Roger made good his opportunity. Getting off the bus at the corner of Bond Street and Oxford Street, he hailed a taxi, and gave Mrs. Verreker-le-Flemming's address. He thought it better to take advantage of her permission at a time when he would not have to pay for it a second time over.

The parlor-maid seemed to think there was nothing odd in his mission, and took him up to the drawing room at once. A corner of the room was devoted to the silver-framed photographs of Mrs. Verreker-le-Flemming's friends, and there were many of them. Roger, who had never seen Sir William in the flesh, had to seek the parlor-maid's help. The girl, like her mistress, was inclined to be loquacious, and to prevent either of them getting ideas into their heads which might be better not there, he removed from their frames not one photograph but five, those of Sir William, Mrs. Beresford, Beresford himself, and two strange males who appeared to belong to the Sir William period of Mrs. Verreker-le-Flemming's collection. Finally he obtained, by means of a small bribe, a likeness of Mrs. Verreker-le-Flemming herself and added that to his collection.

For the rest of the day he was very busy.

His activities would have seemed, no doubt, to Mrs. Verreker-le-Flemming not merely baffling but pointless. He paid a visit to a public library, for instance, and consulted a work of reference, after which he took a taxi and drove to the offices of the Anglo-Eastern Perfumery Company, where he inquired for a certain Mr. Joseph Lea Hardwick and seemed much put out on hearing that no such gentleman was known to the firm and was certainly not employed in any of their numerous branches. Many questions had to be put about the firm and its branches before he consented to abandon the quest. After that he drove to Messrs. Weall and Wilson, the well-known institution which protects the trade interests of individuals and advises its subscribers regarding investments. Here he entered his name as a subscriber, and explaining that he had a large sum of money to invest, filled in one of the special inquiry forms which are headed Strictly Confidential.

Then he went to the Rainbow Club, in Piccadilly.

Introducing himself to the porter without a blush as connected with Scotland Yard, he asked the man a number of questions, more or less trivial, concerning the tragedy. "Sir William, I understand," he said finally, as if by the way, "did not dine here the evening before?"

There it appeared that Roger was wrong. Sir William had dined in the club, as he did about three times a week.

"But I quite understood he wasn't here that evening?" Roger said plaintively.

The porter was emphatic. He remembered quite well. So did a waiter, whom the porter summoned to corroborate him. Sir William had dined rather late, and had not left the dining-room till about nine o'clock. He spent the evening there too, the waiter knew, or at least some of it, for he himself had taken him a whiskey-and-soda in the lounge not less than half an hour later.

Roger retired.

He retired to Merton's, in a taxi.

It seemed that he wanted some new notepaper printed, of a very special kind, and to the young woman behind the counter he specified at great length and in wearisome detail exactly what he did want. The young woman handed him the book of specimen pieces and asked him to see if there was any style there which would suit him. Roger glanced through it, remarking garrulously to the young woman that he had been recommended to Merton's by a very dear friend, whose photograph he happened to have on him at that moment. Wasn't that a curious coincidence? The young woman agreed that it was.

"About a fortnight ago, I think my friend was in here last," said Roger, producing the photograph. "Recognize this?"

The young woman took the photograph, without apparent interest. "Oh, yes. I remember. About some notepaper too, wasn't it? So that's your friend. Well, it's a small world. Now this is a line we're selling a good deal of just now."

Roger went back to his rooms to dine. Afterwards, feeling restless, he wandered out of the Albany and turned down Piccadilly. He wandered round the Circus, thinking hard, and paused for a moment out of habit to inspect the photographs of the new revue hung outside the Pavilion. The next thing he realized was that he had got as far as Jermyn Street and was standing outside the Imperial Theatre. The advertisements of *The Creaking Skull* informed him that it began at half-past eight. Glancing at his watch he saw that the time was twenty-nine minutes past that hour. He had an evening to get through somehow. He went inside.

The next morning, very early for Roger, he called Moresby at Scotland Yard.

"Moresby," he said without preamble, "I want you to do something for me. Can you find me a taximan who took a fare from Piccadilly Circus or its neighborhood at about ten past nine on the evening before the Beresford crime, to the Strand somewhere near the bottom of Southampton Street, and another who took a fare back between those points. I'm not sure about the first. Or one taxi might have been used for the double journey, but I doubt that. Anyhow, try to find out for me, will you?"

"What are you up to now, Mr. Sheringham?" Moresby asked suspiciously.

"Breaking down an interesting alibi," replied Roger serenely. "By the way, I know who sent those chocolates to Sir William. I'm just building up a nice structure of evidence for you. Ring up my rooms when you've got those taximen."

He strolled out, leaving Moresby positively gaping after him. Roger had his annoying moments.

The rest of the day he spent apparently trying to buy a second-hand typewriter. He was very particular that it should be a Hamilton No. 4. When the shop people tried to induce him to consider other makes he refused to look at them, saying that he had had the Hamilton No. 4 so strongly recommended to him by a friend, who had bought one about three weeks ago. Perhaps it was at this very shop? No? They hadn't sold a Hamilton No. 4 for the last three months? How odd.

But at one shop they had sold a Hamilton No. 4 within the last month, and that was odder still.

At half-past four Roger got back to his rooms to await the telephone message from Moresby. At half-past five it came.

"There are fourteen taxi drivers here, littering up my office," said Moresby offensively. "They all took fares from the Strand to Piccadilly Circus at your time. What do you want me to do with 'em, Mr. Sheringham?"

"Keep them till I come, Chief Inspector," returned Roger with dignity. He had not expected more than three at the most, but he was not going to let Moresby know that. He grabbed his hat.

The interview with the fourteen was brief enough, however. To each grinning man (Roger deduced a little heavy humor on the part of Moresby before his arrival) he showed in turn a photograph, holding it so that Moresby could not see it, and asked if he could recognize his fare. The ninth man did so, without hesitation. At a nod from Roger Moresby dismissed the others.

"How dressed?" Roger asked the man laconically, tucking the photograph away in his pocket.

"Evening togs," replied the other, equally laconic.

Roger took a note of his name and address and sent him away with a ten shilling tip. "The case," he said to Moresby, "is at an end."

Moresby sat at his table and tried to look official. "And now, Mr. Sheringham, sir, perhaps you'll tell me what you've been doing."

"Certainly," Roger said blandly, seating himself on the table and swinging his legs. As he did so, a photograph fell unnoticed out of his pocket and fluttered, face downwards, under the table. Moresby eyed it but did not pick it up. "Certainly, Moresby," said Roger. "Your work for you. It was a simple case," he added languidly, "once one had grasped the essential factor. Once, that is to say, one had cleared one's eyes of the soap that the murderer had stuffed into them."

"Is that so, Mr. Sheringham?" said Moresby politely. And yawned.

Roger laughed. "All right, Moresby. We'll get down to it. I really have solved the thing, you know. Here's the evidence for you." He took from his note-case an old letter and handed it to the chief inspector. "Look at the slightly crooked s's and the chipped capital H. Was that typed on the same machine as the forged letter from Mason's, or was it not?"

Moresby studied it for a moment, then drew the forged letter from a drawer of his table and compared the two minutely. When he looked up there was no lurking amusement in his eyes. "You've got it in one, Mr. Sheringham," he said soberly. "Where did you get hold of this?"

"In a secondhand typewriter shop in St. Martin's Lane. The machine was sold to an unknown customer about a month ago. They identified the customer from that photograph. By a lucky chance this machine had been used in the office after it had been repaired, to see that it was OK, and I easily got hold of that specimen of its work. I'd deduced, of course, from the precautions taken all through this crime, that the typewriter would be bought for that one special purpose and then destroyed, and so far as the murderer could see there was no need to waste valuable money on a new one."

"And where is the machine now?"

"Oh, at the bottom of the Thames, I expect," Roger smiled. "I tell you, this criminal takes no unnecessary chances. But that doesn't matter. There's your evidence."

"Humph! It's all right so far as it goes," conceded Moresby. "But what about Mason's paper?"

"That," said Roger calmly, "was extracted from Merton's book of sample notepapers, as I'd guessed from the very yellowed edges might be the case. I can prove contact of the criminal with the book, and there is a gap which will certainly turn out to have been filled by the piece of paper."

"That's fine," Moresby said more heartily.

"As for that taximan, the criminal had an alibi. You've heard it broken down. Between ten past nine and twenty-five past, in fact during the time when the parcel must have been posted, the murderer took a hurried journey to that neighborhood, going probably by bus or underground, but returning, as I expected, by taxi, because time would be getting short."

"And the murderer, Mr. Sheringham?"

"The person whose photograph is in my pocket," Roger said unkindly. "By the way, do you remember what I was saying the other day about Chance the Avenger, my excellent film-title? Well, it's worked again. By a chance meeting in Bond Street with a silly woman I was put, by the merest accident, in possession of a piece of information which showed me then and there who had sent those chocolates addressed to Sir William. There were other possibilities of course, and I tested them, but then and there on the pavement I saw the whole thing, from first to last. It was the merest accident that this woman should have been a friend of mine, of course, and I don't want to blow my own trumpet," said Roger modestly, "but I do think I deserve a little credit for realizing the significance of what she told me and recognizing the hand of Providence at work."

"Who was the murderer, then, Mr. Sheringham?" repeated Moresby, disregarding for the moment this bashful claim.

"It was so beautifully planned," Roger went on dreamily. "We were taken in completely. We never grasped for one moment that we were making the fundamental mistake that the murderer all along intended us to make."

He paused, and in spite of his impatience Moresby obliged. "And what was that?"

"Why, that the plan had miscarried. That the wrong person had been killed. That was just the beauty of it. The plan had *not* miscarried. It had been brilliantly successful. The wrong person was *not* killed. Very much the right person was."

Moresby gaped. "Why, how on earth do you make that out, sir?"

"Mrs. Beresford was the objective all the time. That's why the plot was so ingenious. Everything was anticipated. It was perfectly natural that Sir William would hand the chocolates over to Beresford. It was foreseen that we should look for the criminal among Sir William's associates and not the dead woman's. It was probably even foreseen that the crime would be considered the work of a woman; whereas really, of course, chocolates were employed because it was a woman who was the objective. Brilliant!"

Moresby, unable to wait any longer, snatched up the photograph and gazed at it incredulously. He whistled. "Good heavens! But Mr. Sheringham, you don't mean to tell me that—Sir William himself!"

"He wanted to get rid of Mrs. Beresford," Roger continued, gazing dreamily at his swinging feet. "He had liked her well enough at the beginning, no doubt, though it was her money he was after all the time. But she must have bored him dreadfully very soon. And I really do think there is some excuse for him there. Any woman, however charming otherwise, would bore a normal man if she does nothing but prate about honor and playing the game. She'd never have overlooked the slightest peccadillo. Every tiny lapse would be thrown up at him for years.

"But the real trouble was that she was too close with her money. She sentenced herself to death there. He wanted it, or some of it, pretty badly; and she wouldn't part. There's no doubt about the motive. I made a list of the firms he's interested in and got a report on them. They're all rocky, every one of them. They all need money to save them. He'd got through all he had of his own, and he had to get more. Nobody seems to have gathered it, but he's a rotten business man. And half a million—Well!

"As for the nitrobenzene, that was simple enough. I looked it up and found that beside the uses you told me, it's used largely in perfumery. And he's got a perfumery business. The Anglo-Eastern Perfumery Company. That's how he'd know about it being poisonous of course. But I shouldn't think he got his supply from there. He'd be cleverer than that. He probably made the stuff himself. I discovered, quite by chance, that he has at any rate an elementary knowledge of chemistry (at least, he was on the modern side at Selchester) and it's the simplest operation. Any schoolboy knows how to treat benzol with nitric acid to get nitrobenzene."

"But," stammered Moresby, "but Sir William—He was at Eton."

"Sir William?" said Roger sharply. "Who's talking about Sir William? I told you the photograph of the murderer was in my pocket." He whipped out the photograph in question and confronted the astounded chief inspector with it. "Beresford, man! Beresford's the murderer, of his own wife." Roger studied the other's dumbfounded face and smiled secretly. He felt avenged now for the humor that had been taking place with the taximen.

"Beresford, who still had hankerings after a gay life," he went on more mildly, "didn't want his wife but did want her money. He contrived this plot, providing, as he thought, against every contingency that could possibly arise. He established a mild alibi, if suspicion ever should arise, by taking his wife to the Imperial, and slipped out of the theatre at the first interval (I sat through the first act of the dreadful thing myself last night to see when the interval came). Then he hurried down to the Strand, posted his parcel, and took a taxi back. He had ten minutes, but nobody was going to remark if he got back to the box a minute or two late; you may be able to find that he did.

"And the rest simply followed. He knew Sir William came to the Club every morning at ten thirty, as regularly as clockwork; he knew that for a psychological certainty he could get the chocolates handed over to him if he hinted for them; he knew that the police would go chasing after all sorts of false trails starting from Sir William. That's one reason why he chose him. He could have shadowed anyone else to the Club if necessary. And as for the wrapper and the forged letter, he carefully didn't destroy them because they were calculated not only to divert suspicion but actually to point away from him to some anonymous lunatic. Which is exactly what they did."

"Well, it's very smart of you, Mr. Sheringham," Moresby said, with a little sigh but quite ungrudgingly. "Very smart indeed. By the way, what was it the lady told you that showed you the whole thing in a flash?"

"Why, it wasn't so much what she actually told me as what I heard between her words, so to speak. What she told me was that Mrs. Beresford knew the answer to that bet; what I deduced was that, being the sort of person she sounded to be, it was almost incredible that Mrs. Beresford should have made a bet to which she knew the answer. Unless she had been the most dreadful little hypocrite (which I did not for a moment believe), it would have been a psychological impossibility for her. *Ergo*, she didn't. *Ergo*, there never was such a bet. *Ergo*, Beresford was lying. *Ergo*, Beresford wanted to get hold of those chocolates for some reason other than he stated. And, as events turned out, there was only one other reason. That was all.

"After all, we only had Beresford's word for the bet, didn't we? And only his word for the conversation in the drawing room— though most of that undoubtedly happened. Beresford must be far too good a liar not to make all possible use of the truth. But of course he wouldn't have left her till he'd seen her take, or somehow made her take, at least six of the chocolates, more than a lethal dose. That's why the stuff was in those meticulous six minim doses. And so that he could take a couple himself, of course. A clever stroke, that. Took us all in again. Though of course he exaggerated his symptoms considerably."

Moresby rose to his feet. "Well, Mr. Sheringham, I'm much obliged to you, sir. I shall make a report of course to the assistant commissioner of what you've done, and he'll thank you officially on behalf of the department. And now I shall have to get busy, because naturally I shall have to check your evidence myself, if only as a matter of form, before I apply for a warrant against Beresford." He scratched his head. "Chance, the Avenger, eh? Yes, it's an interesting notion. But I can tell you one pretty big thing Beresford left to Chance, the Avenger, Mr. Sheringham. Suppose Sir William hadn't handed over the chocolates after all? Supposing he'd kept them, to give to one of his own ladies? That was a nasty risk to take."

Roger positively snorted. He felt a personal pride in Beresford by this time, and it distressed him to hear a great man so maligned.

"Really, Moresby! It wouldn't have had any serious results if Sir William had. Do give my man credit for being what he is. You don't imagine he sent the poisoned ones to Sir William, do you? Of course not! He'd send harmless ones, and exchange them for the others on his way home. Dash it all, he wouldn't go right out of his way to present opportunities to Chance.

"If," added Roger, "Chance really is the right word."

The Absent-Minded Coterie

Robert Barr

I WELL remember the November day when I first heard of the Summertrees case, because there hung over London a fog so thick that
two or three times I lost my way, and no cab was to be had at any
price. The few cabmen then in the streets were leading their animals
slowly along, making for their stables. It was one of those depressing
London days which filled me with *ennui* and a yearning for my own
clear city of Paris, where, if we are ever visited by a slight mist, it is at
least clean, white vapor, and not this horrible London mixture satu-
rated with suffocating carbon. The fog was too thick for any passer to
read the contents bills of the newspapers plastered on the pavement,
and as there were probably no races that day the newsboys were
shouting what they considered the next most important event—the
election of an American President. I bought a paper and thrust it
into my pocket. It was late when I reached my flat, and, after dining
there, which was an unusual thing for me to do, I put on my slippers,
took an easy-chair before the fire, and began to read my evening
journal. I was distressed to learn that the eloquent Mr. Bryan had
been defeated. I knew little about the silver question, but the man's
oratorical powers had appealed to me, and my sympathy was aroused
because he owned many silver mines, and yet the price of the metal
was so low that apparently he could not make a living through the
operation of them. But, of course, the cry that he was a plutocrat,
and a reputed millionaire over and over again, was bound to defeat
him in a democracy where the average voter is exceedingly poor
and not comfortably well-to-do, as is the case with our peasants in
France. I always took great interest in the affairs of the huge republic
to the west, having been at some pains to inform myself accurately
regarding its politics; and although, as my readers know, I seldom
quote anything complimentary that is said of me, nevertheless, an
American client of mine once admitted that he never knew the true

81

inwardness—I think that was the phrase he used—of American politics until he heard me discourse upon them. But then, he added, he had been a very busy man all his life.

I had allowed my paper to slip to the floor, for in very truth the fog was penetrating even into my flat, and it was becoming difficult to read, notwithstanding the electric light. My man came in, and announced that Mr. Spenser Hale wished to see me, and, indeed, any night, but especially when there is rain or fog outside, I am more pleased to talk with a friend than to read a newspaper.

"*Mon Dieu*, my dear Monsieur Hale, it is a brave man you are to venture out in such a fog as is abroad to-night."

"Ah, Monsieur Valmont," said Hale with pride, "you cannot raise a fog like this in Paris!"

"No. There you are supreme," I admitted, rising and saluting my visitor, then offering him a chair.

"I see you are reading the latest news," he said, indicating my newspaper. "I am very glad that man Bryan is defeated. Now we shall have better times."

I waved my hand as I took my chair again. I will discuss many things with Spenser Hale, but not American politics; he does not understand them. It is a common defect of the English to suffer complete ignorance regarding the internal affairs of other countries.

"It is surely an important thing that brought you out on such a night as this. The fog must be very thick in Scotland Yard."

This delicate shaft of fancy completely missed him, and he answered stolidly:

"It's thick all over London, and, indeed, throughout most of England."

"Yes, it is," I agreed, but he did not see that either.

Still, a moment later, he made a remark which, if it had come from some people I know, might have indicated a glimmer of comprehension.

"You are a very, very clever man, Monsieur Valmont, so all I need say is that the question which brought me here is the same as that on which the American election was fought. Now, to a countryman, I should be compelled to give further explanation, but to you, monsieur, that will not be necessary."

There are times when I dislike the crafty smile and partial closing of the eyes which always distinguishes Spenser Hale when he places on the table a problem which he expects will baffle me. If I said he never did baffle me, I would be wrong, of course, for sometimes the utter simplicity of the puzzles which trouble him leads me into an intricate involution entirely unnecessary in the circumstances.

I pressed my finger tips together, and gazed for a few moments at the ceiling. Hale had lit his black pipe, and my silent servant placed at his elbow the whisky and soda, then tiptoed out of the room. As the door closed my eyes came from the ceiling to the level of Hale's expansive countenance.

"Have they eluded you?" I asked quietly.

"Who?"

"The coiners."

Hale's pipe dropped from his jaw, but he managed to catch it before it reached the floor. Then he took a gulp from the tumbler.

"That was just a lucky shot," he said.

"*Parfaitement*," I replied carelessly.

"Now, own up, Valmont, wasn't it?"

I shrugged my shoulders. A man cannot contradict a guest in his own house.

"Oh, stow that!" cried Hale impolitely. He is a trifle prone to strong and even slangy expressions when puzzled. "Tell me how you guessed it."

"It is very simple, *mon ami*. The question on which the American election was fought is the price of silver, which is so low that it has ruined Mr. Bryan, and threatens to ruin all the farmers of the West who possess silver mines on their farms. Silver troubled America, *ergo* silver troubles Scotland Yard."

"Very well; the natural inference is that some one has stolen bars of silver. But such a theft happened three months ago, when the metal was being unloaded from a German steamer at Southampton, and my dear friend Spenser Hale ran down the thieves very cleverly as they were trying to dissolve the marks off the bars with acid. Now crimes do not run in series, like the numbers in roulette at Monte Carlo. The thieves are men of brains. They say to themselves, 'What chance is there successfully to steal bars of silver while Mr. Hale is at Scotland Yard?' Eh, my good friend?"

"Really, Valmont," said Hale, taking another sip, "sometimes you almost persuade me that you have reasoning powers."

"Thanks, comrade. Then it is not a *theft* of silver we have now to deal with. But the American election was fought on the *price* of silver. If silver had been high in cost, there would have been no silver question. So the crime that is bothering you arises through the low price of silver, and this suggests that it must be a case of illicit coinage, for there the low price of the metal comes in. You have, perhaps, found a more subtle illegitimate act going forward than heretofore. Some one is making your shillings and your half crowns from real silver, instead of from baser metal, and yet there is a large profit which has not hitherto been possible through the high price of silver. With the old conditions you were familiar, but this new element sets at naught all your previous formulas. That is how I reasoned the matter out."

"Well, Valmont, you have hit it, I'll say that for you; you have hit it. There is a gang of expert coiners who are putting out real silver money, and making a clear shilling on the half crown. We can find no trace of the coiners, but we know the man who is shoving the stuff."

"That ought to be sufficient," I suggested.

"Yes, it should, but it hasn't proved so up to date. Now I came to-night to see if you would do one of your French tricks for us, right on the quiet."

"What French trick, Monsieur Spenser Hale?" I inquired with some asperity, forgetting for the moment that the man invariably became impolite when he grew excited.

"No offense intended," said this blundering officer, who really is a good-natured fellow, but always puts his foot in it, and then apologizes. "I want some one to go through a man's house without a search warrant, spot the evidence, let me know, and then we'll rush the place before he has time to hide his tracks."

"Who is this man, and where does he live?"

"His name is Ralph Summertrees, and he lives in a very natty little *bijou* residence, as the advertisements call it, situated in no less a fashionable street than Park Lane."

"I see. What has aroused your suspicions against him?"

"Well, you know, that's an expensive district to live in; it takes a bit of money to do the trick. This Summertrees has no ostensible business, yet every Friday he goes to the United Capital Bank in Piccadilly, and deposits a bag of swag, usually all silver coin."

"Yes; and this money?"

"This money, so far as we can learn, contains a good many of these new pieces which never saw the British Mint."

"It's not all the new coinage, then?"

"Oh, no, he's a bit too artful for that! You see, a man can go round London, his pockets filled with new-coined five-shilling pieces, buy this, that, and the other, and come home with his change in legitimate coins of the realm—half crowns, florins, shillings, sixpences, and all that."

"I see. Then why don't you nab him one day when his pockets are stuffed with illegitimate five-shilling pieces?"

"That could be done, of course, and I've thought of it, but, you see, we want to land the whole gang. Once we arrested him, without knowing where the money came from, the real coiners would take flight."

"How do you know he is not the real coiner himself?"

Now poor Hale is as easy to read as a book. He hesitated before answering this question, and looked confused as a culprit caught in some dishonest act.

"You need not be afraid to tell me," I said soothingly, after a pause. "You have had one of your men in Mr. Summertrees' house, and so learned that he is not the coiner. But your man has not succeeded in getting you evidence to incriminate other people."

"You've about hit it again, Monsieur Valmont. One of my men has been Summertrees' butler for two weeks, but, as you say, he has found no evidence."

"Is he still butler?"

"Yes."

"Now tell me how far you have got. You know that Summertrees deposits a bag of coin every Friday in the Piccadilly Bank, and I suppose the bank has allowed you to examine one or two of the bags."

"Yes, sir, they have, but, you see, banks are very difficult to treat with. They don't like detectives bothering round, and while they do not stand out against the law, still they never answer any more questions than they're asked, and Mr. Summertrees has been a good customer at the United Capital for many years."

"Haven't you found out where the money comes from?"

"Yes, we have; it is brought there night after night by a man who looks like a respectable city clerk, and he puts it into a large safe, of which he holds the key, this safe being on the ground floor, in the dining room."

"Haven't you followed the clerk?"

"Yes. He sleeps in the Park Lane house every night and goes up in the morning to an old curiosity shop in Tottenham Court

Road, where he stays all day, returning with his bag of money in the evening."

"Why don't you arrest and question him?"

"Well, Monsieur Valmont, there is just the same objection to his arrest as to that of Summertrees himself. We could easily arrest both, but we have not the slightest evidence against either of them, and then, although we put the go-betweens in clink, the worst criminals of the lot would escape."

"Nothing suspicious about the old curiosity shop?"

"No. It appears to be perfectly regular."

"This game has been going on under your noses for how long?"

"For about six weeks."

"Is Summertrees a married man?"

"No."

"Are there any women servants in the house?"

"No, except that three charwomen come in every morning to do up the rooms."

"Of what is his household comprised?"

"There is the butler, then the valet, and last the French cook."

"Ah," cried I, "the French cook! This case interests me. So Summertrees has succeeded in completely disconcerting your man? Has he prevented him going from top to bottom of the house?"

"Oh, no! He has rather assisted him than otherwise. On one occasion he went to the safe, took out the money, had Podgers—that's my chap's name—help him to count it, and then actually sent Podgers to the bank with the bag of coin."

"And Podgers has been all over the place?"

"Yes."

"Saw no signs of a coining establishment?"

"No. It is absolutely impossible that any coining can be done there. Besides, as I tell you, that respectable clerk brings him the money."

"I suppose you want me to take Podger's position?"

"Well, Monsieur Valmont, to tell you the truth, I would rather you didn't. Podgers has done everything a man can do, but I thought if you got into the house, Podgers assisting, you might go through it night after night at your leisure."

"I see. That's just a little dangerous in England. I think I should prefer to assure myself the legitimate standing of being amiable Podgers's successor. You say that Summertrees has no business?"

"Well, sir, not what you might call a business. He is by way of being an author, but I don't count that any business."

"Oh, an author, is he? When does he do his writing?"

"He locks himself up most of the day in his study."

"Does he come out for lunch?"

"No; he lights a little spirit lamp inside, Podgers tells me, and makes himself a cup of coffee, which he takes with a sandwich or two."

"That's rather frugal fare for Park Lane."

"Yes. Monsieur Valmont, it is, but he makes it up in the evening, when he has a long dinner, with all them foreign kickshaws you people like, done by his French cook."

"Sensible man! Well, Hale, I see I shall look forward with pleasure to making the acquaintance of Mr. Summertrees. Is there any restriction on the going and coming of your man Podgers?"

"None in the least. He can get away either night or day."

"Very good, friend Hale; bring him here to-morrow, as soon as our author locks himself up in his study, or rather, I should say, as soon as the respectable clerk leaves for Tottenham Court Road, which I should guess, as you put it, is about half an hour after his master turns the key of the room in which he writes."

"You are quite right in that guess, Valmont. How did you hit it?"

"Merely a surmise, Hale. There is a good deal of oddity about that Park Lane house, so it doesn't surprise me in the least that the master gets to work earlier in the morning than the man. I have also a suspicion that Ralph Summertrees knows perfectly well what the estimable Podgers is there for."

"What makes you think that?"

"I can give no reason except that my opinion of the acuteness of Summertrees has been gradually rising all the while you were speaking, and at the same time my estimate of Podgers's craft has been as steadily declining. However, bring the man here to-morrow, that I may ask him a few questions."

Next day, about eleven o'clock, the ponderous Podgers, hat in hand, followed his chief into my room. His broad, impassive, immobile, smooth face gave him rather more the air of a genuine butler than I had expected, and this appearance, of course, was enhanced by his livery. His replies to my questions were those of a well-trained servant who will not say too much unless it is made worth his while.

All in all, Podgers exceeded my expectations, and really my friend
Hale had some justification for regarding him, as he evidently did, a
triumph in his line.

"Sit down, Mr. Hale, and you, Podgers."

The man disregarded my invitation, standing like a statue until his
chief made a motion; then he dropped into a chair. The English are
great on discipline.

"Now, Mr. Hale, I must first congratulate you on the make-up of
Podgers. It is excellent. You depend less on artificial assistance than
we do in France, and in that I think you are right."

"Oh, we know a bit over here, Monsieur Valmont!" said Hale, with
pardonable pride.

"Now then, Podgers, I want to ask you about this clerk. What time
does he arrive in the evening?"

"At prompt six, sir."

"Does he ring, or let himself in with a latchkey?"

"With a latchkey, sir."

"How does he carry the money?"

"In a little locked leather satchel, sir, flung over his shoulder."

"Does he go direct to the dining room?"

"Yes, sir."

"Have you seen him unlock the safe, and put in the money?"

"Yes, sir."

"Does the safe unlock with a word or a key?"

"With a key, sir. It's one of the old-fashioned kind."

"Then the clerk unlocks his leather money bag?"

"Yes, sir."

"That's three keys used within as many minutes. Are they separate
or in a bunch?"

"In a bunch, sir."

"Did you ever see your master with this bunch of keys?"

"No, sir."

"You saw him open the safe once, I am told?"

"Yes, sir."

"Did he use a separate key, or one of a bunch?"

Podgers slowly scratched his head, then said:

"I don't just remember, sir."

"Ah, Podgers, you are neglecting the big things in that house! Sure
you can't remember?"

"No, sir."

"Once the money is in and the safe locked up, what does the clerk do?"

"Goes to his room, sir."

"Where is this room?"

"On the third floor, sir."

"Where do you sleep?"

"On the fourth floor with the rest of the servants, sir."

"Where does the master sleep?"

"On the second floor, adjoining his study."

"The house consists of four stories and a basement, does it?"

"Yes, sir."

"I have somehow arrived at the suspicion that it is a very narrow house. Is that true?"

"Yes, sir."

"Does the clerk ever dine with your master?"

"No, sir. The clerk don't eat in the house at all, sir."

"Does he go away before breakfast?"

"No, sir."

"No one takes breakfast to his room?"

"No, sir."

"What time does he leave the house?"

"At ten o'clock, sir."

"When is breakfast served?"

"At nine o'clock, sir."

"At what hour does your master retire to his study?"

"At half past nine, sir."

"Locks the door on the inside?"

"Yes, sir."

"Never rings for anything during the day?"

"Not that I know of, sir."

"What sort of a man is he?"

Here Podgers was on familiar ground, and he rattled off a description minute in every particular.

"What I meant was, Podgers, is he silent, or talkative, or does he get angry? Does he seem furtive, suspicious, anxious, terrorized, calm, excitable, or what?"

"Well, sir, he is by way of being very quiet, never has much to say for hisself; never saw him angry or excited."

"Now, Podgers, you've been at Park Lane for a fortnight or more. You are a sharp, alert, observant man. What happens there that strikes you as unusual?"

"Well, I can't exactly say, sir," replied Podgers, looking rather help-lessly from his chief to myself, and back again.

"Your professional duties have often compelled you to enact the part of butler before, otherwise you wouldn't do it so well. Isn't that the case?"

Podgers did not reply, but glanced at his chief. This was evidently a question pertaining to the service, which a subordinate was not allowed to answer. However, Hale said at once:

"Certainly. Podgers has been in dozens of places."

"Well, Podgers, just call to mind some of the other households where you have been employed, and tell me any particulars in which Mr. Summertrees' establishment differs from them."

Podgers pondered a long time.

"Well, sir, he do stick to writing pretty close."

"Ah, that's his profession, you see, Podgers. Hard at it from half past nine till toward seven, I imagine?"

"Yes, sir."

"Anything else, Podgers? No matter how trivial."

"Well, sir, he's fond of reading, too; leastways, he's fond of newspapers."

"When does he read?"

"I never seen him read 'em, sir; indeed, so far as I can tell, I never knew the papers to be opened, but he takes them all in, sir."

"What, all the morning papers?"

"Yes, sir, and all the evening papers, too."

"Where are the morning papers placed?"

"On the table in his study, sir."

"And the evening papers?"

"Well, sir, when the evening papers come, the study is locked. They are put on a side table in the dining room, and he takes them upstairs with him to his study."

"This has happened every day since you've been there?"

"Yes, sir."

"You reported that very striking fact to your chief, of course?"

"No, sir, I don't think I did," said Podgers, confused.

"You should have done so. Mr. Hale would have known how to make the most of a point so vital."

"Oh, come now, Valmont," interrupted Hale, "you're chaffing us! Plenty of people take in all the papers!"

"I think not. Even clubs and hotels subscribe to the leading journals only. You said *all*, I think, Podgers?"

"Well, *nearly* all, sir."

"But which is it? There's a vast difference."

"He takes a good many, sir."

"How many?"

"I don't just know, sir."

"That's easily found out, Valmont," cried Hale, with some impatience, "if you think it really important."

"I think it so important that I'm going back with Podgers myself. You can take me into the house, I suppose, when you return?"

"Oh, yes, sir!"

"Coming back to these newspapers for a moment, Podgers. What is done with them?"

"They are sold to the ragman, sir, once a week."

"Who takes them from the study?"

"I do, sir."

"Do they appear to have been read very carefully?"

"Well, no, sir; leastways, some of them seem never to have been opened, or else folded up very carefully again."

"Did you notice that extracts have been clipped from any of them?"

"No, sir."

"Does Mr. Summertrees keep a scrapbook?"

"Not that I know of, sir."

"Oh, the case is perfectly plain!" said I, leaning back in my chair, and regarding the puzzled Hale with that cherubic expression of self-satisfaction which I know is so annoying to him.

"*What's* perfectly plain?" he demanded, more gruffly perhaps than etiquette would have sanctioned.

"Summertrees is no coiner, nor is he linked with any band of coiners."

"What is he, then?"

"Ah, that opens another avenue of inquiry! For all I know to the contrary, he may be the most honest of men. On the surface it would appear that he is a reasonably industrious tradesman in Tottenham Court Road, who is anxious that there should be no visible connection between a plebeian employment and so aristocratic a residence as that in Park Lane."

At this point Spenser Hale gave expression to one of those rare flashes of reason which are always an astonishment to his friends.

"That is nonsense, Monsieur Valmont," he said; "the man who is ashamed of the connection between his business and his house is one who is trying to get into society, or else the women of his family are trying it, as is usually the case. Now Summertrees has no family. He himself goes nowhere, gives no entertainments, and accepts no invitations. He belongs to no club; therefore, to say that he is ashamed of his connection with the Tottenham Court Road shop is absurd. He is concealing the connection for some other reason that will bear looking into."

"My dear Hale, the Goddess of Wisdom herself could not have made a more sensible series of remarks. Now, *mon ami*, do you want my assistance, or have you enough to go on with?"

"Enough to go on with? We have nothing more than we had when I called on you last night."

"Last night my dear Hale, you supposed this man was in league with coiners. To-day you know he is not."

"I know you *say* he is not."

I shrugged my shoulders, and raised my eyebrows, smiling at him.

"It is the same thing, Monsieur Hale."

"Well, of all the conceited—" and the good Hale could get no farther.

"If you wish my assistance, it is yours."

"Very good. Not to put too fine a point upon it, I do."

"In that case, my dear Podgers, you will return to the residence of our friend Summertrees, and get together for me in a bundle all of yesterday's morning and evening papers that were delivered to the house. Can you do that, or are they mixed up in a heap in the coal cellar?"

"I can do it, sir. I have instructions to place each day's papers in a pile by itself in case they should be wanted again. There is always one week's supply in the cellar, and we sell the papers of the week before to the ragman."

"Excellent. Well, take the risk of abstracting one day's journals, and have them ready for me. I will call upon you at half past three o'clock exactly, and then I want you to take me upstairs to the clerk's bedroom in the third story, which I suppose is not locked during the daytime?"

"No, sir, it is not."

With this the patient Podgers took his departure. Spenser Hale rose when his assistant left.

"Anything further I can do?" he asked.

"Yes; give me the address of the shop in Tottenham Court Road. Do you happen to have about you one of those new five-shilling pieces which you believe to be illegally coined?"

He opened his pocketbook, took out the bit of white metal, and handed it to me.

"I'm going to pass this off before evening," I said, putting it in my pocket, "and I hope none of your men will arrest me."

"That's all right," laughed Hale as he took his leave.

At half past three Podgers was waiting for me, and opened the front door as I came up the steps, thus saving me the necessity of ringing. The house seemed strangely quiet. The French cook was evidently down in the basement, and we had probably all the upper part to ourselves, unless Summertrees was in his study, which I doubted. Podgers led me directly upstairs to the clerk's room on the third floor, walking on tiptoe, with an elephantine air of silence and secrecy combined, which struck me as unnecessary.

"I will make an examination of this room," I said. "Kindly wait for me down by the door of the study."

The bedroom proved to be of respectable size when one considers the smallness of the house. The bed was all nicely made up, and there were two chairs in the room, but the usual washstand and swing mirror were not visible. However, seeing a curtain at the farther end of the room, I drew it aside, and found, as I expected, a fixed lavatory in an alcove of perhaps four feet deep by five in width. As the room was about fifteen feet wide, this left two-thirds of the space unaccounted for. A moment later I opened a door which exhibited a closet filled with clothes hanging on hooks. This left a space of five feet between the clothes closet and the lavatory. I thought at first that the entrance to the secret stairway must have issued from the lavatory, but examining the boards closely, although they sounded hollow to the knuckles, they were quite evidently plain match boarding, and not a concealed door. The entrance to the stairway, therefore, must issue from the clothes closet. The right-hand wall proved similar to the match boarding of the lavatory, so far as the casual eye or touch was concerned, but I saw at once it was a door. The latch turned out to be somewhat ingeniously operated by one of the hooks which held a pair of old trousers. I found that the hook, if pressed upward,

allowed the door to swing outward, over the stairhead. Descending to
the second floor, a similar latch let me into a similar clothes closet in
the room beneath. The two rooms were identical in size, one directly
above the other, the only difference being that the lower-room door
gave into the study, instead of into the hall, as was the case with the
upper chamber.

The study was extremely neat, either not much used, or the abode
of a very methodical man. There was nothing on the table except a
pile of that morning's papers. I walked to the farther end, turned the
key in the lock, and came out upon the astonished Podgers.

"Well, I'm blowed!" exclaimed he.

"Quite so," I rejoined; "you've been tiptoeing past an empty room
for the last two weeks. Now, if you'll come with me, Podgers, I'll
show you how the trick is done."

When he entered the study I locked the door once more, and led
the assumed butler, still tiptoeing through force of habit, up the stair
into the top bedroom, and so out again, leaving everything exactly as
we found it. We went down the main stair to the front hall, and there
Podgers had my parcel of papers all neatly wrapped up. This bundle
I carried to my flat, gave one of my assistants some instructions, and
left him at work on the papers.

I took a cab to the foot of Tottenham Court Road, and walked up
that street till I came to J. Simpson's old curiosity shop. After gazing
at the well-filled windows for some time, I stepped inside, having
selected a little iron crucifix displayed behind the pane; the work of
some ancient craftsman.

I knew at once from Podger's description that I was waited upon
by the veritable respectable clerk who brought the bag of money
each night to Park Lane, and who, I was certain, was no other than
Ralph Summertrees himself.

There was nothing in his manner differing from that of any other
quiet salesman. The price of the crucifix proved to be seven-and-six,
and I threw down a sovereign to pay for it.

"Do you mind the change being all in silver, sir?" he asked, and
I answered without any eagerness, although the question aroused a
suspicion that had begun to be allayed:

"Not in the least."

He gave me half a crown, three two-shilling pieces, and four
separate shillings, all coins being well-worn silver of the realm, the
undoubted inartistic product of the reputable British Mint. This

seemed to dispose of the theory that he was palming off illegitimate money. He asked me if I were interested in any particular branch of antiquity, and I replied that my curiosity was merely general, and exceedingly amateurish, whereupon he invited me to look around. This I proceeded to do, while he resumed the addressing and stamping of some wrapped-up pamphlets which I surmised to be copies of his catalogue.

He made no attempt either to watch me or to press his wares upon me. I selected at random a little ink-stand, and asked its price. It was two shillings, he said, whereupon I produced my fraudulent five-shilling piece. He took it, gave me the change without comment, and the last doubt about his connection with coiners flickered from my mind.

At this moment a young man came in who, I saw at once, was not a customer. He walked briskly to the farther end of the shop, and disappeared behind a partition which had one pane of glass in it that gave an outlook toward the front door.

"Excuse me a moment," said the shopkeeper, and he followed the young man into the private office.

As I examined the curious heterogeneous collection of things for sale, I heard the clink of coins being poured out on the lid of a desk or an uncovered table, and the murmur of voices floated out to me. I was now near the entrance of the shop, and by a sleight-of-hand trick, keeping the corner of my eye on the glass pane of the private office, I removed the key of the front door without a sound, and took an impression of it in wax, returning the key to its place unobserved. At this moment another young man came in, and walked straight past me into the private office. I heard him say:

"Oh, I beg pardon, Mr. Simpson! How are you, Rogers?"

"Hello, Macpherson," saluted Rogers, who then came out, bidding good night to Mr. Simpson, and departed, whistling, down the street, but not before he had repeated his phrase to another young man entering, to whom he gave the name of Tyrrel.

I noted these three names in my mind. Two others came in together, but I was compelled to content myself with memorizing their features, for I did not learn their names. These men were evidently collectors, for I heard the rattle of money in every case; yet here was a small shop, doing apparently very little business, for I had been within it for more than half an hour, and yet remained the only customer. If credit were given, one collector would certainly have been sufficient, yet five had come in, and had poured their contributions into the pile Summertrees was to take home with him that night.

I determined to secure one of the pamphlets which the man had been addressing. They were piled on a shelf behind the counter, but I had no difficulty in reaching across and taking the one on top, which I slipped into my pocket. When the fifth young man went down the street Summertrees himself emerged, and this time he carried in his hand the well-filled locked leather satchel, with the straps dangling. It was now approaching half past five, and I saw he was eager to close up and get away.

"Anything else you fancy, sir?" he asked me.

"No, or, rather, yes and no. You have a very interesting collection here, but it's getting so dark I can hardly see."

"I close at half past five, sir."

"Ah! In that case," I said, consulting my watch, "I shall be pleased to call some other time."

"Thank you, sir," replied Summertrees quietly, and with that I took my leave.

From the corner of an alley on the other side of the street I saw him put up the shutters with his own hands, then he emerged with overcoat on, and the money satchel slung across his shoulder. He locked the door, tested it with his knuckles, and walked down the street, carrying under one arm the pamphlets he had been addressing. I followed him at some distance, saw him drop the pamphlets into the box at the first post office he passed, and walk rapidly toward his house in Park Lane.

When I returned to my flat and called in my assistant, he said:

"After putting to one side the regular advertisements of pills, soap, and what not, here is the only one common to all the newspapers, morning and evening alike. The advertisements are not identical, sir, but they have two points of similarity, or perhaps I should say three. They all profess to furnish a cure for absent-mindedness; they all ask that the applicant's chief hobby shall be stated, and they all bear the same address: Dr. Willoughby, in Tottenham Court Road."

"Thank you," said I, as he placed the scissored advertisements before me.

I read several of the announcements. They were all small, and perhaps that is why I had never noticed one of them in the newspapers, for certainly they were odd enough. Some asked for lists of absent-minded men, with the hobbies of each, and for these lists, prizes of from one shilling to six were offered. In other clippings Dr. Willoughby professed to be able to cure absent-mindedness. There were no fees and no treatment, but a pamphlet would be sent, which, if it did not benefit the receiver, could do no harm. The doctor was unable to meet patients personally, nor could he enter into correspondence with them. The address was the same as that of the old curiosity shop in Tottenham Court Road. At this juncture I pulled the pamphlet from my pocket, and saw it was entitled, "Christian Science and Absent-Mindedness," by Dr. Stamford Willoughby, and at the end of the article was the statement contained in the advertisements, that Dr. Willoughby would neither see patients nor hold any correspondence with them.

I drew a sheet of paper toward me, wrote to Dr. Willoughby, alleging that I was a very absent-minded man, and would be glad of his pamphlet, adding that my special hobby was the collecting of first editions. I then signed myself, "Alport Webster, Imperial Flats, London, W."

I may here explain that it is often necessary for me to see people under some other name than the well-known appellation of Eugène Valmont. There are two doors to my flat, and on one of these is painted, "Eugène Valmont"; on the other there is a receptacle, into which can be slipped a sliding panel bearing any *nom de guerre* I choose. The same device is arranged on the ground floor, where the names of all the occupants of the building appear on the right-hand wall.

I sealed, addressed, and stamped my letter, then told my man to put out the name of Alport Webster, and if I did not happen to be in when any one called upon that mythical person, he was to make an appointment for me.

It was nearly six o'clock next afternoon when the card of Angus Macpherson was brought in to Mr. Alport Webster. I recognized the young man at once as the second who had entered the little shop, carrying his tribute to Mr. Simpson the day before. He held three volumes under his arm, and spoke in such a pleasant, insinuating sort of way, that I knew at once he was an adept in his profession of canvasser.

"Will you be seated, Mr. Macpherson? In what can I serve you?"
He placed the three volumes, backs upward, on my table.

"Are you interested at all in first editions, Mr. Webster?"

"It is the one thing I am interested in," I replied; "but unfortunately they often run into a lot of money."

"That is true," said Macpherson sympathetically, "and I have here three books, one of which is an exemplification of what you say. This one costs a hundred pounds. The last copy that was sold by auction in London brought a hundred and twenty-three pounds. This next one is forty pounds, and the third ten pounds. At these prices I am certain you could not duplicate three such treasures in any bookshop in Britain."

I examined them critically, and saw at once that what he said was true. He was still standing on the opposite side of the table.

"Please take a chair, Mr. Macpherson. Do you mean to say you go round London with a hundred and fifty pounds' worth of goods under your arm in this careless way?"

The young man laughed.

"I run very little risk, Mr. Webster. I don't suppose any one I meet imagines for a moment there is more under my arm than perhaps a trio of volumes I have picked up in the fourpenny box to take home with me."

I lingered over the volume for which he asked a hundred pounds, then said, looking across at him:

"How came you to be possessed of this book, for instance?"

He turned upon me a fine, open countenance, and answered without hesitation in the frankest possible manner:

"I am not in actual possession of it, Mr. Webster. I am by way of being a connoisseur in rare and valuable books myself, although, of course, I have little money with which to indulge in the collection of them. I am acquainted, however, with the lovers of desirable books in different quarters of London. These three volumes, for instance, are from the library of a private gentleman in the West End. I have sold many books to him, and he knows I am trustworthy. He wishes to dispose of them at something under their real value, and has kindly allowed me to conduct the negotiations. I make it my business to find out those who are interested in rare books, and by such trading I add considerably to my income."

"How, for instance, did you learn that I was a bibliophile?"

Mr. Macpherson laughed genially.

"Well, Mr. Webster, I must confess that I chanced it. I do that very often. I take a flat like this, and send in my card to the name on the door. If I am invited in, I ask the occupant the question I asked you just now: 'Are you interested in rare editions?' If he says no, I simply beg pardon and retire. If he says yes, then I show my wares."

"I see," said I, nodding. What a glib young liar he was, with that innocent face of his, and yet my next question brought forth the truth.

"As this is the first time you have called upon me, Mr. Macpherson, you have no objection to my making some further inquiry, I suppose. Would you mind telling me the name of the owner of these books in the West End?"

"His name is Mr. Ralph Summertrees, of Park Lane."

"Of Park Lane? Ah, indeed!"

"I shall be glad to leave the books with you, Mr. Webster, and if you care to make an appointment with Mr. Summertrees, I am sure he will not object to say a word in my favor."

"Oh, I do not in the least doubt it, and should not think of troubling the gentleman."

"I was going to tell you," went on the young man, "that I have a friend, a capitalist, who, in a way, is my supporter; for, as I said, I have little money of my own. I find it is often inconvenient for people to pay down any considerable sum. When, however, I strike a bargain, my capitalist buys the books, and I make an arrangement with my customer to pay a certain amount each week, and so even a large purchase is not felt, as I make the installments small enough to suit my client."

"You are employed during the day, I take it?"

"Yes, I am a clerk in the City."

Again we were in the blissful realms of fiction!

"Suppose I take this book at ten pounds, what installments should I have to pay each week?"

"Oh, what you like, sir. Would five shillings be too much?"

"I think not."

"Very well, sir; if you pay me five shillings now, I will leave the book with you, and shall have pleasure in calling this day week for the next installment."

I put my hand into my pocket, and drew out two half crowns, which I passed over to him.

"Do I need to sign any form or undertaking to pay the rest?"

The young man laughed cordially.

"Oh, no, sir, there is no formality necessary. You see, sir, this is largely a labor of love with me, although I don't deny I have my eye

on the future. I am getting together what I hope will be a very valuable connection with gentlemen like yourself who are fond of books,
and I trust some day that I may be able to resign my place with the
insurance company and set up a choice little business of my own,
where my knowledge of values in literature will prove useful."

And then, after making a note in a little book he took from his
pocket, he bade me a most graceful good-by and departed, leaving
me cogitating over what it all meant.

Next morning two articles were handed to me. The first came
by post and was a pamphlet on "Christian Science and Absent-
Mindedness," exactly similar to the one I had taken away from the
old curiosity shop; the second was a small key made from my wax
impression that would fit the front door of the same shop—a key
fashioned by an excellent anarchist friend of mine in an obscure
street near Holborn.

That night at ten o'clock I was inside the old curiosity shop, with
a small storage battery in my pocket, and a little electric glowlamp
at my buttonhole, a most useful instrument for either burglar or
detective.

I had expected to find the books of the establishment in a safe,
which, if it was similar to the one in Park Lane, I was prepared to
open with the false keys in my possession, or to take an impression
of the keyhole and trust to my anarchist friend for the rest. But to
my amazement I discovered all the papers pertaining to the concern
in a desk which was not even locked. The books, three in number,
were the ordinary daybook, journal, and ledger referring to the shop;
bookkeeping of the older fashion; but in a portfolio lay half a dozen
foolscap sheets, headed, "Mr. Rogers's List," "Mr. Macpherson's,"
"Mr. Tyrrel's," the names I had already learned, and three others. These
lists contained in the first column, names; in the second column,
addresses; in the third, sums of money; and then in the small, square
places following were amounts ranging from two-and-sixpence to a
pound. At the bottom of Mr. Macpherson's list was the name Alport
Webster, Imperial Flats, £10; then in the small, square place, five
shillings. These six sheets, each headed by a canvasser's name, were
evidently the record of current collections, and the innocence of the
whole thing was so apparent that, if it were not for my fixed rule
never to believe that I am at the bottom of any case until I have come
on something suspicious, I would have gone out empty-handed as I
came in.

The six sheets were loose in a thin portfolio, but standing on a shelf above the desk were a number of fat volumes, one of which I took down, and saw that it contained similar lists running back several years. I noticed on Mr. Macpherson's current list the name of Lord Semptam, an eccentric old nobleman whom I knew slightly. Then turning to the list immediately before the current one the name was still there; I traced it back through list after list until I found the first entry, which was no less than three years previous, and there Lord Semptam was down for a piece of furniture costing fifty pounds, and on that account he had paid a pound a week for more than three years, totaling a hundred and seventy pounds at the least, and instantly the glorious simplicity of the scheme dawned upon me, and I became so interested in the swindle that I lit the gas, fearing my little lamp would be exhausted before my investigation ended, for it promised to be a long one.

In several instances the intended victim proved shrewder than old Simpson had counted upon, and the word "Settled" had been written on the line carrying the name when the exact number of installments was paid. But as these shrewd persons dropped out, others took their places, and Simpson's dependence on their absent-mindedness seemed to be justified in nine cases out of ten. His collectors were collecting long after the debt had been paid. In Lord Semptam's case, the payment had evidently become chronic, and the old man was giving away his pound a week to the suave Macpherson two years after his debt had been liquidated.

From the big volume I detached the loose leaf, dated 1893, which recorded Lord Semptam's purchase of a carved table for fifty pounds, and on which he had been paying a pound a week from that time to the date of which I am writing, which was November, 1896. This single document, taken from the file of three years previous, was not likely to be missed, as would have been the case if I had selected a current sheet. I nevertheless made a copy of the names and addresses of Macpherson's present clients; then, carefully placing everything exactly as I had found it, I extinguished the gas, and went out of the shop, locking the door behind me. With the 1893 sheet in my pocket I resolved to prepare a pleasant little surprise for my suave friend Macpherson when he called to get his next installment of five shillings.

Late as was the hour when I reached Trafalgar Square, I could not deprive myself of the felicity of calling on Mr. Spenser Hale, who I knew was then on duty. He never appeared at his best during office hours, because officialism stiffened his stalwart frame. Mentally he was impressed with the importance of his position, and added to this he was not then allowed to smoke his big black pipe and terrible tobacco. He received me with the curtness I had been taught to expect when I inflicted myself upon him at his office. He greeted me abruptly with:

"I say. Valmont, how long do you expect to be on this job?"

"What job?" I asked mildly.

"Oh, you know what I mean: the Summertrees affair?"

"Oh, *that*!" I exclaimed, with surprise. "The Summertrees case is already completed, of course. If I had known you were in a hurry, I should have finished up everything yesterday, but as you and Podgers, and I don't know how many more, have been at it sixteen or seventeen days, if not longer, I thought I might venture to take as many hours, as I am working entirely alone. You said nothing about haste, you know."

"Oh, come now, Valmont, that's a bit thick. Do you mean to say you have already got evidence against the man?"

"Evidence absolute and complete."

"Then who are the coiners?"

"My most estimable friend, how often have I told you not to jump at conclusions? I informed you when you first spoke to me about the matter that Summertrees was neither a coiner nor a confederate of coiners. I secured evidence sufficient to convict him of quite another offense, which is probably unique in the annals of crime. I have penetrated the mystery of the shop, and discovered the reason for all those suspicious actions which quite properly set you on his trail. Now I wish you to come to my flat next Wednesday night at a quarter to six, prepared to make an arrest."

"I must know whom I am to arrest, and on what counts."

"Quite so, *mon ami* Hale; I did not say you were to make an arrest, but merely warned you to be prepared. If you have time now to listen to the disclosures, I am quite at your service. I promise you there are some original features in the case. If, however, the present moment is inopportune, drop in on me at your convenience, previously telephoning so that you may know whether I am there or not, and thus your valuable time will not be expended purposelessly."

With this I presented to him my most courteous bow, and although his mystified expression hinted a suspicion that he thought I was chaffing him, as he would call it, official dignity dissolved somewhat, and he intimated his desire to hear all about it then and there. I had succeeded in arousing my friend Hale's curiosity. He listened to the evidence with perplexed brow, and at last ejaculated he would be blessed.

"This young man," I said, in conclusion, "will call upon me at six on Wednesday afternoon, to receive his second five shillings. I propose that you, in your uniform, shall be seated there with me to receive him, and I am anxious to study Mr. Macpherson's countenance when he realizes he has walked in to confront a policeman. If you will then allow me to cross-examine him for a few moments, not after the manner of Scotland Yard, with a warning lest he incriminate himself, but in the free and easy fashion we adopt in Paris, I shall afterwards turn the case over to you to be dealt with at your discretion."

"You have a wonderful flow of language, Monsieur Valmont," was the officer's tribute to me. "I shall be on hand at a quarter to six on Wednesday."

"Meanwhile," said I, "kindly say nothing of this to any one. We must arrange a complete surprise for Macpherson. That is essential. Please make no move in the matter at all until Wednesday night."

Spenser Hale, much impressed, nodded acquiescence, and I took a polite leave of him.

The question of lighting is an important one in a room such as mine, and electricity offers a good deal of scope to the ingenious. Of this fact I have taken full advantage. I can manipulate the lighting of my room so that any particular spot is bathed in brilliancy, while the rest of the space remains in comparative gloom, and I arranged the lamps so that the full force of their rays impinged against the door that Wednesday evening, while I sat on one side of the table in semidarkness and Hale sat on the other, with a light beating down on him from above which gave him the odd, sculptured look of a living statue of Justice, stern and triumphant. Any one entering the room would first be dazzled by the light, and next would see the gigantic form of Hale in the full uniform of his order.

When Angus Macpherson was shown into this room, he was quite visibly taken aback, and paused abruptly on the threshold, his gaze riveted on the huge policeman. I think his first purpose was to turn and run, but the door closed behind him, and he doubtless heard, as we all did, the sound of the bolt being thrust in its place, thus locking him in.

"I—I beg your pardon," he stammered, "I expected to meet Mr. Webster."

As he said this, I pressed the button under my table, and was instantly enshrouded with light. A sickly smile overspread the countenance of Macpherson as he caught sight of me, and he made a very creditable attempt to carry off the situation with nonchalance.

"Oh, there you are, Mr. Webster; I did not notice you at first."

It was a tense moment. I spoke slowly and impressively.

"Sir, perhaps you are not unacquainted with the name of Eugène Valmont."

He replied brazenly:

"I am sorry to say, sir, I never heard of the gentleman before."

At this came a most inopportune "Haw-haw" from that block-head Spenser Hale, completely spoiling the dramatic situation I had elaborated with such thought and care. It is little wonder the English possess no drama, for they show scant appreciation of the sensational moments in life; they are not quickly alive to the lights and shadows of events.

"Haw-haw," brayed Spenser Hale, and at once reduced the emotional atmosphere to a fog of commonplace. However, what is a man to do? He must handle the tools with which it pleases Providence to provide him. I ignored Hale's untimely laughter.

"Sit down, sir," I said to Macpherson, and he obeyed.

"You have called on Lord Semptam this week," I continued sternly.

"Yes, sir."

"And collected a pound from him?"

"Yes, sir."

"In October, 1893, you sold Lord Semptam a carved antique table for fifty pounds?"

"Quite right, sir."

"When you were here last week you gave me Ralph Summertrees as the name of a gentleman living in Park Lane. You knew at the time that this man was your employer?"

Macpherson was not looking fixedly at me, and on this occasion made no reply. I went on calmly:

"You also knew that Summertrees, of Park Lane, was identical with Simpson, of Tottenham Court Road?"

"Well, sir," said Macpherson, "I don't exactly see what you're driving at, but it's quite usual for a man to carry on a business under an assumed name. There is nothing illegal about that."

"We will come to the illegality in a moment, Mr. Macpherson. You and Rogers and Tyrrel and three others are confederates of this man Simpson."

"We are in his employ; yes, sir, but no more confederates than clerks usually are."

"I think, Mr. Macpherson, I have said enough to show you that the game is what you call up. You are now in the presence of Mr. Spenser Hale, from Scotland Yard, who is waiting to hear your confession."

Here the stupid Hale broke in with his:

"And remember, sir, that anything you say will be—"

"Excuse me, Mr. Hale," I interrupted hastily, "I shall turn over the case to you in a very few moments, but I ask you to remember our compact, and to leave it for the present entirely in my hands. Now, Mr. Macpherson, I want your confession, and I want it at once."

"Confession? Confederates?" protested Macpherson, with admirably simulated surprise. "I must say you use extraordinary terms, Mr.—. Mr.— What did you say the name was?"

"Haw-haw," roared Hale. "His name is Monsieur Valmont."

"I implore you, Mr. Hale, to leave this man to me for a very few moments. Now, Macpherson, what have you to say in your defense?"

"Where nothing criminal has been alleged, Monsieur Valmont, I see no necessity for defense. If you wish me to admit that somehow you have acquired a number of details regarding our business, I am perfectly willing to do so, and to subscribe to their accuracy. If you will be good enough to let me know of what you complain, I shall endeavor to make the point clear to you, if I can. There has evidently been some misapprehension, but for the life of me, without further explanation, I am as much in a fog as I was on my way coming here, for it is getting a little thick outside."

Macpherson certainly was conducting himself with great discretion, and presented, quite unconsciously, a much more diplomatic figure than my friend Spenser Hale, sitting stiffly opposite me. His tone was one of mild expostulation, mitigated by the intimation that all misunderstanding speedily would be cleared away. To outward view he offered a perfect picture of innocence, neither protesting too much nor too little. I had, however, another surprise in store for him, a trump card, as it were, and I played it down on the table.

"There!" I cried with vim, "have you ever seen that sheet before?"

He glanced at it without offering to take it in his hand.

"Oh, yes," he said, "that has been abstracted from our file. It is what I call my visiting list."

"Come, come, sir," I cried sternly, "you refuse to confess, but I warn you we know all about it. You never heard of Dr. Willoughby, I suppose?"

"Yes, he is the author of the silly pamphlet on Christian Science."

"You are in the right, Mr. Macpherson; on Christian Science and Absent-Mindedness."

"Possibly. I haven't read it for a long while."

"Have you ever met this learned doctor, Mr. Macpherson?"

"Oh, yes. Dr. Willoughby is the pen name of Mr. Summertrees. He believes in Christian Science and that sort of thing, and writes about it."

"Ah, really. We are getting your confession bit by bit, Mr. Macpherson. I think it would be better to be quite frank with us."

"I was just going to make the same suggestion to you, Monsieur Valmont. If you will tell me in a few words exactly what is your charge against either Mr. Summertrees or myself, I will know then what to say."

"We charge you, sir, with obtaining money under false pretenses, which is a crime that has landed more than one distinguished financier in prison."

Spenser Hale shook his fat forefinger at me, and said:

"Tut, tut, Valmont; we mustn't threaten, we mustn't threaten, you know"; but I went on without heeding him.

"Take, for instance, Lord Semptam. You sold him a table for fifty pounds, on the installment plan. He was to pay a pound a week, and in less than a year the debt was liquidated. But he is an absent-minded man, as all your clients are. That is why you came to me. I had answered the bogus Willoughby's advertisement. And so you kept on collecting and collecting for something more than three years. Now do you understand the charge?"

Mr. Macpherson's head, during this accusation, was held slightly inclined to one side. At first his face was clouded by the most clever imitation of anxious concentration of mind I had ever seen, and this was gradually cleared away by the dawn of awakening perception. When I had finished, an ingratiating smile hovered about his lips.

"Really, you know," he said, "that is rather a capital scheme. The absent-minded league, as one might call them. Most ingenious. Summertrees, if he had any sense of humor, which he hasn't, would be rather taken by the idea that his innocent fad for Christian Science had led him to be suspected of obtaining money under false pretenses. But, really, there are no pretensions about the matter at all. As I understand it, I simply call and receive the money through the forgetfulness of the persons on my list, but where I think you would have both Summertrees and myself, if there was anything in your audacious theory, would be an indictment for conspiracy. Still, I quite see how the mistake arises. You have jumped to the conclusion that we sold nothing to Lord Semptam except that carved table three years ago. I have pleasure in pointing out to you that his lordship is a frequent customer of ours, and has had many things from us at one time or another. Sometimes he is in our debt; sometimes we are in his. We keep a sort of running contract with him by which he pays us a pound a week. He and several other customers deal on the same plan, and in return, for an income that we can count upon, they get the first offer of anything in which they are supposed to be interested. As I have told you, we call these sheets in the office our visiting lists, but to make the visiting lists complete you need what we term our encyclopedia. We call it that because it is in so many volumes; a volume for each year, running back I don't know how long. You will notice little figures here from time to time above the amount stated on this visiting list. These figures refer to the page of the encyclopedia for the current year, and on that page is noted the new sale and the amount of it, as it might be set down, say, in a ledger."

"That is a very entertaining explanation, Mr. Macpherson. I suppose this encyclopedia, as you call it, is in the shop at Tottenham Court Road?"

"Oh, no, sir. Each volume of the encyclopedia is self-locking. These books contain the real secret of our business, and they are kept in the safe at Mr. Summertrees' house in Park Lane. Take Lord Semptam's account, for instance. You will find in faint figures under a certain date, 102. If you turn to page 102 of the encyclopedia for that year, you will then see a list of what Lord Semptam has bought, and the prices he was charged for them. It is really a very simple matter. If you will allow me to use your telephone for a moment, I will ask

Mr. Summertrees, who has not yet begun dinner, to bring with him here the volume for 1893, and within a quarter of an hour you will be perfectly satisfied that everything is quite legitimate."

I confess that the young man's naturalness and confidence staggered me, the more so as I saw by the sarcastic smile on Hale's lips that he did not believe a single word spoken. A portable telephone stood on the table, and as Macpherson finished his explanation, he reached over and drew it toward him. Then Spenser Hale interfered.

"Excuse *me*," he said, "I'll do the telephoning. What is the call number of Mr. Summertrees?"

"One forty Hyde Park."

Hale at once called up Central, and presently was answered from Park Lane. We heard him say:

"Is this the residence of Mr. Summertrees? Oh, is that you, Podgers? Is Mr. Summertrees in? Very well. This is Hale. I am in Valmont's flat—Imperial Flats—you know. Yes, where you went with me the other day. Very well, go to Mr. Summertrees, and say to him that Mr. Macpherson wants the encyclopedia for 1893. Do you get that? Yes, encyclopedia. Oh, don't understand what it is, Mr. Macpherson. No, don't mention my name at all. Just say Mr. Macpherson wants the encyclopedia for the year 1893, and that you are to bring it. Yes, you may tell him that Mr. Macpherson is at Imperial Flats, but don't mention my name at all. Exactly. As soon as he gives you the book, get into a cab, and come here as quickly as possible with it. If Summertrees doesn't want to let the book go, then tell him to come with you. If he won't do that, place him under arrest, and bring both him and the book here. All right. Be as quick as you can; we're waiting."

Macpherson made no protest against Hale's use of the telephone: he merely sat back in his chair with a resigned expression on his face which, if painted on canvas, might have been entitled, "The Falsely Accused." When Hale rang off, Macpherson said:

"Of course you know your business best, but if your man arrests Summertrees, he will make you the laughing-stock of London. There is such a thing as unjustifiable arrest, as well as getting money under false pretenses, and Mr. Summertrees is not the man to forgive an insult. And then, if you will allow me to say so, the more I think over your absent-minded theory, the more absolutely grotesque it seems, and if the case ever gets into the newspapers, I am sure, Mr. Hale, you'll experience an uncomfortable half hour with your chiefs at Scotland Yard."

"I'll take the risk of that, thank you," said Hale stubbornly.

"Am I to consider myself under arrest?" inquired the young man.

"No, sir."

"Then, if you will pardon me, I shall withdraw. Mr. Summertrees will show you everything you wish to see in his books, and can explain his business much more capably than I, because he knows more about it; therefore, gentlemen, I bid you good night."

"No, you don't. Not just yet awhile," exclaimed Hale, rising to his feet simultaneously with the young man.

"Then I *am* under arrest," protested Macpherson.

"You're not going to leave this room until Podgers brings that book."

"Oh, very well," and he sat down again.

And now, as talking is dry work, I set out something to drink, a box of cigars, and a box of cigarettes. Hale mixed his favorite brew, but Macpherson, shunning the wine of his country, contented himself with a glass of plain mineral water, and lit a cigarette. Then he awoke my high regard by saying pleasantly, as if nothing had happened:

"While we are waiting, Monsieur Valmont, may I remind you that you owe me five shillings?"

I laughed, took the coin from my pocket, and paid him, whereupon he thanked me.

"Are you connected with Scotland Yard, Monsieur Valmont?" asked Macpherson, with the air of a man trying to make conversation to bridge over a tedious interval; but before I could reply Hale blurted out:

"Not likely!"

"You have no official standing as a detective, then, Monsieur Valmont?"

"None whatever," I replied quickly, thus getting in my oar ahead of Hale.

"That is a loss to our country," pursued this admirable young man, with evident sincerity.

I began to see I could make a good deal of so clever a fellow if he came under my tuition.

"The blunders of our police," he went on, "are something deplorable. If they would but take lessons in strategy, say, from France, their unpleasant duties would be so much more acceptably performed, with much less discomfort to their victims."

"France," snorted Hale in derision, "why, they call a man guilty there until he's proven innocent."

"Yes, Mr. Hale, and the same seems to be the case in Imperial Flats. You have quite made up your mind that Mr. Summertrees is guilty, and will not be content until he proves his innocence. I venture to predict that you will hear from him before long in a manner that may astonish you."

Hale grunted and looked at his watch. The minutes passed very slowly as we sat there smoking and at last even I began to get uneasy. Macpherson, seeing our anxiety, said that when he came in the fog was almost as thick as it had been the week before, and that there might be some difficulty in getting a cab. Just as he was speaking the door was unlocked from the outside, and Podgers entered, bearing a thick volume in his hand. This he gave to his superior, who turned over its pages in amazement, and then looked at the back, crying:

"'Encyclopedia of Sport, 1893'! What sort of a joke is this, Mr. Macpherson?"

There was a pained look on Mr. Macpherson's face as he reached forward and took the book. He said with a sigh.

"If you had allowed me to telephone, Mr. Hale, I should have made it perfectly plain to Summertrees what was wanted. I might have known this mistake was liable to occur. There is an increasing demand for out-of-date books of sport, and no doubt Mr. Summertrees thought this was what I meant. There is nothing for it but to send your man back to Park Lane and tell Mr. Summertrees that what we want is the locked volume of accounts for 1893, which we call the encyclopedia. Allow me to write an order that will bring it. Oh, I'll show you what I have written before your man takes it," he said, as Hale stood ready to look over his shoulder.

On my note paper he dashed off a request such as he had outlined, and handed it to Hale, who read it and gave it to Podgers.

"Take that to Summertrees, and get back as quickly as possible. Have you a cab at the door?"

"Yes, sir."

"Is it foggy outside?"

"Not so much, sir, as it was an hour ago. No difficulty about the traffic now, sir."

"Very well, get back as soon as you can."

Podgers saluted, and left with the book under his arm. Again the door was locked, and again we sat smoking in silence until the stillness was broken by the tinkle of the telephone. Hale put the receiver to his ear.

"Yes, this is the Imperial Flats. Yes. Valmont. Oh, yes; Macpherson is here. What? Out of what? Can't hear you. Out of print. What, the encyclopedia's out of print? Who is that speaking? Dr. Willoughby; thanks."

Macpherson rose as if he would go to the telephone, but instead (and he acted so quietly that I did not notice what he was doing until the thing was done) he picked up the sheet which he called his visiting list, and walking quite without haste, held it in the glowing coals of the fireplace until it disappeared in a flash of flame up the chimney. I sprang to my feel indignant, but too late to make even a motion toward saving the sheet. Macpherson regarded us both with that self-depreciatory smile which had several times lighted up his face.

"How dared you burn that sheet?" I demanded.

"Because, Monsieur Valmont, it did not belong to you; because you do not belong to Scotland Yard; because you stole it; because you had no right to it; and because you have no official standing in this country. If it had been in Mr. Hale's possession I should not have dared, as you put it, to destroy the sheet, but as this sheet was abstracted from my master's premises by you, an entirely unauthorized person, whom he would have been justified in shooting dead if he had found you housebreaking, and you had resisted him on his discovery, I took the liberty of destroying the document. I have always held that these sheets should not have been kept, for, as has been the case, if they fell under the scrutiny of so intelligent a person as Eugène Valmont, improper inferences might have been drawn. Mr. Summertrees, however, persisted in keeping them, but made this concession, that if I ever telegraphed him or telephoned him the word 'Encyclopedia,' he would at once burn these records, and he, on his part, was to telegraph or telephone to me 'The encyclopedia is out of print,' whereupon I would know that he had succeeded.

"Now, gentlemen, open this door, which will save me the trouble of forcing it. Either put me formally under arrest, or cease to restrict my liberty. I am very much obliged to Mr. Hale for telephoning, and I have made no protest to so gallant a host as Monsieur Valmont is, because of the locked door. However, the farce is now terminated. The proceedings I have sat through were entirely illegal, and if you will pardon me, Mr. Hale, they have been a little too French to go down here in old England, or to make a report in the newspapers that would be quite satisfactory to your chiefs. I demand either my formal arrest or the unlocking of that door."

In silence I pressed a button, and my man threw open the door. Macpherson walked to the threshold, paused, and looked back at Spenser Hale, who sat there silent as a sphinx.

"Good evening, Mr. Hale."

There being no reply, he turned to me with the same ingratiating smile:

"Good evening, Monsieur Eugène Valmont," he said. "I shall give myself the pleasure of calling next Wednesday at six for my five shillings."

The Problem of Cell 13

Jacques Futrelle

I

PRACTICALLY ALL those letters remaining in the alphabet after Augustus
S. F. X. Van Dusen was named were afterward acquired by that gentleman in the course of a brilliant scientific career, and, being honorably
acquired, were tacked on to the other end. His name, therefore, taken
with all that belonged to it, was a wonderfully imposing structure.
He was a Ph.D., an LL.D., an F.R.S., an M.D., and an M.D.S. He was
also some other things—just what he himself couldn't say—through
recognition of his ability by various foreign educational and scientific
institutions.

In appearance he was no less striking than in nomenclature. He
was slender with the droop of the student in his thin shoulders and
the pallor of a close, sedentary life on his clean-shaven face. His eyes
wore a perpetual, forbidding squint—of a man who studies little
things—and when they could be seen at all through his thick spectacles, were mere slits of watery blue. But above his eyes was his
most striking feature. This was a tall, broad brow, almost abnormal in
height and width, crowned by a heavy shock of bushy, yellow hair.
All these things conspired to give him a peculiar, almost grotesque,
personality.

Professor Van Dusen was remotely German. For generations his
ancestors had been noted in the sciences; he was the logical result, the
master mind. First and above all he was a logician. At least thirty-five
years of the half-century or so of his existence had been devoted
exclusively to proving that two and two always equal four, except in
unusual cases, where they equal three or five, as the case may be. He
stood broadly on the general proposition that all things that start must
go somewhere, and was able to bring the concentrated mental force

of his forefathers to bear on a given problem. Incidentally it may be remarked that Professor Van Dusen wore a No. 8 hat.

The world at large had heard vaguely of Professor Van Dusen as The Thinking Machine. It was a newspaper catch-phrase applied to him at the time of a remarkable exhibition at chess; he had demonstrated then that a stranger to the game might, by the force of inevitable logic, defeat a champion who had devoted a lifetime to its study. The Thinking Machine! Perhaps that more nearly described him than all his honorary initials, for he spent week after week, month after month, in the seclusion of his small laboratory from which had gone forth thoughts that staggered scientific associates and deeply stirred the world at large.

It was only occasionally that The Thinking Machine had visitors, and these were usually men who, themselves high in the sciences, dropped in to argue a point and perhaps convince themselves. Two of these men, Dr. Charles Ransome and Alfred Fielding, called one evening to discuss some theory which is not of consequence here.

"Such a thing is impossible," declared Dr. Ransome emphatically, in the course of the conversation.

"Nothing is impossible," declared The Thinking Machine with equal emphasis. He always spoke petulantly. "The mind is master of all things. When science fully recognizes that fact a great advance will have been made."

"How about the airship?" asked Dr. Ransome.

"That's not impossible at all," asserted The Thinking Machine. "It will be invented some time. I'd do it myself, but I'm busy."

Dr. Ransome laughed tolerantly.

"I've heard you say such things before," he said. "But they mean nothing. Mind may be master of matter, but it hasn't yet found a way to apply itself. There are some things that can't be *thought* out of existence, or rather which would not yield to any amount of thinking."

"What, for instance?" demanded The Thinking Machine.

Dr. Ransome was thoughtful for a moment as he smoked. "Well, say prison walls," he replied. "No man can *think* himself out of a cell. If he could, there would be no prisoners."

"A man can so apply his brain and ingenuity that he can leave a cell, which is the same thing," snapped The Thinking Machine.

Dr. Ransome was slightly amused.

"Let's suppose a case," he said, after a moment. "Take a cell where prisoners under sentence of death are confined—men who are des-

perate and, maddened by fear, would take any chance to escape—
suppose you were locked in such a cell. Could you escape?"

"Certainly," declared The Thinking Machine.

"Of course," said Mr. Fielding, who entered the conversation for
the first time, "you might wreck the cell with an explosive—but
inside, a prisoner, you couldn't have that."

"There would be nothing of that kind," said The Thinking Machine.
"You might treat me precisely as you treated prisoners under sentence
of death, and I would leave the cell."

"Not unless you entered it with tools prepared to get out," said Dr.
Ransome.

The Thinking Machine was visibly annoyed and his blue eyes
snapped.

"Lock me in any cell in any prison anywhere at any time, wearing only what is necessary, and I'll escape in a week," he declared,
sharply.

Dr. Ransome sat up straight in the chair, interested. Mr. Fielding
lighted a new cigar.

"You mean you could actually *think* yourself out?" asked Dr.
Ransome.

"I would get out," was the response.

"Are you serious?"

"Certainly I am serious."

Dr. Ransome and Mr. Fielding were silent for a long time.

"Would you be willing to try it?" asked Mr. Fielding, finally.

"Certainly," said Professor Van Dusen, and there was a trace of irony
in his voice. "I have done more asinine things than that to convince
other men of less important truths."

The tone was offensive and there was an undercurrent strongly
resembling anger on both sides. Of course it was an absurd thing,
but Professor Van Dusen reiterated his willingness to undertake the
escape and it was decided upon.

"To begin now," added Dr. Ransome.

"I'd prefer that it begin to-morrow," said The Thinking Machine,
"because—"

"No, now," said Mr. Fielding, flatly. "You are arrested, figuratively,
of course, without any warning locked in a cell with no chance to
communicate with friends, and left there with identically the same
care and attention that would be given to a man under sentence of
death. Are you willing?"

"All right, now, then," said The Thinking Machine, and he arose.

"Say, the death-cell in Chisholm Prison."

"The death-cell in Chisholm Prison."

"And what will you wear?"

"As little as possible," said The Thinking Machine. "Shoes, stockings, trousers and a shirt."

"You will permit yourself to be searched, of course?"

"I am to be treated precisely as all prisoners are treated," said The Thinking Machine. "No more attention and no less."

There were some preliminaries to be arranged in the matter of obtaining permission for the test, but all three were influential men and everything was done satisfactorily by telephone, albeit the prison commissioners, to whom the experiment was explained on purely scientific grounds, were sadly bewildered. Professor Van Dusen would be the most distinguished prisoner they had ever entertained.

When The Thinking Machine had donned those things which he was to wear during his incarceration he called the little old woman who was his housekeeper, cook and maid-servant all in one.

"Martha," he said, "it is now twenty-seven minutes past nine o'clock. I am going away. One week from to-night, at half-past nine, these gentlemen and one, possibly two, others will take supper with me here. Remember Dr. Ransome is very fond of artichokes."

The three men were driven to Chisholm Prison, where the warden was awaiting them, having been informed of the matter by telephone. He understood merely that the eminent Professor Van Dusen was to be his prisoner, if he could keep him, for one week; that he had committed no crime, but that he was to be treated as all other prisoners were treated.

"Search him," instructed Dr. Ransome.

The Thinking Machine was searched. Nothing was found on him; the pockets of the trousers were empty; the white, stiff-bosomed shirt had no pocket. The shoes and stockings were removed, examined, then replaced. As he watched all these preliminaries—the rigid search and noted the pitiful, childlike physical weakness of the man, the colorless face, and the thin, white hands—Dr. Ransome almost regretted his part in the affair.

"Are you sure you want to do this?" he asked.

"Would you be convinced if I did not?" inquired The Thinking Machine in turn.

"No."

"All right. I'll do it."

What sympathy Dr. Ransome had was dissipated by the tone. It nettled him, and he resolved to see the experiment to the end; it would be a stinging reproof to egotism.

"It will be impossible for him to communicate with any one outside?" he asked.

"Absolutely impossible," replied the warden. "He will not be permitted writing materials of any sort."

"And your jailers, would they deliver a message from him?"

"Not one word, directly or indirectly," said the warden. "You may rest assured of that. They will report anything he might say or turn over to me anything he might give them."

"That seems entirely satisfactory," said Mr. Fielding, who was frankly interested in the problem.

"Of course, in the event he fails," said Dr. Ransome, "and asks for his liberty, you understand you are to set him free?"

"I understand," replied the warden.

The Thinking Machine stood listening, but had nothing to say until this was all ended, then:

"I should like to make three small requests. You may grant them or not, as you wish."

"No special favors, now," warned Mr. Fielding.

"I am asking none," was the stiff response. "I would like to have some tooth powder—buy it yourself to see that it is tooth powder— and I should like to have one five-dollar and two ten-dollar bills."

Dr. Ransome, Mr. Fielding and the warden exchanged astonished glances. They were not surprised at the request for tooth powder, but were at the request for money.

"Is there any man with whom our friend would come in contact that he could bribe with twenty-five dollars?" asked Dr. Ransome of the warden.

"Not for twenty-five hundred dollars," was the positive reply.

"Well, let him have them," said Mr. Fielding. "I think they are harmless enough."

"And what is the third request?" asked Dr. Ransome.

"I should like to have my shoes polished."

Again the astonished glances were exchanged. This last request was the height of absurdity, so they agreed to it. These things all being attended to, The Thinking Machine was led back into the prison from which he had undertaken to escape.

"Here is Cell 13," said the warden, stopping three doors down the steel corridor. "This is where we keep condemned murderers. No one can leave it without my permission; and no one in it can communicate with the outside. I'll stake my reputation on that. It's only three doors back of my office and I can readily hear any unusual noise."

"Will this cell do, gentlemen?" asked The Thinking Machine. There was a touch of irony in his voice.

"Admirably," was the reply.

The heavy steel door was thrown open, there was a great scurrying and scampering of tiny feet, and The Thinking Machine passed into the gloom of the cell. Then the door was closed and double locked by the warden.

"What is that noise in there?" asked Dr. Ransome, through the bars.

"Rats—dozens of them," replied The Thinking Machine, tersely.

The three men, with final good nights, were turning away when The Thinking Machine called:

"What time is it exactly, warden?"

"Eleven seventeen," replied the warden.

"Thanks. I will join you gentlemen in your office at half-past eight o'clock one week from to-night," said The Thinking Machine.

"And if you do not?"

"There is no 'if' about it."

II

Chisholm Prison was a great, spreading structure of granite, four stories in all, which stood in the center of acres of open space. It was surrounded by a wall of solid masonry eighteen feet high, and so smoothly finished inside and out as to offer no foothold to a climber, no matter how expert. Atop of this fence, as a further precaution, was a five-foot fence of steel rods, each terminating in a keen point. This fence in itself marked an absolute deadline between freedom and imprisonment, for, even if a man escaped from his cell, it would seem impossible for him to pass the wall.

The yard, which on all sides of the prison building was twenty-five feet wide, that being the distance from the building to the wall, was by day an exercise ground for those prisoners to whom was granted the boon of occasional semi-liberty. But that was not for those in Cell 13.

At all times of the day there were armed guards in the yard, four of them, one patrolling each side of the prison building.

By night the yard was almost as brilliantly lighted as by day. On each of the four sides was a great arc light which rose above the prison wall and gave to the guards a clear sight. The lights, too, brightly illuminated the spiked top of the wall. The wires which fed the arc lights ran up the side of the prison building on insulators and from the top story led out to the poles supporting the arc lights.

All these things were seen and comprehended by The Thinking Machine, who was only enabled to see out his closely barred cell window by standing on his bed. This was on the morning following his incarceration. He gathered, too, that the river lay over there beyond the wall somewhere, because he heard faintly the pulsation of a motor boat and high up in the air saw a river bird. From that same direction came the shouts of boys at play and the occasional crack of a batted ball. He knew then that between the prison wall and the river was an open space, a playground.

Chisholm Prison was regarded as absolutely safe. No man had ever escaped from it. The Thinking Machine, from his perch on the bed, seeing what he saw, could readily understand why. The walls of the cell, though built he judged twenty years before, were perfectly solid, and the window bars of new iron had not a shadow of rust on them. The window itself, even with the bars out, would be a difficult mode of egress because it was small.

Yet, seeing these things, The Thinking Machine was not discouraged. Instead, he thoughtfully squinted at the great arc light—there was bright sunlight now—and traced with his eyes the wire which led from it to the building. That electric wire, he reasoned, must come down the side of the building not a great distance from his cell. That might be worth knowing.

Cell 13 was on the same floor with the offices of the prison—that is, not in the basement, not yet upstairs. There were only four steps up to the office floor, therefore the level of the floor must be only three or four feet above the ground. He couldn't see the ground directly beneath his window, but he could see it further out toward the wall. It would be an easy drop from the window. Well and good.

Then The Thinking Machine fell to remembering how he had come to the cell. First, there was the outside guard's booth, a part of the wall. There were two heavily barred gates there, both of steel. At this gate was one man always on guard. He admitted persons to the prison after much clanking of keys and locks, and let them out when ordered to do so. The warden's office was in the prison building, and in order to reach that official from the prison yard one had to pass a gate of solid steel with only a peep-hole in it. Then coming from that inner office to Cell 13, where he was now, one must pass a heavy wooden door and two steel doors into the corridors of the prison; and always there was the double-locked door to Cell 13 to reckon with.

There were then, The Thinking Machine recalled, seven doors to be overcome before one could pass from Cell 13 into the outer world, a free man. But against this was the fact that he was rarely interrupted. A jailer appeared at his cell door at six in the morning with a breakfast of prison fare; he would come again at noon, and again at six in the afternoon. At nine o'clock at night would come the inspection tour. That would be all.

"It's admirably arranged, this prison system," was the mental tribute paid by The Thinking Machine. "I'll have to study it a little when I get out. I had no idea there was such great care exercised in the prisons."

There was nothing, positively nothing, in his cell, except his iron bed, so firmly put together that no man could tear it to pieces save with sledges or a file. He had neither of these. There was not even a chair, or a small table, or a bit of tin or crockery. Nothing! The jailer stood by when he ate, then took away the wooden spoon and bowl which he had used.

One by one these things sank into the brain of The Thinking Machine. When the last possibility had been considered he began an examination of his cell. From the roof, down the walls on all sides, he examined the stones and the cement between them. He stamped over the floor carefully time after time, but it was cement, perfectly solid. After the examination he sat on the edge of the iron bed and was lost in thought for a long time. For Professor Augustus S. F. X. Van Dusen, The Thinking Machine, had something to think about.

He was disturbed by a rat, which ran across his foot, then scampered away into a dark corner of the cell, frightened at its own daring. After a while The Thinking Machine, squinting steadily into the darkness of the corner where the rat had gone, was able to make out in the gloom many little beady eyes staring at him. He counted six pair, and there were perhaps others; he didn't see very well.

Then The Thinking Machine, from his seat on the bed, noticed for the first time the bottom of his cell door. There was an opening there of two inches between the steel bar and the floor. Still looking steadily at this opening, The Thinking Machine backed suddenly into the corner where he had seen the beady eyes. There was a great scampering of tiny feet, several squeaks of frightened rodents, and then silence.

None of the rats had gone out the door, yet there were none in the cell. Therefore there must be another way out of the cell, however small. The Thinking Machine, on hands and knees, started a search for this spot, feeling in the darkness with his long, slender fingers.

At last his search was rewarded. He came upon a small opening in the floor, level with the cement. It was perfectly round and somewhat larger than a silver dollar. This was the way the rats had gone. He put his fingers deep into the opening; it seemed to be a disused drainage pipe and was dry and dusty.

Having satisfied himself on this point, he sat on the bed again for an hour, then made another inspection of his surroundings through the small cell window. One of the outside guards stood directly opposite, beside the wall, and happened to be looking at the window of Cell 13 when the head of The Thinking Machine appeared. But the scientist didn't notice the guard.

Noon came and the jailer appeared with the prison dinner of repulsively plain food. At home The Thinking Machine merely ate to live; here he took what was offered without comment. Occasionally he spoke to the jailer who stood outside the door watching him.

"Any improvements made here in the last few years?" he asked.

"Nothing particularly," replied the jailer. "New wall was built four years ago."

"Anything done to the prison proper?"

"Painted the woodwork outside, and I believe about seven years ago a new system of plumbing was put in."

"Ah!" said the prisoner. "How far is the river over there?"

"About three hundred feet. The boys have a baseball ground between the wall and the river."

The Thinking Machine had nothing further to say just then, but when the jailer was ready to go he asked for some water.

"I get very thirsty here," he explained. "Would it be possible for you to leave a little water in a bowl for me?"

"I'll ask the warden," replied the jailer, and he went away.

Half an hour later he returned with water in a small earthen bowl.

"The warden says you may keep this bowl," he informed the prisoner. "But you must show it to me when I ask for it. If it is broken, it will be the last."

"Thank you," said The Thinking Machine. "I shan't break it."

The jailer went on about his duties. For just the fraction of a second it seemed that The Thinking Machine wanted to ask a question, but he didn't.

Two hours later this same jailer, in passing the door of Cell No. 13, heard a noise inside and stopped. The Thinking Machine was down on his hands and knees in a corner of the cell, and from that same corner came several frightened squeaks. The jailer looked on interestedly.

"Ah, I've got you," he heard the prisoner say.

"Got what?" he asked, sharply.

"One of these rats," was the reply. "See?" And between the scientist's long fingers the jailer saw a small gray rat struggling. The prisoner brought it over to the light and looked at it closely. "It's a water rat," he said.

"Ain't you got anything better to do than to catch rats?" asked the jailer.

"It's disgraceful that they should be here at all," was the irritated reply. "Take this one away and kill it. There are dozens more where it came from."

The jailer took the wriggling, squirmy rodent and flung it down on the floor violently. It gave one squeak and lay still. Later he reported the incident to the warden, who only smiled.

Still later that afternoon the outside armed guard on Cell 13 side of the prison looked up again at the window and saw the prisoner looking out. He saw a hand raised to the barred window and then something white fluttered to the ground directly under the window of Cell 13. It was a little roll of linen, evidently of white shirting material, and tied around it was a five-dollar bill. The guard looked up at the window again, but the face had disappeared.

With a grim smile he took the little linen roll and the five-dollar bill to the warden's office. There together they deciphered something which was written on it with a queer sort of ink, frequently blurred. On the outside was this:

"Finder of this please deliver to Dr. Charles Ransome."

"Ah," said the warden, with a chuckle. "Plan of escape number one has gone wrong." Then, as an afterthought: "But why did he address it to Dr. Ransome?"

"And where did he get the pen and ink to write with?" asked the guard.

The warden looked at the guard and the guard looked at the warden. There was no apparent solution of that mystery. The warden studied the writing carefully, then shook his head.

"Well, let's see what he was going to say to Dr. Ransome," he said at length, still puzzled, and he unrolled the inner piece of linen.

"Well, if that—what—what do you think of that?" he asked, dazed.

The guard took the bit of linen and read this:

"*Epa cseot d'net niiy awe htto n'si sih. T.*"

III

The warden spent an hour wondering what sort of a cipher it was, and half an hour wondering why his prisoner should attempt to communicate with Dr. Ransome, who was the cause of him being there. After this the warden devoted some thought to the question of where the prisoner got writing materials, and what sort of writing materials he had. With the idea of illuminating this point, he examined the linen again. It was a torn part of a white shirt and had ragged edges.

Now it was possible to account for the linen, but what the prisoner had used to write with was another matter. The warden knew it would have been impossible for him to have either pen or pencil, and, besides, neither pen nor pencil had been used in this writing. What, then? The warden decided to personally investigate. The Thinking Machine was his prisoner: he had orders to hold his prisoners; if this one sought to escape by sending cipher messages to persons outside, he would stop it, as he would have stopped it in the case of any other prisoner.

The warden went back to Cell 13 and found The Thinking Machine on his hands and knees on the floor, engaged in nothing more alarming than catching rats. The prisoner heard the warden's step and turned to him quickly.

"It's disgraceful," he snapped, "these rats. There are scores of them."

"Other men have been able to stand them," said the warden. "Here is another shirt for you—let me have the one you have on."

"Why?" demanded The Thinking Machine, quickly. His tone was hardly natural, his manner suggested actual perturbation.

"You have attempted to communicate with Dr. Ransome," said the warden severely. "As my prisoner, it is my duty to put a stop to it."

The Thinking Machine was silent for a moment.

"All right," he said, finally. "Do your duty."

The warden smiled grimly. The prisoner arose from the floor and removed the white shirt, putting on instead a striped convict shirt the warden had brought. The warden took the white shirt eagerly, and then and there compared the pieces of linen on which was written the cipher with certain torn places in the shirt. The Thinking Machine looked on curiously.

"The guard brought *you* those, then?" he asked.

"He certainly did," replied the warden triumphantly. "And that ends your first attempt to escape."

The Thinking Machine watched the warden as he, by comparison, established to his own satisfaction that only two pieces of linen had been torn from the white shirt.

"What did you write this with?" demanded the warden. "I should think it a part of your duty to find out," said The Thinking Machine, irritably.

The warden started to say some harsh things, then restrained himself and made a minute search of the cell and of the prisoner instead. He found absolutely nothing; not even a match or toothpick which might have been used for a pen. The same mystery surrounded the fluid with which the cipher had been written. Although the warden left Cell 13 visibly annoyed, he took the torn shirt in triumph.

"Well, writing notes on a shirt won't get him out, that's certain," he told himself with some complacency. He put the linen scraps into his desk to await developments. "If that man escapes from that cell I'll—hang it—I'll resign."

On the third day of his incarceration The Thinking Machine openly attempted to bribe his way out. The jailer had brought his dinner and was leaning against the barred door, waiting, when The Thinking Machine began the conversation.

"The drainage pipes of the prison lead to the river, don't they?" he asked.

"Yes," said the jailer.

"I suppose they are very small?"

"Too small to crawl through, if that's what you're thinking about," was the grinning response.

There was silence until The Thinking Machine finished his meal. Then:

"You know I'm not a criminal, don't you?"

"Yes."

"And that I've a perfect right to be freed if I demand it?"

"Yes."

"Well, I came here believing that I could make my escape," said the prisoner, and his squint eyes studied the face of the jailer. "Would you consider a financial reward for aiding me to escape?"

The jailer, who happened to be an honest man, looked at the slender, weak figure of the prisoner, at the large head with its mass of yellow hair, and was almost sorry.

"I guess prisons like these were not built for the likes of you to get out of," he said, at last.

"But would you consider a proposition to help me get out?" the prisoner insisted, almost beseechingly.

"No," said the jailer, shortly.

"Five hundred dollars," urged The Thinking Machine. "I am not a criminal."

"No," said the jailer.

"A thousand?"

"No," again said the jailer, and he started away hurriedly to escape further temptation. Then he turned back. "If you should give me ten thousand dollars I couldn't get you out. You'd have to pass through seven doors, and I only have the keys to two."

Then he told the warden all about it.

"Plan number two fails," said the warden, smiling grimly. "First a cipher, then bribery."

When the jailer was on his way to Cell 13 at six o'clock, again bearing food to The Thinking Machine, he paused, startled by the unmistakable scrape, scrape of steel against steel. It stopped at the sound of his steps, then craftily the jailer, who was beyond the prisoner's range of vision, resumed his tramping, the sound being apparently that of a man going away from Cell 13. As a matter of fact he was in the same spot.

After a moment there came again the steady scrape, scrape, and the jailer crept cautiously on tiptoes to the door and peered between the bars. The Thinking Machine was standing on the iron bed working at the bars of the little window. He was using a file, judging from the backward and forward swing of his arms.

Cautiously the jailer crept back to the office, summoned the warden in person, and they returned to Cell 13 on tiptoes. The steady scrape was still audible. The warden listened to satisfy himself and then suddenly appeared at the door.

"Well?" he demanded, and there was a smile on his face.

The Thinking Machine glanced back from his perch on the bed and leaped suddenly to the floor, making frantic efforts to hide something. The warden went in, with hand extended.

"Give it up," he said.

"No," said the prisoner, sharply.

"Come, give it up," urged the warden. "I don't want to have to search you again."

"No," repeated the prisoner.

"What was it, a file?" asked the warden.

The Thinking Machine was silent and stood squinting at the warden with something very nearly approaching disappointment on his face—nearly, but not quite. The warden was almost sympathetic.

"Plan number three fails, eh?" he asked, good-naturedly. "Too bad, isn't it?"

The prisoner didn't say.

"Search him," instructed the warden.

The jailer searched the prisoner carefully. At last, artfully concealed in the waistband of the trousers, he found a piece of steel about two inches long, with one side curved like a half moon.

"Ah," said the warden, as he received it from the jailer. "From your shoe heel," and he smiled pleasantly.

The jailer continued his search and on the other side of the trousers waistband another piece of steel identical with the first. The edges showed where they had been worn against the bars of the window.

"You couldn't saw a way through those bars with these," said the warden.

"I could have," said The Thinking Machine firmly.

"In six months, perhaps," said the warden, good-naturedly.

The warden shook his head slowly as he gazed into the slightly flushed face of his prisoner.

"Ready to give it up?" he asked.

"I haven't started yet," was the prompt reply.

Then came another exhaustive search of the cell. Carefully the two men went over it, finally turning out the bed and searching that. Nothing. The warden in person climbed upon the bed and examined the bars of the window where the prisoner had been sawing. When he looked he was amused.

"Just made it a little bright by hard rubbing," he said to the prisoner, who stood looking on with a somewhat crestfallen air. The warden grasped the iron bars in his strong hands and tried to shake them. They were immovable, set firmly in the solid granite. He examined each in turn and found them all satisfactory. Finally he climbed down from the bed.

"Give it up, professor," he advised.

The Thinking Machine shook his head and the warden and jailer passed on again. As they disappeared down the corridor The Thinking Machine sat on the edge of the bed with his head in his hands.

"He's crazy to try to get out of that cell," commented the jailer.

"Of course he can't get out," said the warden. "But he's clever. I would like to know what he wrote that cipher with."

★   ★   ★

It was four o'clock next morning when an awful, heart-racking shriek of terror resounded through the great prison. It came from a cell, somewhere about the center, and its tone told a tale of horror, agony, terrible fear. The warden heard and with three of his men rushed into the long corridor leading to Cell 13.

IV

As they ran there came again that awful cry. It died away in a sort of wail. The white faces of prisoners appeared at cell doors upstairs and down, staring out wonderingly, frightened.

"It's that fool in Cell 13," grumbled the warden.

He stopped and stared in as one of the jailers flashed a lantern. "That fool in Cell 13" lay comfortably on his cot, flat on his back with his mouth open, snoring. Even as they looked there came again the piercing cry, from somewhere above. The warden's face blanched a little as he started up the stairs. There on the top floor he found a man in Cell 43, directly above Cell 13, but two floors higher, cowering in a corner of his cell.

"What's the matter?" demanded the warden.

"Thank God you've come," exclaimed the prisoner, and he cast himself against the bars of his cell.

"What is it?" demanded the warden again.

He threw open the door and went in. The prisoner dropped on his knees and clasped the warden about the body. His face was white with terror, his eyes were widely distended, and he was shuddering. His hands, icy cold, clutched at the warden's.

"Take me out of this cell, please take me out," he pleaded.

"What's the matter with you, anyhow?" insisted the warden, impatiently.

"I heard something—something," said the prisoner, and his eyes roved nervously around the cell.

"What did you hear?"

"I—I can't tell you," stammered the prisoner. Then, in a sudden burst of terror: "Take me out of this cell—put me anywhere—but take me out of here."

The warden and the three jailers exchanged glances.

"Who is this fellow? What's he accused of?" asked the warden.

"Joseph Ballard," said one of the jailers. "He's accused of throwing acid in a woman's face. She died from it."

"But they can't prove it," gasped the prisoner. "They can't prove it. Please put me in some other cell."

He was still clinging to the warden, and that official threw his arms off roughly. Then for a time he stood looking at the cowering wretch, who seemed possessed of all the wild, unreasoning terror of a child.

"Look here, Ballard," said the warden, finally, "if you heard anything, I want to know what it was. Now tell me."

"I can't, I can't," was the reply. He was sobbing.

"Where did it come from?"

"I don't know. Everywhere—nowhere. I just heard it."

"What was it—a voice?"

"Please don't make me answer," pleaded the prisoner.

"You must answer," said the warden, sharply.

"It was a voice—but—but it wasn't human," was the sobbing reply.

"Voice, but not human?" repeated the warden, puzzled.

"It sounded muffled and—and far away—and ghostly," explained the man.

"Did it come from inside or outside the prison?"

"It didn't seem to come from anywhere—it was just here, here, everywhere. I heard it. I heard it."

For an hour the warden tried to get the story, but Ballard had become suddenly obstinate and would say nothing—only pleaded to be placed in another cell, or to have one of the jailers remain near him until daylight. These requests were gruffly refused.

"And see here," said the warden, in conclusion, "if there's any more of this screaming I'll put you in the padded cell."

Then the warden went his way, a sadly puzzled man. Ballard sat at his cell door until daylight, his face, drawn and white with terror, pressed against the bars, and looked out into the prison with wide, staring eyes.

That day, the fourth since the incarceration of The Thinking Machine, was enlivened considerably by the volunteer prisoner, who spent most of his time at the little window of his cell. He began proceedings by throwing another piece of linen down to the guard, who picked it up dutifully and took it to the warden. On it was written:

"Only three days more."

The warden was in no way surprised at what he read; he understood that The Thinking Machine meant only three days more of his imprisonment, and he regarded the note as a boast. But how was the thing written? Where had The Thinking Machine found his new piece of linen? Where? How? He carefully examined the linen. It was white, of fine texture, shirting material. He took the shirt which he had taken and carefully fitted the two original pieces of the linen to the torn places. This third piece was entirely superfluous; it didn't fit anywhere, and yet it was unmistakably the same goods.

"And where—where does he get anything to write with?" demanded the warden of the world at large.

Still later on the fourth day The Thinking Machine, through the window of his cell, spoke to the armed guard outside.

"What day of the month is it?" he asked.

"The fifteenth," was the answer.

The Thinking Machine made a mental astronomical calculation and satisfied himself that the moon would not rise until after nine o'clock that night. Then he asked another question:

"Who attends to those arc lights?"

"Man from the company."

"You have no electricians in the building?"

"No."

"I should think you could save money if you had your own man."

"None of my business," replied the guard.

The guard noticed The Thinking Machine at the cell window frequently during that day, but always the face seemed listless and there was a certain wistfulness in the squint eyes behind the glasses. After a while he accepted the presence of the leonine head as a matter of course. He had seen other prisoners do the same thing; it was the longing for the outside world.

That afternoon, just before the day guard was relieved, the head appeared at the window again, and The Thinking Machine's hand held something out between the bars. It fluttered to the ground and the guard picked it up. It was a five-dollar bill.

"That's for you," called the prisoner.

As usual, the guard took it to the warden. That gentleman looked at it suspiciously; he looked at everything that came from Cell 13 with suspicion.

"He said it was for me," explained the guard.

"It's a sort of a tip, I suppose," said the warden. "I see no particular reason why you shouldn't accept—"

Suddenly he stopped. He had remembered that The Thinking Machine had gone into Cell 13 with one five-dollar bill and two ten-dollar bills; twenty-five dollars in all. Now a five-dollar bill had been tied around the first pieces of linen that came from the cell. The warden still had it, and to convince himself he took it out and looked at it. It was five dollars; yet here was another five dollars, and The Thinking Machine had only had ten-dollar bills.

"Perhaps somebody changed one of the bills for him," he thought at last, with a sigh of relief.

But then and there he made up his mind. He would search Cell 13 as a cell was never before searched in this world. When a man could write at will, and change money, and do other wholly inexplicable things, there was something radically wrong with his prison. He planned to enter the cell at night—three o'clock would be an excellent time. The Thinking Machine must do all the weird things he did some time. Night seemed the most reasonable.

Thus it happened that the warden stealthily descended upon Cell 13 that night at three o'clock. He paused at the door and listened. There was no sound save the steady, regular breathing of the prisoner. The keys unfastened the double locks with scarcely a clank, and the warden entered, locking the door behind him. Suddenly he flashed his dark-lantern in the face of the recumbent figure.

If the warden had planned to startle The Thinking Machine he was mistaken, for that individual merely opened his eyes quietly, reached for his glasses and inquired, in a most matter-of-fact tone:

"Who is it?"

It would be useless to describe the search that the warden made. It was minute. Not one inch of the cell or the bed was overlooked. He found the round hole in the floor, and with a flash of inspiration thrust his thick fingers into it. After a moment of fumbling there he drew up something and looked at it in the light of his lantern.

"Ugh!" he exclaimed.

The thing he had taken out was a rat—a dead rat. His inspiration fled as a mist before the sun. But he continued the search.

The Thinking Machine, without a word, arose and kicked the rat out of the cell into the corridor.

The warden climbed on the bed and tried the steel bars in the tiny window. They were perfectly rigid; every bar of the door was the same.

Then the warden searched the prisoner's clothing, beginning at the shoes. Nothing hidden in them! Then the trousers waistband. Still nothing! Then the pockets of the trousers. From one side he drew out some paper money and examined it.

"Five one-dollar bills," he gasped.

"That's right," said the prisoner.

"But the—you had two tens and a five—what the —how do you do it?"

"That's my business," said The Thinking Machine.

"Did any of my men change this money for you—on your word of honor?"

The Thinking Machine paused just a fraction of a second.

"No," he said.

"Well, do you make it?" asked the warden. He was prepared to believe anything.

"That's my business," again said the prisoner.

The warden glared at the eminent scientist fiercely. He felt—he knew—that this man was making a fool of him, yet he didn't know how. If he were a real prisoner he would get the truth—but, then, perhaps, those inexplicable things which had happened would not have been brought before him so sharply. Neither of the men spoke for a long time, then suddenly the warden turned fiercely and left the cell, slamming the door behind him. He didn't dare to speak, then.

He glanced at the clock. It was ten minutes to four. He had hardly settled himself in bed when again came that heart-breaking shriek through the prison. With a few muttered words, which, while not elegant, were highly expressive, he relighted his lantern and rushed through the prison again to the cell on the upper floor.

Again Ballard was crushing himself against the steel door, shrieking, shrieking at the top of his voice. He stopped only when the warden flashed his lamp in the cell.

"Take me out, take me out," he screamed. "I did it, I did it, I killed her. Take it away."

"Take what away?" asked the warden.

"I threw the acid in her face—I did it—I confess. Take me out of here."

Ballard's condition was pitiable; it was only an act of mercy to let him out into the corridor. There he crouched in a corner, like an animal at bay, and clasped his hands to his ears. It took half an hour to calm him sufficiently for him to speak. Then he told incoherently what had happened. On the night before at four o'clock he had heard a voice—a sepulchral voice, muffled and wailing in tone.

"What did it say?" asked the warden, curiously.

"Acid—acid—acid!" gasped the prisoner. "It accused me. Acid! I threw the acid, and the woman died. Oh!" It was a long, shuddering wail of terror.

"Acid?" echoed the warden, puzzled. The case was beyond him.

"Acid. That's all I heard—that one word, repeated several times. There were other things, too, but I didn't hear them."

"That was last night, eh?" asked the warden. "What happened to-night—what frightened you just now?"

"It was the same thing," gasped the prisoner. "Acid—acid—acid." He covered his face with his hands and sat shivering. "It was acid I used on her, but I didn't mean to kill her. I just heard the words. It was something accusing me—accusing me." He mumbled, and was silent.

"Did you hear anything else?"

"Yes—but I couldn't understand—only a little bit—just a word or two."

"Well, what was it?"

"I heard 'acid' three times, then I heard a long, moaning sound, then—then—I heard 'No. 8 hat.' I heard that voice."

"No. 8 hat," repeated the warden. "What the devil—No. 8 hat? Accusing voices of conscience have never talked about No. 8 hats, so far as I ever heard."

"He's insane," said one of the jailers, with an air of finality.

"I believe you," said the warden. "He must be. He probably heard something and got frightened. He's trembling now. No. 8 hat! What the—"

V

When the fifth day of The Thinking Machine's imprisonment rolled around the warden was wearing a hunted look. He was anxious for the end of the thing. He could not help but feel that his distinguished prisoner had been amusing himself. And if this were so, The Thinking Machine had lost none of his sense of humor. For on this fifth day he flung down another linen note to the outside guard, bearing the words: "Only two days more." Also he flung down half a dollar.

Now the warden knew—he *knew*—that the man in Cell 13 didn't have any half dollars—he *couldn't* have any half dollars, no more than he could have pen and ink and linen, and yet he did have them. It was a condition, not a theory; that is one reason why the warden was wearing a hunted look.

That ghastly, uncanny thing, too, about "Acid" and "No. 8 hat" clung to him tenaciously. They didn't mean anything, of course, merely the ravings of an insane murderer who had been driven by fear to confess his crime, still there were so many things that "didn't mean anything" happening in the prison now since The Thinking Machine was there.

On the sixth day the warden received a postal stating that Dr. Ransome and Mr. Fielding would be at Chisholm Prison on the following evening, Thursday, and in the event Professor Van Dusen had not yet escaped—and they presumed he had not because they had not heard from him—they would meet him there.

"In the event he had not yet escaped!" The warden smiled grimly. Escaped!

The Thinking Machine enlivened this day for the warden with three notes. They were on the usual linen and bore generally on the appointment at half-past eight o'clock Thursday night, which appointment the scientist had made at the time of his imprisonment.

On the afternoon of the seventh day the warden passed Cell 13 and glanced in. The Thinking Machine was lying on the iron bed, apparently sleeping lightly. The cell appeared precisely as it always did from a casual glance. The warden would swear that no man was going to leave it between that hour—it was then four o'clock—and half-past eight o'clock that evening.

On his way back past the cell the warden heard the steady breathing again, and coming close to the door looked in. He wouldn't have done so if The Thinking Machine had been looking, but now—well, it was different.

A ray of light came through the high window and fell on the face of the sleeping man. It occurred to the warden for the first time that his prisoner appeared haggard and weary. Just then The Thinking Machine stirred slightly and the warden hurried on up the corridor guiltily. That evening after six o'clock he saw the jailer.

"Everything all right in Cell 13?" he asked.

"Yes, sir," replied the jailer. "He didn't eat much, though."

It was with a feeling of having done his duty that the warden received Dr. Ransome and Mr. Fielding shortly after seven o'clock. He intended to show them the linen notes and lay before them the full story of his woes, which was a long one. But before this came to pass the guard from the river side of the prison yard entered the office.

"The arc light in my side of the yard won't light," he informed the warden.

"Confound it, that man's a hoodoo," thundered the official. "Everything has happened since he's been here."

The guard went back to his post in the darkness, and the warden 'phoned to the electric light company.

"This is Chisholm Prison," he said through the 'phone. "Send three or four men down here quick, to fix an arc light."

The reply was evidently satisfactory, for the warden hung up the receiver and passed out into the yard. While Dr. Ransome and Mr. Fielding sat waiting, the guard at the outer gate came in with a special delivery letter. Dr. Ransome happened to notice the address, and, when the guard went out, looked at the letter more closely.

"By George!" he exclaimed.

"What is it?" asked Mr. Fielding.

Silently the doctor offered the letter. Mr. Fielding examined it closely.

"Coincidence," he said. "It must be."

It was nearly eight o'clock when the warden returned to his office. The electricians had arrived in a wagon, and were now at work. The warden pressed the buzz-button communicating with the man at the outer gate in the wall.

"How many electricians came in?" he asked, over the short 'phone. "Four? Three workmen in jumpers and overalls and the manager? Frock coat and silk hat? All right. Be certain that only four go out. That's all."

He turned to Dr. Ransome and Mr. Fielding. "We have to be careful here—particularly," and there was broad sarcasm in his tone, "since we have scientists locked up."

The warden picked up the special delivery letter carelessly, and then began to open it.

"When I read this I want to tell you gentlemen something about how— Great Caesar!" he ended, suddenly, as he glanced at the letter. He sat with mouth open, motionless, from astonishment.

"What is it?" asked Mr. Fielding.

"A special delivery letter from Cell 13," gasped the warden. "An invitation to supper."

"What?" and the two others arose, unanimously.

The warden sat dazed, staring at the letter for a moment, then called sharply to a guard outside in the corridor.

"Run down to Cell 13 and see if that man's in there."

The guard went as directed, while Dr. Ransome and Mr. Fielding examined the letter.

"It's Van Dusen's handwriting; there's no question of that," said Dr. Ransome. "I've seen too much of it."

Just then the buzz on the telephone from the outer gate sounded, and the warden, in a semi-trance, picked up the receiver.

"Hello! Two reporters, eh? Let 'em come in." He turned suddenly to the doctor and Mr. Fielding. "Why, the man *can't* be out. He must be in his cell."

Just at that moment the guard returned.

"He's still in his cell, sir," he reported. "I saw him. He's lying down."

"There, I told you so," said the warden, and he breathed freely again. "But how did he mail that letter?"

There was a rap on the steel door which led from the jail yard into the warden's office.

"It's the reporters," said the warden. "Let them in," he instructed the guard; then to the two other gentlemen: "Don't say anything about this before them, because I'd never hear the last of it."

The door opened, and the two men from the front gate entered.

"Good-evening, gentlemen," said one. That was Hutchinson Hatch; the warden knew him well.

"Well?" demanded the other, irritably. "I'm here."

That was The Thinking Machine.

He squinted belligerently at the warden, who sat with mouth agape. For the moment that official had nothing to say. Dr. Ransome and Mr. Fielding were amazed, but they didn't know what the warden knew. They were only amazed; he was paralyzed. Hutchinson Hatch, the reporter, took in the scene with greedy eyes.

"How—how—how did you do it?" gasped the warden, finally.

"Come back to the cell," said The Thinking Machine, in the irritated voice which his scientific associates knew so well.

The warden, still in a condition bordering on trance, led the way.

"Flash your light in there," directed The Thinking Machine.

The warden did so. There was nothing unusual in the appearance of the cell, and there—there on the bed lay the figure of The Thinking Machine. Certainly! There was the yellow hair! Again the warden looked at the man beside him and wondered at the strangeness of his own dreams.

With trembling hands he unlocked the cell door and The Thinking Machine passed inside.

"See here," he said.

He kicked at the steel bars in the bottom of the cell door and three of them were pushed out of place. A fourth broke off and rolled away in the corridor.

"And here, too," directed the erstwhile prisoner as he stood on the bed to reach the small window. He swept his hand across the opening and every bar came out.

"What's this in the bed?" demanded the warden, who was slowly recovering.

"A wig," was the reply. "Turn down the cover."

The warden did so. Beneath it lay a large coil of strong rope, thirty feet or more, a dagger, three files, ten feet of electric wire, a thin, powerful pair of steel pliers, a small tack hammer with its handle, and—and a Derringer pistol.

"How did you do it?" demanded the warden.

"You gentlemen have an engagement to supper with me at half-past nine o'clock," said The Thinking Machine. "Come on, or we shall be late."

"But how did you do it?" insisted the warden.

"Don't ever think you can hold any man who can use his brain," said The Thinking Machine. "Come on; we shall be late."

VI

It was an impatient supper party in the rooms of Professor Van Dusen and a somewhat silent one. The guests were Dr. Ransome, Albert Fielding, the warden, and Hutchinson Hatch, reporter. The meal was served to the minute, in accordance with Professor Van Dusen's instructions of one week before; Dr. Ransome found the artichokes delicious. At last the supper was finished and The Thinking Machine turned full on Dr. Ransome and squinted at him fiercely.

"Do you believe it now?" he demanded.

"I do," replied Dr. Ransome.

"Do you admit that it was a fair test?"

"I do."

With the others, particularly the warden, he was waiting anxiously for the explanation.

"Suppose you tell us how—" began Mr. Fielding.

"Yes, tell us how," said the warden.

The Thinking Machine readjusted his glasses, took a couple of preparatory squints at his audience, and began the story. He told it from the beginning logically; and no man ever talked to more interested listeners.

"My agreement was," he began, "to go into a cell, carrying nothing except what was necessary to wear, and to leave that cell within a week. I had never seen Chisholm Prison. When I went into the cell I asked for tooth powder, two ten- and one five-dollar bills, and also to have my shoes blacked. Even if these requests had been refused it would not have mattered seriously. But you agreed to them.

"I knew there would be nothing in the cell which you thought I might use to advantage. So when the warden locked the door on me I was apparently helpless, unless I could turn three seemingly innocent things to use. They were things which would have been permitted any prisoner under sentence of death, were they not, warden?"

"Tooth powder and polished shoes, yes, but not money," replied the warden.

"Anything is dangerous in the hands of a man who knows how to use it," went on The Thinking Machine. "I did nothing that first night but sleep and chase rats." He glared at the warden. "When the matter was broached I knew I could do nothing that night, so suggested next day. You gentlemen thought I wanted time to arrange an escape with outside assistance, but this was not true. I knew I could communicate with whom I pleased, when I pleased."

The warden stared at him a moment, then went on smoking solemnly.

"I was aroused next morning at six o'clock by the jailer with my breakfast," continued the scientist. "He told me dinner was at twelve and supper at six. Between these times, I gathered, I would be pretty much to myself. So immediately after breakfast I examined my outside surroundings from my cell window. One look told me it would be useless to try to scale the wall, even should I decide to leave my cell by the window, for my purpose was to leave not only the cell, but the prison. Of course, I could have gone over the wall, but it would have taken me longer to lay my plans that way. Therefore, for the moment, I dismissed all idea of that.

"From this first observation I knew the river was on that side of the prison, and that there was also a playground there. Subsequently these surmises were verified by a keeper. I knew then one important thing—that any one might approach the prison wall from that side if necessary without attracting any particular attention. That was well to remember. I remembered it.

"But the outside thing which most attracted my attention was the feed wire to the arc light which ran within a few feet—probably three or four—of my cell window. I knew that would be valuable in the event I found it necessary to cut off that arc light."

"Oh, you shut it off to-night, then?" asked the warden.

"Having learned all I could from that window," resumed The Thinking Machine, without heeding the interruption, "I considered the idea of escaping through the prison proper. I recalled just how I had come into the cell, which I knew would be the only way. Seven doors lay between me and the outside. So, also for the time being, I gave up the idea of escaping that way. And I couldn't go through the solid granite walls of the cells."

The Thinking Machine paused for a moment and Dr. Ransome lighted a new cigar. For several minutes there was silence, then the scientific jail-breaker went on:

"While I was thinking about these things a rat ran across my foot. It suggested a new line of thought. There were at least half a dozen rats in the cell—I could see their beady eyes. Yet I had noticed none come under the cell door. I frightened them purposely and watched the cell door to see if they went out that way. They did not, but they were gone. Obviously they went another way. Another way meant another opening.

"I searched for this opening and found it. It was an old drain pipe, long unused and partly choked with dirt and dust. But this was the way the rats had come. They came from somewhere. Where? Drain pipes usually lead outside prison grounds. This one probably led to the river, or near it. The rats must therefore come from that direction. If they came a part of the way, I reasoned that they came all the way, because it was extremely unlikely that a solid iron or lead pipe would have any hole in it except at the exit.

"When the jailer came with my luncheon he told me two important things, although he didn't know it. One was that a new system of plumbing had been put in the prison seven years before; another that the river was only three hundred feet away. Then I knew positively that the pipe was a part of an old system; I knew, too, that it slanted generally toward the river. But did the pipe end in the water or on land?

"This was the next question to be decided. I decided it by catching several of the rats in the cell. My jailer was surprised to see me engaged in this work. I examined at least a dozen of them. They were perfectly dry; they had come through the pipe, and, most important of all, they were *not house rats, but field rats.* The other end of the pipe was on land, then, outside the prison walls. So far, so good.

"Then, I knew that if I worked freely from this point I must attract the warden's attention in another direction. You see, by telling the warden that I had come there to escape you made the test more severe, because I had to trick him by false scents."

The warden looked up with a sad expression in his eyes.

"The first thing was to make him think I was trying to communicate with you, Dr. Ransome. So I wrote a note on a piece of linen I tore from my shirt, addressed it to Dr. Ransome, tied a five-dollar bill around it and threw it out the window. I knew the guard would take it to the warden, but I rather hoped the warden would send it as addressed. Have you that first linen note, warden?"

The warden produced the cipher.

"What the deuce does it mean, anyhow?" he asked.

"Read it backward, beginning with the 'T' signature and disregard the division into words," instructed The Thinking Machine.

The warden did so.

"T-h-i-s, this," he spelled, studied it a moment, then read it off, grinning:

"This is not the way I intend to escape."

"Well, now what do you think o' that?" he demanded, still grinning.

"I knew that would attract your attention, just as it did," said The Thinking Machine, "and if you really found out what it was it would be a sort of gentle rebuke."

"What did you write it with?" asked Dr. Ransome, after he had examined the linen and passed it to Mr. Fielding.

"This," said the erstwhile prisoner, and he extended his foot. On it was the shoe he had worn in prison, though the polish was gone— scraped off clean. "The shoe blacking, moistened with water, was my ink; the metal tip of the shoe lace made a fairly good pen."

The warden looked up and suddenly burst into a laugh, half of relief, half of amusement.

"You're a wonder," he said, admiringly. "Go on."

"That precipitated a search of my cell by the warden, as I had intended," continued The Thinking Machine. "I was anxious to get the warden into the habit of searching my cell, so that finally, constantly finding nothing, he would get disgusted and quit. This at last happened, practically."

The warden blushed.

"He then took my white shirt away and gave me a prison shirt. He was satisfied that those two pieces of the shirt were all that was missing. But while he was searching my cell I had another piece of that same shirt, about nine inches square, rolled into a small ball in my mouth."

"Nine inches of that shirt?" demanded the warden. "Where did it come from?"

"The bosoms of all stiff white shirts are of triple thickness," was the explanation. "I tore out the inside thickness, leaving the bosom only two thicknesses. I knew you wouldn't see it. So much for that."

There was a little pause, and the warden looked from one to another of the men with a sheepish grin.

"Having disposed of the warden for the time being by giving him something else to think about, I took my first serious step toward freedom," said Professor Van Dusen. "I knew, within reason, that the pipe led somewhere to the playground outside; I knew a great many boys played there; I knew that rats came into my cell from out there. Could I communicate with some one outside with these things at hand?

"First was necessary, I saw, a long and fairly reliable thread, so—but here," he pulled up his trousers legs and showed that the tops of both stockings, of fine, strong lisle, were gone. "I unraveled those—after I got them started it wasn't difficult—and I had easily a quarter of a mile of thread that I could depend on.

"Then on half of my remaining linen I wrote, laboriously enough, I assure you, a letter explaining my situation to this gentleman here," and he indicated Hutchinson Hatch. "I knew he would assist me—for the value of the newspaper story. I tied firmly to this linen letter a ten-dollar bill—there is no surer way of attracting the eye of any one—and wrote on the linen: 'Finder of this deliver to Hutchinson Hatch, *Daily American*, who will give another ten dollars for the information.'

"The next thing was to get this note outside on that playground where a boy might find it. There were two ways, but I chose the best. I took one of the rats—I became adept in catching them—tied the linen and money firmly to one leg, fastened my lisle thread to another, and turned him loose in the drain pipe. I reasoned that the natural fright of the rodent would make him run until he was outside the pipe and then out on earth he would probably stop to gnaw off the linen and money.

"From the moment the rat disappeared into that dusty pipe I became anxious. I was taking so many chances. The rat might gnaw the string, of which I held one end; other rats might gnaw it; the rat might run out of the pipe and leave the linen and money where they would never be found; a thousand other things might have happened. So began some nervous hours, but the fact that the rat ran on until only a few feet of the string remained in my cell made me think he was outside the pipe. I had carefully instructed Mr. Hatch what to do in case the note reached him. The question was: Would it reach him?

"This done, I could only wait and make other plans in case this one failed. I openly attempted to bribe my jailer, and learned from him that he held the keys to only two of seven doors between me and freedom. Then I did something else to make the warden nervous. I took the steel supports out of the heels of my shoes and made a pretense of sawing the bars of my cell window. The warden raised a pretty row about that. He developed, too, the habit of shaking the bars of my cell window to see if they were solid. They were—then."

Again the warden grinned. He had ceased being astonished.

"With this one plan I had done all I could and could only wait to see what happened," the scientist went on. "I couldn't know whether my note had been delivered or even found, or whether the rat had gnawed it up. And I didn't dare to draw back through the pipe that one slender thread which connected me with the outside.

"When I went to bed that night I didn't sleep, for fear there would come the slight signal twitch at the thread which was to tell me that Mr. Hatch had received the note. At half-past three o'clock, I judge, I felt this twitch, and no prisoner actually under sentence of death ever welcomed a thing more heartily."

The Thinking Machine stopped and turned to the reporter.

"You'd better explain just what you did," he said.

"The linen note was brought to me by a small boy who had been playing baseball," said Mr. Hatch. "I immediately saw a big story in it, so I gave the boy another ten dollars, and got several spools of silk, some twine, and a roll of light, pliable wire. The professor's note suggested that I have the finder of the note show me just where it was picked up, and told me to make my search from there, beginning at two o'clock in the morning. If I found the other end of the thread I was to twitch it gently three times, then a fourth.

"I began to search with a small bulb electric light. It was an hour and twenty minutes before I found the end of the drain pipe, half hidden in weeds. The pipe was very large there, say twelve inches across. Then I found the end of the lisle thread, twitched it as directed and immediately I got an answering twitch.

"Then I fastened the silk to this and Professor Van Dusen began to pull it into his cell. I nearly had heart disease for fear the string would break. To the end of the silk I fastened the twine, and when that had been pulled in I tied on the wire. Then that was drawn into the pipe and we had a substantial line, which the rats couldn't gnaw, from the mouth of the drain into the cell."

The Thinking Machine raised his hand and Hatch stopped.

"All this was done in absolute silence," said the scientist. "But when the wire reached my hand I could have shouted. Then we tried another experiment, which Mr. Hatch was prepared for. I tested the pipe as a speaking tube. Neither of us could hear very clearly, but I dared not speak loud for fear of attracting attention in the prison. At last I made him understand what I wanted immediately. He seemed to have great difficulty in understanding when I asked for nitric acid, and I repeated the word 'acid' several times.

"Then I heard a shriek from a cell above me. I knew instantly that some one had overheard, and when I heard you coming, Mr. Warden, I feigned sleep. If you had entered my cell at that moment that whole plan of escape would have ended there. But you passed on. That was the nearest I ever came to being caught.

"Having established this improvised trolley it is easy to see how I got things in the cell and made them disappear at will. I merely dropped them back into the pipe. You, Mr. Warden, could not have reached the connecting wire with your fingers; they are too large. My fingers, you see, are longer and more slender. In addition I guarded the top of that pipe with a rat—you remember how."

"I remember," said the warden, with a grimace.

"I thought that if any one were tempted to investigate that hole the rat would dampen his ardor. Mr. Hatch could not send me anything useful through the pipe until next night, although he did send me change for ten dollars as a test, so I proceeded with other parts of my plan. Then I evolved the method of escape, which I finally employed.

"In order to carry this out successfully it was necessary for the guard in the yard to get accustomed to seeing me at the cell window.

I arranged this by dropping linen notes to him, boastful in tone, to make the warden believe, if possible, one of his assistants was communicating with the outside for me. I would stand at my window for hours gazing out, so the guard could see, and occasionally I spoke to him. In that way I learned that the prison had no electricians of its own, but was dependent upon the lighting company if anything should go wrong.

"That cleared the way to freedom perfectly. Early in the evening of the last day of my imprisonment, when it was dark, I planned to cut the feed wire which was only a few feet from my window, reaching it with an acid-tipped wire I had. That would make that side of the prison perfectly dark while the electricians were searching for the break. That would also bring Mr. Hatch into the prison yard.

"There was only one more thing to do before I actually began the work of setting myself free. This was to arrange final details with Mr. Hatch through our speaking tube. I did this within half an hour after the warden left my cell on the fourth night of my imprisonment. Mr. Hatch again had serious difficulty in understanding me, and I repeated the word 'acid' to him several times, and later the words: 'Number eight hat'—that's my size—and these were the things which made a prisoner upstairs confess to murder, so one of the jailers told me next day. This prisoner heard our voices, confused of course, through the pipe, which also went to his cell. The cell directly over me was not occupied, hence no one else heard.

"Of course the actual work of cutting the steel bars out of the window and door was comparatively easy with nitric acid, which I got through the pipe in thin bottles, but it took time. Hour after hour on the fifth and sixth and seventh days the guard below was looking at me as I worked on the bars of the window with the acid on a piece of wire. I used the tooth powder to prevent the acid spreading. I looked away abstractedly as I worked and each minute the acid cut deeper into the metal. I noticed that the jailers always tried the door by shaking the upper part, never the lower bars, therefore I cut the lower bars, leaving them hanging in place by thin strips of metal. But that was a bit of dare-deviltry. I could not have gone that way so easily."

The Thinking Machine sat silent for several minutes.

"I think that makes everything clear," he went on. "Whatever points I have not explained were merely to confuse the warden and jailers. These things in my bed I brought in to please Mr. Hatch, who wanted to improve the story. Of course, the wig was necessary in my plan. The special delivery letter I wrote and directed in my cell with Mr. Hatch's fountain pen, then sent it out to him and he mailed it. That's all, I think."

"But your actually leaving the prison grounds and then coming in through the outer gate to my office?" asked the warden.

"Perfectly simple," said the scientist. "I cut the electric light wire with acid, as I said, when the current was off. Therefore when the current was turned on the arc didn't light. I knew it would take some time to find out what was the matter and make repairs. When the guard went to report to you the yard was dark. I crept out the window—it was a tight fit, too—replaced the bars by standing on a narrow ledge and remained in a shadow until the force of electricians arrived. Mr. Hatch was one of them.

"When I saw him I spoke and he handed me a cap, a jumper and overalls, which I put on within ten feet of you, Mr. Warden, while you were in the yard. Later Mr. Hatch called me, presumably as a workman, and together we went out the gate to get something out of the wagon. The gate guard let us pass out readily as two workmen who had just passed in. We changed our clothing and reappeared, asking to see you. We saw you. That's all."

There was silence for several minutes. Dr. Ransome was first to speak.

"Wonderful!" he exclaimed. "Perfectly amazing."

"How did Mr. Hatch happen to come with the electricians?" asked Mr. Fielding.

"His father is manager of the company," replied The Thinking Machine.

"But what if there had been no Mr. Hatch outside to help?"

"Every prisoner has one friend outside who would help him escape if he could."

"Suppose—just suppose—there had been no old plumbing system there?" asked the warden, curiously.

"There were two other ways out," said The Thinking Machine, enigmatically.

Ten minutes later the telephone bell rang. It was a request for the warden.

"Light all right, eh?" the warden asked, through the 'phone. "Good. Wire cut beside Cell 13? Yes, I know. One electrician too many? What's that? Two came out?"

The warden turned to the others with a puzzled expression.

"He only let in four electricians, he had let out two and says there are three left."

"I was the odd one," said The Thinking Machine.

"Oh," said the warden. "I see." Then through the 'phone: "Let the fifth man go. He's all right."

The Invisible Man

G. K. Chesterton

IN THE cool blue twilight of two steep streets in Camden Town, the shop at the corner, a confectioner's, glowed like the butt of a cigar. One should rather say, perhaps, like the butt of a firework, for the light was of many colors and some complexity, broken up by many mirrors and dancing on many gilt and gaily-colored cakes and sweetmeats. Against this one fiery glass were glued the noses of many gutter-snipes, for the chocolates were all wrapped in those red and gold and green metallic colors which are almost better than chocolate itself; and the huge white wedding-cake in the window was somehow at once remote and satisfying, just as if the whole North Pole were good to eat. Such rainbow provocations could naturally collect the youth of the neighborhood up to the ages of ten or twelve. But this corner was also attractive to youth at a later stage; and a young man, not less than twenty-four, was staring into the same shop window. To him, also, the shop was of fiery charm, but this attraction was not wholly to be explained by chocolates; which, however, he was far from despising.

He was a tall, burly, red-haired young man, with a resolute face but a listless manner. He carried under his arm a flat, grey portfolio of black-and-white sketches, which he had sold with more or less success to publishers ever since his uncle (who was an admiral) had disinherited him for Socialism, because of a lecture which he had delivered against that economic theory. His name was John Turnbull Angus.

Entering at last, he walked through the confectioner's shop into the back room, which was a sort of pastry-cook restaurant, merely raising his hat to the young lady who was serving there. She was a dark, elegant, alert girl in black, with a high color and very quick, dark eyes; and after the ordinary interval she followed him into the inner room to take his order.

His order was evidently a usual one. "I want, please," he said with precision, "one halfpenny bun and a small cup of black coffee." An instant before the girl could turn away he added, "Also, I want you to marry me."

The young lady of the shop stiffened suddenly, and said, "Those are jokes I don't allow."

The red-haired young man lifted grey eyes of an unexpected gravity.

"Really and truly," he said, "it's as serious—as serious as the halfpenny bun. It is expensive, like the bun; one pays for it. It is indigestible, like the bun. It hurts."

The dark young lady had never taken her dark eyes off him, but seemed to be studying him with almost tragic exactitude. At the end of her scrutiny she had something like the shadow of a smile, and she sat down in a chair.

"Don't you think," observed Angus, absently, "that it's rather cruel to eat these halfpenny buns? They might grow up into penny buns. I shall give up these brutal sports when we are married."

The dark young lady rose from her chair and walked to the window, evidently in a state of strong but not unsympathetic cogitation. When at last she swung round again with an air of resolution she was bewildered to observe that the young man was carefully laying out on the table various objects from the shop window. They included a pyramid of highly colored sweets, several plates of sandwiches, and the two decanters containing that mysterious port and sherry which are peculiar to pastry-cooks. In the middle of this neat arrangement he had carefully let down the enormous load of white sugared cake which had been the huge ornament of the window.

"What on earth are you doing?" she asked.

"Duty, my dear Laura," he began.

"Oh, for the Lord's sake, stop a minute," she cried, "and don't talk to me in that way. I mean, what is all that?"

"A ceremonial meal, Miss Hope."

"And what is *that?*" she asked impatiently, pointing to the mountain of sugar.

"The wedding-cake, Mrs. Angus," he said.

The girl marched to that article, removed it with some clatter, and put it back in the shop window; she then returned, and, putting her elegant elbows on the table, regarded the young man not unfavorably but with considerable exasperation.

"You don't give me any time to think," she said.

"I'm not such a fool," he answered; "that's my Christian humility."

She was still looking at him; but she had grown considerably graver behind the smile.

"My Angus," she said steadily, "before there is a minute more of this nonsense I must tell you something about myself as shortly as I can."

"Delighted," replied Angus gravely. "You might tell me something about myself, too, while you are about it."

"Oh, do hold your tongue and listen," she said. "It's nothing that I'm ashamed of, and it isn't even anything that I'm specially sorry about. But what would you say if there were something that is no business of mine and yet is my nightmare?"

"In that case," said the man seriously, "I should suggest that you bring back the cake."

"Well, you must listen to the story first," said Laura, persistently. "To begin with, I must tell you that my father owned the inn called the 'Red Fish' at Ludbury, and I used to serve people in the bar."

"I have often wondered," he said, "why there was a kind of a Christian air about this one confectioner's shop."

"Ludbury is a sleepy, grassy little hole in the Eastern Counties, and the only kind of people who ever came to the 'Red Fish' were occasional commercial travelers, and for the rest, the most awful people you can see, only you've never seen them. I mean little, loungy men, who had just enough to live on and had nothing to do but lean about in bar-rooms and bet on horses, in bad clothes that were just too good for them. Even these wretched young rotters were not very common at our house; but there were two of them that were a lot too common—common in every sort of way. They both lived on money of their own, and were wearisomely idle and over-dressed. But yet I was a bit sorry for them, because I half believe they slunk into our little empty bar because each of them had a slight deformity; the sort of thing that some yokels laugh at. It wasn't exactly a deformity either; it was more an oddity. One of them was a surprisingly small man, something like a dwarf, or at least like a jockey. He was not at all jockeyish to look at, though; he had a round black head and a well-trimmed black beard, bright eyes like a bird's; he jingled money in his pockets; he jangled a great gold watch chain; and he never turned up except dressed just too much like a gentleman to be one. He was no fool though, though a futile idler; he was curiously clever at all kinds of things that couldn't be the slightest use; a sort of impromptu conjuring; making fifteen matches set fire to each other like a regular firework; or cutting a banana or some such thing into a dancing doll. His name was Isidore Smythe; and I can see him still, with his little dark face, just coming up to the counter, making a jumping kangaroo out of five cigars.

"The other fellow was more silent and more ordinary; but somehow he alarmed me much more than poor little Smythe. He was very tall and slight, and light-haired; his nose had a high bridge, and he might almost have been handsome in a spectral sort of way; but he had one of the most appalling squints I have ever seen or heard of. When he looked straight at you, you didn't know where you were yourself, let alone what he was looking at. I fancy this sort of disfigurement embittered the poor chap a little; for while Smythe was ready to show off his monkey tricks anywhere, James Welkin (that was the squinting man's name) never did anything except soak in our bar parlor, and go for great walks by himself in the flat, grey country all round. All the same, I think Smythe, too, was a little sensitive about being so small, though he carried it off more smartly. And so it was that I was really puzzled, as well as startled, and very sorry, when they both offered to marry me in the same week.

"Well, I did what I've since thought was perhaps a silly thing. But, after all, these freaks were my friends in a way; and I had a horror of their thinking I refused them for the real reason, which was that they were so impossibly ugly. So I made up some gas of another sort, about never meaning to marry anyone who hadn't carved his way in the world. I said it was a point of principle with me not to live on money that was just inherited like theirs. Two days after I had talked in this well-meaning sort of way, the whole trouble began. The first thing I heard was that both of them had gone off to seek their fortunes, as if they were in some silly fairy tale.

"Well, I've never seen either of them from that day to this. But I've had two letters from the little man called Smythe, and really they were rather exciting."

"Ever heard of the other man?" asked Angus.

"No, he never wrote," said the girl, after an instant's hesitation. "Smythe's first letter was simply to say that he had started out walking with Welkin to London; but Welkin was such a good walker that the little man dropped out of it, and took a rest by the roadside. He happened to be picked up by some traveling show, and, partly because he was nearly a dwarf, and partly because he was really a clever little wretch, he got on quite well in the show business, and was soon sent up to the Aquarium, to do some tricks that I forget. That was his first letter. His second was much more of a startler, and I only got it last week."

The man called Angus emptied his coffee-cup and regarded her with mild and patient eyes. Her own mouth took a slight twist of laughter as she resumed, "I suppose you've seen on the hoardings all about this 'Smythe's Silent Service'? Or you must be the only person that hasn't. Oh, I don't know much about it, it's some clockwork invention for doing all the housework by machinery. You know the sort of thing: 'Press a button—A Butler who Never Drinks.' 'Turn a Handle—Ten Housemaids who Never Flirt.' You must have seen the advertisements. Well, whatever these machines are, they are making pots of money; and they are making it all for that little imp whom I knew down in Ludbury. I can't help feeling pleased the poor little chap has fallen on his feet; but the plain fact is, I'm in terror of his turning up any minute and telling me he's carved his way in the world—as he certainly has."

"And the other man?" repeated Angus with a sort of obstinate quietude.

Laura Hope got to her feet suddenly. "My friend," she said, "I think you are a witch. Yes, you are quite right. I have not seen a line of the other man's writing; and I have no more notion than the dead of what or where he is. But it is of him that I am frightened. It is he who is all about my path. It is he who has half driven me mad. Indeed, I think he has driven me mad; for I have felt him where he could not have been, and I have heard his voice when he could not have spoken."

"Well, my dear," said the young man, cheerfully, "if he were Satan himself, he is done for now you have told somebody. One goes mad all alone, old girl. But when was it you fancied you felt and heard our squinting friend?"

"I heard James Welkin laugh as plainly as I hear you speak," said the girl, steadily. "There was nobody there, for I stood just outside the shop at the corner, and could see down both streets at once. I had forgotten how he laughed, though his laugh was as odd as his squint. I had not thought of him for nearly a year. But it's a solemn truth that a few seconds later the first letter came from his rival."

"Did you ever make the specter speak or squeak, or anything?" asked Angus, with some interest.

Laura suddenly shuddered, and then said, with an unshaken voice, "Yes. Just when I had finished reading the second letter from Isidore Smythe announcing his success, just then, I heard Welkin say, 'He shan't have you, though.' It was quite plain, as if he were in the room. It is awful; I think I must be mad."

"If you really were mad," said the young man, "you would think you must be sane. But certainly there seems to me to be something a little rum about this unseen gentleman. Two heads are better than one—I spare you allusions to any other organs—and really, if you would allow me, as a sturdy, practical man, to bring back the wedding-cake out of the window—"

Even as he spoke, there was a sort of steely shriek in the street outside, and a small motor, driven at devilish speed, shot up to the door of the shop and stuck there. In the same flash of time a small man in a shiny top hat stood stamping in the outer room.

Angus, who had hitherto maintained hilarious ease from motives of mental hygiene, revealed the strain of his soul by striding abruptly out of the inner room and confronting the newcomer. A glance at him was quite sufficient to confirm the savage guesswork of a man in love. This very dapper but dwarfish figure, with the spike of black beard carried insolently forward, the clever unrestful eyes, the neat but very nervous fingers, could be none other than the man just described to him: Isidore Smythe, who made dolls out of banana skins and match-boxes; Isidore Smythe, who made millions out of undrinking butlers and unflirting housemaids of metal. For a moment the two men, instinctively understanding each other's air of posses-sion, looked at each other with that curious cold generosity which is the soul of rivalry.

Mr. Smythe, however, made no allusion to the ultimate ground of their antagonism, but said simply and explosively, "Has Miss Hope seen that thing on the window?"

"On the window?" repeated the staring Angus.

"There's no time to explain other things," said the small million-aire shortly. "There's some tomfoolery going on here that has to be investigated."

He pointed his polished walking-stick at the window, recently depleted by the bridal preparations of Mr. Angus; and that gentleman was astonished to see along the front of the glass a long strip of paper pasted, which had certainly not been on the window when he had looked through it some time before. Following the energetic Smythe outside into the street, he found that some yard and a half of stamp paper had been carefully gummed along the glass outside, and on this was written in straggly characters, "If you marry Smythe, he will die."

"Laura," said Angus, putting his big red head into the shop, "you're not mad."

"It's the writing of that fellow Welkin," said Smythe gruffly. "I haven't seen him for years, but he's always bothering me. Five times in the last fortnight he's had threatening letters left at my flat, and I can't even find out who leaves them, let alone if it is Welkin himself. The porter of the flats swears that no suspicious characters have been seen, and here he has pasted up a sort of dado on a public shop window, while the people in the shop—"

"Quite so," said Angus modestly, "while the people in the shop were having tea. Well, sir, I can assure you I appreciate your common sense in dealing so directly with the matter. We can talk about other things afterwards. The fellow cannot be very far off yet, for I swear there was no paper there when I went last to the window, ten or fifteen minutes ago. On the other hand, he's too far off to be chased, as we don't even know the direction. If you'll take my advice, Mr. Smythe, you'll put this at once in the hands of some energetic inquiry man, private rather than public. I know an extremely clever fellow, who has set up in business five minutes from here in your car. His name's Flambeau, and though his youth was a bit stormy, he's a strictly honest man now, and his brains are worth money. He lives in Lucknow Mansions, Hampstead."

"That is odd," said the little man, arching his black eyebrows. "I live, myself, in Himalaya Mansions, round the corner. Perhaps you might care to come with me; I can go to my rooms and sort out these queer Welkin documents, while you run round and get your friend the detective."

"You are very good," said Angus politely. "Well, the sooner we act the better."

Both men, with a queer kind of impromptu fairness, took the same sort of formal farewell of the lady, and both jumped into the brisk little car. As Smythe took the handles and they turned the great corner of the street, Angus was amused to see a gigantesque poster of "Smythe's Silent Service," with a picture of a huge headless iron doll, carrying a saucepan with legend, "A Cook Who is Never Cross."

"I use them in my own flat," said the little black-bearded man, laughing, "partly for advertisement, and partly for real convenience.

Honestly, and all above board, those big clockwork dolls of mine do bring you coals or claret or a time-table quicker than any live servants I've ever known, if you know which knob to press. But I'll never deny, between ourselves, that such servants have their disadvantages, too."

"Indeed?" said Angus; "is there something they can't do?"

"Yes," replied Smythe coolly; "they can't tell me who left those threatening letters at my flat."

The man's motor was small and swift like himself; in fact, like his domestic service, it was of his own invention. If he was an advertising quack, he was one who believed in his own wares. The sense of something tiny and flying was accentuated as they swept up long white curves of road in the dead but open daylight of evening. Soon the white curves came sharper and dizzier; they were upon ascending spirals, as they say in the modern religions. For, indeed, they were cresting a corner of London which is almost as precipitous as Edinburgh, if not quite so picturesque. Terrace rose above terrace, and the special tower of flats they sought rose above them all to almost Egyptian height, gilt by the level sunset. The change, as they turned the corner and entered the crescent known as Himalaya Mansions, was as abrupt as the opening of a window; for they found that pile of flats sitting above London as above a green sea of slate. Opposite to the mansions, on the other side of the gravel crescent, was a bushy enclosure more like a steep hedge or dyke than a garden, and some way below that ran a strip of artificial water, a sort of canal, like the moat of that embowered fortress. As the car swept round the crescent it passed, at one corner, the stray stall of a man selling chestnuts; and right away at the other end of the curve, Angus could see a dim blue policeman walking slowly. These were the only human shapes in that high suburban solitude; but he had an irrational sense that they expressed the speechless poetry of London. He felt as if they were figures in a story.

The little car shot up to the right house like a bullet, and shot out its owner like a bomb shell. He was immediately inquiring of a tall commissionaire in shining braid, and a short porter in shirt sleeves, whether anybody or anything had been seeking his apartments. He was assured that nobody and nothing had passed these officials since his last inquiries; whereupon he and the slightly bewildered Angus were shot up in the lift like a rocket, till they reached the top floor.

"Just come in for a minute," said the breathless Smythe. "I want to show you those Welkin letters. Then you might run round the corner and fetch your friend." He pressed a button concealed in the wall, and the door opened of itself.

It opened on a long, commodious ante-room, of which the only arresting features, ordinarily speaking, were the rows of tall half-human mechanical figures that stood up on both sides like tailors' dummies. Like tailors' dummies they were headless; and like tailors' dummies they had a handsome unnecessary humpiness in the shoulders, and a pigeon-breasted protuberance of chest; but barring this, they were not much more like a human figure than any automatic machine at a station that is about the human height. They had two great hooks like arms, for carrying trays; and they were painted pea-green, or vermilion, or black for convenience of distinction; in every other way they were only automatic machines and nobody would have looked twice at them. On this occasion, at least, nobody did. For between the two rows of these domestic dummies lay something more interesting than most of the mechanics of the world. It was a white, tattered scrap of paper scrawled with red ink; and the agile inventor had snatched it up almost as soon as the door flew open. He handed it to Angus without a word. The red ink on it actually was not dry, and the message ran, "If you have been to see her today, I shall kill you."

There was a short silence, and then Isidore Smythe said quietly, "Would you like a little whisky? I rather feel as if I should."

"Thank you; I should like a little Flambeau," said Angus, gloomily. "This business seems to me to be getting rather grave. I'm going round at once to fetch him."

"Right you are," said the other, with admirable cheerfulness. "Bring him round here as quick as you can."

But as Angus closed the front door behind him he saw Smythe push back a button, and one of the clockwork images glided from its place and slid along a groove in the floor carrying a tray with siphon and decanter. There did seem something a trifle weird about leaving the little man alone among those dead servants, who were coming to life as the door closed.

Six steps down from Smythe's landing the man in shirt sleeves was doing something with a pail. Angus stopped to extract a promise, fortified with a prospective bribe, that he would remain in that place until the return with the detective, and would keep count of any kind of stranger coming up those stairs. Dashing down to the front hall he then laid similar charges of vigilance on the commissionaire at the front door, from whom he learned the simplifying circumstance that

there was no back door. Not content with this, he captured the float-
ing policeman and induced him to stand opposite the entrance and
watch it; and finally paused an instant for a pennyworth of chestnuts,
and an inquiry as to the probable length of the merchant's stay in the
neighborhood.

The chestnut seller, turning up the collar of his coat, told him he
should probably be moving shortly, as he thought it was going to
snow. Indeed, the evening was growing grey and bitter, but Angus,
with all his eloquence, proceeded to nail the chestnut man to his
post.

"Keep yourself warm on your own chestnuts," he said earnestly.
"Eat up your whole stock; I'll make it worth your while. I'll give
you a sovereign if you'll wait here till I come back, and then tell me
whether any man, woman, or child has gone into that house where
the commissionaire is standing."

He then walked away smartly, with a last look at the besieged
tower.

"I've made a ring round that room, anyhow," he said. "They can't
all four of them be Mr. Welkin's accomplices."

Lucknow Mansions were, so to speak, on a lower platform of that
hill of houses, of which Himalaya Mansions might be called the peak.
Mr. Flambeau's semi-official flat was on the ground floor, and presented in every way a marked contrast to the American machinery
and cold hotel-like luxury of the flat of the Silent Service. Flambeau,
who was a friend of Angus, received him in a rococo artistic den
behind his office, of which the ornaments were sabers, harquebuses,
Eastern curiosities, flasks of Italian wine, savage cooking-pots, a plumy
Persian cat, and a small dusty-looking Roman Catholic priest, who
looked particularly out of place.

"This is my friend Father Brown," said Flambeau. "I've often
wanted you to meet him. Splendid weather, this; a little cold for
Southerners like me."

"Yes, I think it will keep clear," said Angus, sitting down on a
violet-striped Eastern ottoman.

"No," said the priest quietly, "it has begun to snow."

And, indeed, as he spoke, the first few flakes, foreseen by the man
of chestnuts, began to drift across the darkening windowpane.

"Well," said Angus heavily. "I'm afraid I've come on business, and
rather jumpy business at that. The fact is, Flambeau, within a stone's
throw of your house is a fellow who badly wants your help; he's

perpetually being haunted and threatened by an invisible enemy—a scoundrel whom nobody has even seen." As Angus proceeded to tell the whole tale of Smythe and Welkin, beginning with Laura's story, and going on with his own, the supernatural laugh at the corner of two empty streets, the strange distinct words spoken in an empty room, Flambeau grew more and more vividly concerned, and the little priest seemed to be left out of it, like a piece of furniture. When it came to the scribbled stamp paper pasted on the window, Flambeau rose, seeming to fill the room with his huge shoulders.

"If you don't mind," he said, "I think you had better tell me the rest on the nearest road to this man's house. It strikes me, somehow, that there is no time to be lost."

"Delighted," said Angus, rising also, "though he's safe enough for the present, for I've set four men to watch the only hole to his burrow."

They turned out into the street, the small priest trundling after them with the docility of a small dog. He merely said, in a cheerful way, like one making conversation, "How quick the snow gets thick on the ground."

As they threaded the steep side streets already powdered with silver, Angus finished his story; and by the time they reached the crescent with the towering flats, he had leisure to turn his attention to the four sentinels. The chestnut seller, both before and after receiving a sovereign, swore stubbornly that he had watched the door and seen no visitor enter. The policeman was even more emphatic. He said he had had experience of crooks of all kinds, in top hats and in rags; he wasn't so green as to expect suspicious characters to look suspicious; he looked out for anybody, and, so help him, there had been nobody. And when all three men gathered round the gilded commissionaire, who still stood smiling astride of the porch, the verdict was more final still.

"I've got a right to ask any man, duke or dustman, what he wants in these flats," said the genial and gold-laced giant, "and I'll swear there's been nobody to ask since this gentleman went away."

The unimportant Father Brown, who stood back, looking modestly at the pavement, here ventured to say meekly, "Has nobody been up and down stairs, then, since the snow began to fall? It began while we were all round at Flambeau's."

"Nobody's been in here, sir, you can take it from me," said the official, with beaming authority.

"Then I wonder what that is?" said the priest, and stared at the ground blankly like a fish.

The others all looked down also; and Flambeau used a fierce exclamation and a French gesture. For it was unquestionably true that down the middle of the entrance guarded by the man in gold lace, actually between the arrogant, stretched legs of that colossus, ran a stringy pattern of grey footprints stamped upon the white snow.

"God!" cried Angus involuntarily, "the Invisible Man!"

Without another word he turned and dashed up the stairs, with Flambeau following; but Father Brown still stood looking about him in the snowclad street as if he had lost interest in his query.

Flambeau was plainly in a mood to break down the door with his big shoulder; but the Scotsman, with more reason, if less intuition, fumbled about on the frame of the door till he found the invisible button; and the door swung slowly open.

It showed substantially the same serried interior; the hall had grown darker, though it was still struck here and there with the last crimson shafts of sunset, and one or two of the headless machines had been moved from their places for this or that purpose, and stood here and there about the twilit place. The green and red of their coats were all darkened in the dusk; and their likeness to human shapes slightly increased by their very shapelessness. But in the middle of them all, exactly where the paper with the red ink had lain, there lay something that looked very like red ink spilt out of its bottle. But it was not red ink.

With a French combination of reason and violence Flambeau simply said "Murder!" and, plunging into the flat, had explored every corner and cupboard of it in five minutes. But if he expected to find a corpse he found none. Isidore Smythe simply was not in the place, either dead or alive. After the most tearing search the two men met each other in the outer hall, with streaming faces and staring eyes. "My friend," said Flambeau, talking French in his excitement, "not only is your murderer invisible, but he makes invisible also the murdered man."

Angus looked round at the dim room full of dummies, and in some Celtic corner of his Scotch soul a shudder started. One of the life-size dolls stood immediately overshadowing the blood stain, summoned, perhaps, by the slain man an instant before he fell. One of the high-shouldered hooks that served the thing for arms, was a little lifted, and

Angus had suddenly the horrid fancy that poor Smythe's own iron child had struck him down. Matter had rebelled, and these machines had killed their master. But even so, what had they done with him?

"Eaten him?" said the nightmare at his ear; and he sickened for an instant at the idea of rent, human remains absorbed and crushed into all that acephalous clockwork.

He recovered his mental health by an emphatic effort, and said to Flambeau, "Well, there it is. The poor fellow has evaporated like a cloud and left a red streak on the floor. The tale does not belong to this world."

"There is only one thing to be done," said Flambeau, "whether it belongs to this world or the other, I must go down and talk to my friend."

They descended, passing the man with the pail, who again asseverated that he had let no intruder pass, down to the commissionaire and the hovering chestnut man, who rigidly reasserted their own watchfulness. But when Angus looked round for his fourth confirmation he could not see it, and called out with some nervousness, "Where is the policeman?"

"I beg your pardon," said Father Brown; "that is my fault. I just sent him down the road to investigate something—that I just thought worth investigating."

"Well, we want him back pretty soon," said Angus abruptly, "for the wretched man upstairs has not only been murdered, but wiped out."

"How?" asked the priest.

"Father," said Flambeau, after a pause, "upon my soul I believe it is more in your department than mine. No friend or foe has entered the house, but Smythe is gone, as if stolen by the fairies. If that is not supernatural, I—"

As he spoke they were all checked by an unusual sight; the big blue policeman came round the corner of the crescent, running. He came straight up to Brown.

"You're right, sir," he panted, "they've just found poor Mr. Smythe's body in the canal down below."

Angus put his hand wildly to his head. "Did he run down and drown himself?" he asked.

"He never came down, I'll swear," said the constable, "and he wasn't drowned either, for he died of a great stab over the heart."

"And yet you saw no one enter?" said Flambeau in a grave voice.

"Let us walk down the road a little," said the priest.

As they reached the other end of the crescent he observed abruptly, "Stupid of me! I forgot to ask the policeman something. I wonder if they found a light brown sack."

"Why a light brown sack?" asked Angus, astonished.

"Because if it was any other colored sack, the case must begin over again," said Father Brown; "but if it was a light brown sack, why, the case is finished."

"I am pleased to hear it," said Angus with hearty irony. "It hasn't begun, so far as I am concerned."

"You must tell us all about it," said Flambeau with a strange heavy simplicity, like a child.

Unconsciously they were walking with quickening steps down the long sweep of road on the other side of the high crescent, Father Brown leading briskly, though in silence. At last he said with an almost touching vagueness, "Well, I'm afraid you'll think it so prosy. We always begin at the abstract end of things, and you can't begin this story anywhere else.

"Have you ever noticed this—that people never answer what you say? They answer what you mean—or what they think you mean. Suppose one lady says to another in a country house, "Is anybody staying with you?" the lady doesn't answer "Yes; the butler, the three footmen, the parlormaid, and so on," though the parlormaid may be in the room, or the butler behind her chair. She says "There is *nobody* staying with us," meaning nobody of the sort you mean. But suppose a doctor inquiring into an epidemic asks, "Who is staying in the house?" then the lady will remember the butler, parlormaid, and the rest. All language is used like that; you never get a question answered literally, even when you get it answered truly. When those four quite honest men said that no man had gone into the Mansions, they did not really mean that *no man* had gone into them. They meant no man whom they could suspect of being your man. A man did go into the house, and did come out of it, but they never noticed him."

"An invisible man?" inquired Angus, raising his red eyebrows.

"A mentally invisible man," said Father Brown.

A minute or two after he resumed in the same unassuming voice, like a man thinking his way. "Of course you can't think of such a man, until you do think of him. That's where his cleverness comes in. But I came to think of him through two or three little things in the tale Mr. Angus told us. First, there was the fact that this Welkin went for long walks. And then there was the vast lot of stamp paper on the window. And then, most of all, there were the two things the young lady said—things that couldn't be true. Don't get annoyed," he added hastily, noting a sudden movement of the Scotsman's head; "she thought they were true all right, but they couldn't be true. A person *can't* be quite alone in a street a second before she receives a letter. She can't be quite alone in a street when she starts reading a letter just received. There must be somebody pretty near her; he must be mentally invisible."

"Why must there be somebody near her?" asked Angus.

"Because," said Father Brown, "barring carrier-pigeons, somebody must have brought her the letter."

"Do you really mean to say," asked Flambeau, with energy, "that Welkin carried his rival's letters to his lady?"

"Yes," said the priest. "Welkin carried his rival's letters to his lady. You see, he had to."

"Oh, I can't stand much more of this," exploded Flambeau. "Who is this fellow? What does he look like? What is the usual get-up of a mentally invisible man?"

"He is dressed rather handsomely in red, blue and gold," replied the priest promptly with precision, "and in this striking, and even showy, costume he entered Himalaya Mansions under eight human eyes; he killed Smythe in cold blood, and came down into the street again carrying the dead body in his arms——"

"Reverend sir," cried Angus, standing still, "are you raving mad, or am I?"

"You are not mad," said Brown, "only a little unobservant. You have not noticed such a man as this, for example."

He took three quick strides forward, and put his hand on the shoulder of an ordinary passing postman who had bustled by them unnoticed under the shade of the trees.

"Nobody ever notices postmen somehow," he said thoughtfully; "yet they have passions like other men, and even carry large bags where a small corpse can be stowed quite easily."

The postman, instead of turning naturally, had ducked and tumbled against the garden fence. He was a lean fair-bearded man of very ordinary appearance, but as he turned an alarmed face over his shoulder, all three men were fixed with an almost fiendish squint.

Flambeau went back to his sabers, purple rugs and Persian cat, having many things to attend to. John Turnbull Angus went back to the lady at the shop, with whom that imprudent young man contrives to be extremely comfortable. But Father Brown walked those snow-covered hills under the stars for many hours with a murderer, and what they said to each other will never be known.

Naboth's Vineyard

Melville D. Post

ONE HEARS a good deal about the sovereignty of the people in this republic; and many persons imagine it a sort of fiction, and wonder where it lies, who are the guardians of it, and how they would exercise it if the forms and agents of the law were removed. I am not one of those who speculate upon this mystery, for I have seen this primal ultimate authority naked at its work. And, having seen it, I know how mighty and how dread a thing it is. And I know where it lies, and who are the guardians of it, and how they exercise it when the need arises.

There was a great crowd, and for the whole country was in the courtroom. It was a notorious trial.

Elihu Marsh had been shot down in his house. He had been found lying in a room, with a hole through his body that one could put his thumb in. He was an irascible old man, the last of his family, and so, lived alone. He had rich lands, but only a life estate in them, the remainder was to some foreign heirs. A girl from a neighboring farm came now and then to bake and put his house in order, and he kept a farm hand about the premises.

Nothing had been disturbed in the house when the neighbors found Marsh; no robbery had been attempted, for the man's money, a considerable sum, remained on him.

There was not much mystery about the thing, because the farm hand had disappeared. This man was a stranger in the hills. He had come from over the mountains some months before, and gone to work for Marsh. He was a big blond man, young and good looking; of better blood, one would say, than the average laborer. He gave his name as Taylor, but he was not communicative, and little else about him was known.

The country was raised, and this man was overtaken in the foothills of the mountains. He had his clothes tied into a bundle, and a long-

163

barreled fowling-piece on his shoulder. The story he told was that
he and Marsh had settled that morning, and he had left the house
at noon, but that he had forgotten his gun and had gone back for it;
had reached the house about four o'clock, gone into the kitchen,
got his gun down from the dogwood forks over the chimney, and
at once left the house. He had not seen Marsh, and did not know
where he was.

He admitted that this gun had been loaded with a single huge lead
bullet. He had so loaded it to kill a dog that sometimes approached
the house, but not close enough to be reached with a load of shot.
He affected surprise when it was pointed out that the gun had been
discharged. He said that he had not fired it, and had not, until then,
noticed that it was empty. When asked why he had so suddenly
determined to leave the country, he was silent.

He was carried back and confined in the county jail, and now he
was on trial at the September term of the circuit court.

The court sat early. Although the Judge, Simon Kilrail, was a landowner and lived on his estate in the country some half dozen miles
away, he rode to the courthouse in the morning, and home at night,
with his legal papers in his saddle-pockets. It was only when the
court sat that he was a lawyer. At other times he harvested his hay
and grazed his cattle, and tried to add to his lands like any other man
in the hills, and he was as hard in a trade and as hungry for an acre
as any.

It was the sign and insignia of distinction in Virginia to own land.
Mr. Jefferson had annulled the titles that George the Third had
granted, and the land alone remained as a patent of nobility. The
Judge wished to be one of these landed gentry, and he had gone a
good way to accomplish it. But when the court convened he became
a lawyer and sat upon the bench with no heart in him, and a cruel
tongue like the English judges.

I think everybody was at this trial. My Uncle Abner and the
strange old doctor, Storm, sat on a bench near the center aisle of the
courtroom, and I sat behind them, for I was a half-grown lad, and
permitted to witness the terrors and severities of the law.

The prisoner was the center of interest. He sat with a stolid countenance like a man careless of the issues of life. But not everybody
was concerned with him, for my Uncle Abner and Storm watched
the girl who had been accustomed to bake for Marsh and red up his
house.

She was a beauty of her type; dark haired and dark eyed like a gypsy, and with an April nature of storm and sun. She sat among the witnesses with a little handkerchief clutched in her hands. She was nervous to the point of hysteria, and I thought that was the reason the old doctor watched her. She would be taken with a gust of tears, and then throw up her head with a fine defiance; and she kneaded and knotted and worked the handkerchief in her fingers. It was a time of stress and many witnesses were unnerved, and I think I should not have noticed this girl but for the whispering of Storm and my Uncle Abner.

The trial went forward, and it became certain that the prisoner would hang. His stubborn refusal to give any reason for his hurried departure had but one meaning, and the circumstantial evidence was conclusive. The motive, only, remained in doubt, and the Judge had charged on this with so many cases in point, and with so heavy a hand, that any virtue in it was removed. The Judge was hard against this man, and indeed there was little sympathy anywhere, for it was a foul killing—the victim an old man and no hot blood to excuse it.

In all trials of great public interest, where the evidences of guilt overwhelmingly assemble against a prisoner, there comes a moment when all the people in the courtroom, as one man, and without a sign of the common purpose, agree upon a verdict; there is no outward or visible evidence of this decision, but one feels it, and it is a moment of the tensest stress.

The trial of Taylor had reached this point, and there lay a moment of deep silence, when this girl sitting among the witnesses suddenly burst into a very hysteria of tears. She stood up shaking with sobs, her voice choking in her throat, and the tears gushing through her fingers.

What she said was not heard at the time by the audience in the courtroom, but it brought the Judge to his feet and the jury crowding about her, and it broke down the silence of the prisoner, and threw him into a perfect fury of denials. We could hear his voice rise above the confusion, and we could see him struggling to get to the girl and stop her. But what she said was presently known to everybody, for it was taken down and signed; and it put the case against Taylor, to use a lawyer's term, out of court.

The girl had killed Marsh herself. And this was the manner and the reason of it: She and Taylor were sweethearts and were to be married. But they had quarreled the night before Marsh's death and the following morning Taylor had left the country. The point of the quarrel was some remark that Marsh had made to Taylor touching the girl's reputation. She had come to the house in the afternoon, and finding her lover gone, and maddened at the sight of the one who had robbed her of him, had taken the gun down from the chimney and killed Marsh. She had then put the gun back into its place and left the house. This was about two o'clock in the afternoon, and about an hour before Taylor returned for his gun.

There was a great veer of public feeling with a profound sense of having come at last upon the truth, for the story not only fitted to the circumstantial evidence against Taylor, but it fitted also to his story and it disclosed the motive for the killing. It explained, too, why he had refused to give the reason for his disappearance. That Taylor denied what the girl said and tried to stop her in her declaration, meant nothing except that the prisoner was a man, and would not have the woman he loved make such a sacrifice for him.

I cannot give all the forms of legal procedure with which the closing hours of the court were taken up, but nothing happened to shake the girl's confession. Whatever the law required was speedily got ready, and she was remanded to the care of the sheriff in order that she might come before the court in the morning.

Taylor was not released, but was also held in custody, although the case against him seemed utterly broken down. The Judge refused to permit the prisoner's counsel to take a verdict. He said that he would withdraw a juror and continue the case. But he seemed unwilling to release any clutch of the law until some one was punished for this crime.

It was on our way, and we rode out with the Judge that night. He talked with Abner and Storm about the pastures and the price of cattle, but not about the trial, as I hoped he would do, except once only, and then it was to inquire why the prosecuting attorney had not called either of them as witnesses, since they were the first to find Marsh, and Storm had been among the doctors who examined him. And Storm had explained how he had mortally offended the prosecutor in his canvass, by his remark that only a gentleman should hold office. He did but quote Mr. Hamilton, Storm said, but the man had received it as a deadly insult, and thereby proved the truth of Mr. Hamilton's expression, Storm added. And Abner said that as no circumstance about Marsh's death was questioned, and others arriving about the same time had been called, the prosecutor doubtless considered further testimony unnecessary.

The Judge nodded, and the conversation turned to other questions. At the gate, after the common formal courtesy of the country, the Judge asked us to ride in, and, to my astonishment, Abner and Storm accepted his invitation. I could see that the man was surprised, and I thought annoyed, but he took us into his library.

I could not understand why Abner and Storm had stopped here, until I remembered how from the first they had been considering the girl, and it occurred to me that they thus sought the Judge in the hope of getting some word to him in her favor. A great sentiment had leaped up for this girl. She had made a staggering sacrifice, and with a headlong courage, and it was like these men to help her if they could.

And it was to speak of the woman that they came, but not in her favor. And while Simon Kilrail listened, they told this extraordinary story: They had been of the opinion that Taylor was not guilty when the trial began, but they had suffered it to proceed in order to see what might develop. The reason was that there were certain circumstantial evidences, overlooked by the prosecutor, indicating the guilt of the woman and the innocence of Taylor. When Storm examined the body of Marsh he discovered that the man had been killed by poison, and was dead when the bullet was fired into his body. This meant that the shooting was a fabricated evidence to direct the suspicion against Taylor. The woman had baked for Marsh on this morning, and the poison was in the bread which he had eaten at noon.

Abner was going on to explain something further, when a servant entered and asked the Judge what time it was. The man had been greatly impressed, and he now sat in a profound reflection. He took his watch out of his pocket and held it in his hand, then he seemed to realize the question and replied that his watch had run down. Abner gave the hour, and said that perhaps his key would wind the watch. The Judge gave it to him, and he wound it and laid it on the table. Storm observed my Uncle with, what I thought, a curious interest, but the Judge paid no attention. He was deep in his reflection and oblivious to everything. Finally he roused himself and made his comment.

"This clears the matter up," he said. "The woman killed Marsh from the motive which she gave in her confession, and she created this false evidence against Taylor because he had abandoned her. She thereby avenged herself desperately in two directions. . . . It would be like a woman to do this, and then regret it and confess."

He then asked my Uncle if he had anything further to tell him, and although I was sure that Abner was going on to say something further when the servant entered, he replied now that he had not, and asked for the horses. The Judge went out to have the horses brought, and we remained in silence. My Uncle was calm, as with some consuming idea, but Storm was as nervous as a cat. He was out of his chair when the door was closed, and hopping about the room looking at the law books standing on the shelves in their leather covers. Suddenly he stopped and plucked out a little volume. He whipped through it with his forefinger, smothered a great oath, and shot it into his pocket, then he crooked his finger to my Uncle, and they talked together in a recess of the window until the Judge returned.

We rode away. I was sure that they intended to say something to the Judge in the woman's favor, for, guilty or not, it was a fine thing she had done to stand up and confess. But something in the interview had changed their purpose. Perhaps when they had heard the Judge's comment they saw it would be of no use. They talked closely together as they rode, but they kept before me and I could not hear. It was of the woman they spoke, however, for I caught a fragment.

"But where is the motive?" said Storm.

And my Uncle answered, "In the twenty-first chapter of the Book of Kings."

We were early at the county seat, and it was a good thing for us, because the court-room was crowded to the doors. My Uncle had got a big record book out of the county clerk's office as he came in, and I was glad of it, for he gave it to me to sit on, and it raised me up so I could see. Storm was there, too, and, in fact, every man of any standing in the country.

The sheriff opened the court, the prisoners were brought in, and the Judge took his seat on the bench. He looked haggard like a man who had not slept, as, in fact, one could hardly have done who had so cruel a duty before him. Here was every human feeling pressing to save a woman, and the law to hang her. But for all his hagridden face, when he came to act, the man was adamant.

He ordered the confession read, and directed the girl to stand up. Taylor tried again to protect, but he was forced down into his chair. The girl stood up bravely, but she was white as plaster, and her eyes dilated. She was asked if she still adhered to the confession and understood the consequences of it, and, although she trembled from head to toe, she spoke out distinctly. There was a moment of silence and the Judge was about to speak, when another voice filled the court-room. I turned about on my book to find my head against my Uncle Abner's legs.

"I challenge the confession!" he said.

The whole court-room moved. Every eye was on the two tragic figures standing up: the slim, pale girl and the big, somber figure of my Uncle. The Judge was astounded.

"On what ground?" he said.

"On the ground," replied my Uncle, "that the confession is a lie!"

One could have heard a pin fall anywhere in the whole room. The girl caught her breath in a little gasp, and the prisoner, Taylor, half rose and then sat down as though his knees were too weak to bear him. The Judge's mouth opened, but for a moment or two he did not speak, and I could understand his amazement. Here was Abner assailing a confession which he himself had supported before the Judge, and speaking for the innocence of a woman whom he himself had shown to be guilty and taking one position privately, and another publicly. What did the man mean? And I was not surprised that the Judge's voice was stern when he spoke.

"This is irregular," he said. "It may be that this woman killed Marsh, or it may be that Taylor killed him, and there is some collusion between these persons, as you appear to suggest. And you may know something to throw light on the matter, or you may not. However that may be, this is not the time for me to hear you. You will have ample opportunity to speak when I come to try the case."

"But you will never try this case!" said Abner.

I cannot undertake to describe the desperate interest that lay on the people in the courtroom. They were breathlessly silent; one could hear the voices from the village outside, and the sounds of men and horses that came up through the open windows. No one knew what hidden thing Abner drove at. But he was a man who meant what he said, and the people knew it.

The Judge turned on him with a terrible face.

"What do you mean?" he said.

"I mean," replied Abner, and it was in his deep, hard voice, "that you must come down from the bench."

The Judge was in a heat of fury.

"You are in contempt," he roared. "I order your arrest. Sheriff!" he called.

But Abner did not move. He looked the man calmly in the face.

"You threaten me," he said, "but God Almighty threatens you." And he turned about to the audience. "The authority of the law," he said, "is in the hands of the electors of this county. Will they stand up?"

I shall never forget what happened then, for I have never in my life seen anything so deliberate and impressive. Slowly, in silence, and without passion, as though they were in a church of God, men began to get up in the courtroom.

Randolph was the first. He was a justice of the peace, vain and pompous, proud of the abilities of an ancestry that he did not inherit. And his superficialities were the annoyance of my Uncle Abner's life. But whatever I may have to say of him hereafter I want to say this thing of him here, that his bigotry and his vanities were builded on the foundations of a man. He stood up as though he stood alone, with no glance about him to see what other men would do, and he faced the Judge calmly above his great black stock. And I learned then that a man may be a blusterer and a lion.

Hiram Arnold got up, and Rockford, and Armstrong, and Alkire, and Coopman, and Monroe, and Elnathan Stone, and my father, Lewis, and Dayton and Ward, and Madison from beyond the mountains. And it seemed to me that the very hills and valleys were standing up.

It was a strange and instructive thing to see. The loudmouthed and the reckless were in that courtroom, men who would have shouted in a political convention, or run howling with a mob, but they were not the persons who stood up when Abner called upon the authority of the people to appear. Men rose whom one would not have looked to see—the blacksmith, the saddler, and old Asa Divers. And I saw that law and order and all the structure that civilization had builded up, rested on the sense of justice that certain men carried in their breasts, and that those who possessed it not, in the crisis of necessity, did not count.

Father Donovan stood up; he had a little flock beyond the valley river, and he was as poor, and almost as humble as his Master, but he was not afraid; and Bronson, who preached Calvin, and Adam Rider, who traveled a Methodist circuit. No one of them believed in what the other taught; but they all believed in justice, and when the line was drawn, there was but one side for them all.

The last man up was Nathaniel Davisson, but the reason was that he was very old, and he had to wait for his sons to help him. He had been time and again in the Assembly of Virginia, at a time when only a gentleman and landowner could sit there. He was a just man, and honorable and unafraid.

The Judge, his face purple, made a desperate effort to enforce his authority. He pounded on his desk and ordered the sheriff to clear the courtroom. But the sheriff remained standing apart. He did not lack for courage, and I think he would have faced the people if his duty had been that way. His attitude was firm, and one could mark no uncertainty upon him, but he took no step to obey what the Judge commanded.

The Judge cried out at him in a terrible voice.

"I am the representative of the law here. Go on!"

The sheriff was a plain man, and unacquainted with the nice expressions of Mr. Jefferson, but his answer could not have been better if that gentleman had written it out for him.

"I would obey the representative of the law," he said, "if I were not in the presence of the law itself!"

The Judge rose. "This is revolution," he said; "I will send to the Governor for the militia."

It was Nathaniel Davisson who spoke then. He was very old and the tremors of dissolution were on him, but his voice was steady.

"Sit down, your Honor," he said, "there is no revolution here, and you do not require troops to support your authority. We are here to support it if it ought to be lawfully enforced. But the people have elevated you to be the Bench because they believed in your integrity, and if they have been mistaken they would know it." He paused, as though to collect his strength, and then went on. "The presumptions of right are all with your Honor. You administer the law upon our authority and we stand behind you. Be assured that we will not suffer our authority to be insulted in your person." His voice grew deep and resolute. "It is a grave thing to call us up against you, and not lightly, nor for a trivial reason shall any man dare to do it." Then he turned about. "Now, Abner," he said, "what is this thing?"

Young as I was, I felt that the old man spoke for the people standing in the courtroom, with their voice and their authority, and I began to fear that the measure which my Uncle had taken was high-handed. But he stood there like the shadow of a great rock.

"I charge him," he said, "with the murder of Elihu Marsh! And I call upon him to vacate the Bench."

When I think about this extraordinary event now, I wonder at the calmness with which Simon Kilrail met this blow, until I reflect that he had seen it on its way, and had got ready to meet it. But even with that preparation, it took a man of iron nerve to face an assault like that and keep every muscle in its place. He had tried violence and had failed with it, and he had recourse now to the attitudes and mannerisms of a judicial dignity. He sat with his elbows on the table, and his clenched fingers propping up his jaw. He looked coldly at Abner, but he did not speak, and there was silence until Nathaniel Davisson spoke for him. His face and his voice were like iron.

"No, Abner," he said, "he shall not vacate the Bench for that, nor upon the accusation of any man. We will have your proofs, if you please."

The Judge turned his cold face from Abner to Nathaniel Davisson, and then he looked over the men standing in the courtroom.

"I am not going to remain here," he said, "to be tried by a mob, upon the *viva voce* indictment of a bystander. You may nullify your court, if you like, and suspend the forms of law for yourselves, but you cannot nullify the constitution of Virginia, nor suspend my right as a citizen of that commonwealth."

"And now," he said, rising, "if you will kindly make way, I will vacate this courtroom, which your violence has converted into a chamber of sedition."

The man spoke in a cold, even voice, and I thought he had presented a difficulty that could not be met. How could these men before him undertake to keep the peace of this frontier, and force its lawless elements to submit to the forms of law for trial, and deny any letter of those formalities to this man? Was the grand jury, and the formal indictment, and all the right and privilege of an orderly procedure for one, and not for another?

It was Nathaniel Davisson who met this dangerous problem.

"We are not concerned," he said, "at this moment with your rights as a citizen; the rights of private citizenship are inviolate, and they remain to you, when you return to it. But you are not a private citizen. You are our agent. We have selected you to administer the law for us, and your right to act has been challenged. Well, as the authority behind you, we appear and would know the reason."

The Judge retained his imperturbable calm.

"Do you hold me a prisoner here?" he said.

"We hold you an official in your office," replied Davisson, "not only do we refuse to permit you to leave the courtroom, but we refuse to permit you to leave the Bench. This court shall remain as we have set it up until it is our will to readjust it. And it shall not be changed at the pleasure or demand of any man but by us only, and for a sufficient cause shown to us."

And again I was anxious for my Uncle, for I saw how grave a thing it was to interfere with the authority of the people as manifested in the forms and agencies of the law. Abner must be very sure of the ground under him.

And he was sure. He spoke now, with no introductory expressions, but directly and in the simplest words.

"These two persons," he said, indicating Taylor and the girl, "have each been willing to die in order to save the other. Neither is guilty of this crime. Taylor has kept silent, and the girl has lied, to the same end. This is the truth: There was a lovers' quarrel, and Taylor left the country precisely as he told us, except the motive, which he would not tell lest the girl be involved. And the woman, to save him, confesses to a crime that she did not commit.

"Who did commit it?" He paused and included Storm with a gesture. "We suspected this woman because Marsh had been killed by poison in his bread, and afterwards mutilated with a shot. Yesterday we rode out with the Judge to put those facts before him." Again he paused. "An incident occurring in that interview indicated that we were wrong; a second incident assured us, and still later, a third convinced us. These incidents were, first, that the Judge's watch had run down; second, that we found in his library a book with all the leaves in it uncut, except at one certain page; and, third, that we found in the county clerk's office an unindexed record in an old deed book." There was deep quiet and he went on:

"In addition to the theory of Taylor's guilt or this woman's, there was still a third; but it had only a single incident to support it, and we feared to suggest it until the others had been explained. This theory was that some one, to benefit by Marsh's death, had planned to kill him in such a manner as to throw suspicion on this woman who baked his bread, and finding Taylor gone, and the gun above the mantel, yielded to an afterthought to create a further false evidence. It was overdone!

"The trigger guard of the gun in the recoil caught in the chain of the assassin's watch and jerked it out of his pocket; he replaced the watch, but not the key which fell to the floor, and which I picked up beside the body of the dead man."

Abner turned toward the Judge.

"And so," he said, "I charge Simon Kilrail with this murder; because the key winds his watch; because the record in the old deed book is a conveyance by the heirs of Marsh's lands to him at the life tenant's death; and because the book we found in his library is a book on poisons with the leaves uncut, except at the very page describing that identical poison with which Elihu Marsh was murdered."

The strained silence that followed Abner's words was broken by a voice that thundered in the courtroom. It was Randolph's.

"Come down!" he said.

And this time Nathaniel Davisson was silent.

The Judge got slowly on his feet, a resolution was forming in his face, and it advanced swiftly.

"I will give you my answer in a moment," he said.

Then he turned about and went into his room behind the Bench. There was but one door, and that opening into the court, and the people waited.

The windows were open and we could see the green fields, and the sun, and the far-off mountains, and the peace and quiet and serenity of autumn entered. The Judge did not appear. Presently there was the sound of a shot from behind the closed door. The sheriff threw it open, and upon the floor, sprawling in a smear of blood, lay Simon Kilrail, with a dueling pistol in his hand.

The Gioconda Smile

Aldous Huxley

I

"MISS SPENCE will be down directly, sir."

"Thank you," said Mr. Hutton, without turning round. Janet Spence's parlormaid was so ugly—ugly on purpose, it always seemed to him, malignantly, criminally ugly—that he could not bear to look at her more than was necessary. The door closed. Left to himself, Mr. Hutton got up and began to wander round the room, looking with meditative eyes at the familiar objects it contained.

Photographs of Greek statuary, photographs of the Roman Forum, colored prints of Italian masterpieces, all very safe and well known. Poor, dear Janet, what a prig—what an intellectual snob! Her real taste was illustrated in that water-color by the pavement artist, the one she had paid half a crown for (and thirty-five shillings for the frame). How often he had heard her tell the story, how often expatiate on the beauties of that skillful imitation of an oleograph! "A real Artist in the streets," and you could hear the capital A in Artist as she spoke the words. She made you feel that part of his glory had entered into Janet Spence when she tendered him that half-crown for the copy of the oleograph. She was implying a compliment to her own taste and penetration. A genuine Old Master for half a crown. Poor, dear Janet!

Mr. Hutton came to a pause in front of a small oblong mirror. Stooping a little to get a full view of his face, he passed a white, well-manicured finger over his moustache. It was as curly, as freshly auburn as it had been twenty years ago. His hair still retained its color, and there was no sign of baldness yet—only a certain elevation of the brow. "Shakespearean," thought Mr. Hutton, with a smile, as he surveyed the smooth and polished expanse of his forehead.

175

Others abide our question, thou are free. . . . Footsteps in the sea . . .
Majesty. . . . Shakespeare, thou shouldst be living at this hour. No, that
was Milton, wasn't it? Milton, the Lady of Christ's. There was no lady
about him. He was what the women would call a manly man. That
was why they liked him—for the curly auburn moustache and the
discreet redolence of tobacco. Mr. Hutton smiled again; he enjoyed
making fun of himself. Lady of Christ's? No, no. He was the Christ
of Ladies. Very pretty, very pretty. The Christ of Ladies. Mr. Hutton
wished there were somebody he could tell the joke to. Poor, dear
Janet wouldn't appreciate it, alas!

He straightened himself up, patted his hair, and resumed his
peregrination. Damn the Roman Forum; he hated those dreary
photographs.

Suddenly he became aware that Janet Spence was in the room,
standing near the door. Mr. Hutton started, as though he had been
taken in some felonious act. To make these silent and spectral appearances was one of Janet Spence's peculiar talents. Perhaps she had been
there all the time, had seen him looking at himself in the mirror.
Impossible! But, still, it was disquieting.

"Oh, you gave me such a surprise," said Mr. Hutton, recovering his
smile and advancing with outstretched hand to meet her.

Miss Spence was smiling too: her Gioconda smile, he had once
called it in a moment of half-ironical flattery. Miss Spence had taken
the compliment seriously, and always tried to live up to the Leonardo
standard. She smiled on in silence while Mr. Hutton shook hands;
that was part of the Gioconda business.

"I hope you're well," said Mr. Hutton. "You look it."

What a queer face she had! That small mouth pursed forward by
the Gioconda expression into a little snout with a round hole in
the middle as though for whistling—it was like a penholder seen
from the front. Above the mouth a well-shaped nose, finely aquiline.
Eyes large, lustrous, and dark, with the largeness, luster, and darkness
that seems to invite sties and an occasional bloodshot suffusion. They
were fine eyes, but unchangingly grave. The penholder might do its
Gioconda trick, but the eyes never altered in their earnestness. Above
them, a pair of boldly arched, heavily penciled black eyebrows lent a
surprising air of power, as of a Roman matron, to the upper portion
of the face. Her hair was dark and equally Roman; Agrippina from
the brows upward.

"I thought I'd just look in on my way home," Mr. Hutton went on. "Ah, it's good to be back here"—he indicated with a wave of his hand the flowers in the vases, the sunshine and greenery beyond the windows—"it's good to be back in the country after a stuffy day of business in town."

Miss Spence, who had sat down, pointed to a chair at her side.

"No, really, I can't sit down," Mr. Hutton protested. "I must get back to see how poor Emily is. She was rather seedy this morning." He sat down, nevertheless. "It's these wretched liver chills. She's always getting them. Women——" He broke off and coughed, so as to hide the fact that he had uttered. He was about to say that women with weak digestions ought not to marry; but the remark was too cruel, and he didn't really believe it. Janet Spence, moreover, was a believer in eternal flames and spiritual attachments. "She hopes to be well enough," he added, "to see you at luncheon to-morrow. Can you come? Do!" He smiled persuasively. "It's my invitation too, you know."

She dropped her eyes, and Mr. Hutton almost thought that he detected a certain reddening of the cheek. It was a tribute; he stroked his moustache.

"I should like to come if you think Emily's really well enough to have a visitor."

"Of course. You'll do her good. You'll do us both good. In married life three is often better company than two."

"Oh, you're cynical."

Mr. Hutton always had a desire to say "Bow-wow-wow" whenever that last word was spoken. It irritated him more than any other word in the language. But instead of barking he made haste to protest.

"No, no. I'm only speaking a melancholy truth. Reality doesn't always come up to the ideal, you know. But that doesn't make me believe any the less in the ideal. Indeed, I believe in it passionately—the ideal of a matrimony between two people in perfect accord. I think it's realizable. I'm sure it is."

He paused significantly and looked at her with an arch expression. A virgin of thirty-six, but still unwithered; she had her charms. And there was something really rather enigmatic about her. Miss Spence made no reply, but continued to smile. There were times when Mr. Hutton got rather bored with the Gioconda. He stood up.

"I must really be going now. Farewell, mysterious Gioconda." The smile grew intenser, focused itself, as it were, in a narrower snout. Mr.

Hutton made a Cinquecento gesture, and kissed her extended hand.
It was the first time he had done such a thing; the action seemed not
to be resented. "I look forward to to-morrow."

"Do you?"

For answer Mr. Hutton once more kissed her hand, then turned to
go. Miss Spence accompanied him to the porch.

"Where's your car?" she asked.

"I left it at the gate of the drive."

"I'll come and see you off."

"No, no." Mr. Hutton was playful, but determined. "You must do
no such thing. I simply forbid you."

"But I should like to come," Miss Spence protested, throwing a
rapid Gioconda at him.

Mr. Hutton held up his hand. "No," he repeated, and then, with
a gesture that was almost the blowing of a kiss, he started to run
down the drive, lightly, on his toes, with long, bounding strides
like a boy's. He was proud of that run; it was quite marvelously
youthful. Still, he was glad the drive was no longer. At the last
bend, before passing out of sight of the house, he halted and turned
round. Miss Spence was still standing on the steps, smiling her
smile. He waved his hand, and this time quite definitely and overtly
wafted a kiss in her direction. Then, breaking once more into his
magnificent center, he rounded the last dark promontory of trees.
Once out of sight of the house he let his high paces decline to a
trot, and finally to a walk. He took out his handkerchief and began
wiping his neck inside his collar. What fools, what fools! Had there
ever been such an ass as poor, dear Janet Spence? Never, unless it
was himself. Decidedly he was the more malignant fool, since he,
at least, was aware of his folly and still persisted in it. Why did he
persist? Ah, the problem that was himself, the problem that was
other people. . .

He had reached the gate. A large prosperous-looking motor was
standing at the side of the road.

"Home, M'Nab." The chauffeur touched his cap. "And stop at the
cross-roads on the way, as usual," Mr. Hutton added, as he opened
the door of the car. "Well?" he said, speaking into the obscurity that
lurked within.

"Oh, Teddy Bear, what an age you've been!" It was a fresh and
childish voice that spoke the words. There was the faintest hint of
Cockney impurity about the vowel sounds.

Mr. Hutton bent his large form and darted into the car with the agility of an animal regaining its burrow.

"Have I?" he said, as he shut the door. The machine began to move. "You must have missed me a lot if you found the time so long." He sat back in the low seat; a cherishing warmth enveloped him.

"Teddy Bear. . ." and with a sigh of contentment a charming little head declined on to Mr. Hutton's shoulder. Ravished, he looked down sideways at the round, babyish face.

"Do you know, Doris, you look like the pictures of Louise de Kéroual." He passed his fingers through a mass of curly hair.

"Who's Louise de Kera-whatever-it-is?" Doris spoke from remote distances.

"She was, alas! *Fuit.* We shall all be 'was' one of these days. Meanwhile. . ."

Mr. Hutton covered the babyish face with kisses. The car rushed smoothly along. M'Nab's back, through the front window, was stonily impressive, the back of a statue.

"Your hands," Doris whispered. "Oh, you mustn't touch me. They give me electric shocks."

Mr. Hutton adored her for the virgin imbecility of the words. How late in one's existence one makes the discovery of one's body!

"The electricity isn't in me, it's in you." He kissed her again, whispering her name several times: Doris, Doris, Doris. The scientific appellation of the sea-mouse, he was thinking as he kissed the throat she offered him, white and extended like the throat of a victim awaiting the sacrificial knife. The sea-mouse was a sausage with iridescent fur: very peculiar. Or was Doris the sea-cucumber, which turns itself inside out in moments of alarm? He would really have to go to Naples again, just to see the aquarium. These sea creatures were fabulous, unbelievably fantastic.

"Oh, Teddy Bear!" (More zoology; but he was only a land animal. His poor little jokes!) "Teddy Bear, I'm so happy."

"So am I," said Mr. Hutton. Was it true?

"But I wish I knew if it were right. Tell me, Teddy Bear, is it right or wrong?"

"Ah, my dear, that's just what I've been wondering for the last thirty years."

"Be serious, Teddy Bear. I want to know if this is right; if it's right that I should be here with you and that we should love one another, and that it should give me electric shocks when you touch me."

"Right? Well, it's certainly good that you should have electric shocks rather than sexual repressions, Read Freud; repressions are the devil."

"Oh, you don't help me. Why aren't you ever serious? If only you knew how miserable I am sometimes, thinking it's not right. Perhaps, you know, there is a hell, and all that. I don't know what to do. Sometimes I think I ought to stop loving you."

"But could you?" asked Mr. Hutton, confident in the powers of his seduction and his moustache.

"No. Teddy Bear, you know I couldn't. But I could run away, I could hide from you, I could lock myself up and force myself not to come to you."

"Silly little thing!" He tightened his embrace.

"Oh, dear, I hope it isn't wrong. And there are times when I don't care if it is."

Mr. Hutton was touched. He had a certain protective affection for this little creature. He laid his cheek against her hair and so, interlaced, they sat in silence, while the car, swaying and pitching a little as it hastened along, seemed to draw in the white road and the dusty hedges towards it devouringly.

"Good-bye, good-bye."

The car moved on, gathered speed, vanished round a curve, and Doris was left standing by the sign-post at the cross-roads, still dizzy and weak with the languor born of those kisses and the electrical touch of those gentle hands. She had to take a deep breath, to draw herself up deliberately, before she was strong enough to start her homeward walk. She had half a mile in which to invent the necessary lies.

Alone, Mr. Hutton suddenly found himself the prey of an appalling boredom.

II

Mrs. Hutton was lying on the sofa in her boudoir, playing Patience. In spite of the warmth of the July evening a wood fire was burning on the hearth. A black Pomeranian, extenuated by the heat and the fatigues of digestion, slept before the blaze.

"Phew! Isn't it rather hot in here?" Mr. Hutton asked as he entered the room.

"You know I have to keep warm, dear." The voice seemed breaking on the verge of tears. "I get so shivery."

"I hope you're better this evening."

"No much, I'm afraid."

The conversation stagnated. Mr. Hutton stood leaning his back against the mantelpiece. He looked down at the Pomeranian lying at his feet, and with the toe of his right boot he rolled the little dog over and rubbed its white-flecked chest and belly. The creature lay in an inert ecstasy. Mrs. Hutton continued to play Patience. Arrived at an *impasse*, she altered the position of one card, took back another, and went on playing. Her Patiences always came out.

"Dr. Libbard thinks I ought to go to Llandrindod Wells this summer."

"Well, go, my dear—go, most certainly."

Mr. Hutton was thinking of the events of the afternoon: how they had driven, Doris and he, up to the hanging wood, had left the car to wait for them under the shade of the trees, and walked together out into the windless sunshine of the chalk down.

"I'm to drink the waters for my liver, and he thinks I ought to have massage and electric treatment, too."

Hat in hand, Doris had stalked four blue butterflies that were dancing together round a scabious flower with a motion that was like the flickering of blue fire. The blue fire burst and scattered into whirling sparks; she had given chase, laughing and shouting like a child.

"I'm sure it will do you good, my dear."

"I was wondering if you'd come with me, dear."

"But you know I'm going to Scotland at the end of the month."

Mrs. Hutton looked up at him entreatingly. "It's the journey," she said. "The thought of it is such a nightmare. I don't know if I can manage it. And you know I can't sleep in hotels. And then there's the luggage and all the worries. I can't go alone."

"But you won't be alone. You'll have your maid with you." He spoke impatiently. The sick woman was usurping the place of the healthy one. He was being dragged back from the memory of the sunlit down and the quick, laughing girl, back to this unhealthy, overheated room and its complaining occupant.

"I don't think I shall be able to go."

"But you must, my dear, if the doctor tells you to. And, besides, a change will do you good."

"I don't think so."

"But Libbard thinks so, and he knows what he's talking about."

"No, I can't face it. I'm too weak. I can't go alone." Mrs. Hutton pulled a handkerchief out of her black silk bag, and put it to her eyes.

"Nonsense, my dear, you must make the effort."

"I had rather be left in peace to die here." She was crying in earnest now.

"O Lord! Now do be reasonable. Listen now, please." Mrs. Hutton only sobbed more violently. "Oh, what is one to do?" He shrugged his shoulders and walked out of the room.

Mr. Hutton was aware that he had not behaved with proper patience; but he could not help it. Very early in his manhood he had discovered that not only did he not feel sympathy for the poor, the weak, the diseased, and deformed; he actually hated them. Once, as an undergraduate, he spent three days at a mission in the East End. He had returned, filled with a profound and ineradicable disgust. Instead of pitying, he loathed the unfortunate. It was not, he knew, a very comely emotion, and he had been ashamed of it at first. In the end he had decided that it was temperamental, inevitable, and had felt no further qualms. Emily had been healthy and beautiful when he married her. He had loved her then. But now—was it his fault that she was like this?

Mr. Hutton dined alone. Food and drink left him more benevolent than he had been before dinner. To make amends for his show of exasperation he went up to his wife's room and offered to read to her. She was touched, gratefully accepted the offer, and Mr. Hutton, who was particularly proud of his accent, suggested a little light reading in French.

"French? I am so fond of French." Mrs. Hutton spoke of the language of Racine as though it were a dish of green peas.

Mr. Hutton ran down to the library and returned with a yellow volume. He began reading. The effort of pronouncing perfectly absorbed his whole attention. But how good his accent was! The fact of its goodness seemed to improve the quality of the novel he was reading.

At the end of fifteen pages an unmistakable sound aroused him. He looked up; Mrs. Hutton had gone to sleep. He sat still for a little while, looking with a dispassionate curiosity at the sleeping face. Once it had been beautiful; once, long ago, the sight of it, the recollection of it, had moved him with an emotion profounder, perhaps, than any he had felt before or since. Now it was lined and cadaverous. The skin was stretched tightly over the cheekbones, across the bridge of the sharp, bird-like nose. The closed eyes were set in profound bone-rimmed sockets. The lamplight striking on the face from the side emphasized with light and shade its cavities and projections. It was the face of a dead Christ by Morales.

> *Le squelette était invisible*
> *Au temps heureux de l'art païen.*

He shivered a little, and tiptoed out of the room.

On the following day Mrs. Hutton came down to luncheon. She had had some unpleasant palpitations during the night, but she was feeling better now. Besides, she wanted to do honor to her guest. Miss Spence listened to her complaints about Llandrindod Wells, and was loud in sympathy, lavish with advice. Whatever she said was always said with intensity. She leaned forward, aimed, so to speak, like a gun, and fired her words. Bang! the charge in her soul was ignited, the words whizzed forth at the narrow barrel of her mouth. She was a machine-gun riddling her hostess with sympathy. Mr. Hutton had undergone similar bombardments, mostly of a literary or philosophic character—bombardments of Maeterlinck, of Mrs. Besant, of Bergson, of William James. To-day the missiles were medical. She talked about insomnia, she expatiated on the virtues of harmless drugs and beneficent specialists. Under the bombardment Mrs. Hutton opened out, like a flower in the sun.

Mr. Hutton looked on in silence. The spectacle of Janet Spence evoked in him an unfailing curiosity. He was not romantic enough to imagine that every face masked an interior physiognomy of beauty or strangeness, that every woman's small talk was like a vapor hanging over mysterious gulfs. His wife, for example, and Doris; they were nothing more than what they seemed to be. But with Janet Spence it was somehow different. Here one could be sure that there was some kind of a queer face behind the Gioconda smile and the Roman eyebrows. The only question was: What exactly was there? Mr. Hutton could never quite make out.

"But perhaps you won't have to go to Llandrindod after all," Miss Spence was saying. "If you get well quickly Dr. Libbard will let you off."

"I only hope so. Indeed, I do really feel rather better to-day."

Mr. Hutton felt ashamed. How much was it his own lack of sympathy that prevented her from feeling well every day? But he comforted himself by reflecting that it was only a case of feeling, not of being better. Sympathy does not mend a diseased liver or a weak heart.

"My dear, I wouldn't eat those red currants if I were you," he said, suddenly solicitous. "You know that Libbard has banned everything with skins and pips."

"But I am so fond of them," Mrs. Hutton protested, "and I feel so well to-day."

"Don't be a tyrant," said Miss Spence, looking first at him and then at his wife. "Let the poor invalid have what she fancies; it will do her good." She laid her hand on Mrs. Hutton's arm and patted it affectionately two or three times.

"Thank you, my dear." Mrs. Hutton helped herself to the stewed currants.

"Well, don't blame me if they make you ill again."

"Do I ever blame you, dear?"

"You have nothing to blame me for," Mr. Hutton answered playfully. "I am the perfect husband."

They sat in the garden after luncheon. From the island of shade under the old cypress tree they looked out across a flat expanse of lawn, in which the parterres of flowers shone with a metallic brilliance.

Mr. Hutton took a deep breath of the warm and fragrant air. "It's good to be alive," he said.

"Just to be alive," his wife echoed, stretching one pale, knot-jointed hand into the sunlight.

A maid brought the coffee; the silver pots and the little blue cups were set on a folding table near the group of chairs.

"Oh, my medicine!" exclaimed Mrs. Hutton. "Run in and fetch it, Clara, will you? The white bottle on the sideboard."

"I'll go," said Mr. Hutton. "I've got to go and fetch a cigar in any case."

He ran in towards the house. On the threshold he turned round for an instant. The maid was walking back across the lawn. His wife was sitting up in her deck-chair, engaged in opening her white parasol. Miss Spence was bending over the table, pouring out the coffee. He passed into the cool obscurity of the house.

"Do you like sugar in your coffee?" Miss Spence inquired.

"Yes, please. Give me rather a lot. I'll drink it after my medicine to take the taste away."

Mrs. Hutton leaned back in her chair, lowering the sunshade over her eyes, so as to shut out from her vision the burning sky.

Behind her, Miss Spence was making a delicate clinking among the coffee-cups.

"I've given you three large spoonfuls. That ought to take the taste away. And here comes the medicine."

Mr. Hutton had reappeared, carrying a wine-glass, half full of a pale liquid.

"It smells delicious," he said, as he handed it to his wife.

"That's only the flavoring." She drank it off at a gulp, shuddered, and made a grimace. "Ugh, it's so nasty. Give me my coffee."

Miss Spence gave her the cup; she sipped at it. "You've made it like syrup. But it's very nice, after that atrocious medicine."

At half-past three Mrs. Hutton complained that she did not feel as well as she had done, and went indoors to lie down. Her husband would have said something about the red currants, but checked himself; the triumph of an "I told you so" was too cheaply won. Instead, he was sympathetic, and gave her his arm to the house.

"A rest will do you good," he said. "By the way, I shan't be back till after dinner."

"But why? Where are you going?"

"I promised to go to Johnson's this evening. We have to discuss the war memorial, you know."

"Oh, I wish you weren't going." Mrs. Hutton was almost in tears. "Can't you stay? I don't like being alone in the house."

"But, my dear, I promised—weeks ago." It was a bother having to lie like this. "And now I must get back and look after Miss Spence."

He kissed her on the forehead and went out again into the garden. Miss Spence received him aimed and intense.

"Your wife is dreadfully ill," she fired off at him.

"I thought she cheered up so much when you came."

"That was purely nervous, purely nervous. I was watching her closely. With a heart in that condition and her digestion wrecked—yes, wrecked—anything might happen."

"Libbard doesn't take so gloomy a view of poor Emily's health."

Mr. Hutton held open the gate that led from the garden into the drive; Miss Spence's car was standing by the front door.

"Libbard is only a country doctor. You ought to see a specialist."

He could not refrain from laughing. "You have a macabre passion for specialists."

Miss Spence held up her hand in protest. "I am serious. I think poor Emily is in a very bad state. Anything might happen—at any moment."

He handed her into the car and shut the door. The chauffeur started the engine and climbed into his place, ready to drive off.

"Shall I tell him to start?" He had no desire to continue the conversation.

Miss Spence leaned forward and shot a Gioconda in his direction. "Remember, I expect you to come and see me again soon."

Mechanically he grinned, made a polite noise, and, as the car moved forward, waved his hand. He was happy to be alone.

A few minutes afterwards Mr. Hutton himself drove away. Doris was waiting at the cross-roads. They dined together twenty miles from home, at a roadside hotel. It was one of those bad, expensive meals which are only cooked in country hotels frequented by motorists. It revolted Mr. Hutton, but Doris enjoyed it. She always enjoyed things. Mr. Hutton ordered a not very good brand of champagne. He was wishing he had spent the evening in his library.

When they started homewards Doris was a little tipsy and extremely affectionate. It was very dark inside the car, but looking forward, past the motionless form of M'Nab, they could see a bright and narrow universe of forms and colors scooped out of the night by the electric head-lamps.

It was after eleven when Mr. Hutton reached home. Dr. Libbard met him in the hall. He was a small man with delicate hands and well-formed features that were almost feminine. His brown eyes were large and melancholy. He used to waste a great deal of time sitting at the bedside of his patients, looking sadness through those eyes and talking in a sad, low voice about nothing in particular. His person exhaled a pleasing odor, decidedly antiseptic but at the same time suave and discreetly delicious.

"Libbard?" said Mr. Hutton in surprise. "You here? Is my wife ill?"

"We tried to fetch you earlier," the soft, melancholy voice replied. "It was thought you were at Mr. Johnson's, but they had no news of you there."

"No. I was detained. I had a break-down," Mr. Hutton answered irritably. It was tiresome to be caught out in a lie.

"Your wife wanted to see you urgently."

"Well, I can go now." Mr. Hutton moved towards the stairs.

Dr. Libbard laid a hand on his arm. "I am afraid it's too late."

"Too late?" He began fumbling with his watch; it wouldn't come out of the pocket.

"Mrs. Hutton passed away half an hour ago."

The voice remained even in its softness, the melancholy of the eyes did not deepen. Dr. Libbard spoke of death as he would speak of a local cricket match. All things were equally vain and equally deplorable.

Mr. Hutton found himself thinking of Janet Spence's words. At any moment—at any moment. She had been extraordinarily right.

"What happened?" he asked. "What was the cause?"

Dr. Libbard explained. It was heart failure brought on by a violent attack of nausea, caused in its turn by the eating of something of an irritant nature. Red currants? Mr. Hutton suggested. Very likely. It had been too much for the heart. There was chronic valvular disease: something had collapsed under the strain. It was all over; she could not have suffered much.

III

"It's a pity they should have chosen the day of the Eton and Harrow match for the funeral," old General Grego was saying as he stood, his top hat in his hand, under the shadow of the lych gate, wiping his face with his handkerchief.

Mr. Hutton overheard the remark and with difficulty restrained a desire to inflict grievous bodily pain on the General. He would have liked to hit the old brute in the middle of his big red face. Monstrous great mulberry, spotted with meal! Was there no respect for the dead? Did nobody care? In theory he didn't much care; let the dead bury their dead. But here, at the graveside, he had found himself actually sobbing. Poor Emily, they had been pretty happy once. Now she was lying at the bottom of a seven-foot hole. And here was Grego complaining that he couldn't go to the Eton and Harrow match.

Mr. Hutton looked round at the groups of black figures that were drifting slowly out of the churchyard towards the fleet of cabs and motors assembled in the road outside. Against the brilliant background of the July grass and flowers and foliage, they had a horribly

alien and unnatural appearance. It pleased him to think that all these
people would soon be dead too.

That evening Mr. Hutton sat up late in his library reading the life
of Milton. There was no particular reason why he should have chosen
Milton; it was the book that first came to hand, that was all. It was
after midnight when he had finished. He got up from his armchair,
unbolted the French windows, and stepped out on to the little paved
terrace. The night was quiet and clear. Mr. Hutton looked at the stars
and at the holes between them, dropped his eyes to the dim lawns and
hueless flowers of the garden, and let them wander over the farther
landscape, black and grey under the moon.

He began to think with a kind of confused violence. There were the
stars, there was Milton. A man can be somehow the peer of stars and
night. Greatness, nobility. But is there seriously a difference between
the noble and the ignoble? Milton, the stars, death, and himself—
himself. The soul, the body; the higher and the lower nature. Perhaps
there was something in it, after all. Milton had a god on his side and
righteousness. What had he? Nothing, nothing whatever. There were
only Doris's little breasts. What was the point of it all? Milton, the stars,
death, and Emily in her grave, Doris and himself—always himself. . .

Oh, he was a futile and disgusting being. Everything convinced
him of it. It was a solemn moment. He spoke aloud: "I will, I will."
The sound of his own voice in the darkness was appalling; it seemed
to him that he had sworn that infernal oath which binds even the
gods: "I will, I will." There had been New Year's days and solemn
anniversaries in the past, when he had felt the same contritions and
recorded similar resolutions. They had all thinned away, these resolutions, like smoke, into nothingness. But this was a greater moment
and he had pronounced a more fearful oath. In the future it was to
be different. Yes, he would live by reason, he would be industrious,
he would curb his appetites, he would devote his life to some good
purpose. It was resolved and it would be so.

In practice he was himself spending his mornings in agricultural
pursuits, riding round with the bailiff, seeing that his land was farmed
in the best modern way—silos and artificial manures and continuous
cropping, and all that. The remainder of the day should be devoted
to serious study. There was that book he had been intending to write
for so long—*The Effect of Diseases on Civilization*.

Mr. Hutton went to bed humble and contrite, but with a sense that
grace had entered into him. He slept for seven and a half hours, and

woke to find the sun brilliantly shining. The emotions of the evening
before had been transformed by a good night's rest into his customary cheerfulness. It was not until a good many seconds after his return
to conscious life that he remembered his resolution, his Stygian oath.
Milton and death seemed somehow different in the sunlight. As for
the stars, they were not there. But the resolutions were good; even
in the daytime he could see that. He had his horse saddled after
breakfast, and rode round the farm with the bailiff. After luncheon he
read Thucydides on the plague at Athens. In the evening he made a
few notes on malaria in Southern Italy. While he was undressing he
remembered that there was a good anecdote in Skelton's jest-book
about the Sweating Sickness. He would have made a note of it if only
he could have found a pencil.

On the sixth morning of his new life Mr. Hutton found among
his correspondence an envelope addressed in that peculiarly vulgar
handwriting which he knew to be Doris's. He opened it, and began
to read. She didn't know what to say; words were so inadequate. His
wife dying like that, and so suddenly—it was too terrible. Mr. Hutton
sighed, but his interest revived somewhat as he read on:

"Death is so frightening, I never think of it when I can help it. But when
something like this happens, or when I am feeling ill or depressed, then I
can't help remembering it is there so close, and I think about all the wicked
things I have done and about you and me, and I wonder what will happen,
and I am so frightened. I am so lonely, Teddy Bear, and so unhappy, and I
don't know what to do. I can't get rid of the idea of dying, I am so wretched
and helpless without you. I didn't mean to write to you; I meant to wait till
you were out of mourning and could come and see me again, but I was so
lonely and miserable, Teddy Bear, I had to write. I couldn't help it. Forgive
me, I want you so much; I have nobody in the world but you. You are so
good and gentle and understanding; there is nobody like you. I shall never
forget how good and kind you have been to me, and you are so clever and
know so much, I can't understand how you ever came to pay any attention
to me, I am so dull and stupid, much less like me and love me, because you
do love me a little, don't you, Teddy Bear?"

Mr. Hutton was touched with shame and remorse. To be thanked
like this, worshipped for having seduced the girl—it was too much.
It had just been a piece of imbecile wantonness. Imbecile, idiotic:
there was no other way to describe it. For, when all was said, he had

derived very little pleasure from it. Taking all things together, he had probably been more bored than amused. Once upon a time he had believed himself to be a hedonist. But to be a hedonist implies a certain process of reasoning, a deliberate choice of known pleasures, a rejection of known pains. This had been done without reason, against it. For he knew beforehand—so well, so well—that there was no interest or pleasure to be derived from these wretched affairs. And yet each time the vague itch came upon him he succumbed, involving himself once more in the old stupidity. There had been Maggie, his wife's maid, and Edith, the girl on the farm, and Mrs. Pringle, and the waitress in London, and others—there seemed to be dozens of them. It had all been so stale and boring. He knew it would be; he always knew. And yet, and yet. . .Experience doesn't teach.

Poor little Doris! He would write to her kindly, comfortingly, but he wouldn't see her again. A servant came to tell him that his horse was saddled and waiting. He mounted and rode off. That morning the old bailiff was more irritating than usual.

Five days later Doris and Mr. Hutton were sitting together on the pier at Southend; Doris, in white muslin with pink garnishings, radiated happiness; Mr. Hutton, legs outstretched and chair tilted, had pushed the panama back from his forehead, and was trying to feel like a tripper. That night, when Doris was asleep, breathing and warm by his side, he recaptured, in this moment of darkness and physical fatigue, the rather cosmic emotion which had possessed him that evening, not a fortnight ago, when he had made his great resolution. And so his solemn oath had already gone the way of so many other resolutions. Unreason had triumphed; at the first itch of desire he had given way. He was hopeless, hopeless.

For a long time he lay with closed eyes, ruminating his humiliation. The girl stirred in her sleep. Mr. Hutton turned over and looked in her direction. Enough faint light crept in between the half-drawn curtains to show her bare arm and shoulder, her neck, and the dark tangle of hair on the pillow. She was beautiful, desirable. Why did he lie there moaning over his sins? What did it matter? If he were hopeless, then so be it; he would make the best of his hopelessness. A glorious sense of irresponsibility suddenly filled him. He was free, magnificently free. In a kind of exaltation he drew the girl towards him. She woke, bewildered, almost frightened under his rough kisses.

The storm of his desire subsided into a kind of serene merriment. The whole atmosphere seemed to be quivering with enormous silent laughter.

"Could anyone love you as much as I do, Teddy Bear?" The question came faintly from distant worlds of love.

"I think I know somebody who does," Mr. Hutton replied. The submarine laughter was swelling, rising, ready to break the surface of silence and resound.

"Who? Tell me. What do you mean?" The voice had come very close; charged with suspicion, anguish, indignation, it belong to this immediate world.

"A—ah!"

"Who?"

"You'll never guess," Mr. Hutton kept up the joke until it began to grow tedious, and then pronounced the name: "Janet Spence."

Doris was incredulous. "Miss Spence of the Manor? That old woman?" It was too ridiculous. Mr. Hutton laughed too.

"But it's quite true," he said. "She adores me." Oh, the vast joke! He would go and see her as soon as he returned—see and conquer. "I believe she wants to marry me," he added.

"But you wouldn't. . . you don't intend . . ."

The air was fairly crepitating with humor. Mr. Hutton laughed aloud. "I intend to marry you," he said. It seemed to him the best joke he had ever made in his life.

When Mr. Hutton left Southend he was once more a married man. It was agreed that, for the time being, the fact should be kept secret. In the autumn they would go abroad together, and the world should be informed. Meanwhile he was to go back to his own house and Doris to hers.

The day after his return he walked over in the afternoon to see Miss Spence. She received him with the old Gioconda.

"I was expecting you to come."

"I couldn't keep away," Mr. Hutton gallantly replied.

They sat in the summer-house. It was a pleasant place—a little old stucco temple bowered among dense bushes of evergreen. Miss Spence had left her mark on it by hanging up over the seat a blue-and-white Della Robbia plaque.

"I am thinking of going to Italy this autumn," said Mr. Hutton. He felt like a ginger-beer bottle, ready to pop with bubbling humorous excitement.

"Italy. . . ." Miss Spence closed her eyes ecstatically. "I feel drawn there too."

"Why not let yourself be drawn?"

"I don't know. One somehow hasn't the energy and initiative to set out alone."

"Alone. . . ." Ah, sound of guitars and throaty singing! "Yes, traveling alone isn't much fun."

Miss Spence lay back in her chair without speaking. Her eyes were still closed. Mr. Hutton stroked his moustache. The silence prolonged itself for what seemed a very long time.

Pressed to stay to dinner, Mr. Hutton did not refuse. The fun had hardly started. The table was laid in the loggia. Through its arches they looked out on to the sloping garden, to the valley below and the farther hills. Light ebbed away; the heat and silence were oppressive. A huge cloud was mounting up the sky, and there were distant breathings of thunder. The thunder drew nearer, a wind began to blow, and the first drops of rain fell. The table was cleared. Miss Spence and Mr. Hutton sat on in the growing darkness.

Miss Spence broke a long silence by saying meditatively:

"I think everyone has a right to a certain amount of happiness, don't you?"

"Most certainly." But what was she leading up to? Nobody makes generalizations about life unless they mean to talk about themselves. Happiness: he looked back on his own life, and saw a cheerful, placid existence disturbed by no great griefs or discomforts or alarms. He had always had money and freedom; he had been able to do very much as he wanted. Yes, he supposed he had been happy—happier than most men. And now he was not merely happy; he had discovered in irresponsibility the secret of gaiety. He was about to say something about his happiness when Miss Spence went on speaking.

"People like you and me have a right to be happy some time in our lives."

"Me?" said Mr. Hutton, surprised.

"Poor Henry! Fate hasn't treated either of us very well."

"Oh, well, it might have treated me worse."

"You're being cheerful. That's brave of you. But don't think I can't see behind the mask."

Miss Spence spoke louder and louder as the rain came down more and more heavily. Periodically the thunder cut across her utterances. She talked on, shouting against the noise.

"I have understood you so well and for so long."

A flash revealed her, aimed and intent, leaning towards him. Her eyes were two profound and menacing gun-barrels. The darkness re-engulfed her.

"You were a lonely soul seeking a companion soul. I could sympathize with you in your solitude. Your marriage. . ."

The thunder cut short the sentence. Miss Spence's voice became audible once more with the words:

". . . could offer no companionship to a man of your stamp. You needed a soul mate."

A soul mate—he! a soul mate. It was incredibly fantastic. "Georgette Leblanc, the ex-soul mate of Maurice Maeterlinck." He had seen that in the paper a few days ago. So it was thus that Janet Spence had painted him in her imagination—as a soul-mater. And for Doris he was a picture of goodness and the cleverest man in the world. And actually, really, he was what?—Who knows?

"My heart went out to you. I could understand; I was lonely, too." Miss Spence laid her hand on his knee. "You were so patient." Another flash. She was still aimed, dangerously. "You never complained. But I could guess—I could guess."

"How wonderful of you!" So he was an *âme incomprise*. "Only a woman's intuition. . ."

The thunder crashed and rumbled, died away, and only the sound of the rain was left. The thunder was his laughter, magnified, externalized. Flash and crash, there it was again, right on top of them.

"Don't you feel that you have within you something that is akin to this storm?" He could imagine her leaning forward as she uttered the words. "Passion makes one the equal of the elements."

What was his gambit now? Why, obviously, he should have said "Yes," and ventured on some unequivocal gesture. But Mr. Hutton suddenly took fright. The ginger beer in him had gone flat. The woman was serious—terribly serious. He was appalled.

Passion? "No," he desperately answered. "I am without passion."

But his remark was either unheard or unheeded, for Miss Spence went on with a growing exaltation, speaking so rapidly, however, and in such a burningly intimate whisper that Mr. Hutton found it very difficult to distinguish what she was saying. She was telling him, as far as he could make out, the story of her life. The lightning was less frequent now, and there were long intervals of darkness. But at each flash he saw her still aiming towards him, still yearning forward with a terrifying intensity. Darkness, the rain, and then flash! Her face was there, close at hand. A pale mask, greenish white; the large eyes, the narrow barrel of the mouth, the heavy eyebrows. Agrippina, or wasn't it rather—yes, wasn't it rather George Robey?"

He began devising absurd plans for escaping. He might suddenly jump up, pretending he had seen a burglar—Stop thief! stop thief!— and dash off into the night in pursuit. Or should he say that he felt faint, a heart attack? or that he had seen a ghost—Emily's ghost—in the garden? Absorbed in his childish plotting, he had ceased to pay any attention to Miss Spence's words. The spasmodic clutching of her hand recalled his thoughts.

"I honored you for that, Henry," she was saying.

Honored him for what?

"Marriage is a sacred tie, and your respect for it, even when the marriage was, as it was in your case, an unhappy one, made me respect you and admire you, and—shall I dare say the word?—"

Oh, the burglar, the ghost in the garden! But it was too late.

"...yes, love you, Henry, all the more. But we're free now, Henry."

Free? There was a movement in the dark, and she was kneeling on the floor by his chair.

"Oh, Henry, Henry, I have been unhappy too."

Her arms embraced him, and by the shaking of her body he could feel that she was sobbing. She might have been a suppliant crying for mercy.

"You mustn't, Janet," he protested. Those tears were terrible, terrible. "Not now, not now! You must be calm; you must go to bed." He patted her shoulder, then got up, disengaging himself from her embrace. He left her still crouching on the floor beside the chair on which he had been sitting.

Groping his way into the hall, and without waiting to look for his hat, he went out of the house, taking infinite pains to close the front door noiselessly behind him. The clouds had blown over, and the moon was shining from a clear sky. There were puddles all along the road, and a noise of running water rose from the gutters and ditches. Mr. Hutton splashed along, not caring if he got wet.

How heartrendingly she had sobbed! With the emotions of pity and remorse that the recollection evoked in him there was a certain resentment: why couldn't she have played the game that he was playing—the heartless, amusing game? Yes, but he had known all the time that she wouldn't, she couldn't, play that game; he had known and persisted.

What had she said about passion and the elements? Something absurdly stale, but true, true. There she was, a cloud black-bosomed and charged with thunder, and he, like some absurd little Benjamin Franklin, had sent up a kite into the heart of the menace. Now he was complaining that his toy had drawn the lightning.

She was probably still kneeling by that chair in the loggia, crying.

But why hadn't he been able to keep up the game? Why had his irresponsibility deserted him, leaving him suddenly sober in a cold world? There were no answers to any of his questions. One idea burned steady and luminous in his mind—the idea of flight. He must get away at once.

IV

"What are you thinking about, Teddy Bear?"

"Nothing."

There was a silence. Mr. Hutton remained motionless, his elbows on the parapet of the terrace, his chin in his hands, looking down over Florence. He had taken a villa on one of the hilltops to the south of the city. From a little raised terrace at the end of the garden one looked down a long fertile valley on to the town and beyond it to the bleak mass of Monte Morello and, eastward of it, to the peopled hill of Fiesole, dotted with white houses. Everything was clear and luminous in the September sunshine.

"Are you worried about anything?"

"No, thank you."

"Tell me, Teddy Bear."

"But, my dear, there's nothing to tell." Mr. Hutton turned round, smiled, and patted the girl's hand. "I think you'd better go in and have your siesta. It's too hot for you here."

"Very well, Teddy Bear. Are you coming too?"

"When I've finished my cigar."

"All right. But do hurry up and finish it, Teddy Bear." Slowly, reluctantly, she descended the steps of the terrace and walked towards the house.

Mr. Hutton continued his contemplation of Florence. He had need to be alone. It was good sometimes to escape from Doris and the restless solicitude of her passion. He had never known the pains of loving hopelessly, but he was experiencing now the pains of being loved. These last weeks had been a period of growing discomfort. Doris was always with him, like an obsession, like a guilty conscience. Yes, it was good to be alone.

He pulled an envelope out of his pocket and opened it, not without reluctance. He hated letters; they always contained something unpleasant—nowadays, since his second marriage. This was from his sister. He began skimming through the insulting home-truths of which it was composed. The words "indecent haste," "social suicide," "scarcely cold in her grave," "person of the lower classes," all occurred. They were inevitable now in any communication from a well-meaning and right-thinking relative. Impatient, he was about to tear the stupid letter to pieces when his eye fell on a sentence at the bottom of the third page. His heart beat with uncomfortable violence as he read it. It was too monstrous! Janet Spence was going about telling everyone that he had poisoned his wife in order to marry Doris. What damnable malice! Ordinarily a man of the suavest temper, Mr. Hutton found himself trembling with rage. He took the childish satisfaction of calling names—he cursed the woman.

Then suddenly he saw the ridiculous side of the situation. The notion that he should have murdered anyone in order to marry Doris! If they only knew how miserably bored he was. Poor, dear Janet! She had tried to be malicious; she had only succeeded in being stupid.

A sound of footsteps aroused him; he looked round. In the garden below the little terrace the servant girl of the house was picking fruit. A Neapolitan, strayed somehow as far north as Florence, she was a specimen of the classical type—a little debased. Her profile might have been taken from a Sicilian coin of a bad period. Her features, carved floridly in the grand tradition, expressed an almost perfect stupidity. Her mouth was the most beautiful thing about her; the calligraphic hand of nature had richly curved it into an expression of mulish bad temper. . . . Under her hideous black clothes, Mr. Hutton divined a powerful body, firm and massive. He had looked at her before with a vague interest and curiosity. To-day the curiosity defined and focused itself into a desire. An idyll of Theocritus. Here was the woman; he, alas, was not precisely like a goatherd on the volcanic hills. He called to her.

"Armida!"

The smile with which she answered him was so provocative, attested so easy a virtue, that Mr. Hutton took fright. He was on the brink once more—on the brink. He must draw back, oh! quickly, quickly, before it was too late. The girl continued to look up at him.

"*Ha chiamato?*" she asked at last.

Stupidity or reason? Oh, there was no choice now. It was imbecility every time.

"*Scendo,*" he called back to her. Twelve steps led from the garden to the terrace. Mr. Hutton counted them. Down, down, down, down. . . . He saw a vision of himself descending from one circle of the inferno to the next—from a darkness full of wind and hail to an abyss of sinking mud.

V

For a good many days the Hutton case had a place on the front page of every newspaper. There had been no more popular murder trial since George Smith had temporarily eclipsed the European War by drowning in a warm bath his seventh bride. The public imagination was stirred by this tale of a murder brought to light months after the date of the crime. Here, it was felt, was one of those incidents in human life, so notable because they are so rare, which do definitely justify the ways of God to man. A wicked man had been moved by an illicit passion to kill his wife. For months he had lived in sin and fancied security—only to be dashed at last more horribly into the pit he had prepared for himself. Murder will out, and here was a case of it. The readers of the newspapers were in a position to follow every movement of the hand of God. There had been vague, but persistent, rumors in the neighborhood; the police had taken action at last. Then came the exhumation order, the post-mortem examination, the inquest, the evidence of the experts, the verdict of the coroner's jury, the trial, the condemnation. For once Providence had done its duty, obviously, grossly, didactically, as in a melodrama. The newspapers were right in making of the case the staple intellectual food of a whole season.

Mr. Hutton's first emotion when he was summoned from Italy to give evidence at the inquest was one of indignation. It was a monstrous, a scandalous thing that the police should take such idle, malicious gossip seriously. When the inquest was over he would bring an action for malicious prosecution against the Chief Constable; he would sue the Spence woman for slander.

The inquest was opened; the astonishing evidence unrolled itself. The experts had examined the body, and had found traces of arsenic;

they were of opinion that the late Mrs. Hutton had died of arsenic poisoning.

Arsenic poisoning. . . . Emily had died of arsenic poisoning? After that, Mr. Hutton learned with surprise that there was enough arsenicated insecticide in his greenhouses to poison an army.

It was now, quite suddenly, that he saw it: there was a case against him. Fascinated, he watched it growing, growing, like some monstrous tropical plant. It was enveloping him, surrounding him; he was lost in a tangled forest.

When was the poison administered? The experts agreed that it must have been swallowed eight or nine hours before death. About lunch-time? Yes, about lunch-time. Clara, the parlor-maid, was called. Mrs. Hutton, she remembered, had asked her to go and fetch her medicine. Mr. Hutton had volunteered to go instead; he had gone alone. Miss Spence—ah, the memory of the storm, the white aimed face! the horror of it all!—Miss Spence confirmed Clara's statement, and added that Mr. Hutton had come back with the medicine already poured out in a wine-glass, not in the bottle.

Mr. Hutton's indignation evaporated. He was dismayed, frightened. It was all too fantastic to be taken seriously, and yet this nightmare was a fact—it was actually happening.

M'Nab had seen them kissing, often. He had taken them for a drive on the day of Mrs. Hutton's death. He could see them reflected in the wind-screen, sometimes out of the tail of his eye.

The inquest was adjourned. That evening Doris went to bed with a headache. When he went to her room after dinner, Mr. Hutton found her crying.

"What's the matter?" He sat down on the edge of her bed and began to stroke her hair. For a long time she did not answer, and he went on stroking her hair mechanically, almost unconsciously; sometimes, even, he bent down and kissed her bare shoulder. He had his own affairs, however, to think about. What had happened? How was it that the stupid gossip had actually come true? Emily had died of arsenic poisoning. It was absurd, impossible. The order of things had been broken, and he was at the mercy of irresponsibility. What had happened, what was going to happen? He was interrupted in the midst of his thoughts.

"It's my fault—it's my fault!" Doris suddenly sobbed out. "I shouldn't have loved you; I oughtn't to have let you love me. Why was I ever born?"

Mr. Hutton didn't say anything, but looked down in silence at the abject figure of misery lying on the bed.

"If they do anything to you I shall kill myself."

She sat up, held him for a moment at arm's length, and looked at him with a kind of violence, as though she were never to see him again.

"I love you, I love you, I love you." She drew him, inert and passive, towards her, clasped him, pressed herself against him. "I didn't know you loved me as much as that, Teddy Bear. But why did you do it—why did you do it?"

Mr. Hutton undid her clasping arms and got up. His face became very red. "You seem to take it for granted that I murdered my wife," he said. "It's really too grotesque. What do you all take me for? A cinema hero?" He had begun to lose his temper. All the exasperation, all the fear and bewilderment of the day, was transformed into a violent anger against her. "It's all such damned stupidity. Haven't you any conception of a civilized man's mentality? Do I look the sort of man who'd go about slaughtering people? I suppose you imagined I was so insanely in love with you that I could commit any folly. When will you women understand that one isn't insanely in love? All one asks for is a quiet life, which you won't allow one to have. I don't know what the devil ever induced me to marry you. It was all a damned stupid, practical joke. And now you go about saying I'm a murderer. I won't stand it."

Mr. Hutton stamped towards the door. He had said horrible things, he knew—odious things that he ought speedily to unsay. But he wouldn't. He closed the door behind him.

"Teddy Bear!" He turned the handle; the latch clicked into place. "Teddy Bear!" The voice that came to him through the closed door was agonized. Should he go back? He ought to go back. He touched the handle, then withdrew his fingers and quickly walked away. When he was half-way down the stairs he halted. She might try to do something silly—throw herself out of the window or God know what! He listened attentively; there was no sound. But he pictured her very clearly, tiptoeing across the room, lifting the sash as high as it would go, leaning out into the cold night air. It was raining a little. Under the window lay the paved terrace. How far below? Twenty-five or thirty feet? Once, when he was walking along Piccadilly, a dog had jumped out of a third-story window of the Ritz. He had seen it fall; he had heard it strike the pavement. Should he go back? He was damned if he would; he hated her.

He sat for a long time in the library. What had happened? What was happening? He turned the question over and over in his mind and could find no answer. Suppose the nightmare dreamed itself out to its horrible conclusion. Death was waiting for him. His eyes filled with tears; he wanted so passionately to live. "Just to be alive." Poor Emily had wished it too, he remembered: "Just to be alive." There were still so many places in this astonishing world unvisited, so many queer delightful people still unknown, so many lovely women never so much as seen. The huge white oxen would still be dragging their wains along the Tuscan roads, the cypresses would still go up, straight as pillars, to the blue heaven; but he would not be there to see them. And the sweet southern wines—Tear of Christ and Blood of Judas—others would drink them, not he. Others would walk down the obscure and narrow lanes between the bookshelves in the London Library, sniffing the dusty perfume of good literature, peering at strange titles, discovering unknown names, exploring the fringes of vast domains of knowledge. He would be lying in a hole in the ground. And why, why? Confusedly he felt that some extraordinary kind of justice was being done. In the past he had been wanton and imbecile and irresponsible. Now Fate was playing as wantonly, as irresponsibly, with him. It was tit for tat, and God existed after all.

He felt that he would like to pray. Forty years ago he used to kneel by his bed every evening. The nightly formula of his childhood came to him almost unsought from some long unopened chamber of the memory. "God bless Father and Mother, Tom and Cissie and the Baby, Mademoiselle and Nurse, and everyone that I love, and make me a good boy. Amen." They were all dead now—all except Cissie.

His mind seemed to soften and dissolve; a great calm descended upon his spirit. He went upstairs to ask Doris's forgiveness. He found her lying on the couch at the foot of the bed. On the floor beside her stood a blue bottle of liniment, marked "Not to be taken"; she seemed to have drunk about half of it.

"You didn't love me," was all she said when she opened her eyes to find him bending over her.

Dr. Libbard arrived in time to prevent any very serious consequences. "You mustn't do this again," he said while Mr. Hutton was out of the room.

"What's to prevent me?" she asked defiantly.

Dr. Libbard looked at her with his large, sad eyes. "There's nothing to prevent you," he said. "Only yourself and your baby. Isn't it rather bad luck on your baby, not allowing it to come into the world because you want to go out of it?"

Doris was silent for a time. "All right," she whispered. "I won't."

Mr. Hutton sat by her bedside for the rest of the night. He felt himself now to be indeed a murderer. For a time he persuaded himself that he loved this pitiable child. Dozing in his chair, he woke up, stiff and cold, to find himself drained dry, as it were, of every emotion. He had become nothing but a tired and suffering carcass. At six o'clock he undressed and went to bed for a couple of hours' sleep. In the course of the same afternoon the coroner's jury brought in a verdict of "Willful Murder," and Mr. Hutton was committed for trial.

VI

Miss Spence was not at all well. She had found her public appearances in the witness-box very trying, and when it was all over she had something that was very nearly a breakdown. She slept badly, and suffered from nervous indigestion. Dr. Libbard used to call every other day. She talked to him a great deal—mostly about the Hutton case. . . . Her moral indignation was always on the boil? Wasn't it appalling to think that one had had a murderer in one's house? Wasn't it extraordinary that one could have been for so long mistaken about the man's character? (But she had had an inkling from the first.) And then the girl he had gone off with—so low class, so little better than a prostitute. The news that the second Mrs. Hutton was expecting a baby—the posthumous child of a condemned and executed criminal—revolted her; the thing was shocking—an obscenity. Dr. Libbard answered her gently and vaguely, and prescribed bromide.

One morning he interrupted her in the midst of her customary tirade. "By the way," he said in his soft, melancholy voice, "I suppose it was really you who poisoned Mrs. Hutton."

Miss Spence stared at him for two or three seconds with enormous eyes, and then quietly said "Yes." After that she started to cry.

"In the coffee, I suppose."

She seemed to nod assent. Dr. Libbard took out his fountain-pen, and in his neat, meticulous calligraphy wrote out a prescription for a sleeping-draught.

The Yellow Slugs

H. C. Bailey

THE BIG car closed up behind a florid funeral procession which held the middle of the road. On either side was a noisy congestion of lorries. Mr. Fortune sighed and closed his eyes.

When he looked out again he was passing the first carriage of another funeral, and saw beneath the driver's seat the white coffin of a baby. For the road served the popular cemetery of Blaney.

Two slow miles of dingy tall houses and cheap shops slid by, with vistas of meaner streets opening on either side. The car gathered speed across Blaney Common, an expanse of yellow turf and bare sand, turbid pond and scrubwood, and stopped at the brown pile of an old poor law hospital.

Entering its carbolic odor, Mr. Fortune was met by Superintendent Bell. "Here I am," he moaned. "Why am I?"

"Well, she's still alive, sir," said Bell. "They both are."

Mr. Fortune was taken to a ward in which, secluded by a screen, a little girl lay asleep.

Her face had a babyish fatness, but in its pallor looked bloated and unhealthy. Though the close July air was oppressive and she was covered with heavy bedclothes, her skin showed no sign of heat and she slept still as death.

Reggie sat down beside her. His hands moved gently within the bed. . . . He listened . . . he looked . . .

A nurse followed him to the door. "How old, do you think?" he murmured.

"That was puzzling me, sir. She's big enough for seven or eight, but all flabby. And when she came to she was talking almost baby talk. I suppose she may be only about five."

Reggie nodded. "Quite good, yes. All right. Carry on."

From the ward he passed to a small room where a nurse and a doctor stood together watching the one bed.

A boy lay in it, restless and making noises—inarticulate words mixed with moaning and whimpering.

The doctor lifted his eyebrows at Reggie. "Get that?" he whispered. "Still talking about hell. He came absolutely unstuck. I had to risk a shot of morphia. I——" He broke off in apprehension as Reggie's round face hardened to a cold severity. But Reggie nodded and moved to the bed. . . .

The boy tossed into stertorous sleep, one thin arm flung up above a tousled head. His sunken cheeks were flushed, and drops of sweat stood on the upper lip and the brow. Not a bad brow—not an uncomely face but for its look of hungry misery—not the face of a child—a face which had been the prey of emotions and thwarted desires. . . .

Reggie's careful hands worked over him . . . bits of the frail body were laid bar. . . . Reggie stood up, and still his face was set in ruthless, passionless determination.

Outside the door the doctor spoke nervously. "I hope you don't——"

"Morphia's all right," Reggie interrupted. "What do you make of him?"

"Well, Mr. Fortune, I wish you'd seen him at first." The doctor was uncomfortable beneath the cold insistence of a questioning stare. "He was right out of hand—a sort of hysterical fury. I should say he's quite abnormal. Neurotic lad, badly nourished—you can't tell what they won't do, that type."

"I can't. No. What age do you give him?"

"Now you've got me. To hear him raving, you'd think he was grown up, such a flow of language. Bible phrases and preaching. I'd say he was a twelve-year-old, but he might only be eight or ten. His development is all out of balance. He's unhealthy right through."

"Yes, that is so," Reggie murmured. "However. You ought to save him."

"Poor little devil," said the doctor.

In a bare, grim waiting-room Reggie sat down with Superintendent Bell, and Bell looked anxiety. "Well, sir?"

"Possible. Probable," Reggie told him. "On the evidence."

"Ah. Cruel, isn't it? I hate these child cases."

"Any more evidence?" Reggie drawled.

Bell stared at his hard calm gloomily. "I have. Plenty."

The story began with a small boy on the bank of one of the ponds on Blaney Common. That was some time ago. That was the first time anybody in authority had been aware of the existence of Eddie Hill. One of the keepers of the common made the discovery. The pond was that one which children used for the sailing of toy boats. Eddie Hill had no boat, but he loitered round all the morning, watching the boats of other children. There was little wind, and one boat lay becalmed in the middle of the pond when the children had to go home to dinner.

An hour later the keeper saw Eddie Hill wade into the pond and run away. When the children came back from dinner there was no boat to be seen. Its small owner made weeping complaint to the keeper, who promised to keep his eyes open, and some days later found Eddie Hill and his little sister Bessie lurking among the gorse of the common with the stolen boat.

It was taken from them and their sin reported to their mother, who promised vengeance.

Their mother kept a little general shop. She had been there a dozen years—ever since she married her first husband. She was well liked and looked up to; a religious woman, regular chapel-goer and all that. Her second husband, Brightman, was the same sort—hardworking, respectable man; been at the chapel longer than she had.

The day-school teachers had nothing against Eddie or the little girl. Eddie was rather more than usually bright, but dreamy and careless; the girl a bit stodgy. Both of 'em rather less naughty than most.

"Know a lot, don't you?" Reggie murmured. "Got all this to-day?"

"No, this was all on record," Bell said. "Worked out for another business."

"Oh. Small boy and small girl already old offenders. Go on."

The other business was at the chapel Sunday school. Eddie Hill, as the most regular of its pupils, was allowed the privilege of tidying up at the end of the afternoon. On a Sunday in the spring the super-intendent came in unexpectedly upon the process and found Eddie holding the money-box in which had been collected the contribu-tions of the school to the chapel missionary society.

Eddie had no need nor right to handle the money-box. Moreover, on the bench beside him were pennies and a sixpence. Such wealth could not be his own. Only the teachers ever put in silver. Moreover, he confessed that he had extracted the money by rattling the box upside down, and his small sister wept for the sin.

The superintendent took him to the police station and charged him with theft.

"Virtuous man," Reggie murmured.

"It does seem a bit harsh," Bell said. "But they'd had suspicions about the money-box before. They'd been watching for something like this. Well, the boy's mother came and tried to beg him off, but of course the case had to go on. The boy came up in the Juvenile Court—you know the way, Mr. Fortune; no sort of criminal atmosphere, magistrate talking like a father. He let the kid off with a lecture."

"Oh, yes. What did he say? Bringin' down mother's grey hairs in sorrow to the grave—wicked boy—goin' to the bad in this world and the next—anything about hell?"

"I couldn't tell you." Bell was shocked. "I heard he gave the boy a rare old talking to. I don't wonder. Pretty bad, wasn't it, the Sunday-school money-box? What makes you bring hell into it?"

"I didn't. The boy did. He was raving about hell to-day. Part of the evidence. I was only tracin' the origin."

"Ah. I don't like these children's cases," Bell said gloomily. "They don't seem really human sometimes. You get a twisted kind of child and he'll talk the most frightful stuff—and do it too. We can only go by acts, can we?"

"Yes. That's the way I'm goin'. Get on."

The sharp impatience of the tone made Bell look at him with some reproach. "All right, sir. The next thing is this morning's business. I gave you the outline of that on the phone. I've got the full details now. This is what it comes to. Eddie and his little sister were seen on the common; the keepers have got to keep an eye on him. He wandered about with her—he has a casual, drifting sort of way, like some of these queer kids do have—and they came to the big pond. That's not a children's place at all; it's too deep; only dog bathing and fishing. There was nobody near; it was pretty early. Eddie and Bessie went along the bank, and a laborer who was scything thistles says the little girl was crying, and Eddie seemed to be scolding her, and then he fair chucked her in and went in with her. That's what it looked like to the keeper who was watchin' 'em. Him and the other chap, they nipped down and chucked the life-buoy; got it right near, but Eddie didn't take hold of it; he was clutching the girl and sinking and coming up again. So the keeper went in to 'em and had trouble getting 'em out. The little girl was unconscious, and Eddie sort of fought him." Bell stopped and gave a look of inquiry, but Reggie said nothing, and his face showed neither opinion nor feeling. "Well, you know how it is with these rescues from the water," Bell went on. "People often seem to be fighting to drown themselves and it don't mean anything except fright. And about the boy throwing the girl in—that might have been just a bit of a row or play—it's happened often—not meant vicious at all; and then he'd panic, likely enough." Again Bell looked an anxious question at the cold, passionless face. "I mean to say, I wouldn't have bothered you with it, Mr. Fortune, but for the way the boy carried on when they got him out. There he was with his little sister unconscious, and the keeper doing artificial respiration, and he called out, "Don't do it. Bessie's dead. She must be dead." And the keeper asked him, "Do you want her dead, you little devil?" And he said, "Yes, I do. I had to." Then the laborer chap came back with help and they got hold of Eddie; he was raving, flinging himself about and screaming if she lived she'd only get like him and go to hell, so she must be dead. While they brought him along here he was sort of preaching to 'em bits of the Bible, and mad stuff about the wicked being sent to hell and tortures for 'em."

"Curious and interestin'," Reggie drawled. "Any particular torture?"

"I don't know. The whole thing pretty well gave these chaps the horrors. They didn't get all the boy's talk. I don't wonder. There was something about worms not dying, they told me. That almost turned 'em up. Well—there you are, Mr. Fortune. What do you make of it?"

"I should say it happened," Reggie said. "All of it. As stated."

"You feel sure he could have thrown that fat little girl in? He seemed to me such a weed."

"Yes. Quite a sound point. I took that point. Development of both children unhealthy. Girl wrongly nourished. Boy inadequately nourished. Boy's physique frail. However. He could have done it. Lots of nervous energy. Triumph of mind over matter."

Bell drew in his breath. "You take it cool."

"Only way to take it," Reggie murmured, and Bell shifted uncomfortably. He has remarked since that he had seen Mr. Fortune look like that once or twice before—sort of inhuman, heartless, and inquisitive; but there it seemed all wrong, it didn't seem his way at all.

Reggie settled himself in his chair and spoke—so Bell has reported, and this is the only criticism which annoys Mr. Fortune—like a lecturer. "Several possibilities to be considered. The boy may be merely a precocious rascal. Having committed some iniquity which the little girl knew about, he tried to drown her to stop her giving him away. Common type of crime, committed by children as well as their elders."

"I know it is," Bell admitted. "But what could he have done that was worth murdering his sister?"

"I haven't the slightest idea. However. He did steal. Proved twice by independent evidence. Don't blame if you don't want. 'There, but for the grace of God, go I.' I agree. Quite rational to admit that consideration. We shall certainly want it. But he knew he was a thief; he knew it got him into trouble—that's fundamental."

"All right," said Bell gloomily. "We have to take it like that."

"Yes. No help. Attempt to murder sister may be connected with consciousness of sin. I should say it was. However. Other possibilities. He's a poor little mess of nerves; he's unsound, physically, mentally, spiritually. He may not have meant to murder her at all; may have got in a passion and not known what he was doing."

"Ah. That's more likely." Bell was relieved.

"You think so? Then why did he tell everybody he did mean to murder her?"

"Well, he was off his head, as you were saying. That's the best explanation of the whole thing. It's really the only explanation. Look at your first idea: he wanted to kill her so she couldn't tell about some crime he'd done. You get just the same question, why did he say he meant murder? He must know killing is worse than stealing. However you take the thing, you work back to his being off his head." Reggie's eyelids drooped. "I was brought here to say he's mad. Yes. I gather that. You're a merciful man, Bell. Sorry not to satisfy your gentle nature. I could swear he's mentally abnormal. If that would do any good. I couldn't say he's mad. I don't know. I can find you mental experts who would give evidence either way."

"I know which a jury would believe," Bell grunted.

"Yes. So do I. Merciful people, juries. Like you. Not my job. I'm lookin' for the truth. One more possibility. The boy's motive was just what he said it was—to kill his little sister so she shouldn't get wicked and go to hell. That fits the other facts. He'd got into the way of stealing; it had been rubbed into him that he was doomed to hell. So, if he found her goin' the same way, he might think it best she should die while she was still clean."

"Well, if that isn't mad!" Bell exclaimed.

"Abnormal, yes. Mad—I wonder," Reggie murmured.

"But it's sheer crazy, sir. If he believed he was so wicked, the thing for him to do was to pull up and go straight, and see that she did too."

"Yes. That's common sense, isn't it?" A small, contemptuous smile lingered a moment on Reggie's stern face. "What's the use of common sense here? If he was like this—sure he was going to hell; sure she was bein' driven there too—kind of virtuous for him to kill her to save her. Kind of rational. Desperately rational. Ever know any children, Bell? Some of 'em do believe what they're taught. Some of 'em take it seriously. Abnormal, as you say. Eddie Hill is abnormal." He turned and looked full at Bell, his blue eyes dark in the failing light. "Aged twelve or so—too bad to live—or too good. Pleasant case."

Bell moved uneasily. "These things do make you feel queer," he grunted. "What it all comes to though—we mean much the same—the boy ought to be in a home. That can be worked."

"A home!" Reggie's voice went up, and he laughed. "Yes. Official home for mentally defective. Yes. We can do that. I dare say we shall." He stood up and walked to the window and looked out at the dusk. "These children had a home of their own. And a mother. What's she doing about 'em?"

"She's been here, half off her head, poor thing," said Bell. "She wouldn't believe the boy meant any harm. She told me he couldn't, he was so fond of his sister. She said it must have been accident."

"Quite natural and motherly. Yes. But not adequate. Because it wasn't accident, whatever it was. We'd better go and see mother."

"If you like," Bell grunted reluctantly.

"I don't like," Reggie mumbled. "I don't like anything. I'm not here to do what I like." And they went.

People were drifting home from the common. The mean streets of Blaney had already grown quiet in the sultry gloom.

Shutters were up at the little shop which was the home of Eddie Hill, and still bore in faded paint his father's name. No light showed in the windows above. Bell rapped on the door, and they waited in vain. He moved to a house door close beside the shop. "Try this. This may be theirs too," he said, and knocked and rang.

After a minute it was opened by a woman who said nothing, but stared at them. From somewhere inside came the sound of a man's voice, talking fervently.

The light of the street lamp showed her of full figure, in neat black, and a face which was still pretty but distressed.

"You remember me, Mrs. Brightman," said Bell. "I'm Superintendent Bell."

"I know." She was breathless. "What's the matter? Are they—is Eddie—what's happened?"

"They're doing all right. I just want a little talk with you."

"Oh, they're all right. Praise God!" She turned; she called out: "Matthew, Matthew dear, they're all right."

The man's voice went on talking with the same fervor, but not in answer.

"I'll come in, please," said Bell.

"Yes, do. Thank you kindly. Mr. Brightman would like to see you. We were just asking mercy."

She led the way along a passage, shining clean, to a room behind the shop. There a man was on his knees praying, and most of the prayer was texts: "And we shall sing of mercy in the morning. Amen. Amen." He made an end.

He stood up before them, tall and gaunt, a bearded man with melancholy eyes. He turned to his wife. "What is it, my dear? What do the gentlemen want?"

"It's about the children, Matthew." His wife came and took his arm. "It's the police superintendent, I told you. He was so kind."

The man sucked in his breath. "Ay, ay. Please sit down. They must sit down, Florrie." There was a fluster of setting chairs. "This is kind, sir. What can you tell us to-night?"

"Doin' well. Both of 'em," Reggie said.

"There's our answer, Florrie," the man said, and smiled, and his somber eyes glowed. "There's our prayers answered."

"Yes. I think they're going to live," said Reggie. "But that's not the only thing that matters. We have to ask how it was they were nearly drowned."

"It was an accident. It must have been," the woman cried. "I'm sure Eddie wouldn't—he never would, would he, Matthew?"

"I won't believe it," Brightman answered quickly.

"Quite natural you should feel like that," Reggie nodded. "However. We have to deal with the facts."

"You must do what you think right, sir, as it is shown you." Brightman bent his head.

"Yes, I will. Yes. Been rather a naughty boy, hasn't he?"

Brightman looked at his wife's miserable face and turned to them again. "The police know," he said. "He has been a thief—twice he has been a thief—but little things. There is mercy, surely there is mercy for repentance. If his life is spared, he should not be lost; we must believe that."

"I do," Reggie murmured. "Any special reason why he should have been a thief?"

Brightman shook his head. "He's always had a good home, I'm sure," the woman moaned. She looked round her room, which was ugly and shabby, but all in the cleanest order.

"What can I say?" Brightman shook his head. "We've always done our best for him. There's no telling how temptation comes, sir, and it's strong and the little ones are weak."

"That is so. Yes. How much pocket-money did they have?"

"Eddie has had his twopence a week since he was ten," Brightman answered proudly. "And Bessie has her penny."

"I see. And was there anything happened this morning which upset Bessie or Eddie?"

"Nothing at all, sir. Nothing that I know." Brightman turned to his wife. "They went off quite happy, didn't they?"

"Yes, of course they did," she said eagerly. "They always loved to have a day on the common. They took their lunch, and they went running as happy as happy—and then this," she sobbed.

"My dearie." Brightman patted her.

"Well, well." Reggie stood up. "Oh. By the way. Has Eddie—or Bessie—ever stolen anything at home here—money or what not?"

Brightman started and stared at him. "That's not fair, sir. That's not a right thing to ask. There isn't stealing between little ones and their mother and father."

"No. As you say. No," Reggie murmured. "Good night. You'll hear how they go on. Good night."

"Thank you, sir. We shall be anxious to hear. Good night, sir," said Brightman, and Mrs. Brightman showed them out with tearful gratitude. As the door was opened, Brightman called: "Florrie! Don't bolt it. Mrs. Wiven hasn't come back."

"I know. I know," she answered, and bade them good night and shut the door.

A few paces away, Reggie stopped and looked back at the shuttered shop and the dark windows. "Well, well. What does the professional mind make of all that?"

"Just what you'd expect, wasn't it?" Bell grunted.

"Yes. Absolutely. Poor struggling shopkeepers, earnestly religious, keeping the old house like a new pin. All in accordance with the evidence." He sniffed the night air. "Dank old house."

"General shop smell. All sorts of things mixed up."

"As you say. There were. And there would be. Nothing you couldn't have guessed before we went. Except that Mrs. Wiven is expected—whoever Mrs. Wiven is."

"I don't know. Sounds like a lodger."

"Yes, that is so. Which would make another resident in the home of Eddie and Bessie. However. She's not come back yet. So we can go home. The end of a beastly day. And to-morrow's another one. I'll be out to see the children in the morning. Oh, my Lord! Those children." His hand gripped Bell's arm. . . .

By eight o'clock in the morning he was at the bedside of Bessie Hill—an achievement of stupendous but useless energy, for she did not wake till half past.

Then he took charge. A responsible position, which he interpreted as administering to her cups of warm milk and bread and butter. She consumed them eagerly; she took his service as matter of course.

"Good girl." Reggie wiped her mouth. "Feelin' better?"

She sighed and snuggled down, and gazed at him with large eyes. "Umm. Who are you?"

"They call me Mr. Fortune. Is it nice here?"

"Umm. Comfy." The big eyes were puzzled and wondering. "Where is it?"

"Blaney Hospital. People brought you here after you were in the pond. Do you remember?"

She shook her head. "Is Eddie here?"

"Oh, yes. Eddie's asleep. He's all right. Were you cross with Eddie?"

Tears came into the brown eyes. "Eddie was cross wiv me," the child whimpered. "I wasn't. I wasn't. Eddie said must go into ve water. I didn't want. But Eddie was so cross. Love Eddie."

"Yes. Little girl." Reggie stroked her hair. "Eddie shouldn't have been cross. Just a little girl. But Eddie isn't often cross, is he?"

"No. Love Eddie. Eddie's dear."

"Why was he cross yesterday?"

The brown eyes opened wider. "I was naughty. It was Mrs. Wiven. Old Mrs. Wiven. I did go up to her room. I didn't fink she was vere.

Sometimes is sweeties. But she was vere. She scolded me. She said I was little fief. We was all fiefs. And Eddie took me away and oh, he was so cross; he said I would be wicked and must not be. But I aren't. I aren't. Eddie was all funny and angry, and said not to be like him and go to hell, and then he did take me into pond wiv him. I didn't want. I didn't want!"

"No. Of course not. No. Poor little girl. Eddie didn't understand. But it's all right now."

"Is Eddie still cross wiv me?" she whimpered.

"Oh, no. No. Eddie won't be cross any more. Nobody's cross, little girl." Reggie bent over her. "Everybody's going to be kind now. You only have to be quiet and happy. That's all."

"Oooh." She gazed up at him. "Tell Eddie I'm sorry."

"Yes. I'll tell him." Reggie kissed her hand and turned away.

The nurse met him at the door. "Did she wake in the night?" he whispered.

"Yes, sir, asking for Eddie. She's a darling, isn't she? She makes me cry, talking like that of him."

"That won't do any harm," Reggie said, and his face hardened. "But you mustn't talk about him."

He went to the room where Eddie lay. The doctor was there, and turned from the bedside to confer with him. "Not too bad. We've put in a long sleep. Quite quiet since we walked. Very thirsty. Taken milk with a dash of coffee nicely. But we're rather flat."

Reggie sat down by the bed. The boy lay very still. His thin face was white. Only his eyes moved to look at Reggie, so little open, their pupils so small that they seemed all greenish-grey. He gave no sign of recognition, or feeling, or intelligence. Reggie put a hand under the clothes and found him cold and damp, and felt for his pulse.

"Well, young man, does anything hurt you now?"

"I'm tired. I'm awful tired," the boy said.

"Yes. I know. But that's going away."

"No, it isn't; it's worse. I didn't ought to have waked up." The faint voice was drearily peevish. "I didn't want to. It's no good. I thought I was dead. And it was good being dead."

"Was it?" Reggie said sharply.

The boy gave a quivering cry. "Yes, it was!" His face was distorted with fear and wonder. "I thought it would be so dreadful and it was all quiet and nice, and then I wasn't dead, I was alive and everything's awful again. I've got to go on still."

"What's awful in going on?" said Reggie. "Bessie wants you. Bessie sent you her love. She's gettin' well quick."

"Bessie? Bessie's here in bed like I am?" The unnatural greenish eyes stared.

"Of course she is. Only much happier than you are."

The boy began to sob.

"Why do you cry about that?" Reggie said. "She's got to be happy. Boys and girls have to be happy. That's what they're for. You didn't want Bessie to die."

"I did. You know I did," the boy sobbed.

"I know you jumped in the pond with her. That was silly. But you'd got rather excited, hadn't you? What was it all about?"

"They'll tell you," the boy muttered.

"Who will?"

"The keepers, the p'lice, the m-magistrate, everybody. I'm wicked. I'm a thief. I can't help it. And I didn't want Bessie to be wicked too."

"Of course you didn't. And she isn't. What ever made you think she was?"

"But she was." The boy's voice was shrill. "She went to Mrs. Wiven's room. She was looking for pennies. I know she was. She'd seen me. And Mrs. Wiven said we were all thieves. So I had to."

"Oh, no, you hadn't. And you didn't. You see? Things don't happen like that."

"Yes, they do. There's hell. Where their worms don't die."

The doctor made a muttered exclamation.

Reggie's hand held firm at the boy's as he moved and writhed. "There's God too," he murmured. "God's kind. Bessie's not going to be wicked. You don't have to be wicked. That's what's come of it all. Somebody's holding you up now." His hand pressed. "Feel?" The boy's lips parted; he looked up in awe. "Yes. Like that. You'll see me again and again. Now good-bye. Think about me. I'm thinking about you.". . . He stayed a while longer before he said another "Good-bye."

Outside, in the corridor, the doctor spoke: "I say, Mr. Fortune, you got him then. That was the stuff. I thought you were driving hard before. Sorry I spoke."

"I was." Reggie frowned. His round face was again of a ruthless severity. "'Difficult matter to play with souls,'" he mumbled. "We've got to." He looked under drooping eyelids. "Know the name of the keeper who saw the attempted drowning? Fawkes? Thanks."

He left the hospital and walked across the common.

The turf was parched and yellow, worn away on either side, paths loosened by the summer drought. Reggie descried the brown coat of a keeper, made for him, and was directed to where Fawkes would be.

Fawkes was a slow-speaking, slow-thinking old soldier, but he knew his own mind.

There was no doubt in it that Eddie had tried to kill Bessie, no indignation, no surprise. Chewing his words, he gave judgment. He had known Eddie's sort, lots of 'em. 'Igh strung, wanting the earth, kicking up behind and before 'cause they couldn't get it. He didn't mind 'em. Rather 'ave 'em than young 'uns like sheep. But you'ad to dress 'em down proper. They was devils else. Young Eddie would 'ave to be for it.

That business of the boat? Yes, Eddie pinched that all right. Smart kid; you'd got to 'and him that. And yet not so smart. Silly, lying up with it on the common; just the way to get nabbed. Ought to 'ave took it 'ome and sailed it over at Wymond Park. Never been spotted then. But 'im and 'is sister, they made a reg'lar den up in the gorse. Always knew where to look for 'em. Silly. Why, they was up there yesterday, loafing round, before 'e did 'is drowning act.

"Take you there? I can, if you like."

Reggie did like. They went up the brown slopes of the common to a tangle of gorse and bramble over small sand-hills.

"There you are." The keeper pointed his stick to a patch of loose sand in a hollow. "That's young Eddie's funk-'ole. That's where we spotted 'em with the blinking boat."

Reggie came to the place. The sand had been scooped up by small hands into a low wall round a space which was decked out with pebbles, yellow petals of gorse, and white petals of bramble.

"Ain't that just like 'em!" The keeper was angrily triumphant. "They know they didn't ought to pick the flowers. As well as you and me they do, and they go and do it."

Reggie did not answer. He surveyed the pretense of a garden and looked beyond. "Oh, my Lord!" he muttered. On the ground lay a woman's bag.

"'Allo, 'allo." The keeper snorted. "They've been pinching something else."

Reggie took out his handkerchief, put his hand in it, and thus picked up the bag. He looked about him; he wandered to and fro, going delicately, examining the confusion of small footmarks, further and further away.

"Been all round, ain't they?" the keeper greeted him on his return.

"That is so. Yes." Reggie mumbled and looked at him with searching eyes. "Had any notice of a bag lost or stolen?"

"Not as I've 'eard. Better ask the 'ead keeper. 'E'll be up at the top wood about now."

The wood was a thicket of birch and crab-apple and thorn. As they came near, they saw on its verge the head keeper and two other men who were not in the brown coats of authority. One of these was Superintendent Bell. He came down the slope in a hurry.

"I tried to catch you at the hospital, Mr. Fortune," he said. "But I suppose you've heard about Mrs. Wiven?"

"Oh. The Mrs. Wiven who hadn't come back," Reggie said slowly. "No. I haven't heard anything."

"I thought you must have, by your being out here on the common. Well, she didn't come back at all. This morning Brightman turned up at the station very fussy and rattled to ask if they had any news of his lodger, Mrs. Wiven. She never came in last night, and he thought she must have had an accident or something. She'd been lodging with them for years. Old lady, fixed in her habits. Never went anywhere, that he knew of, except to chapel and for a cup o' tea with some of her chapel friends, and none of them had seen her. These fine summer days she'd take her food out and sit on the common here all day long. She went off yesterday morning with sandwiches and a vacuum flask of tea and her knitting. Often she wouldn't come home till it was getting dark. They didn't think much of her being late; sometimes she went in and had a bit o' supper with a friend. She had her key, and they left the door unbolted, like we heard, and went to bed, being worn out with the worry of the kids. But when Mrs. Brightman took up her cup of tea this morning and found she wasn't in her room, Brightman came running round to the station. Queer business, eh?"

"Yes. Nasty business. Further you go the nastier."

Bell looked at him curiously and walked him away from the keeper. "You feel it that way? So do I. Could you tell me what you were looking for out here—as you didn't know she was missing?"

"Oh, yes. I came to verify the reports of Eddie's performances."

"Ah! Have you found any error?"

"No. I should say everything happened as stated."

"The boy's going to get well, isn't he?"

"It could be. If he gets the chance."

"Poor little beggar," Bell grunted. "What do you really think about him, Mr. Fortune?"

"Clever child, ambitious child, imaginative child. What children ought to be—twisted askew."

"Kind of perverted, you mean."

"That is so. Yes. However. Question now is, not what I think of the chances of Eddie's soul, but what's been happening. Evidence inadequate, curious, and nasty. I went up to the private lair of Eddie and Bessie. Same where he was caught with the stolen boat. I found this." He showed Bell the woman's bag.

"My oath!" Bell muttered, and took it from him gingerly. "You wrapped it up! Thinkin' there might be fingerprints."

"Yes. Probably are. They might even be useful."

"And you went looking for this—not knowing the woman was missing?"

"Wasn't lookin' for it," Reggie snapped. "I was lookin' for anything there might be. Found a little pretense of a garden they'd played at—and this."

"Ah, but you heard last night about Mrs. Wiven, and this morning you go up where Eddie hides what he's stolen. Don't that mean you made sure there was something fishy? You see when we're blind, Mr. Fortune."

"Oh, no. I don't see. I knew more than you did. Little Bessie told me this morning she was in Mrs. Wiven's room yesterday, privily and by stealth, and Mrs. Wiven caught her and called her a thief, and said they were all thieves. I should think little Bessie may have meant to be a thief. Which would agree with Eddie's effort to drown her so she should die good and honest. But I don't see my way."

"All crazy, isn't it?" Bell grunted.

"Yes. The effort of Eddie is an incalculable factor. However. You'd better look at the bag."

Bell opened it with cautious fingers. A smell of peppermint came out. Within was a paper bag of peppermint lozenges, two unclean handkerchiefs marked E. W., an empty envelope addressed to Mrs. Wiven, a bottle of soda-mint tablets, and some keys.

"Evidence that it is the bag of the missing Mrs. Wiven strong," Reggie murmured. He peered into it. "But no money. Not a penny." He looked up at Bell with that cold, ruthless curiosity which Bell always talks about in discussing the case. "Stealin' is the recurrin' motive. You notice that?"

"I do." Bell started at him. "You take it cool, Mr. Fortune. I've got to own it makes me feel queer."

"No use feelin' feelings," Reggie drawled. "We have to go on. We want the truth, whatever it is."

"Well, all right, I know," Bell said gloomily. "They're searching the common for her. That's why I came out here. They knew her. She did sit about here in summer." He went back to the head keeper and conferred again. . . .

Reggie purveyed himself a deck-chair, and therein sat extended and lit a pipe and closed his eyes. . . .

"Mr. Fortune!" Bell stood over him. His lips emitted a stream of smoke. No other part of him moved. "They've found her. I suppose you expected that."

"Yes. Obvious possibility. Probable possibility." It has been remarked that Mr. Fortune has a singular capacity for becoming erect from a supine position. A professor of animal morphology once delivered a lecture upon him—after a hospital dinner—as the highest type of the invertebrates. He stood up from the deck-chair in one undulating motion. "Well, well. Where is the new fact?" he moaned.

Bell took him into the wood. No grass grew in it. Where the sandy soil was not bare, dead leaves made a carpet. Under the crab-apple trees, between the thorn-brakes, were nooks obviously much used by pairs of lovers. By one of these, not far from the whale-back edge of rising ground which was the wood's end, some men stood together.

On the grey sand there lay a woman's body. She was small; she was dressed in a coat and skirt of dark grey cloth and a black and white blouse. The hat on her grey hair was pulled to one side, giving her a look of absurd frivolity in ghastly contrast to the distortion of her pallid face. Her lips were closely compressed and almost white. The dead eyes stared up at the trees with dilated pupils.

Reggie walked round the body, going delicately, rather like a dog in doubt how to deal with another dog.

Beside the body was a raffia bag which held some knitting, a vacuum flask, and an opened packet of sandwiches.

Reggie's discursive eyes looked at them and looked again at the dead face, but not for long. He was more interested in the woman's skirt. He bent over that, examined it from side to side, and turned away and went on prowling further and further away, and as he went he scraped at the dry sand here and there.

When he came back to the body, his lips were curved in a grim, mirthless smile. He looked at Bell. "Photographer," he mumbled.

"Sent a man to phone, sir," Bell grunted.

Reggie continued to look at him. "Have you? Why have you?"

"Just routine." Bell was startled.

"Oh. Only that. Well, well." Reggie knelt down by the body. His hands went to the woman's mouth. . . . He took something from his pocket and forced the mouth open and looked in. . . . He closed the mouth again, and sat down on his heels and contemplated the dead woman with dreamy curiosity. . . . He opened her blouse. Upon the underclothes was a dark stain. He bent over that and smelt it; he drew the clothes from her chest.

"No wound, is there?" Bell muttered.

"Oh, no. No." Reggie put back the clothes and stood up and went to the flask and the sandwiches. He pulled the bread of an unfinished sandwich apart, looked at it, and put it down. He took the flask and shook it. It was not full. He poured some of the contents into its cup.

"Tea, eh?" said Bell. "Strong tea."

"Yes. It would be," Reggie murmured. He tasted it and spat, and poured what was in the cup back into the flask and corked it again and gave it to Bell.

"There you are. Cause of death, poisoning by oxalic acid or binoxalate of potassium—probably the latter—commonly called salts of lemon. And we shall find some in that awful tea. We shall also find it in the body. Tongue and mouth, white, contracted, eroded. Time of death, probably round about twenty-four hours ago. No certainty."

"My oath! It's too near certainty for my liking," Bell muttered.

"Is it?" Reggie's eyelids drooped. "Wasn't thinkin', about what you'd like. Other interestin' facts converge."

"They do!" Bell glowered at him. "One of the commonest kinds of poisoning, isn't it?"

"Oh, yes. Salts of lemon very popular."

"Anybody can get it."

"As you say. Removes stains, cleans brass and what not. Also quickly fatal, with luck. Unfortunate chemical properties."

"This boy Eddie could have got some easy."

"That is so. Yes. Lethal dose for a penny or two anywhere."

"Well, then—look at it!"

"I have," Reggie murmured. "Weird case. Ghastly case."

"Gives me the horrors," said Bell. "The old lady comes out here to spend the day as usual, and somebody's put a spot of poison in her drop o' tea and she dies; and her bag's stolen, and found without a farthing where the boy Eddie hides his loot. And, about the time the old lady's dying, Eddie tries to drown his sister. What are you going to make of that? What can you make of it? It was a poison any kid could get hold of. One of 'em must have poisoned her to steal her little bit o' money. But the girl's not much more than a baby. It must have been Eddie that did it—and that goes with the rest of his doings. He's got the habit of stealing. But his little sister saw something of it, knew too much, so he put up this drowning to stop her tongue—and then, when she was saved, made up this tale about killing her to keep her honest. Devilish, isn't it? And when you find a child playing the devil—my oath! But it is devilish clever—his tale would put the stealing and all the rest on the baby. And we can't prove anything else. She's too little to be able to get it clear, and he's made himself out driven wild by her goings on. If a child's really wicked, he beats you."

"Yes, that is so," Reggie drawled. "Rather excited, aren't you? Emotions are not useful in investigation. Prejudice the mind into exaggeratin' facts and ignorin' other facts. Both fallacies exhibited in your argument. You mustn't ignore what Bessie did say—that she went into Mrs. Wiven's room yesterday morning and Mrs. Wiven caught her. I shouldn't wonder if you found Bessie's fingerprints on that bag."

"My Lord!" Bell stared at him. "It's the nastiest case I ever had. When it comes to babies in murder——"

"Not nice, no. Discoverin' the possibilities of corruption of the soul. However. We haven't finished yet. Other interestin' facts have been ignored by Superintendent Bell. Hallo!" Several men were approaching briskly. "Is this your photographer and other experts?"

"That's right. Photographer and fingerprint men."

"Very swift and efficient." Reggie went to meet them. "Where did you spring from?"

"By car, sir." The photographer was surprised. "On the road up there. We had the location by phone."

"Splendid. Now then. Give your attention to the lady's skirt. Look." He indicated a shining streak across the dark stuff. "Bring that out."

"Can do, sir," the photographer said, and fell to work.

Reggie turned to Bell. "Then they'll go over the whole of her for fingerprints, what? And the sandwich paper. And the flask. Not forgettin' the bag. That's all. I've finished here. She can be taken to the mortuary for me."

"Very good," Bell said, and turned away to give the orders, but, having given them, stood still to stare at the thin glistening streak on the skirt.

Reggie came quietly to his elbow. "You do notice that? Well, well." Bell looked at him with a puzzled frown and was met for the first time in this case by a small, satisfied smile which further bewildered him. He bent again to pore over the streak. "It's all right." Reggie's voice was soothing. "That's on record now. Come on." Linking arms, he drew Bell away from the photographers and the fingerprint men. "Well? What does the higher intelligence make of the line on the skirt?"

"I don't know. I can't make out why you think so much of it."

"My dear chap! Oh, my dear chap!" Reggie moaned. "Crucial fact. Decisive fact." He led Bell on out of the wood and across the common, and at a respectful distance Bell's two personal satellites followed.

"Decisive, eh?" Bell frowned. "It was just a smear of something to me. You mean salts of lemon would leave a shiny stain?"

"Oh, no. No. Wouldn't shine at all."

"Has she been sick on her skirt?"

"Not there. No. Smear wasn't human material."

"Well, I thought it wasn't. What are you thinking of?"

"I did think of what Eddie said—where their worm dieth not."

"My God!" Bell muttered. "Worms?" He gave a shudder. "I don't get you at all, sir. It sounds mad."

"No. Connection is sort of desperate rational. I told you Eddie was like that. However. Speakin' scientifically, not a worm, but a slug. That streak was a slug's trail."

"Oh. I see." Bell was much relieved. "Now you say so, it did look like that. The sort o' slime a slug leaves behind. It does dry shiny, of course."

"You have noticed that?" Reggie admired him. "Splendid!"

Bell was not pleased. "I have seen slugs before," he grunted. "But what is there to make a fuss about? I grant you, it's nasty to think of a slug crawling over the woman as she lay there dead. That don't mean anything, though. Just what you'd expect, with the body being all night in the wood. Slugs come out when it gets dark."

"My dear chap! Oh, my dear chap!" Reggie moaned. "You mustn't talk like that. Shakes confidence in the police force. Distressin' mixture of inadequate observation and fallacious reasonin'."

"Thank you. I don't know what's wrong with it." Bell was irritated.

"Oh, my Bell! You shock me. Think again. Your general principle's all right. Slugs do come out at night. Slugs like the dark. That's a general truth which has its particular application. But you fail to observe the conditions. The body was in a wood with no herbage on the ground: and the ground was a light dry sand. These are not conditions which attract the slug. I should have been much surprised if I'd found any slugs there, or their tracks. But I looked for 'em—which you didn't, Bell. I'm always careful. And there wasn't a trace. No. I can't let you off. A slug had crawled over her skirt, leavin' his slime from side to side. And yet his slime didn't go beyond her skirt on to the ground anywhere. How do you suppose he managed that? Miracle—by a slug. I don't believe in miracles if I can help it, I object to your simple faith in the miraculous gastropod. It's lazy."

"You go beyond me," said Bell uneasily. "You grasp the whole thing while I'm only getting bits. What do you make of it all?"

"Oh, my Bell!" Reggie reproached him. "Quite clear. When the slug walked over her, she wasn't lying where she was found."

"Is that all?" Bell grunted. "I dare say. She might have had her dose, and felt queer and lay down, and then moved on to die where we found her. Nothing queer in that, is there?"

"Yes. Several things very queer. It could be. Oxalic poisoning might lay her out and still let her drag herself somewhere else to die. Not likely she'd take care to bring her flask and her sandwiches with her. Still less likely she'd lie long enough for a slug to walk over her and then recover enough to move somewhere else—and choose to move into the wood, where she wouldn't be seen. Why should she? She'd try for help if she could try for anything. And, finally, most unlikely she'd find any place here with slugs about. Look at it; it's all arid and sandy and burnt up by the summer. No. Quite unconvincin' explanation. The useful slug got on to her somewhere else. The slug is decisive."

"Then you mean to say she was poisoned some other place, and brought here dead?" Bell frowned. "It's all very well. You make it sound reasonable. But would you like to try this slug argument on a jury? They'd never stand for it, if you ask me. It's all too clever."

"You think so?" Reggie murmured. "Well, well. Then it does give variety to the case. We haven't been very clever so far. However. Study to improve. There is further evidence. She'd been sick. Common symptom of oxalic poisoning. But she'd been sick on her underclothes and not on her outside clothes. That's very difficult. Think about it. Even juries can be made to think sometimes. Even coroners, which is very hard. Even judges. I've done it in my time, simple as I am. I might do it again. Yes, I might. With the aid of the active and intelligent police force. Come on."

"What do you want to do?"

"Oh, my Bell! I want to call on Mr. and Mrs. Brightman. We need their collaboration. We can't get on without it."

"All right. I don't mind trying 'em," Bell agreed gloomily. "We've got to find out all about the old woman somehow. We don't really know anything yet."

"I wouldn't say that. No," Reggie mumbled. "However. One moment."

They had come to the edge of the common by the hospital, where his car waited. He went across to it and spoke to his chauffeur.

"Just calmin' Sam," he apologized on his return. "He gets peevish when forgotten. Come on."

They arrived again at the little general shop. Its unshuttered window now enticed the public with a meager array of canned goods and cartons which had been there some time. The door was shut but not fastened. Opening it rang a bell. They went in, and found the shop empty, and for a minute or two stood in a mixture of smells through which soap was dominant.

Mrs. Brightman came from the room behind, wiping red arms and hands on her apron. Her plump face, which was tired and sweating, quivered alarm at the sight of them. "Oh, it's you!" she cried. "What is it? Is there anything?"

"Your children are doing well," said Reggie. "Thought I'd better let you know that."

She stared at him, and tears came into her eyes. "Praise God!" she gasped. "Thank you, sir, you're very kind."

"No. You don't have to thank me. I'm just doin' my job."

But again she thanked him, and went on nervously: "Have you heard anything of Mrs. Wiven?"

"I want to have a little talk about her. Is Mr. Brightman in?"

"No, he isn't, not just now. Have you got any news of her, sir?"

"Yes. There is some news. Sorry Mr. Brightman's out. Where's he gone?"

"Down to the yard, sir."

"Out at the back here?"

"No. No. Down at his own yard."

"Oh. He has a business of his own?"

"Yes, sir, a little business. Furniture dealing it is. Second-hand furniture."

"I see. Well, well. We could get one of the neighbors to run down and fetch him, what?" Reggie turned to Bell.

"That's the way," Bell nodded. "What's the address, ma'am?"

She swallowed. "It's just round the corner. Smith's Buildings. Anybody would tell you. But he might be out on a job, you know; I couldn't say."

Bell strode out, and the messenger he sent was one of his satellites.

"Well, while we're waitin', we might come into your nice little room," Reggie suggested. "There's one or two things you can tell me."

"Yes, sir, I'm sure, anything as I can, I'll be glad. Will you come through, please?" She lifted the flap of the counter for him, she opened the curtained glass door of the room behind. It was still in exact order, but she had to apologize for it. "I'm sorry we're all in a mess. I'm behindhand with my cleaning, having this dreadful trouble with the children and being so worried I can't get on. I don't half know what I'm doing, and then poor Mrs. Wiven being lost——" She stopped, breathless. "What is it about Mrs. Wiven, sir? What have you heard?"

"Not good news," Reggie said. "Nobody will see Mrs. Wiven alive again."

The full face grew pale beneath its sweat, the eyes stood out. "She's dead! Oh, the poor soul! But how do you know? How was it?"

"She's been found dead on the common."

Mrs. Brightman stared at him: her mouth came open and shook; she flung her apron over her head and bent and was convulsed with hysterical sobbing.

"Fond of her, were you?" Reggie sympathized.

A muffled voice informed him that she was a dear old lady—and so good to everybody.

"Was she? Yes. But I wanted to ask you about the children. What time did they go out yesterday?" Still sobbing under her apron, Mrs. Brightman seemed not to hear. "Yesterday morning," Reggie insisted. "You must remember. What time was it when Eddie and Bessie went out?"

After a moment the apron was pulled down from a swollen, tearful face. "What time?" she repeated looking at her lap and wiping her eyes. "I don't know exactly, sir. Just after breakfast. Might be somewheres about nine o'clock."

"Yes, it might be," Reggie murmured. "They were pulled out of the pond about ten."

"I suppose so," she whimpered. "What's it got to do with Mrs. Wiven?"

"You don't see any connection?"

She stared at him. "How could there be?"

The shop-door bell rang, and she started up to answer it. She found Bell in the shop. "Oh, have you found Mr. Brightman?" she cried.

"No, not yet. Where's Mr. Fortune?"

Reggie called to him, "Come on, Bell," and she brought him into the back room and stood looking from one to the other. "So Mr. Brightman wasn't in his yard?"

"No, sir. Nobody there. At least, they couldn't make anybody hear."

"Well, well," Reggie murmured.

"But I told you he might have gone off on a job. He often has to go to price some stuff or make an offer or something."

"You did say so. Yes," Reggie murmured. "However. I was asking about the children. Before they went out yesterday—Bessie got into trouble with Mrs. Wiven, didn't she?"

The woman looked down and plucked at her apron.

"You didn't tell us that last night," Reggie said.

"I didn't want to. I didn't see as it mattered. And I didn't want to say anything against Bessie. She's my baby." Her eyes were streaming. "Don't you see?"

"Bessie told me," said Reggie.

"Bessie confessed! Oh, it's all too dreadful. The baby! I don't know why this was to come on us. I brought 'em up to be good, I have. And she was such a darling baby. But it's God's will."

"Yes. What did happen?" said Reggie.

"Mrs. Wiven was always hard on the children. She never had a child herself, poor thing. Bessie got into her room, and Mrs. Wiven caught her and said she was prying and stealing like Eddie. I don't know what Bessie was doing there. Children will do such, whatever you do. And there was Bessie crying and Eddie all wild. He does get so out of himself. I packed 'em off, and I told Mrs. Wiven it wasn't nothing to be so cross about, and she got quite nice again. She was always a dear with me and Brightman. A good woman at heart, sir, she was."

"And when did Mrs. Wiven go out?" said Reggie.

"It must have been soon after. She liked her days on the common in summer, she did."

"Oh, yes. That's clear," Reggie stood up and looked out at the yard, where some washing was hung out to dry. "What was Mrs. Wiven wearing yesterday?"

"Let me see———" Mrs. Brightman was surprised by the turn in the conversation. "I don't rightly remember—she had on her dark coat and skirt. She always liked to be nicely dressed when she went." Under the frown of this mental effort swollen eyes blinked at him. "But you said she'd been found. You know what she had on."

"Yes. When she was on the common. Before she got there—what was she wearing?"

Mrs. Brightman's mouth opened and shut.

"I mean, when she caught Bessie in her room. What was she wearing then?"

"The same—she wouldn't have her coat on—I don't know as I remember—but the same—she knew she was going out—she'd dress for it—she wouldn't ever dress twice in a morning."

"Wouldn't she? She didn't have that overall on?" Reggie pointed to a dark garment hanging on the line in the yard which stretched from house to shed.

"No, she didn't, I'm sure. That was in the dirty clothes."

"But you had to wash it to-day. Well, well. Now we want to have a look at Mrs. Wiven's room."

"If you like. Of course, nothing's been done. It's all untidy." She led the way upstairs, lamenting that the house was all anyhow, she'd been so put about.

But Mrs. Wiven's room was primly neat and as clean as the shining passage and stairs. The paint had been worn thin by much washing, the paper was so faded that its rosebud pattern merged into a uniform pinkish grey. An old fur rug by the bedside, a square of threadbare carpet under the rickety round table in the middle of the room, were the only coverings of the scoured floor. The table had one cane chair beside it, and there was a small basket chair by the empty grate— nothing else in the room but the iron bedstead and a combination of chest of drawers, dressing-table, and washstand, with its mirror all brown spots.

Mrs. Brightman passed round the room, pulling this and pushing that. "I haven't even dusted," she lamented.

"Is this her own furniture?" Reggie asked.

"No, sir, she hadn't anything. We had to furnish it for her."

"Quite poor, was she?"

"I don't really know how she managed. And, of course, we didn't ever press her; you couldn't. She had her savings, I suppose. She'd been in good service, by what she used to say."

"No relations?"

"No, sir. She was left quite alone. That was really why she came to us, she was that lonely. She'd say to me she did so want a home, till we took her. When she was feeling down, she used to cry and tell me she didn't know what would become of her. Of course, we wouldn't ever have let her want, poor dear. But it's my belief her bit of money was running out."

Reggie gazed about the room. On the walls were many cards with texts.

"Mr. Brightman put up the good words for her," Mrs. Brightman explained, and gazed at one of the texts and cried.

"'In my Father's house are many mansions.'" Reggie read it out slowly, and again looked round the bare little room.

Mrs. Brightman sobbed. "Ah, she's gone there now. She's happy."

Bell was moving from one to the other of the cupboards beside the grate. Nothing was in them but clothes. He went on to the dressing-table. "She don't seem to have any papers. Only this." He lifted a cash-box, and money rattled in it.

"I couldn't say, I'm sure," Mrs. Brightman whimpered.

Reggie stood by the table. "Did she have her meals up here?" he asked.

Mrs. Brightman thought about that. "Mostly she didn't. She liked to sit down with us. She used to say it was more homey."

Reggie fingered the table-cloth, pulled it off, and looked at the cracked veneer beneath. He stooped, felt the strip of old carpet under the table, drew it back. On the boards beneath was a patch of damp.

Mrs. Brightman came nearer. "Well there!" she said. "That comes of my not doing out the room. She must have had a accident with her slops and never told me. She always would do things for herself."

Reggie did not answer. He wandered round the room, stopped by the window a moment, and turned to the door.

"I'm taking this cash-box, ma'am," said Bell.

"If you think right——" Mrs. Brightman drew back. "It's not for me to say—I don't mind, myself." She looked from one to the other. "Will that be all, then?"

"Nothing more here." Reggie opened the door.

As they went downstairs, the shop bell rang again, and she hurried on to answer it. The two men returned to the room behind the shop.

"Poor old woman," Bell grunted. "You can see what sort of a life she was having—that dingy room and her money running out—I wouldn't wonder if she committed suicide."

"Wouldn't it be wonderful. No," Reggie murmured. "Shut up."

From the shop came a man's voice, lazy and genial.

"Good afternoon, mum. I want a bit o' salts o' lemon. About two penn'worth would do me. 'Ow do you sell it?"

There was a mutter from Mrs. Brightman. "We don't keep it."

"What? They told me I'd be sure to get it 'ere. Run out of it, 'ave you? Ain't that too bad!"

"We never did keep it," Mrs. Brightman said. "Whoever told you we did?"

"All right, all right. Keep your hair on, missus. Where can I get it?"

"How should I know? I don't rightly know what it is."

"Don't you? Sorry I spoke. Used for cleaning, you know."

Bell glowered at Reggie, for the humorous cockney voice was the voice of his chauffeur. But the cold severity of Reggie's round face gave no sign.

"We don't use it, nor we don't keep it, nor any chemist's stuff," Mrs. Brightman was answering.

"Oh, good day!" The bell rang again as the shop door closed.

Mrs. Brightman came back. "Running in and out of the shop all day with silly people," she panted. She looked from one to the other, questioning, afraid.

"I was wonderin'," Reggie murmured. "Did Mrs. Wiven have her meals with you yesterday—or in her room?"

"Down here." The swollen eyes looked at him and looked away. "She did usual, I told you. She liked to."

"And which was the last meal she ever had?"

Mrs. Brightman suppressed a cry. "You do say things! Breakfast was the last she had here. She took out a bit o' lunch and tea."

"Yes. When was that put ready?"

"I had it done first thing, knowing she meant to get out—and she always liked to start early. It was there on the sideboard waiting at breakfast."

"Then it was ready before the children went out? Before she had her quarrel with Bessie?"

Mrs. Brightman swallowed. "So it was."

"Oh. Thank you. Rather strong, the tea in her flask," Reggie mumbled.

"She always had it fairly strong. Couldn't be too strong for her. I'm just the same myself."

"Convenient," Reggie said. "Now you'll take me down into the cellar, Mrs. Brightman."

"What?" She drew back so hastily that she was brought up by the wall. "The cellar?" Her eyes seemed to stand out more than ever, so they stared at him, the whites of them more widely bloodshot. With an unsteady hand she thrust back the hair from her sweating brow. "The cellar? Why ever do you want to go there? There's nothing in the cellar."

"You think not?" Reggie smiled. "Come down and see."

She gave a moaning cry; she stumbled away to the door at the back, and opened it, and stood holding by the door-post, looking out to the paved yard.

From the shed in it appeared Brightman's bearded face. "Were you looking for me, dearie?" he asked, and brought his lank shape into sight, brushing it as it came.

She made a gesture to him; she went to meet him and muttered: "Matthew! They're asking me to take 'em down to the cellar."

"Well, to be sure!" Brightman gave Reggie and Bell a glance of melancholy, pitying surprise. "I don't see any reason in that." He held her up, he stroked her and gently remonstrated. "But there's no reason they shouldn't go to the cellar if they want to, Florrie. We ain't to stand in the way of anything as the police think right. We ain't got anything to hide, have we? Come along, dearie."

An inarticulate quavering sound came from her.

"That's all right, my dearie, that's all right," Brightman soothed her.

"Is it?" Bell growled. "So you've been here all the time, Mr. Brightman. While she sent us to look for you down at your own place. Why didn't you show up before?"

"I've only just come in, sir," Brightman said quietly. "I came in by the back. I was just putting things to rights in the washhouse. The wife's been so pushed. I didn't know you gentlemen were here. You're searching all the premises, are you? I'm agreeable. I'm sure it's in order, if you say so. But I don't know what you're looking for."

"Mrs. Brightman will show us," said Reggie, and grasped her arm.

"Don't, don't," she wailed.

"You mustn't be foolish, dearie," said Brightman. "You know there's nothing in the cellar. Show the gentlemen if they want. It's all right. I'll go with you."

"Got a torch, Bell?" said Reggie.

"I have." Bell went back into the room. "And here's a lamp, too." He lit it.

Reggie draw the shaking woman through the room into the passage. "That's the door to your cellar. Open it. Come on."

Bell held the lamp overhead behind them. Reggie led her stumbling down the stairs, and Brightman followed close.

A musty, dank smell came about them. The lamplight showed a large cellar of brick walls and an earth floor. There was in it a small heap of coal, some sacks and packing-cases and barrels, but most of the dim space was empty. The light glistened on damp.

"Clay soil," Reggie murmured, and smiled at Brightman. "Yes. That was indicated."

"I don't understand you, sir," said Brightman.

"No. You don't. Torch, Bell." He took it and flashed its beam about the cellar. "Oh, yes." He turned to Bell. With a finger he indicated the shining tracks of slugs. "You see?"

"I do," Bell muttered.

Mrs. Brightman gave a choked, hysterical laugh.

Reggie moved to and fro. He stooped. He took out his pocketbook and from it a piece of paper, and with that scraped something from a barrel side, something from the clay floor, and sighed satisfaction.

Standing up, he moved the ray of the torch from place to place, held it steady at last to make a circle of light on the ground beneath the steps. "There," he said, and Mrs. Brightman screamed. "Yes. I know. That's where you put her. Look, Bell." His finger pointed to a slug's trail which came into the circle of light, stopped, and went on again at another part of the circle. "It didn't jump. They don't."

He swung round upon Mrs. Brightman. He held out to her the piece of paper cupped in his hand. On it lay two yellow slugs.

She flung herself back, crying loathing and fear.

"Really, gentlemen, really now," Brightman stammered. "This isn't right. This isn't proper. You've no call to frighten a poor woman so. Come away now, Florrie dearie." He pulled at her.

"Where are you going?" Reggie murmured. She did not go. Her eyes were set on the two yellow slugs. "'Where their worm dieth not,'" Reggie said slowly.

She broke out in the screams of hysterical laughter; she tore herself from Brightman, and reeled and fell down writhing and yelling.

"So that is that, Mr. Brightman." Reggie turned to him.

"You're a wicked soul!" Brightman whined. "My poor dearie!" He fell on his knees by her; he began to pray forgiveness for her sins.

"My oath!" Bell muttered, and ran up the steps shouting to his men. . . .

Some time afterwards the detective left to keep the little shop ushered Reggie out.

On the other side of the street, aloof from the gaping, gossiping crowd, superior and placid, his chauffeur smoked a cigarette. It was thrown away; the chauffeur followed him, fell into step beside him. "Did I manage all right, sir?" The chauffeur invited praise.

"You did. Very neat. Very effective. As you know. Side, Sam, side. We are good at destruction. Efficient incinerators. Humble function. Other justification for existence, doubtful. However. Study to improve. What we want now is a toyshop."

"Sir?" Sam was puzzled.

"I said a toyshop," Reggie complained. "A good toyshop. Quick." . . .

The last of the sunlight was shining into the little room at the hospital where Eddie Hill lay. Upon his bed stood part of a bridge built of strips of metal bolted together, a bridge of grand design. He and Reggie were working on the central span.

There was a tap at the door, a murmur from Reggie, and the nurse brought in Bell. He stood looking at Reggie with reproachful surprise. "So that's what you're doing," he protested.

"Yes. Something useful at last." Reggie sighed. "Well, well. We'll have to call this a day, young man. You've done enough. Mustn't get yourself tired."

"I'm not tired," the boy protested eagerly. "I'm not, really."

"No. Of course not. Ever so much better. But there's another day to-morrow. And you have a big job. Must keep fit to go on with it."

"All right." The boy lay back, looked at his bridge, looked wistfully at Reggie. "I can keep this here, can I, sir?"

"Rather. On the table by the bed. So it'll be there when you wake. Nice, making things, isn't it? Yes. You're going to make a lot now. Good-bye. Jolly, to-morrow, what? Good-bye." He went out with Bell. "Now what's the matter with you?" he complained.

"Well, I had to have a word with you, sir. This isn't going to be so easy. I thought I'd get you at the mortuary doing the post-mortem."

"Minor matter. Simple matter. Only the dead buryin' their dead. The boy was urgent. Matter of savin' life there."

"I'm not saying you're not right," said Bell wearily. "But it is a tangle of a case. The divisional surgeon reports Mrs. Brightman's mad. Clean off her head."

"Yes. I agree. What about it?"

"Seemed to me you pretty well drove her to it. Those slugs—oh, my Lord."

"Got you, did it? It rather got me. I'd heard Eddie talk of 'the worm that dieth not.' I should say he's seen that cellar. Dreamed of it. However. I didn't drive the woman mad. She'd been mad some time. Not medically mad. Not legally mad. But morally. That was the work of our Mr. Brightman. I only clarified the situation. He almost sent the boy the same way. That's been stopped. That isn't going to happen now. That's the main issue. And we win on it. Not too bad. But rather a grim day. Virtue has gone out of me. My dear chap!" He took Bell's arm affectionately. "You're tucked up too."

"I don't mind owning I've had enough," said Bell. "This sort of thing tells me I'm not as young as I was. And it's all a tangle yet."

"My dear chap! Oh, my dear chap!" Reggie murmured. "Empty, aren't we? Come on. Come home with me."

While Sam drove them back, he declined to talk. He stretched in the corner of the car and closed his eyes, and bade Bell do the same. While they ate a deviled sole and an entrecôte Elise, he discussed the qualities of Elise, his cook, and of the Romanée which they drank, and argued bitterly (though he shared it) that the cheese offered in deference to Bell's taste, a bland Stilton, was an insult to the raspberries, the dish of which he emptied.

But when they were established in big chairs in his library, with brandy for Bell and seltzer for himself, and both pipes were lit. "Did you say a tangle?" he murmured. "Oh, no. Not now. The rest is only routine for your young men and the lawyers. It'll work out quite easy. You can see it all. When Mrs. Brightman was left a widow with her little shop, the pious Brightman pounced on her and mastered her. The little shop was only a little living. Brightman wanted more. Children were kept very short—they might fade out, they might go to the bad—either way the devout Brightman would be relieved of their keep; and meanwhile it was pleasant making 'em believe they were wicked. Old Mrs. Wiven was brought in as a lodger—not out of charity as the wretched Mrs. Brightman was trained to say; she must have had a bit of money. Your young men will be able to trace that. And they'll find Brightman got it out of her and used it to set up his second-hand furniture business. Heard of that sort of thing before, what?"

"I should say I have," Bell grunted. "My Lord, how often. The widow that falls for a pious brute—the old woman lodger with a bit of money."

"Oh, yes. Dreary old game. And then the abnormal variations began. Pious bullyin' and starvin' didn't turn the boy into a criminal idiot. He has a mind. He has an imagination, poor child. Mrs. Wiven didn't give herself up to Brightman like his miserable wife. She had a temper. So the old game went wrong. Mrs. Wiven took to fussin' about her money. As indicated by Bessie. Mrs. Wiven was going to be very awkward. Your young men will have to look about and get evidence she'd been grumbling. Quite easy. Lots of gossip will be goin'. Some of it true. Most of it useful at the trial. Givin' the atmosphere."

Bell frowned. "Fighting with the gloves off, aren't you?"

"Oh, no. No. Quite fair. We have to fight the case without the children. I'm not going to have Eddie put in the witness-box, to be tortured about his mad mother helpin' murder. That might break

him up for ever. And he's been tortured enough. The brute Brightman isn't going to hurt him any more. The children won't be givin'
evidence. I'll get half the College of Physicians to certify they're not
fit, if they're asked for. But that's not goin' to leave Mr. Brightman
any way out. Now then. Things bein' thus, Brightman had his motive
to murder Mrs. Wiven. If he didn't stop her mouth she'd have him in
jail. Being a clever fellow, he saw that Eddie's record of stealin' would
be very useful. By the way—notice that queer little incident, Bessie
bein' caught pilferin' by Mrs. Wiven yesterday morning? Brightman
may have fixed that up for another black mark against the children.
I wonder. But it didn't go right. He must have had a jolt when Mrs.
Wiven called out they were all thieves. Kind of compellin' immediate
action. His plan would have been all ready, of course—salts of lemon
in her favorite strong tea; a man don't think of an efficient way of
poisonin' all of sudden. And then the incalculable Eddie intervened.
Reaction of Mrs. Wiven's explosion on him, a sort of divine com-
mand to save his sister from hell by seeing she died innocent. When
Brightman had the news of that effort at drowning, he took it as a
godsend. Hear him thanking heaven? Boy who was wicked enough
to kill a little sister was wicked enough for anything. Mr. Brightman
read his title clear to mansions in the skies. And Mrs. Wiven was
promptly given her cup o' tea. She was sick in her room, sick on
her overall and on her underclothes. Evidence for all that conclusive.
Remember the damp floor. I should say Mrs. Brightman had another
swab at that to-day. She has a craze about cleaning. We saw that. Feels
she never can get clean, poor wretch. Well. Mrs. Wiven died. Oxalic
poisoning generally kills quick. I hope it did. They hid the body in
the cellar. Plan was clever. Take the body out in the quiet of the night
and dump it on the common with a flask of poisoned tea—put her
bag in Eddie's den. All clear for the intelligent police. Devil of a boy
poisoned the old lady to steal her money, and was drownin' his little
sister so she shouldn't tell on him. That's what you thought, wasn't it?
Yes. Well-made plan. It stood up against us last night."

"You did think there was something queer," Bell said.

"I did," Reggie sighed. "Physical smell. Damp musty smell. Probably
the cellar. And the Brightmans didn't smell nice spiritually. However.
Lack of confidence in myself. And I have no imagination. I ought to
have waited and watched. My error. My grave error. Well. It was a
clever plan. But Brightman was rather bustled. That may account for
his errors. Fatal errors. Omission to remove the soiled underclothes

when the messed-up overall was taken off. Failure to allow for the habits of *limax flavus*."

"What's that?" said Bell.

"Official name of yellow slug—cellar slug. The final, damning evidence. I never found any reason for the existence of slugs before. However. To round it off—when you look into Mr. Brightman's furniture business, you'll find that he has a van, or the use of one. You must prove it was used last night. That's all. Quite simple now. But a wearin' case." He gazed at Bell with large, solemn eyes. "His wife! He'd schooled her thorough. Ever hear anything more miserably appealing than her on her dear babies and poor old Mrs. Wiven? Not often? No. Took a lot of breakin' down."

"Ah. You were fierce," Bell muttered.

"Oh, no. No." Reggie sighed. "I was bein' merciful. She couldn't be saved. My job was to save the children. And she—if that brute hadn't twisted her, she'd have done anything to save 'em too. She'd been a decent soul once. No. She won't be giving evidence against me."

"Why, how should she?" Bell gaped.

"I was thinkin' of the day of judgment," Reggie murmured. "Well, well. Post-mortem in the morning. Simple straight job. Then I'll be at the hospital if you want me. Have to finish Eddie's bridge. And then we're going to build a ship. He's keen on ships."

The Genuine Tabard

E. C. Bentley

IT WAS quite by chance, at a dinner party given by the American Naval Attaché, that Philip Trent met the Langleys, who were visiting Europe for the first time. During the cocktail time, before dinner was served, he had gravitated towards George D. Langley, because he was the finest looking man in the room—tall, strongly-built, carrying his years lightly, pink of face, with vigorous, massive features and thick grey hair.

They had talked about the Tower of London, the Cheshire Cheese, and the Zoo, all of which the Langleys had visited that day. Langley, so the Attaché had told Trent, was a distant relative of his own; he had made a large fortune manufacturing engineers' drawing-office equipment, was a prominent citizen of Cordova, Ohio, the headquarters of his business, and had married a Schuyler. Trent, though not sure what a Schuyler was, gathered that it was an excellent thing to marry, and this impression was confirmed when he found himself placed next to Mrs. Langley at dinner.

Mrs. Langley always went on the assumption that her own affairs were the most interesting subject of conversation; and as she was a vivacious and humorous talker and a very handsome and good-hearted woman, she usually turned out to be right. She informed Trent that she was crazy about old churches, of which she had seen and photographed she did not know how many in France, Germany, and England. Trent, who loved thirteenth-century stained glass, mentioned Chartres, which Mrs. Langley said, truly enough, was too perfect for words. He asked if she had been to Fairford in Gloucester-shire. She had; and that was, she declared with emphasis, the greatest day of all their time in Europe; not because of the church, though that was certainly lovely, but because of the treasure they had found that afternoon.

235

Trent asked to be told about this; and Mrs. Langley said that it was quite a story. Mr. Gifford had driven them down to Fairford in his car. Did Trent know Mr. Gifford—W. N. Gifford, who lived at the Suffolk Hotel? He was visiting Paris just now. Trent ought to meet him, because Mr. Gifford knew everything there was to know about stained glass, and church ornaments, and brasses, and antiques in general. They had met him when he was sketching some traceries in Westminster Abbey, and they had become great friends. He had driven them about to quite a few places within reach of London. He knew all about Fairford, of course, and they had a lovely time there.

On the way back to London, after passing through Abingdon, Mr. Gifford had said it was time for a cup of coffee, as he always did around five o'clock; he made his own coffee, which was excellent, and carried it in a thermos. They slowed down, looking for a good place to stop, and Mrs. Langley's eye was caught by a strange name on a signpost at a turning off the road—something Episcopi. She knew that meant bishops, which was interesting; so she asked Mr. Gifford to halt the car while she made out the weather-beaten lettering. The sign said "Silcote Episcopi ½ mile."

Had Trent heard of the place? Neither had Mr. Gifford. But that lovely name, Mrs. Langley said, was enough for her. There must be a church, and an old one; and anyway she would love to have Silcote Episcopi in her collection. As it was so near, she asked Mr. Gifford if they could go there so she could take a few snaps while the light was good, and perhaps have coffee there.

They found the church, with the parsonage near by, and a village in sight some way beyond. The church stood back of the churchyard, and as they were going along the footpath they noticed a grave with tall railings round it; not a standing-up stone but a flat one, raised on a little foundation. They noticed it because, though it was an old stone, it had not been just left to fall into decay, but had been kept clean of moss and dirt, so you could make out the inscription, and the grass around it was trim and tidy. They read Sir Rowland Verey's epitaph; and Mrs. Langley—so she assured Trent—screamed with joy.

There was a man trimming the churchyard boundary hedge with shears, who looked at them, she thought, suspiciously when she screamed. She thought he was probably the sexton; so she assumed a winning manner, and asked him if there was any objection to her taking a photograph of the inscription on the stone. The man said that he didn't know as there was; but maybe she ought to ask vicar, because it was his grave, in a manner of speaking. It was vicar's great-grandfather's grave, that was; and he always had it kep' in good order. He would be in the church now, very like, if they had a mind to see him.

Mr. Gifford said that in any case they would have a look at the church, which he thought might be worth the trouble. He observed that it was not very old—about mid-seventeenth century, he would say—a poor little kid church, Mrs. Langley commented with gay sarcasm. In a place so named, Mr. Gifford said, there had probably been a church for centuries farther back: but it might have been burnt down, or fallen into ruin, and replaced by this building. So they went into the church; and at once Mr. Gifford had been delighted with it. He pointed out how the pulpit, the screen, the pews, the glass, the organ-case in the west gallery, were all of the same period. Mrs. Langley was busy with her camera when a pleasant-faced man of middle age, in clerical attire, emerged from the vestry with a large book under his arm.

Mr. Gifford introduced himself and his friends as a party of chance visitors who had been struck by the beauty of the church and had ventured to explore its interior. Could the vicar tell them anything about the armorial glass in the nave windows? The vicar could and did; but Mrs. Langley was not just then interested in any family history but the vicar's own, and soon she broached the subject of his great-grandfather's gravestone.

The vicar, smiling, said that he bore Sir Rowland's name, and had felt it a duty to look after the grave properly, as this was the only Verey to be buried in that place. He added that the living was in the gift of the head of the family, and that he was the third Verey to be vicar of Silcote Episcopi in the course of two hundred years. He said that Mrs. Langley was most welcome to take a photograph of the stone, but he doubted if it could be done successfully with a hand-camera from over the railings—and of course, said Mrs. Langley, he was perfectly right. Then the vicar asked if she would like to have a copy of the epitaph, which he could write for her if they would all come over to his house, and his wife would give them some tea; and at this, as Trent could imagine, they were just tickled to death.

"But what was it, Mrs. Langley, that delighted you so much about the epitaph?" Trent asked. "It seems to have been about a Sir Rowland Verey—that's all I have been told so far."

"I was going to show it to you," Mrs. Langley said, opening her handbag. "Maybe you will not think it so precious as we do. I have had a lot of copies made, to send to friends at home." She unfolded a small typed sheet, on which Trent read what follows:

Within this Vault are interred
the Remains of
Lt.-Gen. Sir Rowland Edmund Verey,
Garter Principal King of Arms,
Gentleman Usher of the Black Rod
and
Clerk of the Hanaper,
who departed this Life
on the 2nd May 1795
in the 73rd Year of his Age
calmly relying
on the Merits of the Redeemer
for the Salvation of
his Soul.
Also of Lavinia Prudence,
Wife of the Above,
who entered into Rest
on the 12th March 1799
in the 68th Year of her Age.
She was a Woman of fine Sense
genteel Behavior,
prudent Oeconomy
and
great Integrity.
"This is the Gate of the Lord:
The Righteous shall enter into it."

"You have certainly got a fine specimen of that style," Trent observed. "Nowadays we don't run to much more, as a rule, than 'in loving memory', followed by the essential facts. As for the titles, I don't wonder at your admiring them; they are like the sound of trumpets. There is also a faint jingle of money, I think. In Sir Rowland's time, Black Rod's was probably a job worth having; and though I don't know what a Hanaper is, I do remember that its Clerkship was one of the fat sinecures that made it well worth while being a courtier."

Mrs. Langley put away her treasure, patting the bag with affection. "Mr. Gifford said the Clerk had to collect some sort of legal fees for the Crown, and that he would draw maybe seven or eight thousand pounds a year for it, paying another man two or three hundred for doing the actual work. Well, we found the vicarage just perfect—an old house with everything beautifully mellow and personal about it. There was a long oar hanging on the wall in the hall, and when I asked about it the vicar said he had rowed for All Souls College when he was at Oxford. His wife was charming, too. And now listen! While she was giving us tea, and her husband was making a copy of the epitaph for me, he was talking about his ancestor, and he said the first duty that Sir Rowland had to perform after his appointment as King of Arms was to proclaim the Peace of Versailles from the steps of the Palace of St. James's. Imagine that, Mr. Trent!"

Trent looked at her uncertainly. "So they had a Peace of Versailles all that time ago."

"Yes, they did," Mrs. Langley said, a little tartly. "And quite an important Peace, at that. We remember it in America, if you don't. It was the first treaty to be signed by the United States, and in that treaty the British Government took a licking, called off the war, and recognized our independence. Now when the vicar said that about his ancestor having proclaimed peace with the United States, I saw George Langley prick up his ears; and I knew why.

"You see, George is a collector of Revolution pieces, and he has some pretty nice things, If I do say it. He began asking questions; and the first thing anybody knew, the vicaress had brought down the old King of Arm's tabard and was showing it off. You know what a tabard is, Mr. Trent, of course. Such a lovely garment! I fell for it on the spot, and as for George, his eyes stuck out like a crab's. That wonderful shade of red satin, and the Royal Arms embroidered in those stunning colors, red and gold and blue and silver, as you don't often see them.

"Presently George got talking to Mr. Gifford in a corner, and I could see Mr. Gifford screwing up his mouth and shaking his head; but George only stuck out his chin, and soon after, when the vicaress was showing off the garden, he got the vicar by himself and talked turkey.

"Mr. Verey didn't like it at all, George told me; but George can be a very smooth worker when he likes, and at last the vicar had to allow that he was tempted, what with having his sons to start in the world, and the income tax being higher than a cat's back, and the death duties and all. And finally he said yes. I won't tell you or anybody what George offered him, Mr. Trent, because George swore me to secrecy; but, as he says, it was no good acting like a piker in this kind of a deal, and he could sense that the vicar wouldn't stand for any bargaining back and forth. And anyway, it was worth every cent of it to George, to have something that no other curio-hunter possessed. He said he would come for the tabard next day and bring the money in notes, and the vicar said very well, then we must all three come to lunch, and he would have a paper ready giving the history of the tabard over his signature. So that was what we did; and the tabard is in our suite at the Greville, locked in a wardrobe, and George has it out and gloats over it first thing in the morning and last thing at night."

Trent said with sincerity that no story of real life had ever interested him more. "I wonder," he said, "if your husband would let me have a look at his prize. I'm not much of an antiquary, but I am interested in heraldry, and the only tabards I have ever seen were quite modern ones."

"Why, of course," Mrs. Langley said. "You make a date with him after dinner. He will be delighted. He has no idea of hiding it under a bushel, believe me!"

The following afternoon, in the Langleys' sitting-room at the Greville, the tabard was displayed on a coat-hanger before the thoughtful gaze of Trent, while its new owner looked on with a pride not untouched with anxiety.

"Well, Mr. Trent," he said. "How do you like it? You don't doubt this is a genuine tabard, I suppose?"

Trent rubbed his chin. "Oh yes, it's a tabard. I have seen a few before, and I have painted one, with a man inside it, when Richmond Herald wanted his portrait down in the complete get-up. Everything about it is right. Such things are hard to come by. Until recent times, I believe, a herald's tabard remained his property, and stayed in the family, and if they got hard up they might perhaps sell it privately, as this was sold to you. It's different now—so Richmond Herald told me. When a herald dies, his tabard goes back to the College of Arms, where he got it from."

Langley drew a breath of relief. "I'm glad to hear you say my tabard is genuine. When you asked me if you could see it, I got the impression you thought there might be something phoney about it."

Mrs. Langley, her keen eyes on Trent's face, shook her head. "He thinks so still, George, I believe. Isn't that so, Mr. Trent?"

"Yes, I am sorry to say it is. You see, this was sold to you as a particular tabard, with an interesting history of its own; and when Mrs. Langley described it to me, I felt pretty sure that you had been swindled. You see, she had noticed nothing odd about the Royal Arms. I wanted to see it just to make sure. It certainly did not belong to the Garter King of Arms in the year 1783."

A very ugly look wiped all the benevolence from Langley's face, and it grew several shades more pink. "If what you say is true, Mr. Trent, and if that old fraud was playing me for a sucker, I will get him jailed if it's my last act. But it certainly is hard to believe—a preacher—and belonging to one of your best families—settled in that lovely, peaceful old place, with his flock to look after and everything. Are you really sure of what you say?"

"What I know is that the Royal Arms on this tabard are all wrong."

An exclamation came from the lady. "Why, Mr. Trent, how you talk! We have seen the Royal Arms quite a few times, and they are just the same as this—and you have told us it is a genuine tabard, anyway. I don't get this at all."

"I must apologize," Trent said unhappily, "for the Royal Arms. You see, they have a past. In the fourteenth century Edward III laid claim to the Kingdom of France, and it took a hundred years of war to convince his descendants that that claim wasn't practical politics. All the same, they went on including the lilies of France in the Royal Arms, and they never dropped them until the beginning of the nineteenth century."

"Mercy!" Mrs. Langley's voice was faint.

"Besides that, the first four Georges and the fourth William were Kings of Hanover; so until Queen Victoria came along, and could not

inherit Hanover because she was a female, the Arms of the House of
Brunswick were jammed in along with our own. In fact, the tabard
of the Garter King of Arms in the year when he proclaimed the
peace with the United States of America was a horrible mess of the
leopards of England, the lion of Scotland, the harp of Ireland, the
lilies of France, together with a few more lions, and a white horse,
and some hearts, as worn in Hanover. It was a fairly tight fit for one
shield, but they managed it somehow—and you can see that the Arms
of this tabard of yours are not nearly such a bad dream as that. It is a
Victorian tabard—a nice, gentlemanly coat, such as no well-dressed
herald should be without."

Langley thumped the table. "Well, I intend to be without it, anyway, if I can get my money back."

"We can but try," Trent said. "It may be possible. But the reason
why I asked to be allowed to see this thing, Mr. Langley, was that I
thought I might be able to save you some unpleasantness. You see,
if you went home with your treasure, and showed it to people, and
talked about its history, and it was mentioned in the newspapers, and
then somebody got inquiring into its authenticity, and found out
what I have been telling you, and made it public—well, it wouldn't
be very nice for you."

Langley flushed again, and a significant glance passed between him
and his wife.

"You're damn right, it wouldn't," he said. "And I know the name
of the buzzard who would do that to me, too, as soon as I had gone
the limit in making a monkey of myself. Why, I would lose the money
twenty times over, and then a bundle, rather than have that happen to
me. I am grateful to you, Mr. Trent—I am indeed. I'll say frankly that
at home we aim to be looked to socially, and we judged that we
would certainly figure if we brought this doggoned thing back and
had it talked about. Gosh! When I think—but never mind that now.
The thing is to go right back to that old crook and make him squeal.
I'll have my money out of him, if I have to use a can-opener."

Trent shook his head. "I don't feel very sanguine about that, Mr.
Langley. But how would you like to run down to his place tomorrow
with me and a friend of mine, who takes an interest in affairs of this
kind, and who would be able to help you if any one can?"

Langley said, with emphasis, that that suited him.

The car which called for Langley next morning did not look as
if it belonged, but did belong, to Scotland Yard; and the same could

be said of its dapper chauffeur. Inside was Trent, with a black-haired, round-faced man whom he introduced as Superintendent Owen. It was at his request that Langley, during the journey, told with as much detail as he could recall the story of his acquisition of the tabard, which he had hopefully brought with him in a suitcase.

A few miles short of Abingdon the chauffeur was told to go slow. "You tell me it was not very far this side of Abingdon, Mr. Langley, that you turned off the main road," the superintendent said. "If you will keep a look-out now, you might be able to point out the spot."

Langley stared at him. "Why, doesn't your man have a map?"

"Yes; but there isn't any place called Silcote Episcopi on his map."

"Nor," Trend added, "on any other map. No, I am not suggesting that you dreamed it all; but the fact is so."

Langley, remarking shortly that this beat him, glared out of the window eagerly; and soon he gave the word to stop. "I am pretty sure this is the turning," he said. "I recognize it by these two haystacks in the meadow, and the pond with osiers over it. But there certainly was a signpost there, and now there isn't one. If I was not dreaming then, I guess I must be now." And as the car ran swiftly down the side-road he went on, "Yes; that certainly is the church on ahead—and the covered gate, and the graveyard—and there is the vicarage, with the yew trees and the garden and everything. Well, gentlemen, right now is when he gets what is coming to him, I don't care what the name of the darn place is."

"The name of the darn place on the map," Trent said, "is Oakhanger."

The three men got out and passed through the lych-gate.

"Where is the gravestone?" Trent asked.

Langley pointed. "Right there." They went across to the railed-in grave, and the American put a hand to his head. "I must be nuts!" he groaned. "I *know* this is the grave—but it says that here is laid to rest the body of James Roderick Stevens, of this parish."

"Who seems to have died about thirty years after Sir Rowland Verey," Trent remarked, studying the inscription; while the superintendent gently smote his thigh in an ecstasy of silent admiration. "And now let us see if the vicar can throw any light on the subject."

They went on to the parsonage; and a dark-haired, bright-faced girl, opening the door at Mr. Owen's ring, smiled recognizingly at Langley. "Well, you're genuine, anyway!" he exclaimed. "Ellen is what they call you, isn't it? And you remember me, I see. Now I feel better. We would like to see the vicar. Is he at home?"

"The canon came home two days ago, sir," the girl said, with a perceptible stress on the term of rank. "He is down in the village now; but he may be back any minute. Would you like to wait for him?"

"We surely would," Langley declared positively; and they were shown into the large room where the tabard had changed hands.

"So he has been away from home?" Trent asked. "And he is a canon, you say?"

"Canon Maberley, sir; yes, sir, he was in Italy for a month. The lady and gentleman who were here till last week had taken the house furnished while he was away. Me and cook stayed on to do for them."

"And did that gentleman—Mr. Verey—do the canon's duty during his absence?" Trent inquired with a ghost of a smile.

"No, sir; the canon had an arrangement with Mr. Giles, the vicar of Cotmore, about that. The canon never knew that Mr. Verey was a clergyman. He never saw him. You see, it was Mrs. Verey who came to see over the place and settled everything; and it seems she never mentioned it. When we told the canon, after they had gone, he was quite took aback. 'I can't make it out at all,' he says. 'Why should he conceal it?' he says. 'Well, sir,' I says, 'they was very nice people, anyhow, and the friends they had to see them here was very nice, and their chauffeur was a perfectly respectable man,' I says."

Trent nodded. "Ah! They had friends to see them."

The girl was thoroughly enjoying this gossip. "Oh yes, sir. The gentleman as brought you down, sir"—she turned to Langley—"he brought down several others before that. They was Americans too, I think."

"You mean they didn't have an English accent, I suppose," Langley suggested dryly.

"Yes, sir; and they had such nice manners, like yourself," the girl said, quite unconscious of Langley's confusion, and of the grins covertly exchanged between Trent and the superintendent, who now took up the running.

"This respectable chauffeur of theirs—was he a small, thin man with a long nose, partly bald, always smoking cigarettes?"

"Oh yes, sir; just like that. You must know him."

"I do," Superintendent Owen said grimly.

"So do I!" Langley exclaimed. "He was the man we spoke to in the churchyard."

"Did Mr. and Mrs. Verey have any—er—ornaments of their own with them?" the superintendent asked.

Ellen's eyes rounded with enthusiasm. "Oh yes, sir—some lovely things they had. But they was only put out when they had friends coming. Other times they was kept somewhere in Mr. Verey's bedroom, I think. Cook and me thought perhaps they was afraid of burglars."

The superintendent pressed a hand over his stubby moustache. "Yes, I expect that was it," he said gravely. "But what kind of lovely things do you mean? Silver—china—that sort of thing?"

"No, sir; nothing ordinary, as you might say. One day they had out a beautiful goblet, like, all gold, with little figures and patterns worked on it in colors, and precious stones, blue and green and white, stuck all round it—regular dazzled me to look at, it did."

"The Debenham Chalice!" exclaimed the superintendent.

"Is it a well-known thing, then, sir?" the girl asked.

"No, not at all," Mr. Owen said. "It is an heirloom—a private family possession. Only we happen to have heard of it."

"Fancy taking such things about with them," Ellen remarked. Then there was a big book they had out once, lying open on that table in the window. It was all done in funny gold letters on yellow paper, with lovely little pictures all round the edges, gold and silver and all colors."

"The Murrane Psalter!" said Mr. Owen. "Come, we're getting on."

"And," the girl pursued, addressing herself to Langley, "there was that beautiful red coat with the arms on it, like you see on a half-crown. You remember they got it out for you to look at, sir; and when I brought in the tea it was hanging up in front of the tallboy."

Langley grimaced. "I believe I do remember it," he said, "now you remind me."

"There is the canon coming up the path now," Ellen said, with a glance through the window. "I will tell him you gentlemen are here."

She hurried from the room, and soon there entered a tall, stooping old man with a gentle face and the indescribable air of a scholar.

The superintendent went to meet him.

"I am a police officer, Canon Maberley," he said. "I and my friends have called to see you in pursuit of an official inquiry in connection with the people to whom your house was let last month. I do not think I shall have to trouble you much, though, because your parlormaid has given us already most of the information we are likely to get, I suspect."

"Ah! That girl," the canon said vaguely. "She has been talking to you, has she? She will go on talking for ever, if you let her. Please sit down, gentlemen. About the Vereys—ah yes! But surely there was nothing wrong about the Vereys? Mrs. Verey was quite a nice, well-bred person, and they left the place in perfectly good order. They paid me in advance, too, because they live in New Zealand, as she explained, and know nobody in London. They were on a visit to England, and they wanted a temporary home in the heart of the country, because that is the real England, as she said. That was so sensible of them, I thought—instead of flying to the grime and turmoil of London, as most of our friends from overseas do. In a way, I was quite touched by it, and I was glad to let them have the vicarage."

The superintendent shook his head. "People as clever as they are make things very difficult for us, sir. And the lady never mentioned that her husband was a clergyman, I understand."

"No, and that puzzled me when I heard of it," the canon said. "But it didn't matter, and no doubt there was a reason."

"The reason was, I think," Mr. Owen said, "that if she had mentioned it, you might have been too much interested, and asked questions which would have been all right for a genuine parson's wife, but which she couldn't answer without putting her foot in it. Her husband could do a vicar well enough to pass with laymen, especially if they were not English laymen. I am sorry to say, canon, that your tenants were impostors. Their name was certainly not Verey, to begin with. I don't know who they are—I wish I did—they are new to us and they have invented a new method. But I can tell you what they are. They are thieves and swindlers."

The canon fell back in his chair. "Thieves and swindlers!" he gasped.

"And very talented performers too," Trent assured him. "Why, they have had in this house of yours part of the loot of several country-house burglaries which took place last year, and which puzzled the police because it seemed impossible that some of the things taken could ever be turned into cash. One of them was a herald's tabard, which Superintendent Owen tells me had been worn by the father of Sir Andrew Ritchie. He was Maltravers Herald in his day. It was taken when Sir Andrew's place in Lincolnshire was broken into, and a lot of very valuable jewelry was stolen. It was dangerous to try to sell the tabard in the open market, and it was worth little, anyhow, apart from any associations it might have. What they did was to fake up a story about the tabard which might appeal to an American purchaser, and, having found a victim, to induce him to buy it. I believe he parted with quite a large sum."

"The poor simp!" growled Langley.

Canon Maberley held up a shaking hand. "I fear I do not understand," he said. "What had their taking my house to do with all this?"

"It was a vital part of the plan. We know exactly how they went to work about the tabard; and no doubt the other things were got rid of in very much the same way. There were found of them in the gang. Besides your tenants, there was an agreeable and cultured person—I should think a man with real knowledge of antiquities and objects of art—whose job was to make the acquaintance of wealthy people visiting London, gain their confidence, take them about to places of interest, exchange hospitality with them, and finally get them down to this vicarage. In this case it was made to appear as if the proposal to look over your church came from the visitors themselves. They could not suspect anything. They were attracted by the romantic name of the place on a signpost up there at the corner of the main road."

The canon shook his head helplessly. "But there is no signpost at that corner."

"No, but there was one at the time when they were due to be passing that corner in the confederate's car. It was a false signpost, you see, with a false name on it—so that if anything went wrong, the place where the swindle was worked would be difficult to trace. Then, when they entered the churchyard their attention was attracted by a certain gravestone with an inscription that interested them. I won't waste your time by giving the whole story—the point is only that the gravestone, or rather the top layer which had been fitted on to it, was false too. The sham inscription on it was meant to lead up to the swindle, and so it did."

The canon drew himself up in his chair. "It was an abominable act of sacrilege!" he exclaimed. "The man calling himself Verey——"

"I don't think," Trent said, "it was the man calling himself Verey who actually did the abominable act. We believe it was the fourth member of the gang, who masqueraded as the Vereys' chauffeur—a very interesting character. Superintendent Owen can tell you about him."

Mr. Owen twisted his moustache thoughtfully. "Yes; he is the only one of them that we can place. Alfred Coveney, his name is; a man of some education and any amount of talent. He used to be a stage-carpenter and property-maker—a regular artist, he was. Give him a tub of papier-mâché, and there was nothing he couldn't model and color to look exactly like the real thing. That was how the false top to the gravestone was made, I've no doubt. It may have been made to fit on like a lid, to be slipped on and off as required. The inscription was a bit above Alf, though—I expect it was Gifford who drafted that for him, and he copied the lettering from other old stones in the churchyard. Of course the fake signpost was Alf's work too—stuck up when required, and taken down when the show was over.

"Well, Alf got into bad company. They found how clever he was with his hands, and he became an expert burglar. He has served two terms of imprisonment. He is one of a few who have always been under suspicion for the job at Sir Andrew Ritchie's place, and the other two when the chalice was lifted from Eynsham Park and the Psalter from Lord Swanbourne's house. With what they collected in this house and the jewelry that was taken in all three burglaries, they must have done very well indeed for themselves; and by this time they are going to be hard to catch."

Canon Maberley, who had now recovered himself somewhat, looked at the others with the beginnings of a smile. "It is a new experience for me," he said, "to be made use of by a gang of criminals. But it is highly interesting. I suppose that when these confiding strangers had been got down here, my tenant appeared in the character of the parson, and invited them into the house, where you tell me they were induced to make a purchase of stolen property. I do not see, I must confess, how anything could have been better designed to prevent any possibility of suspicion arising. The vicar of a parish, at home in his own vicarage! Who could imagine anything being wrong? I only hope, for the credit of my cloth, that the deception was well carried out."

"As far as I know," Trent said, "he made only one mistake. It was a small one; but the moment I heard of it I knew that he must have been a fraud. You see, he was asked about the oar you have hanging up in the hall. I didn't go to Oxford myself, but I believe when a man is given his oar it means that he rowed in an eight that did something unusually good."

A light came into the canon's spectacled eyes. "In the year I got my colors the Wadham boat went up five places on the river. It was the happiest week of my life."

"Yet you had other triumphs," Trent suggested. "For instance, didn't you get a Fellowship at All Souls, after leaving Wadham?"

"Yes, and that did please me, naturally," the canon said. "But that is a different sort of happiness, my dear sir, and, believe me, nothing like so keen. And by the way, how did you know about that?"

"I thought it might be so, because of the little mistake your tenant made. When he was asked about the oar, he said he had rowed for All Souls."

Canon Maberley burst out laughing, while Langley and the super-intendent stared at him blankly.

"I think I see what happened," he said. "The rascal must have been browsing about in my library, in search of ideas for the part he was to play. I was a resident Fellow for five years, and a number of my books have a bookplate with my name and the name and arms of All Souls. His mistake was natural." And again the old gentleman laughed delightedly.

Langley exploded. "I like a joke myself," he said, "but I'll be skinned alive if I can see the point of this one."

"Why, the point is," Trent told him, "that nobody ever rowed for All Souls. There never were more than four undergraduates there at one time, all the other members being Fellows."

Suspicion

Dorothy L. Sayers

As THE atmosphere of the railway carriage thickened with tobacco-smoke, Mr. Mummery became increasingly aware that his breakfast had not agreed with him.

There could have been nothing wrong with the breakfast itself. Brown bread, rich in vitamin-content, as advised by the *Morning Star*'s health expert; bacon fried to a delicious crispness; eggs just nicely set; coffee made as only Mrs. Sutton knew how to make it. Mrs. Sutton had been a real find, and that was something to be thankful for. For Ethel, since her nervous breakdown in the Summer, had really not been fit to wrestle with the untrained girls who had come and gone in tempestuous succession. It took very little to upset Ethel nowadays, poor child. Mr. Mummery, trying hard to ignore his growing internal discomfort, hoped he was not in for an illness. Apart from the trouble it would cause at the office, it would worry Ethel terribly, and Mr. Mummery would cheerfully have laid down his rather uninteresting little life to spare Ethel a moment's uneasiness.

He slipped a digestive tablet into his mouth—he had taken lately to carrying a few tablets about with him—and opened his paper. There did not seem to be very much news. A question had been asked in the House about Government typewriters. The Prince of Wales had smilingly opened an all-British exhibition of foot-wear. A further split had occurred in the Liberal party. The police were still looking for the woman who was supposed to have poisoned a family in Lincoln. Two girls had been trapped in a burning factory. A film-star had obtained her fourth decree nisi.

At Paragon Station, Mr. Mummery descended and took a tram. The internal discomfort was taking the form of a definite nausea. Happily he contrived to reach his office before the worst occurred. He was seated at his desk, pale but in control of himself, when his partner came breezing in.

250

"'Morning, Mummery," said Mr. Brookes in his loud tones, adding inevitably, "Cold enough for you?"

"Quite," replied Mr. Mummery. "Unpleasantly raw, in fact."

"Beastly, beastly," said Mr. Brookes. "Your bulbs all in?"

"Not quite all," confessed Mr. Mummery. "As a matter of fact I haven't been feeling—"

"Pity," interrupted his partner. "Great pity. Ought to get 'em in early. Mine were in last week. My little place will be a picture in the Spring. For a town garden, that is. You're lucky, living in the country. Find it better than Hull, I expect, eh? Though we get plenty of fresh air up in the Avenues. How's the missus?"

"Thank you, she's very much better."

"Glad to hear that, very glad. Hope we shall have her about again this winter as usual. Can't do without her in the Drama Society, you know. By Jove! I shan't forget her acting last year in *Romance*. She and young Welbeck positively brought the house down, didn't they? The Welbecks were asking after her only yesterday."

"Thank you, yes. I hope she will soon be able to take up her social activities again. But the doctor says she mustn't overdo it. No worry, he says—that's the important thing. She is to go easy and not rush about or undertake too much."

"Quite right, quite right. Worry's the devil and all. I cut out worrying years ago and look at me! Fit as a fiddle, for all I shan't see fifty again. *You're* not looking altogether the thing, by the way."

"A touch of dyspepsia," said Mr. Mummery. "Nothing much. Chill on the liver, that's what I put it down to."

"That's what it is," said Mr. Brookes, seizing his opportunity. "Is life worth living? It depends on the liver. Ha, ha! Well now, well now—we must do a spot of work, I suppose. Where's that lease of Ferraby's?"

Mr. Mummery, who did not feel at his conversational best that morning, rather welcomed this suggestion, and for half an hour was allowed to proceed in peace with the duties of an estate agent. Presently, however, Mr. Brookes burst into speech again.

"By the way," he said abruptly. "I suppose your wife doesn't know of a good cook, does she?"

"Well, no," replied Mr. Mummery. "They aren't so easy to find nowadays. In fact, we've only just got suited ourselves. But why? Surely your old Cookie isn't leaving you?"

"Good Lord, no!" Mr. Brookes laughed heartily. "It would take an earthquake to shake off old Cookie. No. It's for the Philipsons. Their girl's getting married. That's the worst of girls. I said to Philipson, 'You mind what you're doing,' I said. 'Get somebody you know something about, or you may find yourself landed with this poisoning woman—what's her name—Andrews. Don't want to be sending wreaths to your funeral yet awhile,' I said. He laughed, but it's no laughing matter and so I told him. What we pay the police for I simply don't know. Nearly a month now, and they can't seem to lay hands on the woman. All they say is, they think she's hanging about the neighborhood and 'may seek situation as cook.' As cook! Now I ask you!"

"You don't think she committed suicide, then?" suggested Mr. Mummery.

"Suicide, my foot!" retorted Mr. Brookes, coarsely. "Don't you believe it, my boy. That coat found in the river was all eyewash. *They* don't commit suicide, that sort don't."

"What sort?"

"Those arsenic-maniacs. They're too damned careful of their own skins. Cunning as weasels, that's what they are. It's only to be hoped they'll manage to catch her before she tries her hand on anybody else. As I told Philipson—"

"You think Mrs. Andrews did it, then?"

"Did it? Of course she did it. It's plain as the nose on your face. Looked after her old father, and he died suddenly—left her a bit of money, too. Then she keeps house for an elderly gentleman, and *he* dies suddenly. Now there's this husband and wife—man dies and woman taken very ill, of arsenic poisoning. Cook runs away, and you ask, did she do it? I don't mind betting that when they dig up the father and the other old bird they'll find *them* bung-full of arsenic, too. Once that sort gets started, they don't stop. Grows on 'em, as you might say."

"I suppose it does," said Mr. Mummery. He picked up his paper again and studied the photograph of the missing woman. "She looks harmless enough," he remarked. "Rather a nice, motherly-looking kind of woman."

"She's got a bad mouth," pronounced Mr. Brookes. He had a theory that character showed in the mouth. "I wouldn't trust that woman an inch."

As the day went on, Mr. Mummery felt better. He was rather nervous about his lunch, choosing carefully a little boiled fish and custard pudding and being particular not to rush about immediately after the meal. To his great relief, the fish and custard remained where they were put, and he was not visited by that tiresome pain which had become almost habitual in the last fortnight. By the end of the day he became quite lighthearted. The bogey of illness and doctor's bills ceased to haunt him. He bought a bunch of bronze chrysanthemums to carry home to Ethel, and it was with a feeling of pleasant anticipation that he left the train and walked up the garden path of *Mon Abri*.

He was a little dashed by not finding his wife in the sitting-room. Still clutching the bunch of chrysanthemums he pattered down the passage and pushed open the kitchen door.

Nobody was there but the cook. She was sitting at the table with her back to him, and started up almost guiltily as he approached.

"Lor', sir," she said, "you give me quite a start. I didn't hear the front door go."

"Where is Mrs. Mummery? Not feeling bad again, is she?"

"Well, sir, she's got a bit of a headache, poor lamb. I made her lay down and took her up a nice cup 'o tea at half-past four. I think she's dozing nicely now."

"Dear, dear," said Mr. Mummery.

"It was turning out the dining-room done it, if you ask me," said Mrs. Sutton. "'Now, don't you overdo yourself, ma'am,' I says to her, but you know how she is, sir. She gets that restless, she can't bear to be doing nothing."

"I know," said Mr. Mummery. "It's not your fault, Mrs. Sutton. I'm sure you look after us both admirably. I'll just run up and have a peep at her. I won't disturb her if she's asleep. By the way, what are we having for dinner?"

"Well, I *had* made a nice steak-and-kidney pie," said Mrs. Sutton, in accents suggesting that she would readily turn it into a pumpkin or a coach-and-four if it was not approved of.

"Oh!" said Mr. Mummery. "Pastry? Well, I—"

"You'll find it beautiful and light," protested the cook, whisking open the oven-door for Mr. Mummery to see. "And it's made with butter, sir, you having said that you found lard indigestible."

"Thank you, thank you," said Mr. Mummery. "I'm sure it will be most excellent. I haven't been feeling altogether the thing just lately, and lard does not seem to suit me nowadays."

"Well, it don't suit some people, and that's a fact," agreed Mrs. Sutton. "I shouldn't wonder if you've got a bit of a chill on the liver. I'm sure this weather is enough to upset anybody."

She bustled to the table and cleared away the picture-paper which she had been reading.

"Perhaps the mistress would like her dinner sent up to her?" she suggested.

Mr. Mummery said he would go and see, and tiptoed his way upstairs. Ethel was lying snuggled under the eider-down and looked very small and fragile in the big double bed. She stirred as he came in and smiled up at him.

"Hullo, darling!" said Mr. Mummery.

"Hullo! You back? I must have been asleep. I got tired and head-achy, and Mrs. Sutton packed me off upstairs."

"You've been doing too much, sweetheart," said her husband, taking her hand in his and sitting down on the edge of the bed.

"Yes—it was naughty of me. What lovely flowers, Harold. All for me?"

"All for you, Tiddley-winks," said Mr. Mummery, tenderly. "Don't I deserve something for that?"

Mrs. Mummery smiled, and Mr. Mummery took his reward several times over.

"That's quite enough, you sentimental old thing," said Mrs. Mummery. "Run away, now, I'm going to get up."

"Much better go to bed, my precious, and let Mrs. Sutton send your dinner up," said her husband.

Ethel protested, but he was firm with her. If she didn't take care of herself, she wouldn't be allowed to go to the Drama Society meet-ings. And everybody was so anxious to have her back. The Welbecks had been asking after her and saying that they really couldn't get on without her.

"Did they?" said Ethel with some animation. "It's very sweet of them to want me. Well, perhaps I'll go to bed after all. And how has my old Hubby been all day?"

"Not too bad, not too bad."

"No more tummy-aches?"

"Well, just a *little* tummy-ache. But it's quite gone now. Nothing for Tiddley-winks to worry about."

Mr. Mummery experienced no more distressing symptoms the next day or the next. Following the advice of the newspaper expert, he took to drinking orange-juice, and was delighted with the results of the treatment. On Thursday, however, he was taken so ill in the night that Ethel was alarmed and insisted on sending for the doctor. The doctor felt his pulse and looked at his tongue and appeared to take the matter lightly. An inquiry into what he had been eating elicited the fact that dinner had consisted of pig's trotters, followed by a milk pudding, and that, before retiring, Mr. Mummery had consumed a large glass of orange-juice, according to his new régime.

"There's your trouble," said Dr. Griffiths cheerfully. "Orange-juice is an excellent thing, and so are trotters, but not in combination. Pigs and oranges together are extraordinarily bad for the liver. I don't know why they should be, but there's no doubt that they are. Now I'll send you round a little prescription and you stick to slops for a day or two and keep off pork. And don't you worry about him, Mrs. Mummery, he's as sound as a trout. You're the one we've got to look after. I don't want to see those black rings under the eyes, you know. Disturbed night, of course—yes. Taking your tonic regularly? That's right. Well, don't be alarmed about your hubby. We'll soon have him out and about again."

The prophecy was fulfilled, but not immediately. Mr. Mummery, though confining his diet to Benger's food, bread-and-milk, and beef-tea skillfully prepared by Mrs. Sutton and brought to his bedside by Ethel, remained very seedy all through Friday, and was only able to stagger rather shakily downstairs on Saturday afternoon. He had evidently suffered a "thorough upset." However, he was able to attend to a few papers which Brookes had sent down from the office for his signature, and to deal with the household books. Ethel was not a business woman, and Mr. Mummery always ran over the accounts with her. Having settled up with the butcher, the baker, the dairy, and the coal-merchant, Mr. Mummery looked up inquiringly.

"Anything more, darling?"

"Well, there's Mrs. Sutton. This is the end of her month, you know."

"So it is. Well, you're quite satisfied with her, aren't you, darling?"

"Yes, rather—aren't you? She's a good cook, and a sweet, motherly old thing, too. Don't you think it was a real brainwave of mine, engaging her like that, on the spot?"

"I do, indeed," said Mr. Mummery.

"It was a perfect providence, her turning up like that, just after that wretched Jane had gone off without even giving notice. I was in absolute *despair*. It was a little bit of a gamble, of course, taking her

without any references, but naturally, if she'd been looking after a
widowed mother, you couldn't expect her to give references."

"N-no," said Mr. Mummery. At the time he had felt uneasy about
the matter, though he had not liked to say much because, of course,
they simply had to have somebody. And the experiment had justified
itself so triumphantly in practice that one couldn't say much about it
now. He had once rather tentatively suggested writing to the clergyman of Mrs. Sutton's parish, but, as Ethel had said, the clergyman
wouldn't have been able to tell them anything about cooking, and
cooking, after all, was the chief point.

Mr. Mummery counted out the month's money.

"And by the way, my dear," he said, "you might just mention to
Mrs. Sutton that if she *must* read the morning paper before I come
down, I should be obliged if she would fold it neatly afterwards."

"What an old fuss-box you are, darling," said his wife.

Mr. Mummery sighed. He could not explain that it was somehow
important that the morning paper should come to him fresh and
prim, like a virgin. Women did not feel these things.

On Sunday, Mr. Mummery felt very much better—quite his old
self, in fact. He enjoyed the *News of the World* over breakfast in bed,
reading the murders rather carefully. Mr. Mummery got quite a lot
of pleasure out of murders—they gave him an agreeable thrill of
vicarious adventure, for, naturally, they were matters quite remote
from daily life in the outskirts of Hull.

He noticed that Brookes had been perfectly right. Mrs. Andrews's
father and former employer had been "dug up" and had, indeed,
proved to be "bung-full" of arsenic.

He came downstairs for dinner—roast sirloin, with the potatoes
done under the meat and Yorkshire pudding of delicious lightness, and
an apple tart to follow. After three days of invalid diet, it was delightful
to savor the crisp fat and underdone lean. He ate moderately, but
with a sensuous enjoyment. Ethel, on the other hand, seemed a little
lacking in appetite, but then, she had never been a great meat-eater.
She was fastidious and, besides, she was (quite unnecessarily) afraid
of getting fat.

It was a fine afternoon, and at three o'clock, when he was quite
certain that the roast beef was "settling" properly, it occurred to Mr.
Mummery that it would be a good thing to put the rest of those
bulbs in. He slipped on his old gardening coat and wandered out to

the potting-shed. Here he picked up a bag of tulips and a trowel, and
then, remembering that he was wearing his good trousers, decided
that it would be wise to take a mat to kneel on. When had he had the
mat last? He could not recollect, but he rather fancied he had put it
away in the corner under the potting-shelf. Stooping down, he felt
about in the dark among the flower-pots. Yes, there it was, but there
was a tin of something in the way. He lifted the tin carefully out. Of
course, yes—the remains of the weed-killer.

Mr. Mummery glanced at the pink label, printed in staring letters with the legend: "ARSENICAL WEED-KILLER. *POISON*," and observed,
with a mild feeling of excitement, that it was the same brand of stuff
that had been associated with Mrs. Andrews's latest victim. He was
rather pleased about it. It gave him a sensation of being remotely but
definitely in touch with important events. Then he noticed, with
surprise and a little annoyance, that the stopper had been put in quite
loosely.

"However'd I come to leave it like that?" he grunted. "Shouldn't
wonder if all the goodness has gone off." He removed the stopper
and squinted into the can, which appeared to be half-full. Then he
rammed the thing home again, giving it a sharp thump with the
handle of the trowel for better security. After that he washed his hands,
carefully at the scullery tap, for he did not believe in taking risks.

He was a trifle disconcerted, when he came in after planting the
tulips, to find visitors in the sitting-room. He was always pleased to
see Mrs. Welbeck and her son, but he would rather have had warning, so that he could have scrubbed the garden-mold out of his nails
more thoroughly. Not that Mrs. Welbeck appeared to notice. She
was a talkative woman and paid little attention to anything but her
own conversation. Much to Mr. Mummery's annoyance, she chose to
prattle about the Lincoln Poisoning Case. A most unsuitable subject
for the tea-table, thought Mr. Mummery, at the best of times. His
own "upset" was vivid enough in his memory to make him queasy
over the discussion of medical symptoms, and besides, this kind of
talk was not good for Ethel. After all, the poisoner was still supposed to be in the neighborhood. It was enough to make even a
strong-nerved woman uneasy. A glance at Ethel showed him that she
was looking quite white and tremulous. He must stop Mrs. Welbeck
somehow, or there would be a repetition of one of the old, dreadful,
hysterical scenes.

He broke into the conversation with violent abruptness.

"Those Forsyth cuttings, Mrs. Welbeck," he said. "Now is just about the time to take them. If you care to come down the garden I will get them for you."

He saw a relieved glance pass between Ethel and young Welbeck. Evidently the boy understood the situation and was chafing at his mother's tactlessness. Mrs. Welbeck, brought up all standing, gasped slightly and then veered off with obliging readiness on the new tack. She accompanied her host down the garden and chattered cheerfully about horticulture while he selected and trimmed the cuttings. She complimented Mr. Mummery on the immaculacy of his garden paths. "I simply *cannot* keep the weeds down," she said.

Mr. Mummery mentioned the weed-killer and praised its efficacy.

"That's stuff!" Mrs. Welbeck started at him. Then she shuddered. "I wouldn't have it in my place for a thousand pounds," she said, with emphasis.

Mr. Mummery smiled. "Oh, we keep it well away from the house," he said. "Even if I were a careless sort of person—"

He broke off. The recollection of the loosened stopper had come to him suddenly, and it was as though, deep down in his mind, some obscure assembling of ideas had taken place. He left it at that, and went into the kitchen to fetch a newspaper to wrap up the cuttings.

Their approach to the house had evidently been seen from the sitting-room window, for when they entered, young Welbeck was already on his feet and holding Ethel's hand in the act of saying goodbye. He maneuvered his mother out of the house with tactful promptness and Mr. Mummery returned to the kitchen to clear up the newspapers he had fished out of the drawer. To clear them up and to examine them more closely. Something had struck him about them, which he wanted to verify. He turned them over very carefully, sheet by sheet. Yes—he had been right. Every portrait of Mrs. Andrews, every paragraph and line about the Lincoln Poisoning Case, had been carefully cut out.

Mr. Mummery sat down by the kitchen fire. He felt as though he needed warmth. There seemed to be a curious cold lump of something at the pit of his stomach—something that he was chary of investigating.

He tried to recall the appearance of Mrs. Andrews as shown in the newspaper photographs, but he had not a good visual memory. He remembered having remarked to Brookes that it was a "motherly" face. Then he tried counting up the time since the disappearance. Nearly a month, Brookes had said—and that was a week ago. Must be over a month now. A month. He had just paid Mrs. Sutton her month's money.

"Ethel!" was the thought that hammered at the door of his brain. At all costs, he must cope with this monstrous suspicion on his own. He must spare her any shock or anxiety. And he must be sure of his ground. To dismiss the only decent cook they had ever had out of sheer, unfounded panic would be wanton cruelty to both women. If he did it at all, it would have to be done arbitrarily, preposterously—he could not suggest horrors to Ethel. However it was done, there would be trouble. Ethel would not understand and he dared not tell her.

But if by chance there was anything in this ghastly doubt—how could he expose Ethel to the appalling danger of having the woman in the house a moment longer? He thought of the family at Lincoln— the husband dead, the wife escaped by a miracle with her life. Was not any shock, any risk, better than that?

Mr. Mummery felt suddenly very lonely and tired. His illness had taken it out of him.

Those illnesses—they had begun, when? Three weeks ago he had had the first attack. Yes, but then he had always been rather subject to gastric troubles. Bilious attacks. Not so violent, perhaps, as these last, but undoubtedly bilious attacks.

He pulled himself together and went, rather heavily, into the sitting-room. Ethel was tucked up in a corner of the chesterfield.

"Tired, darling?"

"Yes, a little."

"That woman has worn you out with talking. She oughtn't to talk so much."

"No." Her head shifted wearily in the cushions. "All about that horrible case. I don't like hearing about such things."

"Of course not. Still, when a thing like that happens in the neighborhood, people will gossip and talk. It would be a relief if they caught the woman. One doesn't like to think—"

"I don't want to think of anything so hateful. She must be a horrible creature."

"Horrible. Brookes was saying the other day—"

"I don't want to hear what he said. I don't want to hear about it at all. I want to be quiet. I want to be quiet!"

He recognized the note of rising hysteria.

"Tiddley-winks shall be quiet. Don't worry, darling. We won't talk about horrors."

No. It would not do to talk about them.

Ethel went to bed early. It was understood that on Sundays Mr. Mummery should sit up till Mrs. Sutton came in. Ethel was a little anxious about this, but he assured her that he felt quite strong enough. In body, indeed, he did; it was his mind that felt weak and confused. He had decided to make a casual remark about the mutilated newspapers—just to see what Mrs. Sutton would say.

He allowed himself the usual indulgence of a whisky-and-soda as he sat waiting. At a quarter to ten he heard the familiar click of the garden gate. Footsteps passed up the gravel—squeak, squeak, to the back-door. Then the sound of the latch, the shutting of the door, the rattle of the bolts being shot home. Then only a pause. Mrs. Sutton would be taking off her hat. The moment was coming.

The step sounded in the passage. The door opened. Mrs. Sutton in her neat black dress stood on the threshold. He was aware of a reluctance to face her. Then he looked up. A plump-faced woman, her face obscured by thick horn-rimmed spectacles. Was there, perhaps, something hard about the mouth? Or was it just that she had lost most of her front teeth?

"Would you be requiring anything tonight, sir, before I go up?"

"No, thank you, Mrs. Sutton."

"I hope you are feeling better, sir." Her eager interest in his health seemed to him almost sinister, but the eyes behind the thick glasses were inscrutable.

"Quite better, thank you, Mrs. Sutton."

"Mrs. Mummery is not indisposed, is she, sir? Should I take her up a glass of hot milk or anything?"

"No, thank you, no." He spoke hurriedly, and fancied that she looked disappointed.

"Very well, sir. Good night, sir."

"Good night. Oh! by the way, Mrs. Sutton—"

"Yes, sir?"

"Oh, nothing," said Mr. Mummery, "nothing."

Next morning Mr. Mummery opened his paper eagerly. He would have been glad to learn that an arrest had been made over the week-end. But there was no news for him. The chairman of a trust company had blown out his brains, and all the headlines were occupied with tales about lost millions and ruined shareholders. Both in his own paper and in those he purchased on the way to the office, the Lincoln Poisoning Tragedy had been relegated to an obscure paragraph on a back page, which informed him that the police were still baffled.

The next few days were the most uncomfortable that Mr. Mummery had ever spent. He developed a habit of coming down early in the morning and prowling about the kitchen. This made Ethel nervous, but Mrs. Sutton offered no remark. She watched him tolerantly, even, he thought, with something like amusement. After all, it was ridiculous. What was the use of supervising the breakfast, when he had to be out of the house every day between half-past nine and six?

At the office, Brookes rallied him on the frequency with which he rang up Ethel. Mr. Mummery paid no attention. It was reassuring to hear her voice and to know that she was safe and well.

Nothing happened, and by the following Thursday he began to think that he had been a fool. He came home late that night. Brookes had persuaded him to go with him to a little bachelor dinner for a friend who was about to get married. He left the others at eleven o'clock, however, refusing to make a night of it. The household was in bed when he got back but a note from Mrs. Sutton lay on the table, informing him that there was cocoa for him in the kitchen, ready for hotting-up. He hotted it up accordingly in the little saucepan where it stood. There was just one good cupful.

He sipped it thoughtfully, standing by the kitchen stove. After the first sip, he put the cup down. Was it his fancy, or was there something queer about the taste? He sipped it again, rolling it upon his tongue. It seemed to him to have a faint tang, metallic and unpleasant. In a sudden dread he ran out to the scullery and spat the mouthful into the sink.

After this, he stood quite still for a moment or two. Then with a curious deliberation, as though his movements had been dictated to him, he fetched an empty medicine-bottle from the pantry-shelf, rinsed it under the tap and tipped the contents of the cup carefully into it. He slipped the bottle into his coat pocket and moved on tiptoe to the back-door. The bolts were difficult to draw without noise, but he managed it at last. Still on tiptoe, he stole across the garden to the potting-shed. Stooping down, he struck a match. He knew exactly where he had left the tin of weed-killer, under the shelf behind the pots at the back. Cautiously he lifted it out. The match flared up and burnt his fingers, but before he could light another his sense of touch had told him what he wanted to know. The stopper was loose again.

Panic seized Mr. Mummery, standing there in the earthy-smelling shed, in his dress-suit and overcoat, holding the tin in one hand and the match-box in the other. He wanted very badly to run and tell somebody what he had discovered.

Instead, he replaced the tin exactly where he had found it and went back to the house. As he crossed the garden again, he noticed a light in Mrs. Sutton's bedroom window. This terrified him more than anything which had gone before. Was she watching him? Ethel's window was dark. If she had drunk anything deadly there would be lights everywhere, movements, calls for the doctor, just as when he himself had been attacked. Attacked—that was the right word, he thought.

Still with the same odd presence of mind and precision, he went in, washed out the utensils and made a second brew of cocoa, which he left standing in the saucepan. He crept quietly to his bedroom. Ethel's voice greeted him on the threshold.

"How late you are, Harold. Naughty old boy! Have a good time?"

"Not bad. You all right, darling?"

"Quite all right. Did Mrs. Sutton leave something hot for you? She said she would."

"Yes, but I wasn't thirsty."

Ethel laughed. "Oh! it was *that* sort of a party, was it?"

Mr. Mummery did not attempt any denials. He undressed and got into bed and clutched his wife to him as though defying death and hell to take her from him. Next morning he would act. He thanked God that he was not too late.

Mr. Dimthorpe, the chemist, was a great friend of Mr. Mummery's. They had often sat together in the untidy little shop on Spring Bank and exchanged views on greenfly and club-root. Mr. Mummery told his story frankly to Mr. Dimthorpe and handed over the bottle of cocoa. Mr. Dimthorpe congratulated him on his prudence and intelligence.

"I will have it ready for you by this evening," he said, "and if it's what you think it is, then we shall have a clear case on which to take action."

Mr. Mummery thanked him, and was extremely vague and inattentive at business all day. But that hardly mattered, for Mr. Brookes, who had seen the party through to a riotous end in the small hours, was in no very observant mood. At half-past four, Mr. Mummery shut up his desk decisively and announced that he was off early, he had a call to make.

Mr. Dimthorpe was ready for him.

"No doubt about it," he said. "I used Marsh's test. It's a heavy dose, no wonder you tasted it. There must be four or five grains of pure arsenic in that bottle. Look, here's the mirror. You can see it for yourself."

Mr. Mummery gazed at the little glass tube with its ominous purple-black stain.

"Will you ring up the police from here?" asked the chemist.

"No," said Mr. Mummery. "No—I want to get home. God knows what's happening there. And I've only just time to catch my train."

"All right," said Mr. Dimthorpe. "Leave it to me. I'll ring them up for you."

The local train did not go fast enough for Mr. Mummery. Ethel—poisoned—dying—dead—Ethel—poisoned—dying—dead—the wheels drummed in his ears. He almost ran out of the station and along the road. A car was standing at his door. He saw it from the end of the street and broke into a gallop. It had happened already. The doctor was there. Fool, murderer that he was to have left things so late.

Then, while he was still a hundred and fifty yards off, he saw the front door open. A man came out followed by Ethel herself. The visitor got into his car and was driven away. Ethel went in again. She was safe—safe!

He could hardly control himself to hang up his hat and coat and go in looking reasonably calm. His wife had returned to the armchair by the fire and greeted him in some surprise. There were tea-things on the table.

"Back early, aren't you?"

"Yes—business was slack. Somebody been to tea?"

"Yes, young Welbeck. About the arrangements for the Drama Society." She spoke briefly but with an undertone of excitement.

A qualm came over Mr. Mummery. Would a guest be any protection? His face must have shown his feelings, for Ethel stared at him in amazement.

"What's the matter, Harold, you look so queer."

"Darling," said Mr. Mummery, "there's something I want to tell you about." He sat down and took her hand in his. "Something a little unpleasant, I'm afraid—"

"Oh, ma'am!"

The cook was in the doorway.

"I beg your pardon, sir—I didn't know you was in. Will you be taking tea or can I clear away? And oh, ma'am, there was a young man at the fishmonger's and he's just come from Grimsby and they've caught that dreadful woman—that Mrs. Andrews. Isn't it a good thing? It worritted me dreadful to think she was going about like that, but they've caught her. Taken a job as housekeeper she had to two elderly ladies and they found the wicked poison on her. Girl as spotted her will get a reward. I been keeping my eyes open for her, but it's at Grimsby she was all the time."

Mr. Mummery clutched at the arm of his chair. It had all been a mad mistake then. He wanted to shout or cry. He wanted to apologize to this foolish, pleasant, excited woman. All a mistake.

But there had been the cocoa. Mr. Dimthorpe. Marsh's test. Five grains of arsenic. Who, then—?

He glanced around at his wife, and in her eyes he saw something that he had never seen before. . . .